Praise for *O.*

"A lovely portrait of Sri Lanka in th   "
                                        —NPR,   ."

"Freeman's powerful second novel focu... on ordinary children living their lives as war clouds build."   —*People*, "Great Reads"

"[A] moving perspective on war . . . riveting [and] powerful."
                  —*Reader's Digest*, "Best Summer Reading for 2013"

"Freeman draws all of her characters artfully as she uses her lane and its inhabitants to reflect a larger, troubled world. . . . Not entirely pessimistic about human nature, Freeman even holds out a faint hope for reconciliation, in well-directed words of kindness."   —*The Miami Herald*

"There is something positively Russian in the feel of this book. . . . For 300 pages, nothing much happens, and it happens beautifully."
                                            —*The Globe and Mail* (Toronto)

"*On Sal Mal Lane* succeeds, gathering gravitas and emotional depth. . . . A choice reading destination."   —*Newsday*

"*On Sal Mal Lane* succeeds because it thrums with vitality. On this one street we can find life in all its joy and pain, life lived by people who are so alive.
                                            —*Star Tribune* (Minneapolis)

"This is a brilliant, beautiful and crushing story about childhood, its kindnesses, comforts, misunderstandings and shifting allegiances, and also about the end of childhood."   —*MORE*

"Ru Freeman's *On Sal Mal Lane* is stupendous. . . . With prose both lingering and breathtaking."   —*Bookslut*

"I finished the novel . . . with a deeper respect for the human spirit, despite what politics, violence, and loss can do to it."   —*The Millions*

"Freeman handles the historical complexities of Sri Lanka's conflict with skill. . . . [A] lovingly wrought story of youthful innocence lost."
                                            —*The Daily Beast*

"The language is beautiful. . . . The writing, the story, the talent is not to be missed."   —*KQED*

"Freeman's gift for verisimilitude is manifest with searing clarity. . . . And in fictionalizing Sri Lankan history, Freeman accomplishes what reportage alone cannot: she blends the journalist's loyalty to fact with impassioned imagination." —*Booklist*

"As witness and storyteller, Freeman never falters, revealing 'what happened' with clarity and resolve in prose both lingering and breathtaking. The result is simply stupendous." —*Library Journal*

"Lovingly written, historically rich and compassionate to all sides of the turmoil." —*Kirkus Reviews*

"Freeman is a tender writer, deftly weaving culture, history and, yes, redemption into a story with a range of rich, earned feeling. It's highly likely that readers will close the book with a different outlook on life, love, and loss." —*ForeWord Reviews*

"Deeply moving and brilliant. . . . Devi reminds me of Scout from *To Kill a Mockingbird* and Swede from *Peace Like a River*, small girls who make very large impressions, and I'm sure that *On Sal Mal Lane* will join their ranks as a new perennial favorite of booksellers, librarians, and of course, readers." —Cathy Langer, Tattered Cover

"Ru Freeman's *On Sal Mal Lane* is a gorgeous novel, lush, life-affirming, and full of love. . . . We don't have to be Sri Lankan, Muslim, Hindu, Buddhist, Christian, or come of age in the '80s to recognize ourselves and our own close and assorted communities in the varied and interconnected lives of the families of Sal Mal Lane. Through the compulsively readable story of these unforgettable characters, Freeman has written a novel that has earned a place alongside *Cutting for Stone* and *To Kill a Mockingbird*." —Kris Kleindienst, Left Bank Books

"This novel is beautiful. It is like a piece of music that floats and rises with countervailing currents both light and tightly wound. Rich in imagery and careful observation *On Sal Mal Lane* inhabits our hearts and senses so deeply we become a member of this community of Sri Lankans experiencing terrible personal upheaval brought on by civil war. *On Sal Mal Lane* is so quietly vivid it will never leave me." —Sheryl Cotleur, Copperfield's Books

"Freeman's graceful narrative deftly explores our common humanity, and the idea of 'vayadamma sankaara,' which translates to: 'nothing lasts.'" —Stacie Williams, Boswell Book Company

"Ru Freeman's writing is spectacular! Her character development is one of the best I've read this year. What at first appears to be an ordinary story about a mix of 'ordinary' people on a simple lane in Sri Lanka in the years leading up to the civil war, soon becomes a fierce tale of war and politics told throughout these ordinary voices. Heartbreaking in its violence, but breathtaking in its prose, *On Sal Mal Lane* is sure to become a bookseller and book club favorite.
—Julie Slavinsky, Warwick's

"Captivating. . . . This beautiful novel gives us children of a Sri Lankan lane at a certain historical moment. . . . Utter heartbreak is here—for the rapacious violence and madness of the world does come—and smile-as-you-read passages of larger spirits and powers being realized to the better. Ru Freeman's excellent *A Disobedient Girl* is now followed by a major leap up in accomplishment, empathy, artistry."   —Rick Simonson, Elliott Bay Book Company

"The book is too beautiful to put down even during its most terrifying moments. This is the book I will be handing to every reader who asks to be exported to a whole new world in the same way I did with *The Kite Runner* and *The God of Small Things* before it. This is the book we will be discussing, and haunted by, for years to come."   —Kenny Coble, King's Books

"Freeman illuminates the tragic upheavals and political complexities of a country and its people through the coming-of-age of four main characters, the Herath children. Political strife touches the children's world in direct and indirect ways, but Freeman's strength is to allow elements of history to emerge through the quotidian actions of Sal Mal Lane's magnificently drawn inhabitants."   —Lacey Dunham, Politics & Prose

"*On Sal Mal Lane* is an entrancing, brave, and passionate book, written by a master storyteller. Told primarily from the perspective of the children of Sal Mal Lane, home to a racially and religiously diverse population, it is the story of the loss of innocence under the relentless onset of war. You will come to care deeply for her richly drawn characters as you yearn to know their fates."
—Tripp Ryder, Carleton College Bookstore

"Tragedy visits Sal Mal Lane as the country erupts in violence, but amid the destruction there are also uplifting, hopeful stories too. This is a powerful story, the writing lively and uplifting, and a delight to read."
—Deon Stonehouse, Sunriver Books & Music

"Piercingly intelligent and shatter-your-heart profound, Ru Freeman's *On Sal Mal Lane* is as luminous as it is wrenching, as fierce as it is generous. This is a riveting, important, beauty of a book."

—Cheryl Strayed, author of *Wild* and *Tiny Beautiful Things*

"An elegiac and powerful portrait of a troubled time. Ru Freeman beautifully interweaves humanity and history, creating a wise, thought-provoking and deeply felt novel."

—Madeline Miller, winner of the Orange Prize for *The Song of Achilles*

"Ru Freeman has written the masterwork of Sri Lanka's *bellum civile*, a novel that patiently and lucidly witnesses the daily lives of children on a single lane as the violence builds. . . . It distills one of the last century's most complicated wars into what it really was on the ground—the everyday reality of that timeless threat, the neighbor turned killer."

—Lorraine Adams, Pulitzer Prize winner and
author of *The Room and The Chair*

"Freeman creates a rich and complex world, and although we know where the story will lead us, we go willingly, because her characters are impossible not to love, impossible not to root for. In the end, despite the wrenching tragedy, we come away uplifted and enriched."

—Naomi Benaron, author of *Running the Rift*,
winner of the 2010 Bellwether Prize

"*On Sal Mal Lane* is a finely wrought sculpture of the capillary systems by which nihilism and violence travel from the political realm to the intimate, and back again." —Rana Dasgupta, author of *Solo*

"From page one, I felt as though I'd moved into Sal Mal Lane, with its minor feuds and secret loyalties, its music recitals and barefoot games and of course, its unforgettable children. Ru Freeman's writing is tender, insightful, and eloquent, even when depicting the brutal realities of a country sliding toward civil war." —Tania James, author of *The Atlas of Unknowns* and *Aerogrammes*

"Ru Freeman's new novel moves like a stage play in a dream. Dread hovers over the richness, childhood's abandon faces the crushing power of adulthood, and we live for a time in a world many of us did not imagine. And we fear what might be coming."

—Luis Alberto Urrea, author of *Queen of America*

On Sal Mal Lane

Also by Ru Freeman

A Disobedient Girl

On Sal Mal Lane

· A Novel ·

RU FREEMAN

Graywolf Press

This publication is made possible, in part, by the voters of Minnesota through a Minnesota State Arts Board Operating Support grant, thanks to a legislative appropriation from the arts and cultural heritage fund, and through grants from the National Endowment for the Arts and the Wells Fargo Foundation Minnesota. Significant support has also been provided by Target, the McKnight Foundation, Amazon.com, and other generous contributions from foundations, corporations, and individuals. To these organizations and individuals we offer our heartfelt thanks.

This book is made possible through a partnership with the College of Saint Benedict, and honors the legacy of S. Mariella Gable, a distinguished teacher at the College. Support has been provided by the Manitou Fund as part of the Warner Reading Program.

Published by Graywolf Press
250 Third Avenue North, Suite 600
Minneapolis, Minnesota 55401

www.graywolfpress.org

Published in the United States of America

ISBN 978-1-55597-642-2 (cloth)
ISBN 978-1-55597-676-7 (paper)

2 4 6 8 9 7 5 3 1
First Graywolf Paperback, 2014

Library of Congress Control Number: 2013958008

Cover design: Kimberly Glyder Design

Cover art: Silhouette at sunset © 2009 by Pallab Seth. Used with the permission
        of Getty Images.

For my brothers, Arjuna & Malinda:
Loka, who provided the music of our childhood,
and Puncha, who kept me as safe as he could.

"Neither a person entirely broken

nor one entirely whole can speak.

In sorrow, pretend to be fearless. In happiness, tremble."

—Jane Hirshfield, "In Praise of Coldness" from
Given Sugar, Given Salt

"'I get down on my knees and do what must be done

and kiss Achilles' hand, the killer of my son.'"

—Michael Longley, from "Ceasefire"

The Families of Sal Mal Lane

The Heraths
Suren
Rashmi
Nihil
Devi
Mr. & Mrs. Herath (parents)

The Bollings
Sonna
Rose
Dolly
Sophia
Francie & Jimmy Bolling (parents)

The Silvas
Mohan
Jith
Mr. & Mrs. Silva (parents)

Other families
Old Mrs. Joseph and her son, Raju
Mr. & Mrs. Niles and their daughter, Kala Niles, the piano teacher
Mr. & Mrs. Nadesan
Mr. & Mrs. Tissera and their son, Ranil
Mr & Mrs. Bin Ahmed and their daughter
Mr. & Mrs. Sansoni and their son, Tony
Alice & Lucas

SAL
MAL
LANE

TISSERA

SANSONI

NADESAN

NILES

HERATH

JOSEPH

SILVA

BOLLING

BIN AHMED

Contents

On Sal Mal Lane

Prologue

In 1976, on the fifth day of the month of May, a month during which most of the people who lived in the country celebrated the birth, death, and attainment of nirvana of the Lord Buddha, with paper lanterns, fragrant incense, fresh flowers, and prayers mingling with temple bells late into the night, in the remote jungles of Jaffna, in the Northern Province of Sri Lanka, a man stood before a group of youth and launched a war that, he promised, would bring his people, the Tamil people, a state of their own. The year before, this man had shot another Tamil man just as that other man, the mayor of Jaffna, was about to enter a Hindu temple in Ponnalai, desecrating the temple and the minds of the faithful alike. Therefore, nobody saw fit to contradict what he had to say on that day, that fifth day of the month of May in the year 1976.

Before that day this island country had withstood a steady march of unwelcome visitors. Invaders from the land that came to be known as India were followed by the Portuguese, the Dutch, and finally, British governors, who deemed that the best way to rule this new colony was to elevate the minority over the majority, to favor the mostly Hindu Tamils over the predominantly Buddhist Sinhalese. To the untrained eye, the physical distinction between the Sinhalese and the Tamil races was so subtle that only the natives could distinguish one from the other, pointing to the drape of a sari, the cheekbones on a face, the scent of hair oil to clarify. But distinctions there were, and the natural order of things would eventually come to pass: resentment would grow, the majority would reclaim their country.

So it was that after the British had left the country behind, when what was said of them was that there was no commonwealth, there was only a common thief, the left-behind majority decided to restore pride of place to the language of the majority, which, among other things, meant that all children would be instructed in their mother tongue: the Sinhalese in Sinhala, the Tamils, Muslims, and Burghers in their language of choice but, in the end, not English, not the language of colonialism, which would now be taught only as a second language. And this policy, along with the corresponding policy of conducting all national business in Sinhala, with translations offered in the newly demoted English and the official Tamil language, created a disruption of order that would forever be known as the Language Policy. As though the Language Policy was itself a period of time and not a policy, debatable, mutable, and man-made, unlike time, which merely came and went no matter what was done in its presence.

If the policies of the British and the politics of language were the kindling, then rumor was the match that was used by men who wanted war to set them ablaze. These rumors were always the same: pregnant women split open, children snapped like dry branches, rape, looting, arson, mass graves, night raids, and other atrocities all happening "before their eyes," that is, "before the eyes of sister, brother, father, wife." The kinds of eyes that ought to be blinded before having to see such things. The kind of sight that once heard of necessitates an equivalent list of atrocities to be committed, in turn, before other sets of eyes. Eyes that also deserved no such sight, for who did? Which of us, taken aside, asked privately, would believe it not only possible but practical and desirable that any other of us ought to witness such acts?

Yes, a man addressed a gathering of young men and women on May 5, 1976. And though the clearing in which he stood was two hundred miles away from the neighborhood where our events take place and its people, his story would become their story, his war, theirs.

Everyone who lived on Sal Mal Lane was implicated in what happened, including Lucas and Alice, who had no last names nor professed religious affiliations, the Tamil Catholics and Hindus, the Burgher Catholics, the Muslims, and the Sinhalese, both Catholic and Buddhist. Their lives were unfolding against a backdrop of conflict that would span decades involving intermarriage, national language policies, births, deaths, marriages, and affairs—never divorces—subletting, cricket matches, water cuts, power outages, curfews, riots, and the occasional bomb. And while this story is about small people, we must consider the fact that their history is long and accord them, too, a story equal to their past.

And who, you might ask, am I? I am nothing more than the air that passed through these homes, lingering in the verandas where husbands and wives revisited their days and examined their prospects in comparison to those of their neighbors. I am the road itself, upon whose bosom the children played French cricket with their knees locked together, their bare feet burning as they scored runs with the aid of a short plank of wood, playing chicken with the rare vehicle that came speeding up my quarter-mile curved spine. I am a composite of dreams, the busy rushing ones that seek their hosts by night and day, and the quiet ones that have just bid farewell to move on to other streets, other countries, an afterlife. I am all those thoughts, the fractious, the lush, the desolate, the ones that are created from small apprehensions to those built block by block from the intimations *of tragedy, the ones that spin upward with determined exuberance or trill in low notes with small joys. To tell a story about divergent lives, the storyteller must be everything and nothing. I am that.*

If at times you detect some subtle preference, an undeserved generosity toward someone, a boy child, perhaps, or an old man, forgive me. It is far easier to be everything and nothing than it is to conceal love.

.... 1979

The Listeners

God was not responsible for what came to pass. People said it was karma, punishment in this life for past sins, fate. People said that no beauty was permitted in the world without some accompanying darkness to balance it out, and, surely, these children were beautiful. But what people said was unimportant; what befell them befell us all.

The Herath children were different from all the others who had come and stayed for a while on Sal Mal Lane. It was not simply the neatness of their clothes, washed, sun-dried, and ironed for them by the live-in servant, or their clean fingernails, or the middle parting on their heads for the girls, on the side for the boys, or their broad foreheads and wise eyes, or even the fact that they didn't smile very often, some inner disquiet keeping their features still. It wasn't their music-making or their devout following of deities of all faiths who came and went through their house with the predictability of monsoon rains. It was the way they stood together even when they were apart. There was never a single Herath child in a conversation, there were four; every word uttered, every challenge made, every secret kept, together.

These things, discovered as the months wore on, came to bear upon a day of loss, a day crystallized into a moment that the whole neighborhood, yes, even those who had encouraged such a day, would have done anything to take back, a day that defined and sundered all of their lives. But let us return to the beginning, to the year when, in a pillared parliamentary building that had been constructed overlooking a wind-nudged blue ocean, a measure was passed under the title the Prevention of Terrorism Act. It was an act that built upon a previous one, an act declaring a State of Emergency, the kind of declaration that made adults skittish, elevated small quarrels into full-blown hatreds, and scuttled the best of intentions, for how could goodwill exist under such preparedness for chaos, such expectations of anarchy? The only goodwill to be had was among children unaware of such declarations, children like the ones on Sal Mal Lane, children moving into a new home that brought with it the possibility of new friends. Let us return then to the first days of that year, the days that filled so many people with hope for what the new family would bring to them. Let us pay attention to their words, to the way they enter this house, alone and together, close or from a distance, intent and wish inseparable. Let us return to observe the very first day that foretold all the days that followed.

On the day that the Heraths moved in to the last empty house on Sal Mal Lane, the one located exactly at the center where the broad road angled, slightly, to continue uphill, the Herath children happened to be learning hymns and hallelujahs from their mother. The children's mother, Mrs. Herath, herself a staunch Buddhist, was given to taking on other faiths based solely on the musicality of their songs, faiths of which she partook like others tasted of side dishes, little plates piled high with crispy fish cutlets and vegetable patties. Right now she was going through a Jesus phase, having not yet discovered the chants of the modern Hindu sage Sathya Sai Baba. On the very first afternoon, even before she tended to her anthuriums and pride of Japans and other potted plants that had been brought over in an old borrowed Citroën, she sat at their piano and played while her sons and daughters, two of each, belted out "What a Friend We Have in Jesus," in perfect harmony.

In the house across the street, an old man, Mr. Niles, long confined to spending his days reclining in his armchair in languorous apathy, stirred. With some degree of exertion he pulled himself up to a sitting position and listened. Although he was, himself, raised in the Catholic tradition, it was not the familiar hymns that moved him, but the voices. He tilted his face this way and that, trying to untangle them, one from the other. He picked out four distinct voices: one imbued with refinement, the word endings clear and elegant, the notes held to beat; another sensitive and rich, the melody heroic; and a third that did not seem to care for timing and so was lifted with a too-soon, too-late delight that was refreshing. The last, a boy's voice, he could not place. It seemed both dogged and resigned. Earnest, as though he wanted to please, yet not entirely committed to this particular form of pleasing, it wavered between ardent expression and the mere articulation of melancholy words set to music. Mr. Niles listened more intently to that voice, which spoke of a spirit that required soothing, curious as to what could trouble a boy so young. Unseen by anybody, not even his wife and daughter, each busy with her own weekend preoccupations, he listened through that afternoon, piecing together the unuttered feelings that lay beneath those angelic voices, conjuring up an image of each child and imagining a life for them in the house into which they had moved.

This house was very much like every other house down Sal Mal Lane, rudimentary if with a little style added by the verandas at the front and the back, both shaded by crisscross wooden half trellises, and the bordering hedges that rimmed all but two of the front gardens. At its heart was a large open space that Mrs. Herath had turned into a sitting room and whose focus was the upright piano. At the back of the house, Mrs. Herath had chosen to install her dining room, which, therefore, sat right next to the kitchen in defiance of the centuries-long tradition that dictated a dining table never to recall the kitchen in which food is prepared. The children shared two rooms, she and Mr. Herath shared a third, and the live-in servant, Kamala, was given the storeroom tucked next to a garage for which Mrs. Herath had found no good use since they did not own a car. Nobody down Sal Mal Lane, a dead end traversed almost exclusively by people on foot, owned a car except for Mr. Niles, who could no longer drive it, but this did not matter since all the neighbors felt able to ask for its use when necessary, and all the neighbors glanced with distant possessiveness at their empty garages and contemplated a future date on which they might convert them into fee-charging flats.

The real reason that Mrs. Herath had wanted this particular house, however, was the potential for a real garden that would meander wide on three sides around her home, the fourth side dedicated to a shared driveway. Unlike her neighbors' properties, which were graced by plumes of dancing hibiscus, bunches of creamy gardenias, and bold thrusts of anthuriums, her own, untended for many years by a previous owner, seemed barren. In little more than a year Mrs. Herath's garden would become a showpiece, decked with ferns, flowering bushes, and fragrant varieties of orchids that many of her neighbors had not heard of, she would become an authority on landscaping, and all the little flower thieves who lived down other lanes would flock to her garden in the early-morning hours and reach for her flowers like large butterflies. Today, however, her garden was depleted and the one person staring at it as he stood, hatless and scorched in the still, noonday heat, wondered why the children who had come to inhabit it, smartly dressed as they were, did not seem less pleased with their surroundings.

Sonna, the Bollings' son, fourteen years of age, had spent the day leaning against his uncle's gate, watching the activity across the street. He had arrived that morning dressed in his Sunday churchgoing clothes, though if someone had pointed out that he was trying to present himself at his best, he would have denied it. Sonna had come to assess potential, which, in his mind, meant one of two things: the ability to bully others or being susceptible to bullying. He had watched the children all day, his face arranged in an expression between scorn and disinterest, trying to gauge to which category they belonged. So far he had not been able to tell, and not even his uncle, Raju, who peered over the gate with him, had a definite opinion.

"Can't tell if they are good or not till we talk to them," his uncle said at last, hitching up his loose trousers as he went inside.

Sonna continued to watch. The boys were not muscular, they were lanky and long-fingered, their mouths full and at ease, which augured well for classifying them as victims. Yet there had been a steadfastness to their gaze when they had first seen him that confused Sonna. They had nodded, their arms full of bags and boxes filled with books, but had not smiled, which he took to mean that they, too, were able to judge character and had him pegged as a neighbor but not one they were likely to befriend. He spat into the ground. They were adversaries, those boys, though the source of their strength was not one that he could identify. The girls, too, had resisted the title of victim that he yearned to pin on them, they with their matching dresses and their laughter. They resisted it by not noticing him at all, though how was that possible? He was tall, good-looking, and strong— and standing right across the street from them! He had been standing there for hours. How could they not have noticed?

"Fuckin' snobs," he said to his uncle, who had come back out to ask him if he wanted some tea. "Think they're too good for us. Probably only wan' to talk to the Silva boys. Probably jus' like them. We'll see about that. We'll see how they manage to live here without talkin' to us Bollings. Think they can jus' talk to themselves?"

"Maybe they are busy today, moving and all," Raju told his nephew. To be proximate to Sonna when he was not happy was not something that Raju ever enjoyed; in the end he always wound up being clobbered for nothing he had said or done. "Youngest looks sweet," he added, watching the little girl, who had abandoned her siblings and was skipping in the veranda, the rope smacking rhythmically both on the floor and on the ceiling above her. After a while she called out to someone they could not see, dropped the rope, and ran inside. Raju craned his neck toward the front doors of the house through which the children had disappeared, one by one. From inside came the strains of a piano being played.

"Din' even smile once," Sonna muttered.

Raju lowered his head, anticipating trouble. He tried to think of something soothing to say, knowing, as he had known on every other such occasion, that words would fail him.

Sonna had accumulated a list of unhappy accomplishments: bullying his twin sisters, riding the buses without paying his fare, cutting the clotheslines in his neighbors' backyards and rejoicing in the way everything clean turned instantly muddy, things he did without a second thought. But what he enjoyed the most was tormenting his uncle. In truth Raju, who hid the ropey muscles of a bodybuilder underneath layers of flesh, could have felled Sonna to the ground with a single swipe, but he lacked two things. He lacked what Sonna had, the idea that he deserved to be top dog, and, though this would change, to Raju's dismay and shame, he lacked, for now, a good enough reason to fight Sonna.

"Don' go an' try to suck up," Sonna said, as Raju hung his head and listened. Sonna smacked him on the side of his head. "You're fuckin' retarded anyway. They won' wan' to talk to you, an' I don' wan' to see you runnin' after them, you hear me?" He shoved his uncle with a fist and Raju staggered back. "You hear me? If I catch you . . ."

"No, no, what to talk, I won't talk. Too much for me to be doing," Raju said, unbuttoning the top of his shirt and trying to get some air down the front of his body. "I have too much to do."

"Too much to do," Sonna scoffed. "You got nothin' to do, you fool. Thirty-five years old an' still livin' with Mummy. Don' even have a job."

It was at that moment that the Herath household erupted into "What a Friend We Have in Jesus," which proved too much for Sonna, who shoved Raju once more, spat again for good measure, and strode down the street, his hands in his pockets as he contemplated his next move. He stumbled over a stone as he went, turned back to make sure that nobody had seen, then kicked the stone into the bushes, wincing as a sharp edge caught the end of his toe.

Raju listened absentmindedly to the music from the house across the street as he watched Sonna walk away. The voices and the piano were equally balanced and the singing was different from anything he had heard before. His immediate neighbors, the Niles family, owned a piano, and their daughter, Kala Niles, was a piano teacher, but there had never been any singing next door, just the strains of scales in quick tempo and difficult pieces of music. He wondered if the children took lessons and, if they did not, whether they would go to Kala Niles to learn. He hoped that if they did, they would not end up simply playing the same pieces over but would continue to sing as they were doing now. He turned his face toward the Nileses' house, wondering if they, too, were listening to the new children. He shaded his eyes and took stock of Kala Niles's rosebushes, which had just begun to show over the top of the wall that separated the two houses. At this time of day, the flowers scented the afternoon air; he tipped his head back and flared his nostrils, inhaling deeply as he listened a while longer to the voices from across the street. He felt his spirits lift. Whatever Sonna had to say about these new people, they could hardly be ignored when they sang so beautifully.

Listening to the hymn, the Heraths' immediate next-door neighbors, the Silvas, exchanged looks. The Herath house had been abandoned due to the joint suicide of its previous owner and Raju's father, the tragic culmination of a found-out affair. That, and the resulting insanity of the left-behind spouse, was a hair-raising tale meant to dissuade hasty purchase and one that the Silvas themselves had told Mrs. Herath the day she came house-hunting. It was a tale that Mrs. Herath had, to their consternation, taken in her stride. Now Mr. Silva sighed audibly as he pulsed his knees together in agitation, irritated by the fervorful notes flowing out through the Heraths' open veranda and in through theirs; the determination and flamboyance of his neighbor threatened, even on this first day, a life buttressed by a few good prejudices and much keeping-to-ourselves.

The Silvas' sons came into the veranda where the couple were seated. Mohan, the older of the two boys, frowned as he peered through the climbing jasmine plant that shaded one side. A bunch of flowers caught in his hair as he did so, and he pushed the vine away aggressively. A few crushed flowers fell to the floor and the veranda was filled with the sudden sweet smell of jasmine, a fragrance that instantly made all four of them think of Poya days at temple, of mounds of flowers and incense and oil lamps flickering in the dark.

"Catholics?" he asked.

"No, not Catholics, Buddhists," Jith, the younger one, said. "The older boy, Suren, is in my class at school." Jith picked up the broken flowers and arranged them in a row on the low ledge that circled the veranda; they were already beginning to turn brown. He flopped down in a chair and tapped the sides of his armrests. He and his brother had been on their way to buy some marbles, but he sensed that this, this singing, was going to delay that trip.

"Then why are they singing hymns?" Mohan made a face that signaled that he was disturbed not merely by the fact that a Buddhist family was singing Christian hymns but that the hymns existed in the first place. He glanced at his father as he said this, searching for his approval.

"Anyway, nice voices," Mrs. Silva said, though she couldn't keep the begrudging note out of her own. She could be excused, having two sons like these, neither of whom had yet revealed much artistic talent and, this being their twelfth and thirteenth years, a revelation of genius in that regard was hardly to be expected. "If there is going to be singing, then it is best that the singing is good," she added and chuckled a little, stretching out a section of the white tablecloth that she was embroidering with pale yellow and lilac blooms that bore no resemblance to any flower grown in soil, tropical or otherwise; she cocked her head this way and that in approval of her own considerable imagination and skill.

Mrs. Silva liked to encourage charity in her sons, though, since the encouragement was limited to words rather than actions, her efforts were not as successful as they could otherwise have been. She felt pleased with her comment and beamed good-naturedly at her family as she returned to her sewing. So long as the Catholics and the Hindus and the Tamils and the Burghers and the poor, or any combination thereof, kept away from her family, she had always felt there was ample room to engage in largesse. Indeed, Mrs. Silva was a respected patron of the temple across the bridge and often collected old clothing to be distributed to the people in the slums. But that was the trouble with such people, she thought, the glow fading a little: they always found a way to creep into her life. The hymn seemed to rise with renewed vigor into the air and Mrs. Silva shuddered in its wake.

> *Have we trials and temptations*
> *Is there trouble anywhere?*
> *We should never be discouraged*
> *Take it to the Lord in prayer*

"Good to have some new children in the neighborhood," Mr. Silva said quickly, noticing her discomfort and trying, as his wife had done, to find the positive note. He prided himself on being an opinionated yet nurturing father, a fine example of a man on whom his sons could model their own behavior.

Mrs. Silva brightened. "Yes, I suppose, at least they are our kind. Far too many Tamils already down this lane. Before long they'll be trying to rename it."

"Instead of Sal Mal Lane, we'll be living down some road with a *vem* at the end of its name!"

This was said by Mohan, for he had recently begun to understand that disliking the mostly Hindu Tamil boys in school, even those Tamil boys who studied with him in the Sinhala medium of instruction, had earned him an influential clique of wealthy, cosmopolitan friends who had shunned him before. Little differences had now become his secret arsenal. Things like the smell of the gingelly oil they used on their hair, which he had deemed disgusting and unlike the dill-fragranced coconut oil he used on his own head. And, even better than his new friends at school was his sense that somehow he had earned the approval of his father, who had always seemed inaccessible, locked as he was in his firm opinions morning and night and his constant gardening in between. Lately, it seemed, Mr. Silva looked to Mohan to make the appropriately disparaging observation about the Tamils. Mohan was getting better at this by the week, his latest contribution being along the lines that the Tamils were always studying and getting the best results at school and that everything they did was for themselves and their own race, nothing at all for the school, a statement that was greeted with many a nod and numerous sighs at the dining table, as well as an extra serving of marrow bones, as if in compensation.

Mrs. Silva named the Tamil people down the lane, unfurling a finger for each one. "Mr. and Mrs. Nadesan, who hardly say a word, those piano people, Mr. and Mrs. Niles and Kala Niles, Old Mrs. Joseph, Tamil by marriage, and her son, Raju, even Jimmy Bolling, grandmother was Tamil, after all, so in that family Jimmy and Francie Bolling, the twins, and that dreadful boy, Sonna, and then the Bin Ahmeds, they are Muslims so they might as well be counted with the Tamils. That makes a total of *fifteen* Tamils down this one lane!" She said this as if it were new information, not a count that she took on a weekly basis. She rubbed her fingers together as if shaking off all the Tamil people she had mentioned, and began the next count. "And Sinhalese? Until now Mr. and Mrs. Tissera and their son, Ranil, and us. Just seven! Now with the Heraths at least we'll be thirteen."

"What about the Sansonis? You usually count them with us," Jith said. He had been turning his rubber slippers inside out repeatedly with his feet, and the strap that went between the toes of his right foot popped out. He picked it up quickly and pressed the thong back in with his fingers before his mother could notice. He need not have worried.

"Oh yes, I forgot. The pure Burghers like them are on our side," Mrs. Silva said. "With them we will be sixteen altogether." She smiled at Jith and settled back in her chair, satisfied with her quorum.

Mr. Silva scratched the front of his chest through the white undershirt he was wearing in deference to the heat, and sighed again in agreement. His legs pumped a little more fiercely in his shorts. "Yes, we have certainly had a narrow escape," he said. "I heard the Nadesans up the road had been eyeing the property for one of their brothers from India. If they had got the house we would have been outnumbered."

This *we* that was mentioned was not a group that Mr. Silva's fellow Sinhalese neighbors, the Heraths and the Tisseras, would have liked to join had they known of its existence. It was a *we* that the Silvas liked to imagine existed, *if things came to that*, though it could be argued that the very existence of the idea was proof that such a division into a *we* and a *them* was not far from becoming fact.

Mr. Silva sat for a while, contemplating this near miss. Each morning at work he and his friends gathered to talk about what The Tamils were demanding. *A full one-third of the island for just 12 percent of the population*, they said, *from Mannar in the west and Pottuvil in the east all the way to Kankesanturai!* And they all sipped their morning tea in amazement, shaking their heads at The Tamils. *The best beaches they want for themselves*, said others, though the best beaches were not owned by any person or group or institution, and there were enough best beaches for everybody in the country, which was, after all, an island.

"Also," Mr. Silva said brightly, leaving one concern behind to take up another, less troubling one, "it will raise the ratio of good to bad among the children at least." The bad to which he referred were the Bolling children, with whom the Heraths were soon to be acquainted, though not in a way that Sonna Bolling could have predicted.

They all grew quiet as they thought about the other children down Sal Mal Lane, the three older Silvas unaware that the youngest, Jith, did not share their opinion about at least one of those children, namely, Dolly Bolling. The strains of a new hymn, "Take My Hand, Precious Lord," washed over the silent listeners, who grew surprisingly rapt with attention.

"Have you gone over with anything?" Mr. Silva asked his wife suddenly, raising his voice a little to cut through the spell that seemed to have descended upon them all. "We should make sure that they are on the right side from the start."

Mrs. Silva clucked her tongue, *pth,* and put down her sewing. "Didn't you notice that those children were here all morning while the movers were coming and going? I looked after them. I even offered to teach the girls to embroider. The older one is talented but the small one had never touched a needle. Can you imagine? A girl? Goodness knows what sort of people they are going to be. Only thing going for them is their race."

"Anyway, better take some plantains or something, don't you think?"

Mrs. Silva pressed her lips together with deep disapproval, but half an hour later she was hovering by the steps leading to the Heraths' veranda, a tray of tea and biscuits in hand.

"Savi? Savi?" she called, using Mrs. Herath's first name and trying to be heard above the piano, which was now being played by one of the boys. The other children were singing yet another hymn, and so was Mrs. Herath, who, Mrs. Silva swore, had seen her standing there and still continued to warble shamelessly. "Savi!" she shouted finally, and this time felt satisfied as the music stopped, singing, piano, and all, and Mrs. Herath came out onto the veranda.

"Ah, didn't mean to disturb you. Lovely singing. *Lovely* singing."

Mrs. Herath smiled. "I try to get the children to sing at least once a day. It's good for them, after all, don't you think? The girls of course have music regularly at the convent, but the boys, you know how it is with them, the boys' schools never do enough in the arts. We have to make sure to civilize them at home."

At this early stage of their acquaintance, it was not possible for Mrs. Herath to tell if Mrs. Silva might share her idea of what constituted civilized behavior. Soon enough, she would discover that just about anything her own children got up to was clearly uncivilized, that making music was just as bad as having a husband who sided with the Communists, and that much more besides would be found severely reproachable by Mrs. Silva. Battles would be fought over boundary lines, walls would go up, words would be said, but that was still to come. For now, they were both blessedly ignorant and, therefore, naturally hoped for friendship.

Mrs. Silva put her tray down and sat in one of the round, high-backed cane chairs that were arranged in the veranda and tried to take in as much as she could see of the interior from where she sat. The quality of furnishings, solid teak, the upholstery hand-loomed and bright, the polish on the floors, the arrangement of several lush potted plants, all of this seemed normal and appealing. Mrs. Silva frowned inwardly. Such impeccable taste in furniture and drapes did not go with hymns. Hymns went with synthetic upholstery and lace, and there wasn't a bit of either in evidence.

Finally Mrs. Silva spoke, setting her conundrums aside to be revisited later in the company of her husband, who could always figure these things out. "I thought you and the children might like some tea. Must not have got your cooker and everything set up yet, no?"

Mrs. Herath reached behind her for the fall of her sari and tucked it into the pleats at her waist before sitting in the chair next to her neighbor. "Yes, my woman, Kamala, is trying to get it started but something is not working," she said. "The wick is not picking up the kerosene. You know how it is with new things, they take time to settle down."

"Where did you get it?" Mrs. Silva asked, absently, her eye on a large brass bowl that seemed far too heavy to have been bought in the city. If it was as old as it appeared, then the Heraths were of a higher pedigree than she had imagined from their erratic song-and-dance behavior.

"Oh, from Sinappa Stores, just up the road," Mrs. Herath said.

Mrs. Silva forgot her contemplation of the brass bowl. "Sinappa Stores? My goodness, Savi, you should know better than to buy from those Tamil places. They're thieves, every one of them!" And Mrs. Silva clapped the back of her palm to her forehead, all the fingers parted, so great was her dismay, but glad that she had made this visit right away while there was still time to get Mrs. Herath on track.

Mrs. Herath looked mildly amused. "Really? I've never had that experience, quite the contrary, I have to say. I used to do all my appliance shopping in the Tamil-owned shops in Pettah and never had a problem. I was quite happy when we decided to move here because we would be so close to Wellawatte and I wouldn't have to go all the way to Pettah to shop anymore, even for fabric and saris."

Mrs. Silva breathed out sharply through her nose in disgust, a reptilian hiss that made the four children, listening from inside, sit up straighter in their chairs. "All the same, Savi, they are *all* the same," she said, bending forward for emphasis and dragging out that second *all* for so long that there was no possibility of there being even one Tamil shopkeeper who might merit being placed outside its reach. "Pettah, Wellawatte, all full of thieves, I tell you. We should get together and boycott, us Sinhalese people. Go exclusively to the Sinhalese shops . . ."

Mrs. Herath listened to Mrs. Silva go on for a while longer about the villainy of the Tamil shopkeepers, every single one of them, from those who sold fabric to those who sold electronics to those who sold jewelry and dry goods. She listened to Mrs. Silva mention, as if this were some particular depravity of the Tamil people, that *they always go for the nonperishable businesses, have you noticed?* She didn't know what to say in response, never having considered that anyone in her acquaintance would subscribe to such opinions as these, and even when she did try to counter Mrs. Silva's arguments about the nonperishable items, saying, *But what about the betel sellers and the fortune tellers and the garland makers?* she was firmly rebutted by Mrs. Silva. But when Mrs. Silva moved on from the Tamils to the Muslims and Burghers, she stopped her by calling out to her children in an unnaturally loud and cheerful voice.

"Children! Come and see, Aunty Rani has brought tea and biscuits for you. Go wake your father. Tell him there's tea."

None of the children went to check on their father, being far more curious about their guest and all the things they had listened to her say, from inside their front door, in her deep and authoritative voice. Furthermore, though they murmured their thanks and waited politely as their mother conversed with Mrs. Silva, who sat so stiffly in a perfectly stitched creamy yellow *lungi* and blouse, her knees together, her back straight, they were sure, one and all, that the visit from Aunty Rani did not bode well. They sat while tea was taken, the biscuits exclaimed over, and much was said about the good fortune of securing a house *in these times* by their mother, and each of them resolved, privately, to discuss all of it, the visit, the biscuits, and such *times* with their siblings when they went to bed that night.

Raju

If the Herath children were gifted, like all children, to see through the facades created by adults, there was one adult on Sal Mal Lane who had learned to see through everybody: Old Mrs. Joseph, who lived in the pale pink and gray house directly opposite the Heraths' and spent much of each day on her veranda, watching the goings-on. Her gardens consisted entirely of washed-out salmon-pink mussaendas except for a single white bush that claimed the center of the mangy lawn, where it flourished beside a crumbling birdbath that was routinely emptied of rainwater so as not to breed mosquitoes. The largest of the vastly overgrown mussaendas provided both shade and cover as she surveyed her neighbors.

On this particular afternoon, Old Mrs. Joseph had taken in the tableau of Mrs. Silva's arrival at the Herath house, the presentation of tea, and the commencement of conversation, as well as Mrs. Silva's hurried departure afterward. She also noticed the two Silva boys watching from their veranda as their mother went over to the neighboring house.

"That older boy is no good," she said, speaking in Tamil to the servant girl, who sat beside her on the floor, waiting for Old Mrs. Joseph to finish her tea.

The girl said nothing and Old Mrs. Joseph searched her face, wondering if the girl was interested in Jith or Mohan Silva, there being no other boys her age for her to consider; well, there was Sonna, but he was an undesirable even for a servant like her.

"The new family has two sons and two daughters," the girl said quietly, itching the back of her head with the fingernail she kept long for this purpose, the one on the little finger of her right hand. "Maybe they are good."

The older two of the Herath children came out of the house and left with their father, cane baskets in hand, obviously to go to the Sunday market.

"A little late in the day for them to get anything good," Old Mrs. Joseph said. "By this time all the fresh *mallun* and fish would be gone."

"Maybe they are just going for dry goods. Or bread," the girl said. She swatted at a fly that buzzed around the spill of tea on the tray next to her. Several red ants were clustering around the Nice sugar biscuit that Old Mrs. Joseph had not eaten, and the girl pressed down lightly on each ant, half taken by the way they felt under the pad of her index finger, grainy and rubbery at the same time, then flicked each one away toward the mussaenda, seemingly unconcerned that most of them fell on the ground near her, unfurled, and scurried back to the biscuit.

After a while, the younger Heraths came out and perched on the parapet bordering one side of their house. Old Mrs. Joseph stretched to her fullest height in her chair to examine them, then slurped the last of her tea in disapproval; if the girl had not been wearing a dress, she could have been mistaken for a boy with that dark skin and short hair. She handed the empty cup and saucer to the servant girl, who had stood up to take it.

"Well, we won't know for a while," Old Mrs. Joseph said, trying to be fair, "but surely they will be an improvement on the Silvas. We'll just have to wait and see what kind of people they are." She let the girl help her to her feet and shuffled indoors to clean her dentures as she did every time she ate anything, quite as though the dentures, like teeth, were irreplaceable.

Old Mrs. Joseph, who wasn't all that old—she had acquired this moniker in deference to the tragic circumstances of her marriage—excelled in the diligent observation of what her neighbors did when they were out of sight of their families. If her neighbor Mr. Niles had transferred his lack of mobility into sharpening his powers of hearing and sight and, therefore, intuition, Old Mrs. Joseph had turned her complicated feelings of shame and anger over the loss of her husband, first to another woman and then to suicide, into a rhadamanthine assessment of people, one based entirely upon concrete and visible evidence of wrongdoing. She knew that Mohan, the Silvas' older boy, did not like the Nadesans or Kala Niles or Raju, because on more than one occasion she had observed him making faces at them behind their backs while his brother looked on. She knew that Kala Niles, who lived next door to her, shortened her skirts by rolling up the waistbands as soon as she reached the edge of her parents' house, an act that belied her air of modesty. And she knew that Mr. Sansoni's son, Tony, was homosexual, because he always walked up the road with his arm around the same boy, but dropped his arm as he drew near to his own house. Though she did not put her knowledge of these things to regular good use—it was sufficient to her that she would never be hoodwinked again—Old Mrs. Joseph had power and it lay in the fact that when she did emerge onto the street to walk over to a neighbor, whatever she whispered usually turned out to be the gospel truth. The children stayed away from her. Her son, Raju, could not stay away from the children.

Raju would not have imagined in his most ardent dreams, and his dreams could make that claim, that the Herath children and, of those, the most treasured of the Herath children, the youngest, Devi, would let him into her world. If he had been only a weak man or only a strong one, this may not have happened, and many highs but also desperate lows might have been avoided. But Raju was both a weak man and a strong one. In his moments of weakness, he cowered and groveled and splattered his speech with the *pleases* and *don'ts* that were the very things that spurred Sonna to torment him. In his moments of strength, however, Raju felt deserving. He felt that he could not only strive but be rewarded for his hope. In those moments he didn't worry about Sonna, he didn't worry about what other people might think of him, he didn't worry about the past or the future, he simply was, here and now, available and prepared. It was this latter iteration of Raju that the younger Heraths first encountered.

"Who is that man?" Nihil, the nine-year-old Herath, asked his younger sister, Devi, aged seven and a half. He didn't ask because she was a font of information—she was usually unaware of anything that was going on unless he had explained it to her—but because she was the only available sibling, the other two having accompanied their father to buy vegetables from the Sunday *pola*.

"That's Raju. He's Old Mrs. Joseph's son, Amma told me," she said, swinging her legs in time to his as they sat on the half parapet that served some unclear purpose at one edge of their yard. The pleasures of Devi's life revolved around her siblings, but most particularly this sibling. Anytime she could do what he did, she was happy. If he threw a ball, she imitated him when she caught it and threw it back. If he rolled his rice and curry into identical spheres, she followed suit. If he walked ahead of her, she liked to place her feet in the impressions made by his.

"Why do you think he looks like that?" Nihil asked, halting the movement of his legs.

She halted her swinging legs and shrugged. "Maybe he's mad."

"He doesn't look mad. He looks like he is going to cry."

Devi looked up from comparing their rubber-slippered feet—Nihil's as always in dark blue, hers as always in red, her one point of diversion from her brother—and gazed at Raju. It was true. Raju did look like he might cry, but he continued to look like that for several minutes so she assumed, correctly, that this was simply how his features were arranged, not an indication of some greater despondency. The latter was incorrect.

Raju had wishes, and wishes as grand as his were usually accompanied by despondency.

What did Raju wish for? Raju wished that his father had not committed suicide along with the wife of the previous owner of the Heraths' house. He wished for a more beautiful mother, the kind of charming woman who might have prevented his father from straying to begin with. He wished that he could migrate to Australia, where, he believed, all was forgiven and anything was possible. But more than all this and despite being very round and just five feet and two inches tall no matter how many novenas he uttered to St. Jude, on his knees, he wished that he could have the physique of a bodybuilder to rival that of his cousin, Jimmy Bolling, who had accrued such credit to his family with his coronation as Mr. Sri Lanka. To this end Raju had converted his mother's garage into a weight-lifting studio and retired there to practice whenever he could. Indeed, he had just completed a session in the garage to cheer himself up after Sonna had left him. He had merely come outside to get some air and to check if there had been any developments with the new family.

"Do you think he had an accident?" Devi asked Nihil, the two of them still staring at Raju.

His face gave them pause. Raju's face was disproportionately large and very odd. It sat barely an inch above his shoulders, an upside-down cone with rumpled, indistinct edges, like a just-ripening jackfruit that had fallen too fast and too long onto the ground below. He had small eyes, and his wide mouth was hung about with thick, loose lips that turned down even when he was laughing, as he had been doing when he had first walked up to his gate and into their line of sight.

"I don't know. Maybe we can ask him."

"Shall we talk to him?" Devi asked. Devi trusted Nihil to guide her in her activities, whether the activity was sanctioned by adults or not. Stealing from other people's fruit trees, for instance, something she did remarkably well, her lithe form balancing with ease on the smallest of tree branches, was an art she had honed under his direction.

"Yes, let's go," Nihil said, deciding for them both by hopping down off the parapet.

Those were the only words that could have been uttered by a child like Nihil, one raised to refrain from judgment until judgment was necessary. By the time Nihil came to regret their friendship with Raju, so much would have happened that even he would forget that the first decision, the one to befriend, had been his, not Devi's. And perhaps it is such lapses of memory that are proof that there is some divine hand in human life, some unseen benevolence that protects child and adult alike, allowing them to believe that what occurs in this world is inevitable and preordained and that nothing that had been done could have been done otherwise.

As they approached, Nihil noticed that all Raju was wearing was a pair of very tiny briefs and, furthermore, that what they covered was a very small bottom and a very large front. He hesitated and ran his fingers through his hair, messing it up and making parts of it stand up on end. He looked down at Devi, who looked up at him, her face tilted, eyebrows raised in expectation. She had tucked her lower lip into her mouth and from this angle, her chin in the air, her face looked even more heart-shaped than usual.

"Stop sucking your lip!" Nihil said to her, which was something the entire family said to her all day long and which had failed to achieve the desired result; saying it now, though, bought him a few seconds.

Devi pulled her lip out and waited for him to look away, then tucked it in again. She usually did it when she was anxious or sleepy, and right now she was very worried. Raju just did not seem to present the possibility of a favorable nod from her mother, who, though generous to strangers, *practiced discernment*, as she often told them. They reached the gray gate over which Raju was hanging and through whose bars they could see the rest of his body in meaty stripes and slices, parts of it pressing toward them and the road.

Nihil considered what he could say to introduce themselves. The thought that was always uppermost in his mind, Devi's birth date, the seventh of July, which foretold misfortune whose magnitude was only increased by the very vagueness of the prediction, was not one he could share with someone he barely knew, and he certainly would not utter it aloud in Devi's presence. He thought hard, wondering what shareable anecdote might set them apart from other, less interesting siblings or, indeed, from any other child down this lane.

"We're new," Nihil said at last, from where they stood halfway between the driveway they shared with the Silvas, and Old Mrs. Joseph's property, settling on something that was both true and indisputably different.

Raju, available prepared hopeful Raju, opened the gate and stepped onto the road, the flesh on his thighs and upper body streaked with sweat from lifting weights. The children were taken aback; if it seemed inappropriate for Raju to be visible to them in his barely clothed state, it seemed ill-bred to emerge onto the center of their lane in what they assumed was his underwear. They hoped that their mother would not decide to sweep her garden just then. They also hoped that Mrs. Silva hadn't seen Raju, for they knew, without having had cause to know this yet, that Mrs. Silva would disapprove. They glanced about nervously, but the road remained empty and hot and unchanged and they took some unspoken comfort in the fact that on these sorts of days when the heat seemed virulently desirous, nobody came out of their homes unless they had to. Except, of course, children.

"Hullo! That's the thing, yes I know, you are new, I saw. I have been watching all this time. Two weeks now there have been preparations, painters and everything. Today, no? You children came today?" He smiled at Devi, "I saw you skipping rope earlier."

Raju's shockingly melodious voice washed over the children. It lifted and cuddled its consonants and aired its vowels; it was unlike anything Nihil and Devi had heard and though they had heard a lot of music in their lives, nothing had ever sounded quite like Raju's voice, the way it rose out of the relentless ugliness of his body and issued forth from his vaguely deformed mouth like an ethereal being released into the world by an enormously charitable god.

"We came from Colombo Seven. My brother and I go to Royal College," Nihil said. "My sisters go to the Convent of the Holy Covenant," he added, and then gave away a little more information, just in case Raju was out of touch with this sort of thing. "The convent is in Colombo Three, by the sea."

"Oh! Oh!" Raju said, his voice rising upward at the end of each word and covering, to the best of Nihil's knowledge, at least a middle C, D, E, and F sharp if not something more complicated. "Those are good schools. The best schools. I went to St. Peter's, but my mother went to that convent too. She tried to enroll me at Royal but they wouldn't take me. We lived too far, and anyway," he added, matter-of-fact, shaking his head sideways, "we were Catholics."

"Catholics also go to my school," Nihil said, not wishing to let a slight go uncorrected. He began to list the Catholic boys in his class for Raju. "David Roberts, Tissa Vancuylumberg, Frank Speldewinde, Dimuth de Fonseka, Norbert Pereira—"

Devi interrupted in her own singsong style, her voice sweet and earnest; she had another two years of this before she would learn to speak like her siblings. "And my school is full of them and I'm one of the few girls who are Buddhist and Muslim and Hindu. We used to sit together during religion and the Catholic girls used to study the Bible. I think. But Tha, that's my father, our father, he said that they made a law and now they have to teach all the religions in all the schools. Some schools don't do it, but recently my convent has started to do it. So now they teach me Buddhism at my convent and all the Muslim girls learn Islam and—"

"He knows all that," Nihil said, irritated by this long speech; the passing of information ought to be left to one's elders.

"No, no, no, I didn't know anything! I didn't know anything about this," Raju said, looking very alarmed, the second, they learned in due course, of his two most frequent expressions. "When did this happen?"

"Tha says that it's a good thing," Nihil said, reassuringly, "so that everybody can learn their own religions and nobody can be forced to learn anybody else's religion."

"Your father works for the government? Is he a big man?"

"Tha is in the Ministry of Education, that's why he knows everything," Devi said, not knowing if this would bestow the title of "big man" on her father, but feeling proud of the weight of *the Ministry of Education* in her mouth.

"Tha is a civil servant," Nihil volunteered, having learned quite recently that to be one of those was considered an honor and that there were no more civil servants left in the country other than those of his father's generation. It seemed that being part of a dwindling brigade of anything should elevate a person in rank, and he felt glad that his father had become one of this group before whatever it was that had happened to put an end to enrollment or selection or other process that conferred such honorifics upon adults.

"Oh! Civil servant?" Raju pouted, and pulled his lips down on either side with great seriousness. He shook his head from side to side, suitably impressed. He glanced up toward their house, so recently painted in a soothing custard color, the sort of color that only refined people like these might choose, and then back at the children with renewed respect. He shuffled from foot to foot, trying desperately to think of something further to say, something that would endear him to these new children and their respectable father. They seemed good to him, polite and forthcoming, and he needed some relief from the children who predated them, the ones who mocked him even when they talked to him, asking him questions about his weight lifting and his garage as though they cared. For his part, Nihil wished that Raju would say something adultlike, something about their new neighborhood, himself, the other children, anything that would add to his own stature at the dining table that night when he might share what he and Devi had learned about their new environment.

"We have to go back inside," he said to Raju after waiting a few moments to see if the power of his wish would cause Raju to stop shuffling and speak. "Come," he said to Devi. He took her hand, which he did not do very frequently; his affection for her was something to be hidden with mild berating rather than demonstrated by kindness or care, which, if shown, might bring his fears forth in an unstoppable flood. Devi knotted her fingers around his and Nihil felt their thinness, the lighter weight of her hand. He held it firmly and led her away from Raju.

"Go and come!" Raju called after their retreating backs. "Come and talk again! I'm always here. Uncle Raju. You can call me Uncle Raju." He said all this, but he wasn't sure they heard. He wished that he had thought to introduce himself that way right at the start. Uncle Raju. It had a magnanimous ring to it. He wished he had thought to tell them about Kala Niles and how she gave piano lessons. Surely the children would have been delighted to hear that and to know that he was, himself, someone who appreciated music and understood its importance in the lives of growing children. They might even have asked him to introduce them to Kala Niles, and how fine would that have been, to be the one to make such introductions between good children and a good teacher? He cursed softly to himself as he went back to his gate, thinking of all that he had not said. He hung there for a few minutes, burning in the sun and wishing for rain and replaying the conversation he had just had and mulling over the information he had received. But, momentous though it felt to him, this extraordinarily civil and, he felt, equal exchange with the two new children, nothing further followed, so Raju went back to his garage. *Sonna be damned*, he thought, *these are nice children and I will be their friend. I will be Uncle Raju.* He heaved a forty-pound dumbbell several times as a bonus step toward his future, then dropped it and went to the main house looking for the white curries and glutinous rice his mother always insisted on for lunch.

Sonna's Sisters Pay a Visit

Nihil and Devi could not have known that Sonna, whom they had yet to meet, would one day, uttering words of hurt yet innocent of premeditation, pierce the sweet sphere of their lives. On this first day, their thoughts on Raju, his form, his voice, the children were contentedly distracted and when Sonna's sisters came to visit that evening, even Nihil felt no cause for alarm. The simpleminded Bolling twins, Rose and Dolly, would, in fact, become closest to the Herath children, and it happened that way not just because they were deserving of such friendship, a gift for the absence of malice on their part in thought or deed, but because they made the first move to visit and that set them apart from the too-timid children, including the Silvas, who had stayed away.

If Sonna had imagined that his sisters would be welcomed into the Herath household by the girls as well as the boys, the boys whose source of strength he did not know, he would have kept the twins home by force, for what was denied to him should, he believed, be also denied to them. Or, if he had imagined that within the grace of their friendship much of what was wrong in his life might have turned right, he may have accompanied them. As it was, the girls did not tell him where they were going, nor ask for his permission as he had taught them to do; they simply slipped out while Sonna was away and went to see for themselves. They came in the evening, which meant that they wore long, thin, sleeveless tanks but no skirts over their underwear.

Mrs. Herath was sweeping the garden when they arrived, and at first she did not notice them. She tugged at old leaves and long-dead roots with the edges of her *ekel* broom, seeing not dirt and decay but potential fertility. She saw green buffalo grass that she would uproot from her own mother's garden and repatriate into hers, she saw a hedge exactly like the one she had grown up with, she saw a wall going up between her new home and that of her neighbors to the left, the Nadesans, with whom she had already broached this topic. Just that morning, when Mrs. Nadesan had brought her husband over to meet the new neighbors, carrying a comb of plantains and a packet of ginger biscuits wrapped in brown paper, Mrs. Herath had steered the conversation to landscaping and from there to the possibility of building a wall.

"I have always wanted to have a bordering wall covered with ivy," she said, while discussing her plans for the garden.

"A climbing flower?" Mrs. Nadesan asked in her low, accented voice, her head moving slightly to the beat of her words. "Like Kala's rose vines?" She pronounced the *v* like a *w*.

"No, no," Mrs. Herath said kindly, putting her palm on Mrs. Nadesan's soft upper arm. She could smell and see the faint traces of Gardenia Talc that the older lady had applied to her face and neck. "Ivy doesn't have flowers, but it is very pretty, you'll see. You know, Mrs. Nadesan, all the English cottages have them. And in our country we can grow anything. Once I plant it, the ivy will climb the walls and eventually it will cover your side too. It will be like having a wall made of plants!"

Mrs. Nadesan had nodded in agreement with a slightly furrowed brow, impressed both by Mrs. Herath's knowledge of growing things and by the idea of a green wall. She was glad that she had retouched the red *pottu* on her forehead and worn a good sari, her emerald green one that she generally reserved for visiting relatives. Her *thali*, too, the gold necklace resting with weight and importance, signifying both wealth and marriage, had made her feel grounded, a worthy neighbor to someone like Mrs. Herath who knew so much about English gardens.

"That Mrs. Herath will soon have a beautiful garden," she told her husband that evening as she served him tea without sugar but with a piece of kitul jaggery on the side, all the better to counter his diabetes. "With ferns and flowers and hedges. Just like the English cottages."

Mr. Nadesan had only smiled. Whatever happened with the garden, he was happy that the new neighbors, though not Hindu Tamils as he had hoped, were good people and clearly without prejudice, so warm had been their welcome to him and his wife. To add to that, Mrs. Herath had not even asked them to share in the cost of putting up the wall. That was a good sign.

Now, standing in her garden, Mrs. Herath remembered that conversation with Mrs. Nadesan. She paused for a moment and surveyed the one tree that stood in the center of her front yard: an Asoka tree, with its dense green foliage and clusters of white flowers whose nectar Nihil and Devi had already discovered, sucking at the thin sweetness like birds. She contemplated the miracle of its survival in the midst of such neglect and considered the impact of its shade on the new grass she was going to plant. Clearly, the Asoka tree would have to go. But with what would it be replaced, and where? She glanced at the far corner, the one closest to the Nadesans' house, and pictured a fruit tree. Jambu, she thought. The red jambu, which usually veered between watery tastelessness and acidic sourness, would give her garden color without its having to translate into plebeian consumption. Moreover, it would provide the right degree of shade for her succulents and potted ferns. It was when she was swiveling back to the corner that bordered the driveway on the Silva side, a flamboyant already taking root there in her imaginings, that she saw the twins. They were standing side by side, each with her weight on one foot, left hand in her mouth, gnawing at the edges of their fingernails. She was so taken aback by their presence and their concentrated activity that it took her a few moments to realize they were mostly naked below the hem of their tops.

"Who are you?" she asked, now taking in the less obvious aspects of their appearance, the big shoulders and knobbly knees, the stringy, light-brown streaked hair, the oval faces grimed with a recent meal, and, could that be, yes it was, mud.

"I'm Rose, she's Dolly," one of them said, and they both grinned. Their smiles were sheepish and challenging at the same time.

That their lives were not going to contain what they perceived as normalcy in other people's houses was something the Bolling twins took for granted. They were not poor enough to accept charity, *Only the servants take hand-me-downs*, their mother, Francie, would say, but not rich enough to possess complete wardrobes, so on weekends they wore skirts by morning and then hung them up to dry and went without. Their father and brother only wore shirts on those Sundays when they all went to the nearest church. Sex was neither special nor secret; it was conducted like daily business, if not exactly in full view then in full knowledge of the children, a favor their oldest had grown up to return before moving away. Yet, despite all this, they were children, and they were here to seek out the new members of their tribe with an interest heightened by difference.

"Where are the children?" Rose asked, nudging Dolly as she spoke. Mrs. Herath, though seemingly benign in her Kandyan sari, and probably only because of her daily life as a schoolteacher, gave out a certain aura of reprobation that was hard to miss.

Just then the Silva boys came out of their house, rattling coins in the pockets of their shorts. They whispered to each other, the older one pointing to Rose's hips. His brother averted his gaze after a quick smile at Dolly, who looked over her shoulder at them and waved with good cheer.

"Hello, Jith! Goin' to the bakery?" she asked him.

"No," Jith said, his eyes never dipping below the hem of her tank top and the effort making him tip his head back and look bug-eyed. He tugged at the hem of his own shirt, a washed-out blue plaid hand-me-down from his brother. "Going to Koralé's shop to see if he has got new marbles. Couldn't go earlier."

"Show us when you get," Dolly said. "Las' ones you got were so pretty. I liked the purple-an'-yellow one the best."

Jith grinned and started to speak but Mohan cuffed his brother on his head and Jith's smile vanished. He followed his brother down the driveway and they disappeared from view. Dolly turned back to Mrs. Herath.

"That Mohan, he doesn' like us, not like Jith, the younger one. Jith is nice. He always talks."

"Talks to *you*," Rose said and smiled at Mrs. Herath. "Jith likes Dolly, that's why," she explained.

"What do you want, girls?" Mrs. Herath asked, feeling just a little overwhelmed by these complexities that were being inflicted upon her and hoping against hope that these urchins would ask for a handout of some sort, something manageable like ice cubes or a telephone call.

"Wan' to play with your children, Aunty," Dolly said, glancing at the house.

"Nice house you have, Aunty," Rose added, "nice chairs an' everythin' no?" She lifted up on her toes and, balancing herself with a hand on her sister's shoulder, peered into the house.

"Do you live here?" Mrs. Herath asked, softening just a little, though she left one hand on her hip, the other keeping the *ekel* broom at arm's length for balance and, also, as a stand-in for her feelings about the girls.

Rose waved her head back over her shoulder, gesturing down the street, "We are Bollings, from down the road. First house on your right when you come. Big fence? Daddy's father and Raju's mother were brother and sister an' when property got divided, our gran'father got more, that's why we have the big piece. That whole fence, behind that is all ours."

"We're the second house," Dolly corrected. "First house is Bin Ahmeds, Muslim people right near the big road. Mr. Bin Ahmed is retired and Mrs. Bin Ahmed never worked but makes very tasty *watalappan* at Ramazan. They have a grown-up daughter who works in a bank. They're nice an' all but don' talk much, that's why Rose din' count them. We're next. Our fence is aluminum, can' miss."

Mrs. Herath digested all of it: the girls, their garb, their terrible English, that staccato speech, and, worst, their proximity. She knew the place and she knew the story. Mrs. Silva had told her about the Bolling children and their parents and all of their doings after she had finished her lecture on the Tamils down the lane, but, unfortunately, Mrs. Silva had also warned her about them, and Mrs. Herath did not like to be warned about anything. So though she did not like the look of the girls, nor their apparent disregard for social norms, and though something told her that encouragement was the last thing that should be given to them, she decided to be kind.

"So, Rose? How old are you?"

"We're almos' ten. Nex' month. How old are they?" and she nodded back toward the Heraths' house. Rose spoke through her nose as though she had a very bad cold. Her words sounded thick and after every two or three, she made a snorting sound as though she were clearing her sinuses. Mrs. Herath's regrets began to mount. Now she was going to expose her children to sickness. She made a mental note to ask her servant woman, Kamala, to put some *kottamalli* on for the children to drink instead of evening tea, as a prophylactic.

"Well, we have four children. The oldest is Suren, who is twelve, and then we have Rashmi, who is ten, and then Nihil and Devi. Nihil is now nine, and the little one is seven and a half. I'll call them." She turned to go, then paused and faced them again. "Girls, wait right there. I'll go and get them."

The twins looked at each other and then back at Mrs. Herath. She had an elegant line, Mrs. Herath did. She was not tall, but she was lean and compact, like a small animal with well-exercised muscles. She moved up the steps straight and deliberate, holding the front of her sari away from the mud with her fingers. Her hips did not sway and tempt a smack the way their own mother's bottom did; Mrs. Herath's backside was a well-brought-up one, they could see. Still, despite the evidence of her sensibilities and refinement, they figured she must have a good heart, for hadn't she almost invited them in? Nobody had ever invited them into their home down that lane. Even Old Mrs. Joseph, their own grandaunt, even she shooed them away when they came begging for ice. Now they would have friends, fresh new ones, and their own age, too.

"Think they'll like us?" Dolly asked her sister, spitting out a bit of nail that she hadn't been able to break down.

Rose laughed, "You? Nobody could like you! Even your face is crooked."

"At leas' I don' have *aluhung* like you." Dolly laughed also, at their shared misfortunes, the ludicrousness of their hope for solid friendship.

"Anyway, I'm getting better," Rose said, holding out some hope for the Ayurvedic treatment her mother had found for the patches of discolored skin on her back, their lighter pigment spreading erratically, a tracery of torn lace. She turned away from her sister and as she did so, she caught a movement out of the corner of her eye; it was a movement of color and peace. "They're coming. My god. Look, Dolly, look how nicely dressed. But why only the girls?"

"Where are the boys, Aunty?" Dolly asked, grinning.

Mrs. Herath ignored her question. "Girls, I am going to give you some extra skirts in case you need—"

"No need, Aunty. We have. We only wear in the mornin'. If we came in the mornin' then would have had skirts," Rose said before bursting into a prolonged bout of giggling. "Why? You don' believe?" she asked through mirthful gusts. "You don' believe no, Aunty? But it's true! That's how we are. Can ask Mummy if you wan'. She'll tell." And she laughed again.

"Never mind if you have, but for now, put these on," Mrs. Herath said, holding the skirts out to them. They hesitated, looking from the garments to the children as if wondering whether the bargain was worth it. Then Dolly stepped forward and took the skirts. She handed one to her sister and pulled one on herself.

"We can return them later," Dolly said.

"No, no, girls. You can keep those. Just to have an extra one. For the evening, that is, since you already have for the morning." Mrs. Herath was irritated by the lilt and lapses in her own sentences. She was mimicking them in an effort to influence them and this was not usual for her. Her more common pattern was to say something and have her students and children, and even her husband, simply up and do her bidding. What was it about these girls? She flung a bitter thought toward Mrs. Silva for having forced this course of action upon her. She waited impatiently until the clothes were on, the girls balancing against each other, and then she called out to the boys.

The Herath children arrayed themselves in front of their mother, who rested her palms on the shoulders of the two in each corner, the older ones. They looked like a flock of angels to the Bolling twins, whose smiles rose to the surface and then retreated several times in awe. Rose and Dolly would come to believe that their lives were graced once and only once and that the grace they remembered came from these four children, but for now they were simply dumbstruck.

"Come inside," Rashmi said, walking over to Rose and taking her hand. Dolly felt her own being held in another hand, the smaller one, Devi. For the first time in their lives, the twins felt shy. They climbed reverently up the five steps to the veranda of the Heraths' house and wiped their feet with gusto on the coir mat at the front door.

"We can play outside if you like, Aunty," Rose said to Mrs. Herath, gratitude flowing through her body.

"No, that's okay," Mrs. Herath said. "You can go inside." Her heart swelled as she uttered these words. She felt good. She *was* good. She would do good. She would turn those children around. She watched until the last of the children had disappeared inside and then turned back to her garden.

Telling Secrets

Inside the house, in the girls' bedroom, the children regarded each other, the Heraths seated on Rashmi's bed, the twins on Devi's. Rose breathed deeply, inhaling the scent of the room, a mix of sandalwood soap, a floral powder, and the outdoors. Dolly simply stared at everything: the almirah with its double doors and inlaid full-length mirror, the dressing table with two combs and a small array of Pears products, powders, and cologne, the one desk and two chairs that sat near the window, one half of it pristine, the other a tumble of books and papers, and not a single cobweb or bit of dust in sight, not even in the highest corners of the ceiling. She looked at the Herath girls. It seemed fitting that the room was meant for girls like them, girls who wore skirts and blouses designed to match, with cotton lace edgings at hems and necklines, their feet scrubbed clean and tucked into slippers.

To the twins, the Herath children seemed beautiful if for no other reason than the degree to which they were different from themselves in the most apparent ways: cleanliness and order. Rashmi and Devi had neatly trimmed hair that lifted in waves off their foreheads, offsetting their faces, and the boys wore shirts whose collars were ironed flat, and in which they seemed perfectly at ease with themselves and the world. When they discussed the children later, the twins would diverge. To Dolly, Nihil and Rashmi were the handsome and pretty ones, respectively. *Such nice eyes*, she'd say, *did you see how long their eyelashes were?* To Rose it was Suren and Devi. *Never seen smiles like that*, she'd say, *like the whole world is good*.

The Heraths saw scruffy girls, unpolished, unwashed, their fingernails gnawed, their toenails caked with dirt. But they also felt, even though they could not name it, the innocence before them. They saw friends. *If she washes herself better, Dolly would be quite pretty*, Rashmi would say later. *Rose has a nice voice, if only someone could teach her how to sing*, Suren would say.

At last Devi stood up, unable to contain her curiosity, walked over to the girls, climbed onto the bed beside them, and examined Dolly's hair, which, unlike her own short style, hung down to Dolly's waist in a brown-tinged matte. She picked up Rose's hair in her other hand to compare the two. They were both the same, she decided, the same color, the same weight.

She ran her fingers through her hair and then tried to do the same to the two heads in front of her. It didn't work. Her fingers got stuck and the girls winced.

"Can I comb your hair?" Devi asked Rose, who seemed the less intimidating of the two.

"If you wan'," Rose said, "but even Mummy hates to comb. Always full of knots, my hair."

Devi hopped off her bed, got her comb, and then, thinking better of it, took her sister's comb instead; it was bigger and had wider teeth and, in any case, anything belonging to Rashmi was more efficient. She started at the ends of Rose's hair and worked her way up just as she had watched her mother do when she unwrapped her hair from its bun and let it fall down, down, down to the backs of her knees. Once, when her mother wasn't home, she had climbed up on the last shelf of her mother's almirah to gaze at the sad Jesus face on the postcard wedged at the back of the top shelf, and her fingers had caught the fold of one of her mother's "good" saris and the whole stack had come sliding out and knocked her to the ground. Devi had decided then and there that what she had felt was the sensation of luxury as silk after silk slid out, unfolded like lotuses, and poured over her head and body. She planned to grow her hair long like her mother's so she could keep that feeling with her and take it wherever she went, cascading and shimmering around her like a special shield. As soon as she turned nine that is, which is when the growing of hair would be permitted by her mother.

Working hard on Rose's head, Devi realized that some hair could be considered the opposite of silk. *Kohu*, she thought. Yes, that was a good approximation for the strands that lay inert, spiky, and without character in her hand just like the strands that Kamala plucked from the sides of half-bald coconuts or that fell out from the bottom of her kitchen broom. If Rose washed it, though, like she and Rashmi did, using Sunsilk Egg Protein or, sometimes, the special bottle of Finesse that one of her mother's students had brought back from America, maybe then their hair would be lovely too. She was just about to suggest this course of action, believing as she did in the power of determination to transform the unpleasant into the better, when Rose spoke.

"Y'all don' talk much, no?" Rose said, smiling good-naturedly at the other three Herath children. "In our house of course, talkin' all the time. My god, no Dolly? Mummy and Daddy talk talk talk and then they fight. Your parents fight?"

This was not a question that Nihil, for one, could answer honestly. It was not that his parents did not fight, it was the fact that their fights were complicated by alternating and often self-contradicting narratives the following morning. According to their mother, their father was always one of two things: a misguided fool or anyway-a-good-man. As far as his father was concerned, no fight had ever taken place, or if it had, it was merely an exchange of ideas the essence of which led back, always, like some ancient river rediscovering its true path, to the doings of the government, and, after swirling there in furious concentric circles to gather its strength, flowed on to the root of all evil: the CIA. Such evenings were also often punctuated by his mother bursting into "God Bless America," "My Country 'Tis of Thee," "God Save the Queen," and sometimes, for variation, Nihil felt, "The Maple Leaf Forever," all of which were songs that Mrs. Herath had faithfully strung on the vocal cords of each of her musically gifted children. Could arguments filled with singing be called fighting? Nihil did not have an answer.

Next to Nihil, Suren began humming, and then, softly, to sing:

> *"In Days of yore,*
> *From Britain's shore*
> *Wolfe the dauntless hero came*
> *And planted firm Britannia's flag*
> *On Canada's fair domain.*
> *Here may it wave,*
> *Our boast, our pride*
> *And joined in love together,*
> *The thistle, shamrock, rose entwined,*
> *The Maple Leaf Forever."*

"Nice voice!" Dolly said, not smiling, which, in the Bolling twins' case, bespoke awe. "Down our lane only Kala Niles has music. They're Tamil people. Her father doesn't go anywhere, but Raju says he can hear even better because he can' move. Kala Niles gives lessons. Children come from other places to their house to learn. And the Sansonis' son, Tony Sansoni, at the top of the lane? Suppose' to have a guitar but we have never heard him play. We only hear Kala Niles."

"Every day she practices and we listen," Rose added. "We don' go too near. They don' like that. Have you heard her playing?"

Suren nodded. Kala Niles's piano playing had been the first thing that had reassured him that their move had been a good one, and though he had not met Kala Niles yet, he had divined in the arrangements she favored—Beethoven's *Pathétique* Sonata, for instance, with its repeated dissonance and resolutions—a keen ear and a complex personality.

Dolly asked him to sing another song, and Suren obliged with a few bars of "Hey Jude" and "Yesterday," two songs that Nihil and he had learned by listening to the radio during the *Beatles Hour,* for one entire week.

"So nice. Makes me feel sad." Dolly said, sighing. "With that voice must 'ave won prizes an' everythin', no? Can be on the radio even. You tried? Mus' tell your parents to try, no. They can probably send you there. To the radio people. To the SLBC."

Rose, who had been alternately tapping and caressing the green cotton sheet on Devi's bed, joined in. "*Velona Hit Parade* has all the hit songs. All from pop stars in America. But you can sing nicely. When you get big an' all you can start a group. You can sing, we can dance," she pushed her sister as she said this. "Yes, she can dance. I can too. Like this, see?" Rose stood up and began moving her hips in a circle, her hands raised in the air.

Rashmi did not care for the look of this dance. It was far too something. Far too vulgar, she decided. That was the word for it. Of the Herath children, Rashmi excelled in the pursuit of perfection; her fingers curved just so on the piano, her voice rose but only as much as was required by each note, and when she danced, as she did in her Oriental dancing classes, her steps moved precisely to the drums. But, as perfection usually goes, her performances lacked joy. For their part, Rose and Dolly had an excess of free spiritedness and moved like reeds in the wind, dipping and swiveling to a completely tuneless rendition of "Ra Ra Rasputin," by Boney M., which was currently dominating the *Velona Hit Parade.*

"I don't think our parents want me to be in a band," Suren said now, in his soft voice. He had always spoken that way, having figured out at a very young age that the softer his own voice, the greater the attention he commanded from his siblings and even, sometimes, his parents.

Rose stopped dancing. "Then don' wait for parents!" she declared. "Our sister, Sophia, she din' wait for our parents. She got a boyfriend, not even Burgher, a Tamil Hindu boy, and ran away in the middle of the night. An' she was only fifteen." Rose flopped down onto Devi's bed as she said this and began cooling herself by flapping the front of her top. She sagged her shoulders, and the part of her belly that protruded over the waistband of Rashmi's old skirt rested gently in her lap like a comfort-seeking mammal.

"You heard? That's what Sophia did. You can too. With a voice like that, sky would be the limit for me. Right, Dolly? I would be in the films. I would be in Hollywood!" She flung herself back on the bed, cackling with laughter.

Devi reached around Rose to rearrange her tank top properly over her belly, then pushed her up to a sitting position so she could resume combing her hair. Once again, however, she was thwarted in her recommendation of the use of shampoo by an interruption, this time from her older sister.

"Did Sophia come back?" Rashmi asked, her voice betraying her shock.

"Sophia came back all right," Dolly said. "She is always comin' back. Whenever she fights with the man, she's back but she won' stay. Comes for the day and goes before night. They are madly in love. Can tell. All the marks on her arms. She says he's always grabbin' an' tellin' her not to go. Three kids even already. An' another one comin'. We're hopin' twins. Like us."

The curtain to their doorway fluttered and all the children looked up. Kamala poked her head in. Her eyes washed over the six faces, but her question was directed to Rashmi: "*Baba*, shall I bring some tea for them?"

"Yes, Kamala. Bring some tea and . . . are there any biscuits?"

Kamala shook her head from side to side in agreement and left. The tea had already been made, the question being simply a courtesy, and she returned almost immediately with six cups of tea and Maliban biscuits arranged in a pretty circle on a pale-blue plate. Rashmi noted with the satisfaction of a true lady of the house that there were six each of every kind, chocolate biscuits, cream wafers, lemon puffs, and plain milk.

The twins looked at each other. They had never had a proper servant, and had never served anybody tea in matching cups and saucers or bothered to place biscuits on a plate, and they certainly did not own a tray. Furthermore, at their house, food was always a problem because there was never enough of one thing to be shared equally among all, which meant that, as their parents insisted, they were left to *sort it out* among themselves. Now, arrayed before them, was an equal part of everything. They sat up straight and crossed their legs the way Rashmi had been doing until she had risen to hand the cups to each of them and her siblings before taking her own.

"If you use some shampoo like Sunsilk Egg Protein, then your hair will be much nicer!" Devi burst out, only to be shushed by her three siblings.

"That's not a nice thing to say, Devi," Rashmi said. "You should apologize to Rose. At once."

Devi hung her head, hiding her eyes behind waves of hair. "I'm just trying to help her to be like us," she said.

Rose laughed, "My god, can' be like you all even in a million years! No need for sorry. My hair is like this all the time. Don' have shampoo, got to use soap even that only if we're lucky, Rexona. Otherwise, Lifebuoy."

All the Heraths grew quiet in the face of this information. Not having shampoo was one thing, but to have to use what their mother referred to as *laborers' soap* on one's hair, this was out of the realm of imagination. Devi resolved to give the twins the two special packets of Sunsilk that had come with the bottle her mother had bought for them and that Devi had been saving just for the sheer delight of feeling the soft-bellied pouches between her palms. It didn't matter what Rashmi said, if she were Rose or Dolly she'd want someone to give her some Sunsilk too. She arranged her treats in a circle in her saucer and separated the two halves of the chocolate biscuit. She brought it to her mouth to scrape the cream off with her teeth, but Rashmi touched her arm and shook her head, no, and Devi obeyed, pasting the biscuit together again and taking a well-mannered bite off one edge.

"Do you have brothers or just Sophia?" Nihil asked after a long silence during which he, too, put his chocolate biscuit back together again before Rashmi could catch him misbehaving.

"Have one brother. Sonna. But he's rotten." Dolly said.

"Rotten? How?" Suren asked.

Dolly shrugged.

"Is he the tall boy who was standing with Uncle Raju?" Devi asked.

"If he was shoutin' or looked angry, then that's him," Dolly said. "Was he shoutin'?"

"No, he wasn't shouting," Rashmi said, thinking about the boy she had seen staring at them during the late morning and part of the afternoon too. She wanted to say she had thought he was handsome but that seemed inappropriate in the presence of the boy's sisters. So she simply mentioned the other thing she had noticed. "He looked sad."

At this the twins broke into a gale of laughter so fierce that the Herath children too began to grin. "Our Sonna sad? You mus' be crazy!" Rose said through her laughter.

"Two things for him," Dolly added, "bullyin' us and fightin' with our father."

"An' hittin' Raju, don' forget that!" Rose said.

Their conversation drifted on to other things and before long they fell into the pattern of all children, sharing secrets unabashedly, secure in the knowledge that what was told would remain confidential.

Rose revealed that her greatest fear was that Sonna would pick a fight with their father and be beaten to death, and that her big dream was to break the Guinness World Record for standing on one foot on a stage in Viharamahadevi Park, a task that she felt was well within her sights.

Dolly said: "I don' like the Silvas nex' door, but I like Jith. But I never get to talk to him because Mrs. Silva won' let him come and play with us. An' Mohan too, he won' let Jith talk to us either. I like Jith. I like him a lot." Rose giggled at this "secret," with which she was obviously very familiar, and Dolly pinched her arm and told her to stop it. "Also, I wish Sophia would come back to stay," Dolly continued, "but since she's not there I'm happy to be a twin," for she did not like her brother, no, she did not like him at all.

Suren's statement was so clear that nobody asked him to explain: he wanted his life to begin and end each day with music and nothing else, and not maths not chess in between but more music.

Rashmi said with great confidence that she intended to rise to the rank of head prefect at her convent, go to university to become a doctor, then get married and raise a family of two boys and two girls with her engineer husband, who would make sure her house would be big enough to include her aging parents, whose senility and deaths she would nurse and mourn accordingly.

"Someday, I'm going to play cricket for the first eleven at Royal," Nihil said into the silence that followed Rashmi's words, which were more revelation than aspiration. "Also, I want Devi to grow up to be fifty soon so I can stop worrying about her." And as he said this he avoided looking at either Suren or Rashmi, but he put his arm around Devi, who was now seated next to him, and those words and that gesture made the Bolling twins feel as though they had been let into a very private club and so they said they, too, would look after Devi since she obviously needed it, being the youngest and all.

"I have three notebooks, one for flowers, one for pictures torn out of the Kiddie Page in the *SatMag* that comes on the weekend, and one for writing, but it's still empty because I don't know what is important enough to write," Devi said, followed by a confession that came out in a rush: "I once ate the whole bag of *hoonu bittara* that Aunty Saddha gave me to share with all of you but now I have been sorry about it for two whole years so you shouldn't be angry," and she flung her head into Rashmi's lap, making everybody laugh.

While these stories were shared inside the girls' bedroom, Mrs. Herath, feeling herself elevated slightly upon the prospect of future merit, sang an old love song as she gardened, Kamala, the servant woman, busied herself washing the teacups and, upon the insistence of his wife, Lucas prepared to venture forth and introduce himself to the new arrivals.

The Keeper of Sal Mal Lane

Sal Mal Lane was named for the trees that surrounded the neighborhood and collected in a grove at the closed top end of it. At the time the Heraths moved in, the grove was visible but not accessible. It was cordoned off by a barbed-wire fence while the local authorities debated the possibility of turning the road into a throughway, a discussion that would be decided favorably for Sal Mal Lane thanks to those trees, whose beauty and religious significance ultimately stopped the plans for expansion, though it would be quite a while before the fence would be taken down. It was located a half mile away from the Pamankade-Dehiwela bridge, which placed it within the capital city of Colombo, but just barely. It was a quiet, residential neighborhood, made even more so by the heavy traffic on the main road that met Sal Mal Lane in a T intersection. The vehicles that moved fast along that road almost never turned into the lane; they simply sped by, taking the furious sound of their speed with them. To the right, on that main road, was a hairpin turn around which the buses raced each other, eager to take on passengers, barely slowing to let any off. To the left was the bus halt where the 120 bus stopped, and also the somewhat more infrequent 135, 116, and 107, and the near-mythical 109, whose route nobody knew but into whose empty belly all the children yearned to climb, even if only to travel two stops they didn't care in which direction they went.

Right across that main road was an empty lot continuing from day to day in the state of dirt and general ugliness preferred by its owner, a widow, Mrs. Ratwatte, who ran a batik business. She wanted to maintain an illusion of decay and lost fortunes even as she chased down her workers with a bandy-legged gait that made them, mostly young Tamil girls from the tea estates up-country, seasick to observe, and raked in cash from her commissioned creations, depicting blue-green peacocks and red-orange Kandyan dancers, for tourist boutiques. Part of Mrs. Ratwatte's stage set, *to ward off the evil eye*, was the donation of a shack to Lucas and his wife, Alice, in the farthest corner of her property and a meager stipend. In her mind, they were respectable beggars, the kind who, she imagined, accrued daily merit for her prospects in the next life and yet were able, by virtue of their impoverished appearance, to dissuade anybody else from setting up camp in the unused portions of her land.

Alice, like her benefactor, was also bowlegged; furthermore, she shared Mrs. Ratwatte's countenance of constant outrage at what the world was perpetrating around them. In Alice's case, this was a look directed almost exclusively toward her husband, Lucas. If the price of bread rose, it was because he had cast his vote for the new government. If the traffic went too fast for her to cross, it was because he had chosen to accept charity. And so on.

This evening, however, Alice was in high spirits. New people had moved in and with them had come the prospect of an improved hierarchy. The Silvas, whom she had never taken to and who had, in turn, never paid her or her husband any mind, could now be even more pointedly ignored as she, Alice, went in and out of the house next door to the Silvas as, surely, a welcome visitor. Here was a chance to create a whole new tale to explain her circumstances, maybe even employment, if they needed her help, and she felt like being generous. Yes, she might cook for them on occasion, to bail them out in an hour of need when a live-in servant went missing, she might do that. But first, she had to be introduced to them properly, and introductions were best handled by her husband. Already she had cooked three straight meals of rice and sambol, two of those with dried fish, to get him to move. She had also spoken of the matter of solidarity, for they were not simply new but, she had heard, they were Sinhalese Buddhists.

"If you don't go today, someone else will get to them," she said, as she squatted by the tap set into the back wall of their dwelling and scrubbed a blackened clay rice pot. "Can't have some Muslim or Tamil women from the Elakandiya going there and inserting themselves."

Lucas considered the possibility of one of the slum dwellers offering their services to the Heraths. Unlikely, he thought, the Heraths were far too new. He clucked his back teeth, dismissing his wife's concerns. "No hurry. Nobody is going there now. The whole family has not even been here a full day," he said, sitting on their one bench and smoking his *beedi*.

Alice sucked at her cheeks in exasperation. Alice had always felt that she had married a fool and that even though his better looks and straight legs evened out the edges of her own less favorable ones, his pedigree could not quite compare with hers.

"You wait then. By tomorrow Silva Madam would have told them a pack of lies and they won't want to have anything to do with us. You wait," Alice said. Invoking the specter of gossip was ordinarily sufficient to galvanize

Lucas, but this time it took a further statement. "Or, what is worse, the *lansis* will get hold of them and who will be able to help them then?"

At that, Lucas carefully snuffed out his *beedi*, tucked the leftover half into the thatch of the roof over their veranda for retrieval later, and left without another word.

And what was it about the Bolling family that so disconcerted both the Silvas and the likes of Lucas and Alice? Poverty, and the shabbiness that went with it, yes, but Francie Bolling, who had once been a movie star, and Jimmy Bolling, a former Mr. Sri Lanka, had done worse: they had not lived up to their potential. The advertisers and pageant officials and filmmakers had disappeared with the birth of their first child, and, as if to confirm that their day in the sun was most definitely over, a freak accident had left Jimmy Bolling with a twisted left arm that he carried folded across his middle, its strength atrophying each year until it resembled not so much a limb as a gnarled twig. All that remained was the memory of a blessed time and decades of anonymity stretching into the future, years that stood no chance when weighed against what had once been. Jimmy Bolling had hoped that one of his children would repeat the glory that he and his wife had enjoyed, but none had. Sophia had forsworn beauty pageants altogether, Rose and Dolly were plain and built so solidly that it prompted people like Mrs. Silva to liken them to oxen, and, as far as Jimmy Bolling was concerned, Sonna was a good-for-nothing.

Lucas thought about all this as he went, picking his way through the mud and detritus of the compound. Even he, passive though he was, could not stand by and let the Bolling folk ingratiate themselves with the new family. That just would not do. No, these new people needed someone to protect them and obviously it would be up to him, like most things down that particular lane.

Despite his sense of importance, Lucas was a frail man. He was narrow from head to toe, with sparse gray hair on his head and chest, thin long arms and legs, and a scrape to his walk from what Sonna referred to as *lazy leg* whenever he saw Lucas. Furthermore, though he always unfurled his sarong from its half-tie above his knees to its full length down to his ankles as soon as he crossed the main road and set foot on the bottom of Sal Mal Lane, there was no disguising the fact that Lucas was not, in his appearance, the kind of man to be taken seriously by the serious-minded.

Safe in his own perceptions, however, as he tended to his sarong that morning, Lucas enjoyed the unknown quality of the new arrivals; his wife's concern for them bode well, he felt, since Alice was usually given to letting her own melancholia sweep over and damn everybody she met, assuming that there was a gloomy order to the universe that she had not been capacitated to overcome. He had to wait a long while before he could get across the busy road, but he did not mind. This was actual work; he was going somewhere with a purpose.

"Ai! Mr. Lucas! Where are you going?" Sonna Bolling yelled from his father's doorway. He had discarded his Sunday church-going clothes and was lounging against the door wearing jeans and suspenders looped and crossed over his bare upper body.

Lucas glanced up as he passed and was startled by what looked like a tattoo that covered the lower part of Sonna's belly, a fist of writhing snakes, some of whose heads disappeared into his waistband. The tattoo was red and blue. It was not really a tattoo, it was simply colored ink from ballpoint pens with which Sonna had drawn a picture, an artful and very realistic one at that, in his effort to disguise three evenly spaced scars that stretched across his stomach. Seeing the effect it had on the old man, Sonna flexed the muscles on his chest. Lucas shuddered inwardly and kept on walking.

"Goin' to talk to the new people?" Sonna asked, his tone mocking. He strode up to Lucas and imitated his walk for a few steps, growling softly and grinning all the while.

He might have seemed menacing from afar, a wiry boy closing in on an old man like that, but Lucas paid no heed. He was waiting until he reached the edge of the Silvas' property with its staked fence and its araliya tree, which is when he usually turned and stamped his good foot and sent Sonna scurrying back to his perch against his father's fence like a bird who could not fly. This morning, though, he was deprived of this fleeting enjoyment by the arrival of Raju, who appeared out of nowhere at top speed, his hands, attached to the ends of his disproportionately long arms, flapping wildly at his side. Raju usually walked with his head tilted sideways and hanging down as if he was helpfully exposing his neck to a tired executioner, but today he walked proudly, in gray trousers and a red T-shirt, with his head up and fire in his eyes.

"Sonna! Leave that poor man alone!" he shouted imperiously as he neared the group. Sonna stepped out from behind Lucas and confronted Raju, whose usual post-body-wash smell of Lifebuoy soap was now overlaid with far too many splashes of Brut.

"Who are you to tell me what to do?" he asked.

Raju, in the full flush of his newfound status as A Friend of the Heraths, stopped a few feet away from them and put his hands on his waist. "Why are you doing this? Look at you. A fine boy. Go and help your father or something instead of disgracing him like this. We're decent people, no? We Bollings and Josephs? Go!"

Lucas, who was wheezing very gently and balancing on his good foot, had put up one hand to shade his eyes so he could take in this new, authoritative Raju properly. As his eyes met Raju's, Lucas had a sinking feeling that he had let down his wife: he had tarried too long. "Where are you going, Mr. Raju?" he asked.

"I'm going to get some . . ." Raju paused and his glance flickered to Sonna, who also seemed curious about his uncle's new sense of purpose. He shuffled in place. "I'm going to get some cigarettes for Mr. Herath," he said. "He doesn't know the shops yet."

They all knew that Raju's cigarette run had nothing to do with Mr. Herath's unfamiliarity with the shops; it had to do with Raju's desire to ingratiate himself with the new people. This was comical to Sonna, who could not imagine any family accepting Raju into their fold as a helper, but it also prickled because, though he wanted to very much, he did not have the guts to approach the new family. He stepped toward Raju and sneered.

"So now you're the servant boy?" Sonna said. "You have no shame, no? Not like us, respectable Bollings, we won' go and do *pakkali* service for other people. Do they call you *kolla*?"

"Give the money to me. I will get the cigarettes." Lucas's voice cut through the taunts raining down on Raju. "You shouldn't be doing these things, Mr. Raju," he added. "You are from a good family, no? You can be their friend. You don't have to do servant jobs. *I* can do them. *We* are here for that."

Lucas was hoping to both reclaim the advantage that Raju appeared to have stolen from under his nose, that of liaising between the new family and the bakery, the vegetable sellers, and the cooperative store, and save Raju from his nephew. He only succeeded in one: Raju reached into his pocket and thrust the money into Lucas's hand at the same time that Sonna put his uncle's head into a vice. Just then they heard the sound of approaching footsteps. The Silva boys were returning from the store. Jith was carrying a very small bag made of used notebook paper. He held it carefully.

"I like the cloudy ones the best," they heard Jith say. He glanced toward his brother and then his eyes darted quickly toward the Bollings' house.

He held the bag against his chest with one hand and put his other hand inside to feel the contents. He held up a milky-white marble streaked with pink and yellow and slowed his steps to examine it.

"I like the clear ones," Mohan said as he reached in and took out two clear marbles, one blue, one green.

Sonna, listening to the irresistible sound of marbles, clamped down harder on Raju, who whimpered in pain. Sonna threw a grimace at Mohan, but he got no response. The Silva boys simply made it a point to walk around the group without making eye contact, quite as though they were stepping around a pile of cow dung, and continued to talk about their marbles as they walked unhurriedly toward their house. Lucas took the money and walked back the way he came, but he stopped at the Bollings' door and banged on it until Jimmy Bolling yelled from inside.

"Why are you bangin' on the bloody door, you fool? Come in!"

"It's me, Lucas, sir," Lucas shouted.

"Lucas! Open the door and come in!"

Lucas was not going to do that. The last time he had peered around that door, Francie Bolling had been striding about in her underwear, fanning herself with a newspaper. The entire Bolling clan seemed to think nothing of spending their days half naked, but he had always imagined that Francie Bolling was a cut above the rest, which had made the sight doubly distressing.

"Sir," he said now, raising his voice against the closed door, "the boy . . . your boy is fighting on the road with Mr. Raju, sir."

Jimmy Bolling let out a curse and Lucas heard the sound of him heaving himself off a chair. He came out in his shorts, his just-softening belly smooth and oddly virile in all its nakedness. He was smoking and his eyes squinted between puffs, and Lucas thought that, if he could overlook the injured arm, Jimmy Bolling, when he smoked, resembled an old actor named Marlon Brando, whose poster had appeared for one night at the Tamil movie theater when they showed an English film. He tried to remember the name of the film but could not, particularly with the sound of Jimmy Bolling hollering so close to his ears.

"Sonna! Get in here. I'm goin' to belt you if I have to come out there!" This was a threat Jimmy Bolling uttered frequently with great success. It was something he carried out infrequently, his right fist was his usual choice of weapon, but his bulk, his collection of unworn leather belts awaiting some unknown purpose, and his bad temper were enough to dissuade any of his children from testing him. Sonna appeared, casting malevolent looks at Lucas.

"I wasn' doin' anythin', Daddy!" Sonna began.

Jimmy Bolling, who had once taken pleasure in teaching Sonna how to walk and talk like a movie star, now found the sight of his son loathsome. Unspoken disappointments were strung like rain-soaked paper Vesak lanterns between them, and, with no hope of the sun ever coming out to restore the colors, let alone permit the lighting of the candles inside, they were miserably estranged. "Shut up," he said. "I know what you are up to. Can' you leave that poor bugger alone?" He looked up the road. Raju was shuffling home, and, farther up the road, Mohan and Jith picked up their pace. "You wan' to fight? Then go an' fight with the Silva boys. That'll toughen you up."

Sonna hung his head. He would never challenge the Silva boys to anything and his father knew it. The Silva boys were so untouchable his son had never even tried to cast a stray remark their way, let alone a punch. He shook his head in fresh disappointment, nodded to Lucas, and went back to his house.

"Don't shame your father this way," Lucas said, riding on the waves of Jimmy Bolling's strength and Sonna's crestfallen face. He left him standing there and went to fetch the cigarettes.

Good Cigarettes

At the bottom of Sal Mal Lane, Lucas rolled up his sarong, saluted Mrs. Bin Ahmed, who was sweeping the front of her yard, crossed quickly in front of a 120 bus, and headed for Koralé's store. This was mostly a wood shop, but the proprietor, Koralé, had decided to expand it and now sold Gold Leaf and Bristol and even a few packets of Marlboro that he bought from one of the workers at the dock who ran a lucrative side business in contraband. He displayed those proudly alongside hand-rolled *beedi* and pink-and-white-striped sugar sticks, exercise books, sticking plasters, and the usual dry goods of rice, lentils, coconuts, canned fish, and spices. It was a good place for Lucas to start. It allowed him to drag out the high of announcing his favored status with the new family.

"Koralé," he called out. Koralé came out of the back of his store where he had been arguing with his wife, who constantly wanted him to give up the wood selling in favor of a more glamorous retail business.

"Lucas Aiyya," he said, rubbing his chest, his smile a mix of obliging and humility, the smile that most irritated his wife, who thought herself far too superior to be the spouse of a *dhara mudalali*.

"I came to buy cigarettes for the new master," Lucas said, before realizing that he did not know what brand to buy. He scanned the boxes, red, gold, blue, and glanced down at the money in his hand. There were two five-rupee notes and two one-rupee coins. "How much are the cigarettes?" Lucas asked.

"One Bristol is twenty-two cents—" Koralé began, but Lucas cut in, his brows coming together in severe disapproval.

"No, no, whole packet. This is the new family that just moved in. They are not poor people. They buy whole packets."

"Ah," Koralé said with the correct amount of reverence. "Then Bristol is four rupees and twenty cents, Gold Leaf is four rupees and sixty cents, and Marlboro, well, Marlboro . . ." Koralé rubbed his belly and turned down the corners of his mouth. He considered the presence of those Marlboro cigarettes in his shop to be a sort of benediction. He liked to look at them and feel their importance, heightened by their cost and overseas origin, wash over him. It made him feel weak and small and put in his place, which was exactly what good things should do. Koralé stole a quick look at Lucas. Yes, he was still waiting to know the price. "Marlboro is of course quite expensive. Most people don't buy those," he said, making a face as if to confirm that they were not only expensive but positively bad.

"How much?"

The words were like a whip on Koralé's back. He sighed. "If you want to buy, then I will check the price." He pulled out a piece of wood with chalk scribbles on it and pretended to consult it. "Marlboro is twelve rupees."

"I'll take Marlboro," Lucas said, satisfied that the correlation between the money in his hand and the price of these cigarettes pointed to it being the correct choice, for, of course, Mr. Herath would have sent Raju with the exact amount of money.

The rest of the transaction was conducted in silence, both men with their mouths turned down; Koralé because of the blow he had just suffered, Lucas because of his new regard for a gentleman who smoked the most expensive foreign cigarettes available. Lucas walked back to Sal Mal Lane with renewed purpose. These were just the sort of people his wife would approve of. People with taste.

He was not prepared, therefore, for the sight of Mr. Herath, who was sitting in the front veranda of his house, bare-bodied but for a thin *banian*, and wearing a sarong. The *banian* he could excuse, given the heat, but Lucas had expected khakis at the very least. Beside Mr. Herath, on a salmon-pink formica-topped stool that did not match the deep mahogany color of the furniture inside or the cane of his chair, was a cup of tea; he held a book in one hand and moved chess pieces around the board balanced in his lap with the other. Lucas had to cough and shuffle several times before Mr. Herath looked up, even though his eyebrows had risen with each cough as though the looking up was imminent for a few moments before it actually happened.

"Ah, my cigarettes," Mr. Herath said. "Thank you."

These words were troubling to Lucas. It indicated a chaotic mind, or, at the very least, an inattentive one. Someone who could not distinguish between Raju, who had been sent out for the cigarettes, and himself, who had returned with them, was not a good fit for Alice. Still, there was something likable about Mr. Herath's voice right then, an affability about his clean-cut features that made Lucas want to plunge ahead anyway.

He cleared his throat and put his palm over his chest. "Sir," he said, "I am Lucas. I live in the Ratwatte compound." He moved his right palm, open-fingered, in a sweep up the hill beyond the Herath property and his left palm in a matching sweep down the hill toward the main road, and he stood that way for a while, for effect. "I know this whole lane. I know everybody. I was here before anybody moved in. As a young man. My wife is Alice. She can cook if necessary. I am here to help you. Anything you want, you call Lucas and I will come."

"Very good," Mr. Herath said, putting his chess board down and picking up his tea. "I am sure you will be very useful, especially for my wife." They both listened to the scrape of the *ekel* broom around the side of the house, where Mrs. Herath continued to contemplate the joint pleasures of gardening and the rehabilitation of the Bolling girls. "That's the *nona*. She likes to garden," Mr. Herath said. He put particular emphasis on the word *garden*. As if it were a foreign concept, this gardening.

Lucas tilted his head. "Any children, sir?" he asked, even though he knew there were and exactly how many.

"Yes, we have children. Four. Two boys and two girls. The boys go to school with my wife, the girls go to the convent in Colpetty. We have to find transport for them from here. That's what we have to do," and Mr. Herath nodded, his brow creased in three parallel horizontals.

Lucas exhaled with relief. First the cigarettes, now this. "I know a man, sir. His name is Banda. He drives a Morris Minor and takes girls to school. Bit packed, but better than putting the girls on the bus, I think. Dirty boys standing there, at the bus halt. Not good for them." He lowered his voice and leaned in, gesturing with his finger and pointing to the house next door. "Even the Silva boys from next door, sir, not good enough for your girls. Even they are bad boys." He straightened up. "Shall I tell Banda to come and see you?"

"Better ask him to speak to *nona*. Maybe tomorrow? She is here after about two o'clock. She is a teacher, so she goes when the children go and on most days she comes back right at the end of the school day."

Lucas felt emboldened by his success. "Sir, where do you work?" he asked, knitting his brows and craning his neck sideways in due deference.

"I am with the government," Mr. Herath said. "Ministry of Education."

Lucas's mouth dropped open. A government servant in a ministry! That would make Mr. Herath's the most important job for the whole lane. Mr. Herath could quite possibly secure their plot from Mrs. Ratwatte so she would not evict them, something his wife worried about constantly. He could probably get a speed bump installed near the Tamil cinema to stop the buses from driving too fast around the bend. Why, he might even be able to get the Elakandiya slums that abutted the stream behind his house cleaned out. He couldn't wait to tell Alice. He looked around the garden and the house and finally at Mr. Herath with a smile.

"Lucas Aiyya," Mr. Herath said, and that Aiyya, the title of older brother, was the first sign that Lucas's dreams were not to be. What kind of master referred to his servant like this? "I don't want to trouble you but I don't smoke Marlboro. I smoke the local cigarettes. Bristol. I wanted a packet of Bristol and a card of Disprin. Do you think you could . . ."

Lucas reeled from disappointment. "Okay, sir. I will get them. But," he added a little bitterly, "Bristol is very bad for your health. Local things are not so good."

"No, no, it's the opposite, actually," Mr. Herath said, but very slowly, the way he always spoke, as if whatever he had to say had been proved beyond a doubt and there was hardly any need to repeat all of it, though he would, as a service to humanity. He ran his hand through the masses of waves in his hair while Lucas watched, entranced, as only a bald man could. Finally, Mr. Herath spoke again. "Our researchers have done several tests on cigarettes and also other things, medicines, for example, and they have found that our local products are far superior to this junk that the Americans are dumping on us."

Lucas hesitated. On the one hand, there was that Aiyya, but on the other was a statement that appeared to be weighted with superior knowledge. Assurance, even. Fact. He took in Mr. Herath's clean-shaven face—at least Alice would approve of that—and shrugged. People like Mr. Herath knew things he didn't, after all. He decided to pass that along to Koralé. Koralé was getting too self-important anyway, stocking marbles, Arpico balls, cigarettes, and things like that instead of sticking to his firewood.

"I'll go, Sir. I'll go and bring the proper things."

Lucas had already turned to leave when he heard a familiar shriek of laughter from inside the house. His heart sank. He shut his eyes and listened for a moment and then turned back to Mr. Herath, who had returned to his game.

"Sir. I must tell you this. I cannot look after your family properly if I don't tell you everything. Those Bolling children are bad," and he made a sideways cutting motion with his palms to indicate the exact degree of worthlessness. "They are badly brought up, they have bad mouths, talking filthy words, and they go about naked in the streets. You must get them out of your house. I was here when all of them were born. Even the oldest, Sophia Miss. She was good. And the mother is not bad, I have to say, but she has done a very poor job with these children." He took a deep breath, his wheeze coming up again due to all the stress. "They are not respectable people like you."

Mr. Herath cocked his head and nodded. "Burgher people, I understand? Down the road?"

"Yes, they're *lansis*. But not like Mr. Sansoni at the top of the road. These are *kabal lansis*. Mrs. Sansoni is different. She dresses nicely and goes to church. Mr. Sansoni doesn't drink and has a proper job. Sansoni son is also a good boy. Even owns a guitar, I have heard, a musical boy. They don't make any noise, those Sansonis, and they speak in English even to me! But this Bolling family, different kind of Burgher. Bolling name is of course a very good one, I know, I know, but even their own relatives have washed their hands of them. Don't even visit. Mr. Bolling's father, he was very rich, all that land, he is the one who gave to Jimmy Bolling but he never took care of it. You know, Sir, poor people and also very loud, always fighting, using bad words . . ." and Lucas fell into silence, his face crumpled into an expression of complete disgust.

Mr. Herath sighed. This was not the sort of discussion he wanted to get into right then on a holiday morning. He was looking forward to his cup of tea, his game of chess, and his cigarette. He was looking forward to settling into his new home. He had a telephone call he needed to make to his friend Vasu, a call during which they were to discuss the possibility of a national strike, all the workers in all the major industries ceasing their work together. It was going to be a difficult call and he had been grateful for this small respite, the tea, the chess, the cigarette, before having to dial that number. But now, here was Lucas and now he had to deal with class and caste and slurs and goodness knows what else. He felt burdened by the weight of all his learning, which, he knew, came with the corresponding responsibility to seize any opportunity to correct, so he reluctantly closed the book he had been using to replay a famous game between Boris Spassky and Robert James Fischer from their world championship in 1972 in Reykjavik, and began to explain class politics to a mystified Lucas.

"Lucas Aiyya," he began, "they are children like my children. We don't turn anybody away from our house . . ."

By the end of it, Lucas had heard all about the contributions to their beloved country of the *lansis*, the fact that the term *kabal* could be applied to anybody, even Sinhalese people like Lucas or himself, the importance therefore of understanding that everybody was equal, the value of human life, and, of course, the need to resist the Americans, whom Lucas had never met and had never known were in evidence in his orbit anyway, which made them, the Americans, seem both invisible and omnipresent and almost thrillingly maleficent, the way Mr. Herath talked about them. By the time Mr. Herath was through, Lucas had sunk to the front steps to listen, his entire body felt numb, and he had decided that he was, indeed, a foolish man, misguided and uninformed, and that he should from that day forth make a concentrated effort to care about the Bolling children. The only problem was his wife; Alice would be sorely disappointed by this turn of events. And he would never be able to tell her what he had deduced from his conversation with Mr. Herath: the Heraths were obviously Communists. Alice hated the Communists, for she had heard they even washed their own plates, which she found inappropriate and insulting to people like her who had always known and observed the proper hierarchy, sticking to her place, assured that her superiors would stick to theirs as they were supposed to do.

After he had been served a cup of tea by the Heraths' servant, a cup, he admitted, he had needed in order to absorb all that was said, Lucas went to return the cigarettes to Koralé.

"You should stop carrying this junk," he said to Koralé, an unusual condescension to his voice. "We should not be supporting those capitalist sons of bitches. We should be supporting ourselves." He reached into Koralé's case and helped himself to a packet of Bristol. "This," he said, tapping the packet imperiously, "this is the future of our country. Right here."

Piano Lessons

Lucas had gained much by the arrival of the Heraths, such a desirable family and one that had so swiftly accepted the offer of his services. Yet Lucas knew, having observed the difficulties of adults in charge of children, having seen the polished piano in the Herath house, having heard the music that issued forth, that if he could secure piano lessons conveniently located across the street, that would be a boon that would cement his status with the new family and make the relationship impermeable to others, including Raju, who might aspire to such an alliance.

We could say, then, that Lucas was the reason for the undoing of this family, for it was at the Nileses' house, in the midst of discussing piano lessons, that Nihil sacrificed his own happiness for the first time, and sacrifice, no matter how pure the intention, can never guarantee outcomes, it merely lulls us into believing it can. Yes, we could blame Lucas, but we would be wrong. We will allow him, then, his good deed, exactly as he intended it. Here he stands, a few weeks after the move, informing Mrs. Herath, much to her delight, that the daughter of the family across the street, whose finger exercises and late-night performances she had been listening to, also gave private piano lessons.

"Kala Madam only gives private classes to children who come in cars from outside, not lane children, but," and here he cast an approving look at Mrs. Herath's Kandyan sari and measured its grace with a sweep of his palm to take in the air between her shoulders and her feet, "for Herath Madam, I think she will make an exception. Definitely. I, Lucas, can promise. I can go and ask if you like," he said, trying to add further value to his clearly welcome role as the primary source of useful information. He twitched his face from side to side and up and down in a birdlike manner, trying to nudge Mrs. Herath into giving him the job.

They were standing outside in the Heraths' garden, and Mrs. Herath swiveled slightly away from Lucas and then turned back to him. "No, that's okay, Lucas," she said, without the Aiyya at the end. Mrs. Herath had never fully absorbed her husband's socialist tendencies though she was not averse to acknowledging a good deed when it was obvious. "You have been of great use to us already, I am sure you know. This is very good news for my children. I will go and speak with her. What is her name?"

"Miss Kala Niles. But one thing," he said, clearing his throat, "Tamil people, Catholics, I have to tell you that." Lucas turned down the corners of his mouth while keeping an eye on Mrs. Herath to see if this mattered to her. It seemed it did not, and so he brightened. "Mr. Niles is now retired, but used to be a Government Agent. Always wore white, always walked very straight down this lane to catch the bus. He only drove his Morris Minor to take Mrs. Niles somewhere. Tamil, yes, but very decent old gentleman." Lucas stared at his feet for a few seconds and frowned. "But he never walked up the lane, though, now that I think of it, only down the lane. Everybody up the lane walked down to talk to him. Very odd. All these years, and never up the lane!" he exclaimed and looked up at Mrs. Herath as if expecting her to explain it all to him.

Mrs. Herath had her own theories about the implications of walking up to greet people and walking down toward them or to leave a place, but she knew that, for a man of Lucas's disposition and circumstances, her thoughts would do more harm than good, so she simply murmured assent and said, "That is indeed very odd, but if he's a good man it doesn't matter, does it?"

Lucas smiled. "No, you are right. If he's good, we won't worry. I don't worry. You don't have to worry either. I promise it. No worries from Mr. Niles."

"I will go this afternoon, then," Mrs. Herath said and, after some consideration of all the assistance the old man had provided as well as with a view to retaining his loyalties, a while later she sent him on his way with a five-rupee note adorned with pale snakes and birds, a note pressed into his palm so quickly that the transaction might never have taken place, their eyes meeting and then fleeing to opposite corners of the doorway as they chatted about her garden and the wisdom of cutting down a flower-producing Asoka tree, a pruning that was still in her plans.

Mrs. Herath took all her children with her when she went to visit the Niles family because they were her strongest advocates. Unbeknownst to her, the younger Heraths were incubating assertiveness, but, for now, Mrs. Herath continued to be soothed by what was on the surface. Reliably well behaved, they went everywhere with their parents, even to the dullest or most boisterous of engagements, where they sat in a row, flipped open a borrowed or found book, and began to read from the moment they arrived until the

moment they left. This was a more innocent time in their circles, very few
having ventured abroad to learn otherwise, so such behavior was considered, by other parents, a gift to be coveted, something to be emulated by
their own children rather than a veneer of functionalism that intimated
of difficulties yet to come. For now, as a way of disarming an unmarried
thirty-seven-year-old woman who lived with her parents and had definite
ideas about child rearing, they were unassailable.

"Kala, if I may call you that," Mrs. Herath began, a little taken aback by
the speed with which they had been ushered from the front door, through
the veranda and to the living room, the bottle of mango cordial she had
brought been taken from her, the plastic covers whisked off the living room
furniture, and they were seated on the cushioned settee and matching dark-
blue chairs that all squeaked in the same key. "I have been thrilled to hear
the music coming from your home and felt I had to say hello to the pianist.
The neighbors told me it was the young daughter of the house."

Kala Niles smiled with a coy primness. "Oh, I'm not so good, not so
young either!" she laughed. She fingered the thick long braid that lay over
her bosom and reached her hips and then tossed it over her shoulder with
a certain degree of gaiety that did not go with her sensible black shoes and
her sensible bottle-green skirt and white pin-tucked blouse.

"No, Mama? I'm not that young," she said to the slightly hunched lady
who had come out of the kitchen wiping her hands on a faded pink-checked
serviette. She put the cloth down, pried loose the fall of her sari from where
she had tucked it into her waistband, and smiled and nodded through the
introductions. Mrs. Herath noted with some interest that Mrs. Niles's solid-
colored yellow sari was made of good-quality cut lawn fabric, and not the
kind usually chosen by women who wore their saris in the Indian fashion.
Had it been a mistake or a deliberate choice? Mistake, she decided, taking
in the haphazard way in which Mrs. Niles had draped her sari, the pleats
uneven, the fall barely reaching her hips. Mrs. Herath smiled indulgently at
her new neighbor.

"Quite young, she is," Mrs. Niles asserted, after everybody had sat
down again, gesturing toward her daughter, whose few gray hairs had
been dismissed as a fluke, by Mrs. Niles herself, just that morning as she
plucked them away with a pair of tweezers. "Kala is a piano teacher at
St. Margaret's and now ready to settle down. Good at embroidery too. See
these lace curtains? All done by her!"

Kala Niles flushed. Her mouth twitched in various directions as though looking for a place to settle. She squeezed her eyes several times instead and smiled, her lips stretching so far that her cheeks became taut. The children watched these facial tics with interest. Clearly there was more to Kala Niles than had first seemed apparent from the well-played classical notes that floated out of her window each evening. They couldn't see themselves, but they would not have been surprised to be told that their heads were cocked at identical forty-five-degree angles, presenting to Kala Niles an impression at once disconcerting in its undiluted intensity and soothing in its chordlike symmetry.

"So, Aunty, these are the children?" she asked Mrs. Herath.

Mrs. Herath, who had let her eyes wander over to the pale, peach walls and the scenes of English pastoral life that were framed and hung in the living room, swallowed hard. Flattery was expected on the part of a supplicant, and certainly, in this instance, she was here as the devotee, but to be referred to as *aunty* by a woman her own age required a sacrifice she was not sure she wished to make. She glanced at her children, at their compliant hands, their variously elongated artistic fingers. She sighed, looked up at Kala Niles, and smiled with a slow open-shut of her eyelids to communicate the burden and grace of motherhood. "Yes, these are the children. Suren, Rashmi, Nihil, and Devi. They are twelve, ten, nine, and the youngest is seven and a half."

"Must be busy, no?" Kala Niles said, sounding as though she hoped this were the case. She had not yet heard Suren play, not yet turned her home into a haven for the neighborhood children, and so she was only what she had been thus far: a usually pleasant woman who was, nonetheless, given to the irritations and little cruelties that are born of boredom and being single in a world where marriage was an expected, if somewhat Herodotean, digression on your way to the grave.

"Yes, but you can see, they are so well behaved I don't have to worry about a thing with them," Mrs. Herath said, without thinking. She recollected herself quickly. "But, you are right, not for me the gay life of a single girl like you!" she said, and laughed as heartily as she could, registering not so much the satisfaction in Kala Niles's face but rather the curious interest of her own children, who had never heard her be this obviously false before.

Kala Niles felt up to making a few concessions in the wake of this last remark. "Your children seem very nice. Much nicer than the Bolling kids down the road. Those ones are just no good. Nicer even than the Silva boys.

Have you met them yet? That Mohan, particularly, I get a very bad feeling about him. Something a little hard about both of them, don't you agree?"

Mrs. Herath would have liked to agree, but she was practiced in the art of Setting an Example for children, the ones she taught at school and the ones at home. She fell back on a slight shrug of her shoulders (to let Kala Niles know that she did agree), and an apologetic, "Well, we haven't really got to know them yet," (to communicate to her children the value of refraining from judgment).

Kala Niles pressed on with anecdotes about the various children who lived down Sal Mal Lane, from the worst, Sonna, to the quietest, the Tisseras' son, and even a few who had once lived there but had moved away.

"One time, I saw that Mohan imitating Raju from behind all the way down the street," she said. "And that Sonna, never up to any good. If you see him, you can be sure that he has just done something wrong or is about to. Bolling girls, too, like ragamuffins, no?"

The children listened, curious about the stories, reconciling what they heard with what they knew of the children that they had already met.

"Have some tea," Mrs. Niles said, appearing again though nobody had seen her leave. "Children must be thirsty. Have. Have." She picked up a Maliban lemon puff and held it out to Devi. She complied, and her siblings followed her example, helping themselves to biscuits and balancing their cups of tea on their laps without spilling a sip.

The return of her mother seemed to agitate Kala Niles, whose voice now took on its former sharpness. "What do the children do, Aunty? Boys must be playing cricket, no?" she inquired at last, getting to this question of extracurriculars when it was impossible to delay inviting the request she knew was coming.

Mrs. Herath took a sip of tea to clear her throat and then launched into her sales pitch. "Oh, they are involved in all kinds of things. All of them take elocution classes, and the older two play chess . . ."

"Chess?" Kala Niles exclaimed with a slip of outrage under the awe. "Such young children. Must be brainy. Are you brainy?" Kala Niles asked Rashmi, who shrugged noncommittedly and looked sideways at Suren.

"We just like chess," Suren said mildly. "Our father taught us." He liked Kala Niles, not because of what she said but because of the elegance of her hands, which sat, folded, in her lap. The way she held them implied reverence for their work.

"And the other two?" Mrs. Niles inquired, more impressed with every bit of new information she was gathering for the price of tea and biscuits, and eager for more, particularly as related in the crisply articulated English that Mrs. Herath used, all the *t*'s hit and *o*'s rounded in a way that slowed her speech and made her sound regal.

"They are also quite creative," Mrs. Herath said. "Nihil and Devi are constantly inventing new games. They put on concerts—"

"I direct and produce them," Nihil interrupted his mother. Interrupting was not something usually tolerated in the Herath household, but under the guise of enhancing a narrative being related by an adult it was permissible, even welcome. Mrs. Herath smiled warmly at him.

"Ah? You direct them, darling?" Mrs. Niles said, charmed. "So talented."

"Odd, no? The older three have names beginning with the soft sounds, *su*, *ra*, and *ni*, but not the youngest. She got the hard sound. Why? Couldn't find an appropriate one?" Kala Niles said, using her voice to take the venerating wind out of her mother's sails.

"Of course *you* would notice, with your ear for music!" Mrs. Herath said, trying not to rise to the bait. "The first three were fortunate, and the *akshara* that were found for them by the astrologer were the softer ones, as you say. But the youngest was born on the seventh of July and had a different sound, *de*, which is why we named her that way."

"Seventh of July? Unlucky date, no? What is that local saying?" Kala Niles pretended to think hard. "About how children born on the seventh of July will have nothing but misfortune?"

"*Chee*, Kala. Mustn't say things like that in front of the little one!" Mrs. Niles reprimanded.

Kala Niles was not to be stopped. "Death, even, I have heard," she continued. "Remember, Mama? Your cousin's daughter, unlucky her whole life and then died in a car accident? Remember her?" She turned to face Mrs. Herath. "Just nineteen years old she was, about to get married too. And not so long ago, in the slums past the bridge, in the Elakandiya, a little boy died from cholera. Born in July on the seventh. So many stories I have heard. What *is* that saying? You know what I'm talking about, right? Oh yes, *jooli hathay mala keliyay*. You know what it means, Aunty? July seventh terrible tragedy—"

"Kala!" Mrs. Niles said and smacked her daughter on her shoulder. She turned to Mrs. Herath. "All nonsense. There are always people who come up with these superstitions. Only some," and she turned back to her daughter as she said this, "only some *foolish* ones believe such tales."

Mrs. Herath squared her shoulders but allowed a mellow note into her voice, which fell, soothing in its ebb and flow, into the room. "Oh, don't worry, Mrs. Niles. We aren't a superstitious family. Why, Nihil's birthday is on the ides of March! A most unfortunate date, according to the Romans."

Kala Niles felt a strange and delightful prickling in her stomach as she pressed on, ignoring the sharp pain in her shoulder and aiming for what she could tell was a fear lurking just beneath that serene voice.

"But not like the Roman tales, the seventh of July matter is one of our own beliefs. Mustn't ignore those, no? Even we aren't superstitious. We go to church. But we are very conscious of these stories. Everyone I know has at least one story about someone who has come to a bad end because of that terrible birth date. Can't be too careful." She felt her mother's glare and quickly added, "Beautiful girl after all."

"Kala can give them piano lessons," Mrs. Niles said, firmly, outraged by her daughter's defiance. She sat down heavily in one of the blue single chairs, which sagged beneath her weight, and continued. "She has time every afternoon after school. After one thirty, you name the time, and you can send the kids. Half price."

"I don't have time—" Kala Niles began.

"Every afternoon she's free. Monday, Tuesday, Wednesday, Thursday, Friday. What days can you send the children?"

"Suren and Nihil can come on Tuesdays, and Rashmi and Devi can come on Fridays," Mrs. Herath said quickly, not wanting to test this bit of good fortune.

What else could Nihil do, in the wake of such a conversation as had just taken place, one steeped in references to Devi's luckless birth date and the many undefinable threats that were waiting for her? He said: "I want to come when Devi comes." He said this very slowly, his child voice seeming especially fragile as it made its way through the tumult of the adult ones all around him. His mother's head turned just as slowly to look at him, transforming her misgivings about Kala Niles into something less destructive and possibly more reparable toward her younger son.

"I will decide when you can and cannot come, Nihil," she said.

He laced his fingers together and squeezed them. "I won't come unless I can come with Devi."

"That can't be done. You have cricket practice on Friday."

"I can stop playing cricket. I don't like cricket."

Mrs. Herath raised her eyebrows and waited to see if Nihil would change his mind, and when it was quite obvious, by his steadfast return of her glare, that he wasn't going to, she decided that dropping out of cricket would be punishment enough and, knowing his passion for the game, one far more severe than any she could dream up. She turned away from him and picked the crumbs that had fallen into her lap and placed them carefully in her saucer.

Speaking the Truth

Nihil listened as the arrangements were made for their lessons, feeling tearful inside, a desire made more palpable by the fact that distress, more than any other emotion, must be kept secret in the face of threat and, to Nihil, Kala Niles was a threat. He sat back against the hard press of the settee and regarded the backs of his siblings, now no longer in harmony with his. Sitting there he discovered the weight of fear and distrust when complicated by the tenderness of love. Devi looked particularly vulnerable, more so when she peered over her shoulder to look at him, and he saw the flecks of lemon puff crumbs on her chin. He dusted at his own chin to alert her, and she grinned as she wiped her face clean.

How long, how long would he have to keep her safe? Now he would have to give up cricket and he would never grow up to make the first eleven, something he had felt he was specially meant to do, even though it was the dream of every boy in grade 4A and probably every boy in every class in every grade in his school. Now he would never hear the crack of his bat against the bright new red leather ball, never feel the stitches of that ball in his hand as he changed his grip to make it spin in different ways, and that perfect green, it would be lost to him forever. He stared at the radiant orange flowers on Rashmi's dress and the orange bow tied around her waist. Tears would not do. Someone had to protect Devi from the ogre who took such pleasure in reminding them of his sister's cursed birth date, and he trusted himself alone to do that work.

"Well then, I suppose we are all settled here," Mrs. Herath said, concluding a long negotiation about dates and times and potential conflicts, not to mention a review of their musical training to date. "Do you take fees at the beginning or the end, Kala?" she asked.

"The beginning," Kala Niles said. "That way no misunderstandings. If the children skip then it's their fault. No refunds. If you have to reschedule, must do at the beginning of each month so I can plan my activities properly."

In the silence that followed, Mrs. Herath listened to the sound of the bread man making his way up the lane, ringing his bicycle bell with his particular song, *ring pause ring ring pause ring ring*. She wondered, absently, what activities, for a woman of Kala Niles's upbringing and circumstances, might take precedence over securing either income or permanent male company. Knitting, perhaps Kala Niles was part of a knitting group. At the convent, or the church, or—

"I belong to the Women's Music Federation," Kala Niles said, reading Mrs. Herath's thoughts with a precision that startled her. "I am the secretary. Also, I play tennis at the Women's Club. Very full life I have. Very full."

"Women's Federation is just the teachers from St. Margaret's," Mrs. Niles informed Mrs. Herath. "And tennis Kala just started. She's taking lessons now with a Mr. Knower who lives in Barnes Place. Two weeks so far."

"Mama, you don't know everything," Kala Niles snapped and rose to her feet. The Heraths followed suit. "Then we'll see you next week," she said to Mrs. Herath, moving a few steps toward the door.

"Thank you very much for the tea and everything, Mrs. Niles," Mrs. Herath said, taking the liberty of squeezing Mrs. Niles's shoulder in camaraderie that had more than a little sympathy attached to it.

"I am glad you moved into that house," Mrs. Niles said. "All that sad business . . ." She tipped forward and scooped up Devi, squeezing her own eyes shut almost as hard as she squeezed the child in her arms. "You are a good girl," she said. When she put Devi down and looked up, she was rewarded by three broad smiles from Devi's brothers and sister.

Nihil was almost persuaded to retract his offer to quit cricket, so affectionate was that embrace from Mrs. Niles; Devi had looked not merely safe but untouchable in her arms. Then, just as they were about to step outside, there was a moan from the corner of the veranda. All the Heraths turned toward the noise. At the end of the enclosure—the Niles household having been at the forefront of the move to hide their open veranda, leaving peepholes on one side by design—they saw an unnaturally tall man dressed in a white *verti* of a very high quality and a white linen shirt. To the children he seemed formidable, though he lay on his back in an armchair whose leg rests had been pulled out to accommodate his feet in a manner that suggested that this was his normal state of being in the world. Nihil realized that the particular scent he had noted when he first arrived came from the old man; it was the smell of sedentary old age overlaid with a men's perfume. His great-grandfather had smelled that way in the years before he passed, and for a moment, before Mrs. Niles spoke, Nihil was transported back in time.

"No need to be scared, darling," Mrs. Niles said to Devi, who had shrunk back into her embrace. "Come, I'll take you to say hello to Uncle." She took Devi by the hand and led her toward the old man. Nihil stepped forward and joined her, Suren and Rashmi a step behind.

Mrs. Niles addressed the man in a loud voice. "These are the new children from across." She turned to the children. "This uncle is Kala Akki's father. You can see how she looks just like him, right?"

Suren and Rashmi said hello almost together, but Nihil and Devi stared wordlessly at Mr. Niles. His hair, which clearly had been white for so long it was yellowing with age, still looked soft and lustrous above severe brows that met over eyes that kept tearing up, and ears sprouting a mass of hair in a non-matching dark. He had long arms, one flung behind his head, the other dragging along the floor, the fingers hovering near a neat pile of white handkerchiefs. For his eyes, Rashmi thought, her own moving from the pile to the fluid escaping slowly down a well-worn path along Mr. Niles's cheek.

"Why is Uncle crying?" Devi asked.

"He's not crying. He had a cataract," Mrs. Niles said, "and something didn't go right with the operation. The doctors are still trying to figure it out." This she addressed to Mrs. Herath, who had left Kala Niles by the ornate front door and joined them.

Devi, her hands behind her back, let her eyes wash over the entirety of the old man, from his head to his toes. "Why doesn't he talk to us?"

"He is probably feeling tired right now, darling," Mrs. Niles replied.

"I talk when there is something to say," said Mr. Niles in a deep voice, looking at Devi. "But it seems Kala has already talked too much and all I can say is that I hope you enjoy playing the piano because you won't enjoy spending time with her when she is in that type of mood."

Nihil grinned at Mr. Niles. Now he was certain he would not have to give up cricket for, surely, between the concern and perception of the old couple, Devi would be quite safe. Right then, Mr. Niles turned his eyes toward Nihil and the thought froze in between remorse that he had made the offer and relief that he could rescind it.

"I heard you singing the first day you were here, and I found myself wondering why your voice sounded different from the other ones," Mr. Niles said. "Now, I know." He spoke deliberately, quite as though he had been mulling the thought over for a long time. "There are very few things in life that are worth the price of giving up on your own dreams, son. Find something to keep for yourself, because in the end, that's all you will have. What you keep for yourself. Come and talk to me when you have found something to keep. You can't keep your little sister to yourself. She won't stay."

Nihil felt a foreboding pierce its way into the soles of his feet and take root there. It inched its way up through his legs, his stomach, and settled somewhere around his chest. He took Devi's hand and turned away.

"It's a kindness to speak the truth," Mr. Niles said behind him, then he added softly, "especially to children."

"We'll go and come," Rashmi said to Mrs. Niles.

Suren nodded his good-bye to Mr. Niles, then said, "I'll tell my brother to come and visit you."

Mr. Niles smiled and nodded. "That will be important for him to do."

Nihil marched out as quickly as he could, tugging Devi along, not even stopping when Devi's skirt caught in a thorny flowering plant placed beside the Nileses' front door and making her cry out *Wait! Nihil! Stop dragging me!* After the gate had shut behind them, his mother admonished him for a multitude of sins: for his inability to conceal what he thought of Kala Niles and thereby almost jeopardizing the musical careers of his siblings, for his brazen and undiscussed decision to stop cricket, at which he was currently excelling, and for forcing his mother to leave the house without a proper conversation with Mr. Niles, who was clearly very sick and in need of companionship.

Listening to their mother as they walked in a wide row behind her, past the long hedges and under the spreading branches of the sal mal trees that hung over the lane, Suren took Nihil's free hand in his. Rashmi took Devi's. Nihil felt vindicated by this clear, if silent, defense of his actions, and by the added security he felt in their combined mass. Suren's quiet fortitude and Rashmi's sensible oversight formed a protective support to the role he, Nihil, had taken on, no questions asked, as Devi's primary guardian. No serpent-tongued piano teacher could do her harm when they walked together like this, he thought, with a measure of pride. It was a feeling that would only last until he had to go to sleep, the time of day Nihil disliked the most, for it meant that Devi had to be given over entirely to Rashmi, who, he felt, though she certainly cared, did not display the same intensity of concern for their sister.

It would have helped Nihil greatly to know that he was mistaken in this belief, that the same fears rested equally within the minds of his older siblings, but it was the kind of information that older siblings did not share, believing it wiser to keep concern to themselves lest it lessen their vigilance. They, too, had taken the information about the fragility of Devi's life, information that was simple superstition and conjecture, but that in their minds carried the authority of the past—when, they were sure, other children had found their lives in jeopardy thanks to a twist of fate that caused their birth to coincide with that unfortunate date—and turned it into their life's responsibility. In fact, Rashmi woke up on most nights to ensure, with the placement of her fingers underneath her sister's nose and the sensation of warm moisture on her skin, that Devi was still alive, and Suren put himself to sleep each night only after a recitation of a self-made prayer uttered softly but aloud in the direction of Devi's bed. Nihil, how-ever, had no such tricks of self-assurance. Nihil had only responsibility and fear, which made his nights fretful and his dreams unerringly morbid.

But this night, the night of meeting Mr. Niles, when time had settled his initial doubts, Nihil felt a small easing in his heart. If he could find something to keep for himself, as the old man had suggested, perhaps it would help him wear his burden with more serenity. But what was it that he could keep? He lay in his bed and pondered the question. Cricket had now been sacrificed. Chess he would willingly give up had he been of an age to demonstrate any prowess. His home-style theatrical productions were an ordinary endeavor. What else was left? Nothing, he thought, nothing at all but this sister who was a sweet-sour blessing, full of need and giving. Just as Nihil's eyes began to well up at the particular misfortune of his birth order, the way her arrival had turned him from being a baby to being an older brother, a caregiver, Suren's voice broke in.

"What about your backwards poems?" he asked, prescient.

"What poems?"

"The ones you recite backwards for our performances," Suren said.

Nihil watched his older brother put on a crimson sarong and remove his khaki shorts from beneath. Suren's induction into the world of sarongs was recent, and the knot untied and the sarong fell down a few times as he executed this adult maneuver. Ordinarily, Nihil would have laughed at the sight or uttered some words about when he might be given a sarong, too, but not this time. This time he simply continued to watch as Suren straight-ened up and took off his shirt in preparation for bed.

"Poems are easy," Nihil said.

"I know. But if it is easy to recite poems and speeches and sing songs backwards, then you must have a special way of looking at words."

"I do. I see them like pictures."

"That can be your special thing to keep for yourself. The kind that Mr. Niles said you must find," Suren said, and lay down in his bed and covered his legs, up to the ankles but feet free, with an old sheet worn soft.

"He said that I have to find something to keep. That means it won't come. I have to go," Nihil said and asked at the same time, seeking assurance.

"You just think about it every day and it will come to you," Suren said, and closed his eyes.

And that is how Nihil discovered that his keep-for-himself was words. Backward words, forward words, words in pictures, words in poetry, but most of all, words in prose. Word upon word that he read in books that Mr. Niles would gift him. Words with which to coax talk out of Mr. Niles and, also, to ease his heart to rest. Words with which to pry secrets out of Raju and good graces from Lucas and a free-pass from Sonna Bolling. Words with which to reclaim the sharp smack of red leather balls against cricket bats. Words to demand explanations and words to curse the world. Words also to soothe Devi and, later, himself, when she slipped through his fingers and passed beyond her never-uttered, constant need for his words.

1980

Elsewhere

While the people on Sal Mal Lane gradually adjusted to each other, the adults to their plans for furnishings and gardening, politics and work, the children to the better games that were possible with enough of them now to form teams, the main road that abutted the lane marked a boundary beyond which lay a country where trouble was brewing. It was the sort of trouble that would soon overflow its banks and flood the nation, turning the small ponds of concern and occasional tears of Sal Mal Lane into their own tributaries of discontent. Let us pause then, to take in the events that were unfolding far from the games that the children played on Sal Mal Lane.

First, the nationwide strike that Mr. Herath had tacitly supported, the one organized by his friend Vasudeva and years in the planning, was a monumental failure, and he came home to say that the decision that was made by senior government officials, to fire every person who had participated in the strike, had been discussed aboard a ship in harbor, there being no government buildings available with all the workers gone.

"They announced that every imaginable enterprise whether public or private was an *essential service*," Mr. Herath told his wife, "and they fired everybody from their jobs for not showing up. Nearly eight thousand. Just like that. Bastards banned all public meetings so the workers' rallies were illegal, but the government, *they* met, *they* had mass gatherings with their supporters."

"What about Vasu? Can he do anything?" she asked.

"Nothing. We are all finished." And he said no more. Mrs. Herath did not have to ask who this *all* were. She knew that they, too, belonged to that group.

To make matters worse, in a move that few had seen coming, the former prime minister, Sirimavo Bandaranaike, was stripped of her civic rights and banned from public office for seven years, and though she remained at the helm, her party, the left-leaning SLFP, was soon in disarray. The one person who would be found to stand in for her during the elections to come, Hector Kobbekaduwa, could not dream of obtaining the stature she had commanded as the first female head of state in the world, a wholly beloved matriarch whom the citizenry had become accustomed to calling not by her name or designation but, simply, *Mother*, the title that was unanimously believed to belong to the unsullied.

Mr. Herath took the downfall of Mrs. Bandaranaike very personally. Lucas may have gleaned that there was something wrong from the steady increase in Mr. Herath's consumption of cigarettes, but he said nothing, even when Koralé asked, simply repeating Alice's mantra, the few words she knew in English: *Ours is not to reason why, ours is but to do and die*, words he uttered with a certain degree of cheerful abandon as he took packet after packet of the right kind of cigarette back to Mr. Herath. Only Mrs. Herath knew the full extent of her husband's despair.

"Things are going to get worse," he said to her the day that the move was announced, speaking these words even before he had put down his leather briefcase, and in a tone that made her so anxious that she forgot to reprimand him for placing a stack of papers on her beloved piano.

She called to Kamala to bring them two cups of tea. She waited as he changed into a sarong and took his work clothes from him, and since Mr. Herath rarely wore a tie, she could be excused for having failed to notice it in the pile of clothes that she dropped into her dirty-linen basket.

"What is going to happen now?" she asked, giving her husband the opening he needed. She sat on the edge of her bed, propped up with a pillow against the window, and combed her hair while she listened as he outlined the various miseries that awaited all of them under the market-driven economic policies of the government of the United National Party, the UNP: debt, deprivation, colonization, privatization, theft of national resources, end of self-sufficiency, luxuries nobody could afford, basics nobody would have access to, and all of this resulting in a reprehensible society of need, greed, and alienation, much like what existed in America, and so on.

Mrs. Herath, accustomed though she was to her husband's pessimistic worldview about the government and his notions about the USA, felt her shoulders slump under the weight of all of this information, the sheer degradation that awaited them all, but when Nihil peered through the curtain to their bedroom to ask if something was wrong, she finished tying the end of the long braid in her hair with a length of ribbon, winding it tight, and smiled warmly.

"Everything is fine," she told him.

Nihil glanced at his father. Devi, who had followed him into the room, also stood waiting for confirmation that all was well so they could get on with the business of playing. She squeezed a variously colored Arpico rubber ball in her hands, pulsing it as she waited, her lips tucked in.

Mr. Herath took a sip of tea. "Mrs. B has been disenfranchised."

"These children don't understand all that," Mrs. Herath said. She smiled again at Nihil. "Nothing for you to worry about. Governments come and governments go, and you are not old enough to vote so you don't have to think about these things," she said.

"They should know—" Mr. Herath began.

"What for?" she said. "They're too young to understand."

Just at that moment Rose's voice was heard, calling for Rashmi, and the younger Heraths turned away from their parents and ran to join her, and so Mrs. Herath did not have to keep her husband's mood and politics from the children, and Mr. Herath was saved from having to rephrase his thoughts in a way that would be understandable to children whose interest in anything he said about politics was usually fleeting. But for the rest of the day Mrs. Herath pampered him with her attentive company and an oxtail stew with bread for dinner, trying in this way to soothe him.

In the end, however, though some of the workers whose suffering Mr. Herath felt at least partly responsible for were eventually reinstated in their jobs, many committed suicide, and in the despondency that followed, there was even less desire, except for the most ardent and committed on the Left, to continue to argue and fight for a consideration of the most pressing problem of the day, the felt-injustices of the Tamil minority, amply fueled by the feelings of people like Mr. Silva, who harbored their own resentments, and hardly mitigated by the feelings of people like the Heraths, who did not feel the need to reassure their Tamil neighbors of their goodwill—it existed, and that, they felt, was enough.

Terms that sprang from the thicket of cross-referenced disquiet, terms that had hardly been mentioned before, like "Tamil minority" and "Sinhalese majority," were now becoming common parlance in drawing rooms across the country, and in the streets the words *The Language Policy* were repeated often and with much shaking of heads, along with rumors that forms required for obtaining this or that thing from post offices or banks were printed only in Sinhala.

"Why should we have anything in Tamil after all?" Mr. Silva inquired of his wife as he gardened. "What's the need for it? We have it in Sinhala, and for those who can't read it in Sinhala, we have it in English. Everybody knows English, and if they don't, it is best that they learn."

"English is a universal language," Mrs. Silva agreed, having recently subscribed to a second English-language newspaper, which she forced her sons to read on the weekends; she ignored the evidence of their lack of scholarship, which found only two sections of the paper crumpled, the sports section and the cartoons.

Nihil and Suren arrived just then, both of them carrying baskets of ferns separated from some of the more rare plants in their mother's garden.

"Amma sent the two ferns you wanted, the pineapple fern and the Japanese bird's-nest fern, and some other ones as well," Suren said.

"Get the boys to help you plant them!" Mrs. Herath called from where she was standing, watering the new jambu tree.

Mr. Silva walked over to the Heraths' side of the driveway and stood there, one hand on his waist, the other holding a spade, and began to discuss the appropriate technique for planting the ferns, their requirements for shade and sun.

"Don't you agree, boys?" Mrs. Silva said. "Shouldn't we all just be speaking in English?"

"Amma wants us to speak very good English, but Tha would like us to also speak very good Sinhala," Nihil informed her, handing over his collection of ferns. As soon as he was relieved of his burden he bent down and itched a mosquito bite on his calf, leaving long muddy marks on his leg.

"We also learn Tamil in school," Suren said. "Tha thinks it is best if we learn all three languages."

Ptha, Mrs. Silva said, clucking her tongue against her teeth, and followed that up with a pursed mouth. She thought about Mohan and how he never seemed to be able to get more than twenty or thirty marks in his Tamil examinations, how he was failing in the subject. He only had a single F on his report card, and that was for Tamil, always Tamil.

"Amma thinks that too," Nihil said, "but most of all she wants to make sure that we are good in English."

"Link languages are nonsense. We already have one. It is called English," and when the boys didn't disagree but certainly did not seem to agree, she called out to Jith and Mohan and set all of them to work. For the rest of the afternoon the boys dug in the soil, carried small pots here and there, and deposited dirt and *goma pohora* as directed, chatting good-naturedly in a mix of languages that did not include Tamil.

"Maybe you should practice your Tamil a little more," Mrs. Silva said to her son after the Herath boys had left, though she made sure that her husband was out of hearing when she said it. "Those Heraths seem to be learning," she added.

"What for?" Mohan asked. He rubbed his palms together to get rid of the dried mud, then wiped his hands on the front of his shorts as his mother watched.

"Don't do that!" Mrs. Silva said. "See what those shorts look like now?"

"I'm not like Suren and Nihil," Mohan said. "They don't know anything." And he stormed into the house, followed by Jith.

Mr. Silva, hearing Mohan's last words as he came around the corner, said, "What happened?"

"No, nothing," Mrs. Silva sighed. "I just told him he should put a little more effort into his studies, that's all." She, too, went inside, thinking that Mohan was probably right. The Herath parents seemed woefully ignorant about important matters, so what chance was there that the boys would know any better?

Around the city, the rumors continued. Rumor had it that the Tamil language would soon be banned altogether, that Tamil shopkeepers were erasing the Tamil from their signs, that Tamil politicians addressed everybody in English and did so out of fear. While none of the rumors were entirely true, there was enough anxiety and fear to make them all believable. As a result, gauntlets were now being thrown down in boardrooms across the country, all of them guaranteed to fan the flames of communal strife. Tamils, within the country and abroad, whether nourished or repulsed by the idea of separatism, diligently followed the fortunes of those self-declared leaders who swore to live by the sword, Uma Maheswaran and Kuttimani and, of course, Prabhakaran, whose followers had grown from the first, diffident, haphazard crowd that had gathered to listen to his declaration of war four years before in Jaffna into a regimented force with multiple wings including public relations, propaganda, and suicide squads in training, all of which now had a name: the Liberation Tigers of Tamil Eelam, the LTTE.

Alliances were being forged, breached, and forged again between not only Tamil factions attempting to fight Prabhakaran and take over the leadership of the guerrilla outfit in Jaffna but also those who were convinced that the right combination of registered political groups could ensure peace. Assassinations began to be ordered, such that, very soon, there would be no elected leaders to represent the Tamils, there would simply be an all-or-nothing leadership that imagined, of course it did, that it would be able to run away with *all*. The prospect of *nothing* never entered their calculations.

And here on Sal Mal Lane, three people were acutely aware that something about the way they lived was changing imperceptibly: Mr Herath, due to his employment and his political work; Mr. Niles, who absorbed everything through the news he listened to, alternately, in Tamil and in English on the radio; and Mr. Silva, who felt energized by the definite lines being drawn between his coworkers. Otherwise, life continued along its usual route. Raju was overwhelmed daily by his weights, Sonna continued to try to understand where, precisely, the Herath boys fell in the social hierarchy of the neighborhood, and the Herath children evolved.

The Musician

First son, oldest child was not a title Suren wore with pride. Indeed, he bequeathed what duties he could to Rashmi with such frequency that Rashmi behaved as though she were the oldest of the siblings, stepping forward to accept instructions and lead the way as if practicing for a lifetime of managing small children. But he could not hand over his gender. That he was stuck with, the maleness of it and, worse, the first-maleness, the oldest-maleness. It came at him each morning like a patriotic flag unfurled and snapping into place in a stiff breeze, calling out to him in the guise of all the expectations that had been organized into his schedule: classical music and chess folded into a rich batter of mathematics, the tried and tested path to the airy adult life of an engineer.

In his thirteenth year, on his birthday, to be precise, Suren attempted to alter the inexorable course of his life. "I don't want to be an engineer," he blurted through the candle smoke hanging over a specially ordered Green Cabin cake shaped like a red railway carriage, a cake far more suitable for a different kind of boy, even a differently aged boy. The cake, settled neatly at the very center of the oval dining table with its new navy blue tablecloth, was surrounded by flat plates filled with elegant tiered tea sandwiches with carrots and beets, and crisp round cutlets filled with fish, Suren's favorite birthday food. In the face of these treats, Suren might have been expected to stay quiet, but he, like the other Herath children, was growing up. And growing up usually meant that good behavior, the kind of behavior expected by good parents who had raised their children properly, was destined to be shrugged off as personalities and tastes and a multitude of other characteristics, and their accompanying difficulties, were discovered. And so, Suren did not stay quiet.

Mrs. Herath, the one who always secured cakes and celebrated milestones, leaned forward to relight one of the blue candles stuck to the blue base of the cake. She waved the match in her hand to put it out, and then smiled indulgently at her older son. "What nonsense! Of course you want to be an engineer. Everybody wants to be one," she said, barely shocked by his words but wanting to make sure that she quelled any unseemly expressions of free will. She knew where that led. It led to unsuitable marriages,

marriages agreed to in moments of spontaneity instead of waited for in the proper way. "Look at the Silva boys, for instance," she continued. "Their mother has told me several times that she is always trying to get them to study and be better than they are. Her dream is to get at least one of them to be an engineer. But unlike them, you, my son, are a genius, you were born to be an engineer." And Mrs. Herath stroked Suren's head reassuringly.

Suren, already seated at the table, looked up at his mother, who appeared to be particularly cheerful in a pink flowered sari. "Geniuses can do other things," he suggested, sullen but hopeful.

"A genius can choose, yes," his mother concurred and corrected at the same time, "but if he chooses foolishly, then what is the use of being a genius? Hmm?" And she moved away from him to set out her favorite small Dankotuwa Porcelain white plates with their delicately pleated edges. As she did, she spared a grateful thought for her husband, who had secured these same plates for her through some connection he had at the factory, the plates being designed for export, not for local consumption, the country being safely led at the time by the fiscally conservative Mrs. B, whose policies of ending imports while simultaneously increasing exports had earned the country a budget surplus and a star even from entities like the World Bank that Mr. Herath preferred to scorn.

Suren watched his mother's activity as he considered this line of reasoning. It seemed to make sense and yet it did not. For what was the worth of being a genius if choice was denied to him? After all, fools were always told what they should do and they were foolish because they obeyed. He was about to share these thoughts when help came from an unexpected quarter. His father spoke up.

"What is it that you want to do, Suren?" he asked, tapping the butt end of a cigarette on the surface of his left thumbnail. *Tap, tap, tap.*

Suren turned to look at his father. Still dressed in his work clothes, a modified version of the national dress, gray pants with a matching Nehru-collared tunic, Mr. Herath was sitting by a chess table, curved teak legs supporting an ornate board of carved brass. He had bought it at the one estate auction that he had attended with his wife, outbidding the competition so fiercely that there had been no money left for her to purchase the hat stand with mirror that she had been eyeing. It did not matter. She had exacted her price by turning it into a side table complete with silk tablecloth and the telephone directory and phone, the latter rubbed frequently with 4711 Eau de Cologne, arranged neatly on top. She had hung a cuckoo clock above it, further reducing its pedigree and worth. Still, it was Mr. Herath's favorite perch, right next to the table, as though in apology.

"I don't want to study to become an engineer," Suren said, a touch of anger creeping in though his face remained uncreased. "I am good at maths, but I am better at music. That's what I want to do. Music."

Rashmi gazed at her older brother in dismay. This was not the sort of passion that bode well for the future. Music was a pastime, not a vocation. Yet there Suren sat, his eyes steady, his mouth firm, indeed, his whole body straight, but obviously at ease with this ludicrous idea.

Mr. Herath nodded slowly, lit his cigarette, and exhaled a first puff of smoke. "You want to study music?"

Suren looked unsure. Studying was related to graded accomplishments and he did not care for the latter, particularly since a steady acquisition of A's at schools where A's were parceled out in single digits each year had kept him from the enjoyment of life in general and music in particular.

"You want to play music?" Mr. Herath asked, watching his son and trying very hard to stay focused. The failure of the recent strike, and the plight of Mrs. B, lay heavy on his mind. Still, although Mr. Herath wanted more than anything else to pick up the perfumed telephone and round up some friends with whom he could discuss what avenues remained for addressing the needs of the fishermen, the rural and urban poor, the voiceless—yes, he did think in such terms—and the possibility of securing the release of comrades who had been incarcerated in the aftermath of the strike, he had decided to make a special effort to be present for the momentous occasion of his oldest son's entry into the teenaged years. This was a heavy price to pay and he wanted his presence to count. So he asked the question again. "You want to play music?"

"Yes, that's what I want. I want to play music."

"That's what you are doing, playing," Mrs. Herath said, her voice sharp as something familiar and bilious rose in her belly the way it had done before the birth of each of her complications. "You *play* the piano. You *play* the flute. And I hear that you are even talking about *playing* the guitar."

"Can we cut the cake now?" Rashmi broke in, knowing full well when her older brother needed to be rescued and hoping that he would be grateful for the diversion, but Suren plunged ahead.

"I want to play music forever. I don't want to do it after school and practice pieces and do it on the side like a . . . like a . . . hobby. I want it to be all I do. I want to be a musician!" He finished, unable to keep the triumphant note from the end of this speech. Both his parents spoke at once, and Suren was momentarily thrown off balance by the equilibrium between them, the joint postponement.

His mother, cake knife emphasizing her words: "And how will you live? Who will support you? Who will want to marry you?"

His father: "Good. But if you want to play music, you must study music first."

"I'm cutting the cake," Rashmi said, glad that at least Nihil and Devi favored her response to the heat rising around them. Nothing good ever came out of such heat. Only tears. In the end, somebody cried. She took the cake knife from her mother's hand and sliced through the cake. Nobody seemed to notice that it was she who blew out the candles on the cake and that they hadn't sung "Happy Birthday" for Suren.

Suren stared despondently at the piece of cake on the plate before him, his mind far away. He thought about Kala Niles, of the way she imparted her own love of music to him, with care, as though the love itself was something to be treasured. He thought about Tony, the Sansonis' grown-up son, who had taken Suren home and shown him his guitar not a week after they had first moved in and suggested that he, Suren, play it. He thought about the Tisseras, who stood each evening by Kala Niles's fence to listen to her practice, still dressed in their workday clothes, and how they, though they clearly did not understand any of her music, still seemed to consider it only right that she should have them among her audience. He thought about the Bolling twins, who were able to sing every song that was played on the radio without any effort at all. He thought about his family and how their lives had been filled with music, between their piano playing and singing, not to mention all the concerts their mother and father dragged them to, each according to his or her taste; their mother to performances of Western music where polite applause was crowned occasionally by standing ovations and many bows, their father to those given by visiting Indian musicians and native ones too who sat low to the ground and seemed unconcerned about their audiences, barely raising their heads to acknowledge that they had even come. How was it possible that he was surrounded by music and yet was being denied the right to live his life in time to the rhythms and subtle equivocations of musical phrasing, the hurry-ups and slow-downs and wait, wait longer, wait in silence of eight notes arranged and rearranged in complement to exactly what was being felt by composer and listener alike? *Diatonic*, he heard the word in his head. *Chromatic, pentatonic, hexatonic, heptatonic, octatonic,* each iteration of the scale opening innumerable possibilities for harmony. He thought about the Pythagorean major third, the Didymus comma, the way the intervals sound out of tune rather than as though they were different notes. This, he thought, was where his brilliance at mathematics bled into his love of music; music was the realm in which his mathematical brain danced.

"If you love music you don't need to study it," Suren said at last, choosing the parent of least threat even though experience had taught him that if something needed to be done, his father was also the parent of last resort.

At this, and over the warning murmurs of his wife, Mr. Herath exercised authority by adjourning the game.

"We can talk about all this another day. Look, Rashmi has cut the cake. Let them eat cake!" he said. He stubbed out his cigarette and launched himself out of his seat with a celebratory rubbing of his palms as though he could, when the occasion warranted it, enjoy such bourgeois things as birthday cakes.

But that other day came and went in an unusual way with the usual result: nothing happened. His father came home one night to announce that he had secured tickets to a performance by Ustad Shahid Parvez Khan. He escorted Suren to this event and then chose a postprandial setting, with the sound of dishes being cleared, Kamala coming and going to wipe away the evidence of dinner, the time of night usually reserved for these useless debates for, after all, what kind of resolution was possible between dinner at eight and bedtime at nine, to opine that Suren should be sent to India, to Bhatkhande, to be precise, for training in music.

"The original music," he said, "the music that began music." In Mr. Herath's opinion, reading, writing, arithmetic, music, coconut cultivation, sanitation, and everything in between had an origin, and nothing could be done in the present unless one retraced one's steps to that origin and, having arrived there, at the origin, read everything ever written about that topic by anybody anywhere in the world. Although, if a choice had to be made, then the Greats would come first. His selection of Greats was scattered and multicultural; not for him the myopic clinging to a particular nation of origin when it came to these matters. Yes, even America had its quota of Greats, though almost exclusively in literature and physics.

"Where?" Mrs. Herath asked, her tone so incredulous at this suggestion that her firstborn child should be sent away from home, that any reasonable husband would have shied away from further discussion. Except that in her case she had an unreasonable spouse, one whose unreasonableness took the form of being inattentive to things like timing, mother-son bonds, years of diligent parenting such as she prided herself in accumulating, and, if nothing else, logistics, for who truly believed that a thirteen-year-old Sri Lankan boy could be so easily shipped off to the Indian wilderness?

"Bhatkhande," he repeated, as though his wife had not heard him clearly the first time.

It might have ended there, for Mrs. Herath was just as skilled at decimating the present evocation of the Greats as her husband was in invoking their power, except for the fact that Suren, thirteen and believing, hope and relief united in his preadolescent body, burst forth in affirmation, *Yes, I want to go to Bhatkhande!* something he said though he had no knowledge of what that place might be, what degree of training it might confer upon him, or the suitability of his level of preparation to its curriculum. He said it, because for the first time he had been told there was *a place* where he could go and study music, nothing but music.

It ended therefore, not then but much later, after many words, all of them bitter, all designed to extract the maximum degree of emotional currency exchanged at black market rates, all of them uttered without foresight or consideration of the subject or his very small desire, until all four children lay wide awake listening, listening, to the way things always are with parents, where the things that concern children fall by the wayside and the adults move on to worrying the same tired bones with the same tired mandibles.

In this case, Mrs. Herath accused her husband with great drama of having destroyed her life, a destruction that, it seemed, had preceded the birth of her older son, though the exact details of how this destruction was effected were not revealed; of interfering in matters he knew nothing about, i.e., the raising of children; and of being in all things, but particularly in the business of family life, incompetent at best and routinely absent at worst for—and could he deny it?—he cared more for politics than he did for them. Mr. Herath in his turn cast aspersions on her mothering and accused her of lacking the foresight necessary to recognize talent when she saw it, of ruining her children's lives, and of forcing them to live not as they chose but as she dictated. These were not new statements, but they had a new source and though none of the things they said were altogether true, none of it was entirely false, and so they both went to bed with bruised hearts.

In the boys' bedroom, where the children had gathered, there was a sense that this latest disappointment for one of them had only tightened their bonds with each other. Somewhere during that prolonged argument, the first one that spilled over into the hours that followed the children's bedtime, Suren and his siblings divined that he would never go to Bhatkhande, not because either of his parents said so, explicitly, but because they realized that Suren's desire to immerse himself in music would, in this house, forever be subsumed by whatever it was that stirred the emotions of adults.

Not Only the Piano

Nothing remained for Suren, it seemed, but the piano lessons that were sanctioned by both his parents, and so off he went to Kala Niles, his music books tucked under his arm, resigned to his fate. Had he been paying closer attention, Suren might have guessed that while Kala Niles knew the extent of his aptitude she also knew the hurt of his disappointments, for when she decided to share her collection of records with him, the first she chose was Brahms 3 Intermezzi, op. 117.

"Brahms referred to the intermezzi as his lullabies to his sorrows," she told him. She handed him the record and pointed out the two lines inscribed on the label at the center: *Schlaf sanft mein Kind, schlaf sanft und Schön! Mich dauert's sehr, dich weinen sehn*. And because she did not translate those lines for him, because she did not say, *sleep softly my child, sleep softly and well, it hurts my heart to see you weeping*, Suren simply listened to the music, a gentle glide between what is heard and what is remembered, each note opening in small blooms, and touched the record with reverence when it finished playing.

"You have to be very careful, Suren, when you use this," she said each time she took off the cloth she used to cover her record player, one that she had embroidered with colorful musical notes when she was just a teenager.

Seated cross-legged on the floor of her bedroom, Suren listened to composers he had only heard of and as he listened he felt that they spoke to him of the lives of his brother and sisters, the difficulties and ease of their daily infatuations. In Debussy's Arabesque no. 2 he heard Devi's footsteps, in Brahms's 6 Pieces, op. 118, Ballade in G Minor he saw the movement of kites, and listening to Chopin's "Ocean Waves" Etude op. 25 no. 12 HQ he sensed his own and his siblings' fears. In the music that lifted so majestically off the spinning grooves of the records, he found his favorite keys, the heroic E flat, the gentle G minor, and the perfection of C-sharp major, the keys he would return to one day when he composed his first piece of music.

What Suren did know, however, was that in Kala Niles he had an adult who embraced him fully, who was ready to support him as well as to let his talent guide her. He knew, because he had been told, by Mrs. Niles, that

Kala Niles talked about him with her peers who also taught the piano, and that when she described his skill, she referred to him as *my prodigy*. Suren's fingers had the twice-blessed curvature of strength and restraint. His *impetuoso* evened out with *incalzando* to draw forth if not the half notes of the ragas he had begun listening to thanks to his father, then at least interpretations hitherto concealed from his teacher. He arrived serious-faced and determined to conquer whatever musty pages she had chosen to set before him. He returned having transformed them into pieces whose notes corresponded with his fingers but whose hesitations and reprieves were foreign to her ears. At his touch, demi-semi-quavers rippled and staccatos clapped with an urgency that, once a week, brought Kala Niles to a state of ecstasy that could only be grounded with the heartbreak of his elongated *breves*, quivering in the silence of a remembered note and making the tick-tock of her metronome sound like guns.

Kala Niles's anticipation of Suren's lessons grew to such a pitch that she took to hovering at the farthest edge of her garden, where, hidden by the bushes that formed her hedge, she could hear him practice, waiting to catch the moment when the taught-piece became his. She would try to guess which piece he had chosen by the scale he first practiced to warm up his fingers. She would close her eyes and picture the piece of paper on which he had dissected the music, the tonic, dominant, and subdominant chords neatly arranged and memorized; if the piece was in the key of A major, she could see the A, D, and E chords written out. She had taught him that trick and he had absorbed it easily, using it to master every piece. But most of all, she listened simply to hear him play. In this, she had company.

The Bolling girls had seamlessly added a new routine to their days: crouching in front of the hedge along Mrs. Herath's garden to listen to Suren practice, though whenever any of the other neighbors appeared they would stand up and pretend to be deep in discussion, faces close together, heads bent, fiddling with their own or each other's fingers as though they were whispering secrets.

"Like heaven," Rose breathed.

"Even better. Like hell!" Dolly murmured, without her usual shriek of laughter.

Suren's music was both inspiration for and antidote to their girlish crushes, but it was a game they could play only as long as he was seated at the piano. The moment he stopped, banality returned and they were left to hope against hope that the decency of his upbringing, which would require him not to dismiss them outright, combined with the purity of their need, would secure Suren for one or the other of them. They agreed that with Dolly's attentions already focused on Jith, Rose was the more likely candidate. In this, despite all that was shabby and by-the-seat-of-their-pants about their existence, the twins were not unlike the Herath children: when it came down to it, they wished the best for each other for they knew that luck, should it find them, would neither tarry nor multiply.

This listening that they did, however, could only occur when Sonna was out of the house. He had greeted their friendship with the Heraths first with astonishment and then with rage.

"They probably think of you like servants!" he had yelled that first day as he cornered them behind Raju's gate.

"No, they gave us biscuits on a tray!" Rose wailed as she tried to get away from Sonna, who held her close with her recently combed and braided hair twisted around his fist. The farther she moved her feet away from him, the more she arched her neck, trying desperately to ease the sharp pain that was shooting through her head.

"On a tray?" Sonna spluttered. "On a tray?"

"Yes! An' had enough for all!" Dolly howled in turn, her head, too, yanked back by Sonna.

"You can' stop us from being friends," Rose sobbed when he finally released them, unable to think of a rejoinder to their claim of biscuits served on trays.

"If I see you there I'll drag you back by your hair like the *vesi* up the street. That's what you are like. Two of you. Like fuckin' prostitutes."

These altercations, which became frequent and painful for them, were never reported to their parents. Both Rose and Dolly believed, and they were right, that should their father find out that Sonna had appointed himself the arbiter of their lives, he would either drive him out of their house to live on the streets or fight him until he was too broken to be mended. And because they wanted Sonna to stay as far away from the Heraths as possible, in the beginning Rose and Dolly came to listen and sometimes talk when there was no chance of Sonna returning to discover their fraternity. Eventually however, they grew bolder and set up their own games in the full light of the neighborhood with not only the Herath children but the Tisseras' quiet son and even the Silva boys, who were lured away from their parents' advice, so delightful were their shouts of play.

To all of this, Sonna had no response.

Meanwhile, Suren's resentment at his parents, both of them, the one for having described a dream for him and the one for having crushed it, had taken root in a corner of his heart. It expressed itself occasionally, in the midterm test that he contrived to fail, for instance, or the fact that he forgot to bring home the results of his London Music School exams, for which his mother had paid extra and to which she had chaperoned him, sitting outside the Masonic Hall while the British examiners, flown in for the occasion, administered the tests in theory and music.

"I had a meeting with your class teacher today, Suren," his mother said one evening. After dinner.

Suren said nothing as his mother watched him. Mrs. Herath found his calm face disconcerting. He had the untroubled look of the blameless, further enhanced by its suggestion of an unshared inner life. No child in her knowledge—and hundreds of them had passed through her hands by then, arriving in their tumbled, mismatched groups and leaving as a single unit, lockstep in their admiration for her—could be as good as Suren appeared to be. Of course, she was right. None of the children were. Not Suren, with his saintly face; certainly not Devi, whose only preoccupation was extracting the maximum amount of fun from each day, and fun is rarely all good; not Nihil, who would willingly trade good for safety; not even Rashmi, who, though she appeared to be given over entirely to the matter of good and perfection, would soon be cozy with the delight of bad behavior.

"Consi tells me that you answered almost half the questions wrong on the math test last week," Mrs. Herath continued. "She took me aside in the staff room. She was quite concerned about you. She said you had finished the paper before anybody else and handed it in. She was shocked to discover that it was mostly wrong."

Suren said nothing, since what he wanted to say could not be uttered. He had decided to cut back on the regurgitation of facts. He was tired of it, and bored. He had tried, and succeeded, in answering the 1979 copy of the national grade 10 GCE O/L paper in mathematics the previous week, and so it seemed pointless to convince his teacher in grade 7A that he knew how to divide and multiply and figure out logarithms when he knew much more than that. Even if his maths teacher *was* his mother's best friend.

"What's the matter? Didn't you study? How could you get so much wrong?" his mother asked, frowning.

Suren shrugged. Divulging his experiment would smack of arrogance.

His continued yearning to dedicate his life to the study of music was even more untranslatable to his practical, strong-willed, and devoted mother. How could he explain that his love of music stemmed from a mind that craved harmony but was constantly in tension with the practical realities of living his life, of minding his siblings, of navigating the thousand bromidic requirements of his birth order?

"I don't know," he said.

"How can you not know?" Mrs. Herath rested her chin in her hands. Her forehead knit itself together in genuine concern. She had neglected him, she thought, that was the only explanation for the dismaying situation in which she found herself. She had simply set him aside as soon as his intelligence and forbearance had been confirmed, like a freshly ironed suit of clothes, and moved on to the next of her children. Rashmi she had not even had to consider: that child had been born perfect. She had been distracted by Nihil, who was constantly throwing one worry or another her way, and by Devi, what with all the terrible things that had been said about her at birth by the astrologer, who reaffirmed his predictions every time she visited him and he unfolded the brown parchment etched with symbols and letters that nobody but he could understand. Warnings seconded by every relative, friend, and stranger over the age of forty. Even the ladies of Sal Mal Lane had echoed Kala Niles's dark predictions about Devi just the other evening when they had stopped by to have a cup of tea with Mrs. Herath after taking a look at the latest addition to her garden, a gorgeous flamboyant, destined to sit a little awkwardly among the graceful sal mal trees that dominated the neighborhood, not unlike a road-tart at a gathering of chaste goddesses.

"Not that there should be anything to worry about," Mrs. Nadesan said, "but it is something all of us have heard at one time or another, this seventh of July business."

"We Muslims don't believe these things," Mrs. Bin Ahmed had said, "but it is always best to be careful. Prevention is better than cure, after all." And she had nodded sagely.

"The first time I heard of anybody dying it was when I was just a child, about nine years old," Mrs. Tissera had added, crossing her legs and rearranging her slight frame until she took up even less space than usual. "The woman who used to cook for us, her son, born on the seventh of July, fell into our well and drowned."

These kinds of conversations, which seemed to occur more and more frequently, had distracted her and kept her from realizing that her older son was at risk, Mrs. Herath thought, still gazing at Suren.

"I'm going to ask Mr. Pieris to give you after-school classes. That will fix this problem. Soon you'll be back on your feet again, Putha. Don't worry."

Suren watched as his mother stood up, strode to the living room, where she picked up her soft brown leather handbag, recovered from it a very small red notebook stuffed with bits of papers, and made a series of phone calls. He listened for the reliable musicality of the whirring dial, his mother's index finger inserted into each numbered section with crisp authority, willing the telephone to speed up. He listened as she discussed his downturn with a clutch of her best friends: Consi, Monica, Lakshmi, and Chubba. She referred to it as a stumble, a little stumble, to be precise. She would muster the forces of private classes and restore him to his former glory. By the time she was done, Suren wondered if the better part of valor might not have been to simply answer the question paper correctly, but it was too late now to harbor regret. Mr. Pieris was coming to regenerate his math skills and he would begin the very next day.

As a further rebellion, therefore, Suren began to borrow Tony Sansoni's guitar, Tony being the only one in the Sansoni family who interacted with the children. Tony Sansoni, who couldn't play the guitar himself, looked forward to lending it whenever Suren asked. Suren's request and careful return of the instrument elevated the transaction and made Tony feel as though he must have once known how to play it even if he could not remember it now since why else would this musical boy bring the guitar back with such reverence? Over time, he came to see the ridiculousness of holding on to an instrument he did not use, one that someone else clearly loved.

"Why don't you keep it, Suren," Tony said one Saturday morning. "I don't need it today." He leaned toward Suren, overwhelming him with the scent of Azzaro Pour Homme, a gift Tony had recently received from his boyfriend.

"I can't play it for the rest of the day anyway, Tony Aiyya," Suren replied, his schedule now further complicated by his math lessons with the tutor. His words were soft and polite, but, Tony noticed, he continued to hold the guitar in his arms.

Tony rearranged a curl that had crept over one eye. "Then tomorrow. You can play tomorrow when you have time."

Suren hesitated for a moment. On Sundays he went with his sisters and brother, all of them dressed in white, to the temple for Dhaham Pāsal, and the rest of the day was usually devoted to getting ready for the next week of school. To bring the guitar back would mean risking more of his mother's interventions, for surely she would trace any new transgressions to his music, and to the guitar in particular, an instrument she found inexplicably crass. He shook his head and laid down the guitar, in its case, on the cane settee in the Sansoni veranda.

His resolve lasted for one more month. Four weeks later, thanks to Tony's feeling increasingly guilty that the guitar belonged to a no-longer-boy who never played it, and to Suren's habit of taking longer and longer to refuse to keep it for an extra day and to lay the instrument down on that settee, the guitar went home with him to stay.

"When you have finished playing, you can give it back if you like," Tony said, understanding that this might be the extra nudge that Suren needed. "But I would really prefer if you kept it. I am going abroad for studies and can't take it with me anyway."

Two facts played in Suren's head and beat in time to his footsteps as he walked back home: *going abroad for study* and *I now have a guitar.*

Nihil's Secret

Kala Niles's affection for Suren had the effect of softening her aspect; she had taken to wearing pastel-colored flared skirts rather than the severely pleated ones she had always favored, and she had gradually become more generous toward all the children. So much so that even Nihil came to look forward to going to the Nileses' house for lessons. Just this past Christmas she had allowed all four of the Herath children to help chop dried fruits, small piles of sultanas, dates, and preserves as well as the nuts, and add them to the batter for the Christmas cake she was making. And before that, during Deepavali celebrations, she had agreed to reschedule their lesson for another day so that Nihil and Devi could go over to the Nadesans and help them decorate the entryway in front of their house for the Hindu festival of lights.

"Take these flowers too," Kala Niles had said, giving Devi a brown paper bag filled with the tiny variety of jasmine that grew at the back of her house, in the kitchen garden. "They will be able to use them for garlands and things."

Devi had stolen a few flowers, one to tuck into her blue Alice band and some extras to press between the covers of her still-blank exercise books. At the Nadesans' house they had crouched for hours on the ground next to Mrs. Nadesan and the Tisseras' son, helping to create the elaborate paisley and swan motifs, carefully outlined with colored rice and filled in with powdered dyes and flower petals. It was slow work, but immensely rewarding for the younger Heraths, who watched the design take shape and marveled at what they were able to create with Mrs. Nadesan's expert guidance. They whiled away the afternoon as they sipped hot plain tea with ginger, and said yes more than once to handfuls of warm, spicy chickpeas.

"So pretty I wished I could take a picture!" Devi said when Nihil and she went back to Kala Niles to hand over the plate of floury sweets that the Nadesans had sent in thanks.

"Better go home and take a nice body-wash to get all the dyes off your face and hands before Amma gets home," Kala Niles said good-naturedly, wiping a particularly large stripe of vermilion on Devi's cheek and getting her own fingers smeared with it in the process.

Yes, Kala Niles had warmed to Suren's siblings, and this warmth had the unintended effect of not only making Nihil feel more relaxed around her, but making him realize that coaxing words out of her father, Mr. Niles, was neither as onerous nor as unrewarding as he had imagined it might be. Indeed, even though some of the time when Nihil came in, the old man seemed to be in considerable pain and he only turned his head slowly toward Nihil, sighed, and said nothing at all, Nihil still found that the most comfortable place to spend the time between the beginning of Devi's lesson and the start of his own was beside Mr. Niles. It was a pleasant place to sit, for Mr. Niles's corner of the partially closed veranda was next to his daughter's lush rose vines and their bright colors, yellow and red, and their thick untroubled fragrance overwhelmed, for the most part, the appearance and smell of age and decay.

Understanding that rituals were important to Mr. Niles, Nihil observed a routine. He sent Devi in for her lesson with a little push between her shoulder blades, then walked over to Mr. Niles, silently counting the handkerchiefs remaining in the stack on the floor next to the old man. He found this to be a good gauge of Mr. Niles's degree of discomfort: the fewer the handkerchiefs, the deeper the sighs; on those days he would sit on a chair and read, after Mr. Niles's breathy acknowledgment of his arrival. Sometimes Mr. Niles would ask him about school, about the world outside, about his parents, but mostly he remained silent.

At last, when the weight of those sighs fell more gently upon him, and after nights of careful consideration, Nihil felt that the time was right to share his keep-for-himself secret. He waited until Mr. Niles had finished his meager contortion toward him before speaking into a silence punctuated by Devi's jerky F-sharp major scale.

"I can say any word backward," he said. "I can sing songs, recite poems, write sentences, all backward. Like this. Instead of singing 'my bonnie lies over the ocean,' I can sing it like this, *naeco eht revo seil einnob ym.*" He sang the line and smiled at Mr. Niles.

"Good," Mr. Niles said, though he did not smile. A tear escaped from his eye and he dabbed at it with a worn white handkerchief that had a light gray line running around the borders.

"*Kced gninrub eht no doots yob eht,*" Nihil recited. "'The boy stood on the burning deck.'"

This time, Mr. Niles smiled. "So you read other things besides those Hardy Boys books you keep appearing with?"

Nihil nodded. "I read poetry," he said. "Amma makes us all read poetry."

Mr. Niles raised his eyebrows. "What is your favorite poem?" he asked, with some amusement.

"'O Captain! My Captain!'" Nihil said without a second thought, the rest of the first lines of the poem flooding into his head even as he named the title.

"Whitman," Mr. Niles said, nodding. "Abraham Lincoln. War." He rested his eyes on Nihil, who sat attentively before him wondering why his favorite poem rather than his backward recitation had caught Mr. Niles's imagination. "Celebrations at the end of a war are still marred by the memory of the dead," Mr. Niles said.

Nihil, whose preoccupations were so close to his heart and to his physical being, Devi uppermost among them, did not understand. He had learned to recite the poem with great feeling, the *aabb, xcxc* of the rhyme scheme clear in his delivery, his *The ship has weather'd every rack, the prize we sought is won* arriving with uplifted voice and bright eyes, his *Rise up— for you the flag is flung—for you the bugle trills* full of pleading, and his *fallen, cold and dead* uttered with the requisite degree of bitter sorrow. But all of it was learned-art, not felt-art, for none of the realities that the poem spoke of, and that resonated with generations since, were realities Nihil could understand.

Mr. Niles, on the other hand, to whom the newspapers were read each day, who listened to the radio in two languages each day, grew quiet as he contemplated the poem in light of the things he had recently heard. For weeks now, there had been fresh reports of Tension in the North with the assassination of people who were standing up to Prabhakaran. These murders were mentioned alongside references to Tension in the halls of parliament, where the Tamil leaders were caught between two untenable propositions, neither wishing to support the terrorist group led by Prabhakaran nor able to wrest any assurances from the government regarding the particular concessions they demanded for the Tamil citizens whom they represented.

In print and on the airwaves, several dates were mentioned: 1956, 1958, 1977. It was as if these were the only years that counted. What had happened to the things that truly mattered? The New Years, Deepavalis, Vels, Ramazans, and Christmases for which the entire country had come to a halt and lightened everybody's spirits? Where was the country in which there were purchases of new schoolbooks with their fresh and promising scent, a scent that children like Nihil inhaled, breathing deeply, eyes shut as they imagined a new grade, a new teacher, the possibility of shaking off earlier reputations for good or bad? What had happened to the country with its parades and cricket matches and its marriage of church bell and the call to prayer, its soothing chants of *pirith* wrapping around minaret, steeple, and stupa alike? That country seemed to have fallen silent, taking all its traditions with it, for the newspapers and radio mentioned only those dates that referred to episodes of violence and upheaval, when ordinary people became extraordinarily angry, when they wielded machetes, guns, and fire as though murder and arson were the norm and not the exception.

"Yes, war," Mr. Niles said, "nobody ever wins." And he said nothing more until it was time for Nihil to take Devi home and return for his own lesson.

A few weeks later when Nihil arrived, however, he was rewarded both with a heartening stack of handkerchiefs—Mr. Niles was clearly doing well—and an immediate greeting.

"So, Nihil, those backward lines," he began, "you are saying each word backward but also each sentence, am I right? You could then begin the song or the poem with the last word and work back to its start, I suppose?"

"I could," Nihil said, frowning a little. "I've only done lines so far, but I suppose I could do it from the very end. Then I'd have to picture the whole poem in front of me, to see what I'm saying."

Mr. Niles nodded. "So you see the words as you are speaking or singing?"

"I *have* to see them, otherwise I don't know how they are spelled. I have to pronounce each letter, which means I have to see each letter."

"Remarkable," Mr. Niles said. The middle finger of his left hand drew circles on the red cement floor as he said it again and then again, "Remarkable. Remarkable."

During a subsequent visit, Mr. Niles handed Nihil two books. "The Twain book was the first I bought with my own money," he said. "The second one, Harper Lee, that one was sent to me by a friend who left back in 1958 to live in America. I don't know if there are other copies of it anywhere in this country."

Nihil sat and examined the books. He had read an abridged version of *Huckleberry Finn* and liked it well enough but not as much as he liked the mysteries he preferred. He thought he might begin with the second, *To Kill a Mockingbird*.

"'The one thing that doesn't abide by majority rule is a person's conscience,'" Mr. Niles said. "Best sentence I have ever read."

Nihil held it up to his nose and flipped the pages of the book. The air that brushed his face seemed to be speaking to him with a scent of cinnamon and camphor. He wondered where Mr. Niles had stored the book. He turned to the last page.

"*Gninrom eht ni pu dekaw mej nehw ereht eb d'eh dna,*" he said. "'And he'd be there when Jem waked up in the morning.'"

Mr. Niles laughed. "Son, you need to learn how to listen to the story as it is told. Start from the beginning, read to the end. That is how you learn the reasons for the way things are."

Nihil, too, laughed. "I will," he promised. "I just wanted to show you how I see words sometimes."

"What else do you see, Nihil?" Mr. Niles asked, looking intently at him.

"Nothing," Nihil said, putting the books on the floor beside him. "That's all I can see. Words." He felt slightly crestfallen that his remarkable skill had been so swiftly set among prior accomplishments and that new work was expected.

"You see other things, son," Mr. Niles said, squinting at him, "you just don't call it seeing. You call it knowing, am I right?"

Nihil said nothing. The hesitant notes produced by Devi's fingers picking out the first notes of a simple allegro filled the silent air, suddenly loud. He wondered if she had improved since the last time, or whether he was simply willing that she had. She should practice more. Maybe he would draw up a timetable for them, study time, cricket time, piano practice, all evenly placed between lunch and dinner. Then again, would the studies have to be broken down by subject or just amorphous time? Would Devi do the required work if she was left to her own devices, just a block of time and instructions to *finish homework?* Besides, cricket would soon give way to kites and that could not be controlled by timetables, but by the quality of the winds. And he knew she would want to follow them when he and Suren started flying those kites, tagging along and begging to hold the strings. She would not know how to twist those strings back and forth, and in the end their kite would be stolen by the slum boys who would send their fighter kite to bring it down. All the neighborhood children would blame her and begin to resent her. Better that he keep her home, even if it meant that he, too, would not be able to participate in the flying. That's okay, he would content himself with helping to build the kites, with making the warm glue in the kitchen with Kamala's help, with stretching the pieces of tissue across the frames that Suren and Rashmi would make. That should placate her.

"She needs to practice more," Mr. Niles said, gesturing slightly toward the inner room from which the music escaped, startling Nihil. "And you need to think about the things you know so you can tell me when you come back next week."

How did Mr. Niles know that he could sense what the future held? Nihil mulled over this question as he walked back home alone after his own lesson. Did it show on his face? Had his older brother or sister told Mr. Niles of the way his fears overwhelmed him? What exactly had they said? He was so deep in thought that he walked past his house and almost to the end of the road and would have kept on walking had Sonna not stopped him.

"Goin' to buy bread?" Sonna asked Nihil. Did such civil words spring to his lips because first his misshapen uncle and then his idiot sisters had been embraced by the Heraths? Did Sonna imagine that there was room in that circle for him too? "Nihil, no? Younger one? Goin' to buy bread?"

Nihil had never gone to buy bread in his life and with his head full of Mr. Niles's question, he did not understand, at first, what Sonna was talking about. He cocked his head and considered what Sonna had said.

"Bread?" he finally asked.

"Yeah men, bread. *Paan!*" And Sonna laughed, a little awkwardly.

"I don't have any bread," Nihil told him.

If Sonna had not been wearing a shirt over his jeans, Nihil may have been frightened by the sight, up close, of the skull and crossbones drawn into his forearm in ballpoint pen and the blood-dripping head held by its hair in a fist which an acquaintance of his had painted onto his entire back using *mehendi*, stealing the henna from his own sister. But all Nihil could see was Sonna looking simply unkempt and a little rakish, asking him about bread.

Sonna's smile left his face, albeit slowly, as though regretting both its own disappearance and its having ventured forth. "You laughin' at me?" Sonna asked.

"No, I'm not laughing," Nihil said. "You asked if I have bread. I don't have bread."

"I din' ask if you *have* bread. I asked if you are goin' to *buy* bread," Sonna clarified.

Nihil, now fully within the conversation, smiled disarmingly. "Oh! I didn't hear you properly. I was thinking about something else." He ran his fingers through his hair sheepishly. "I was on my way home and I didn't even realize that I had passed the gate and walked all the way here."

He looked back up the road, at the distance he had walked. All the way down his quiet street, its cul-de-sac and Mr. Niles's one barely driven car keeping it that way, safe for pedestrians and safe for children like him, all the way past the edge of Kala Niles's hedges, past his mother's garden anchored at each corner that faced the road with her new flamboyant and her red-fruited jambu tree, all of which were no longer visible from where he stood, past Raju's house and past the Silvas' compound with its araliya at one end and its cane and bark fence filled to capacity with shrubs, past the Bollings' long line of aluminum and almost past the Bin Ahmeds' house. He looked back at Sonna, amazement on his face.

"Good thing you stopped me. Otherwise I might have kept on walking all the way to the main road!" A bus rounded the corner at a tear, its exhaust belching fumes, and after it passed, Nihil said, "Imagine? I might have even got hit by a bus! Good thing you were there."

What grace there is to give if only the givers knew that they had the privilege of bestowing it. What grace is often given without intention.

Good thing you stopped me. Good thing you were there. The word *good* had never been applied to Sonna. Nobody had thanked him for anything he had ever said or done. No thanks had been deserved, but, on some long-ago occasion, before he had developed the knots and twists that hurt him from within, surely he had deserved one word of kindness? Sonna frowned and pressed his lips together to quieten the odd softening he felt within him. He stared at Nihil, who was still shaking his head at his own foolishness and smiling, now glancing at the main road where the bus had gone, now looking back at Sonna. There he stood, a good boy from a good home where doing nothing was a choice, not a predicament. A boy who was coming from a piano lesson on his way to a house where he did not have to be sent to dodge buses and drunkards on the way to buy the cheaper bread. *Good thing you stopped me. Good thing you were there.* Sonna squared his shoulders and strode up to Nihil, who stood a head shorter than him, still holding on to his *Easy Piano Sonatas* and *Music Theory Workbook* and his freshly sharpened black-and-yellow-striped Staedtler pencil and his soft Staedtler eraser.

He placed his hands on either side of Nihil's shoulders and bent down. "Don' walk like that again," he said. "Nex' time what if I'm not here? You might go straight an' hit the bus. Thinkin' an' walkin' you cannot do at the same time." He ruffled Nihil's hair and straightened up.

Nihil, his hair now disheveled, grinned. "I know. I know," he said. He looked at his sandals then looked up at Sonna. "I can say things backward," he said, wanting to reward Sonna for his narrow escape.

"Backward? Why?"

"'Kced gninrub eht no doots yob eht,'" Nihil said. "That means, 'the boy stood on the burning deck.'"

"Why he's standin' like that?" Sonna asked, leaning back and crossing his arms over his chest. He pulled his chin into his neck and looked skeptical.

"It's a poem about a boy who drowned with his burning ship because his father couldn't hear him. 'Casabianca.'"

"Tell again."

"'Kced gninrub eht no doots yob eht.' Here, I'll write it for you. Then you'll see." Nihil handed his books to Sonna, flipped to the back of the first one, and tore out a scrap of paper. Balancing it on the stack in Sonna's hands, his head bowed, he wrote in capital letters, KCED GNINRUB EHT NO DOOTS YOB EHT. Then he handed the paper to Sonna.

"What to do with this?" Sonna asked.

"Nothing. Just keep it," Nihil said. And then because such meetings were not unusual in his life, nor momentous, he turned to go.

Sonna did not know if he wanted Nihil to stay. Did not know what they might have talked about had he lingered a while longer. And most of all, he did not know what he could say to make Nihil stay. So he just called out, "Be careful nex' time!" as Nihil half turned and waved.

Jimmy Bolling only heard those words as he approached the door to his house, swearing about something. By the time he came out, Nihil had broken into a run. He watched Nihil for a few moments, then turned to Sonna and said, "You pick someone your own age to fight with. Why are you pickin' small fry like that?"

Sonna said nothing. He put the piece of paper in his pocket and went back inside to lie down and think about boys on burning decks, about Nihil, about himself as an older boy with the wisdom to guide children like the Heraths.

That night at dinner, while everybody chattered about school and friends as they passed around warm loaves of steamed bread and dipped their fingers in fish curry and sambol, Nihil was quiet, keeping a secret from his siblings for the first time. He was too afraid to mention that he had escaped being hit by a bus, and there was no way to speak of Sonna and his good work without referring to the circumstances. In private, while he did not tell Devi the exact details of the story (he substituted some unknown boy for himself), he talked to her at great length about the dangers of daydreaming when walking down not only their street but any street at any time.

"Buses could hit you!" Nihil said, and felt satisfied that Devi seemed suitably impressed with the dangers that awaited people who weren't paying attention.

The Magic of the Stolen Guitar

For a few weeks after that conversation with Sonna, Nihil did not have to time to dwell on Mr. Niles's question, for there was fresh commotion in the Herath household thanks to the discovery, by Mrs. Herath, of Suren's no-longer-on-loan guitar. Nihil stood together in a row with his siblings as Suren answered the questions that were asked at top speed, one after another, as if haste might yield a firmer truth.

"When did you stop borrowing and decide to keep it?"

"Where is that Sansoni boy now? Gone to Australia?"

"Why would he give you the guitar? Did he ask for payment?"

"Did his parents give him permission?"

"When were you going to tell me about this guitar?"

These were the sorts of questions that, Nihil knew, could elicit little more than easy answers, the kind of answers that explained nothing. He listened to his brother's replies: *seven months ago, I don't know, I don't know, he had no use for it, no, I don't know, I don't know.* He wished his mother were not so afraid of his brother's talent. He wished that she could see that being good at something, as Suren was in all his academic work, was a confirmation of intelligence whose reward should be an untethering from the usual in favor of pursuing the as-yet-unknown. But these were not things that he could articulate, they were things he felt, and so he stayed silent, his sisters on either side, waiting for the questions to cease.

In the absence of what she termed *concrete information*, his mother placed the guitar on top of her almirah. It was a confiscation that was supposed to be honored by virtue of her having said so, but it was one designed to fail by virtue of her children's joint understanding, unspoken but known, that it was a travesty to deprive their older brother of an instrument that belonged in his hands. That even Rashmi was outraged by the punishment was sufficient validation of their feeling that this was an injustice that could not be tolerated.

"We will take it in turns to get the guitar down from the almirah for Suren," Rashmi declared.

They were sitting in their usual way, Rashmi and Suren on one bed, his, Devi and Nihil across from them on Nihil's bed. The latest setback had upset them all so much that they had carried their tea into the bedroom and sat drinking it, flecks of sugar dropping off the surfaces of their biscuits onto the bed and not one of them seeming to care about the ants that the crumbs would attract.

"I don't care if I get into trouble," Devi declared, which made the others laugh and lightened their mood, for hardly a day went by when Devi was not being pulled up by a parent or a teacher or even, sometimes, Lucas or Kamala, for engaging in some shenanigan or other—helping herself to sticks of cinnamon, for instance, or making pools of mud in her mother's garden.

"If she finds out, I will say it was my idea," Suren said.

"No, I will say that I asked you to teach me," Nihil said, which brought another round of laughter, Nihil's general antipathy to music being so well known that everybody, even the Bolling twins, teased him about his forced piano lessons.

So they took turns to stand on stools and chairs, each according to his or her height, to fetch the guitar from the top of the almirah every other afternoon when their mother stayed late at school to give private lessons to students who needed extra help, and, in exact backward rotation, to replace it before she returned. On the weekends, Suren himself took it off the top of the almirah while his parents rested and went to the Bollings' house. There, in the side-yard that stretched from the end of the house to the wall bordering Old Mrs. Joseph's property, where there was grass but only the most hardy plant—a single orange bougainvillea—had survived, creeping in fits and starts, blooming lushly in one spot, languishing in mangy despair in another, the twins had created a refuge of sorts. They had hauled unused furniture from around their house and from Old Mrs. Joseph, made a table by stacking a plank of wood over two piles of bricks and covering it with a tablecloth, and even persuaded Jimmy Bolling to construct a "roof" for them from sheets of aluminum rigged between the gutters of his house and Old Mrs. Joseph's wall. It was a makeshift shelter that threatened to keel over during a hard rain, but it was all theirs, and when Suren practiced there, he played the pop songs that the twins requested, one after another until they were drunk with adoration.

"Play 'I Want You to Want Me!'" Rose would yell, only to be drowned out by Dolly.

"No no no! Not that again! Play 'We've Got Tonight!'" Dolly would beg.

"Play 'The Rose,'" Rashmi would say, which made Suren happy, for he liked the slow melody, and it made Rose grow all quiet and dreamy as she listened.

On more than one of those occasions, Jith, the younger of the Silva boys, accompanied them, and though he sat twitching nervously the whole time, beside himself with anxiety that his mother would find out, he did not leave until they did.

"Tell me if you see my brother coming to look for me, Aunty," Jith would whisper to Francie Bolling as he scurried indoors, and she would nod and send him along to find a place to sit next to the other children.

Since his courtyard abutted Raju's house, Sonna, too, was able to listen from his uncle's veranda, alongside Raju, without giving away the fact that he was even remotely interested in the music. This music that Suren played was, to Sonna, a simple extension of the music in the books that he had held in his hands while Nihil wrote out his strange words. And though he wished that it was Nihil, not Suren, who was playing, he felt a sort of kinship with Nihil as he listened, moved this way and that by the rhythms of the guitar, his mind now filling with images of throngs of people and dancing, now emptying out into a sweet sort of sadness that still left him feeling at ease.

Whenever his sisters or any of his fellow hooligans down other streets annoyed him now, he took to simply saying *Kced gninrub eht no doots yob eht!* and stalking off, and because nobody knew what those words meant, they assumed it was a superior curse they were not smart enough to understand. This gave Sonna both more power for himself and created more affection for Nihil, which meant that Sonna no longer harassed his sisters when they went to the Heraths' house, and he restricted himself to tormenting them with questions when they returned, hoping, though he did not know that he hoped for this, that Nihil might have told them of his good deed, that some further emphasis had been placed on this part of his character, the part that looked after the children on the street rather than bullied them. There had been nothing, and so he tried to content himself by listening to the music, and though Suren's skill, a skill that made his sisters worshipful, sometimes made him angry when he thought about it, for now the music itself never failed to calm his heart.

Eventually, though he tried to resist it, even Mohan was drawn into the appreciation of music when, sent to look for his brother, he walked right past Francie Bolling, who had fallen asleep, and found Jith sitting with the twins and the Herath children in the Bollings' backyard.

Mohan was not in a good mood that day. The past Friday, he had got into an argument with a classmate that had ended in blows. He had used a string of epithets, called the boy, Jehan, a name that referred to his race, and said that he should *bugger off to Jaffna.* He had thought that the punishment from his teacher, twenty cuts with a ruler, was worth having been able to scream words he had kept bottled up inside, but he had not bargained for further reprisals, which had come in the form of a visit to his home by Jehan's parents. They had arrived with a comb of plantains and sat down to discuss the matter with his mother just that afternoon.

"We did not know anything about this," Mrs. Silva said.

She served the Canagaratnams their tea in her best cups and saucers, and even offered them imported tea biscuits. She glared at Mohan, who had been directed to sit beside Jehan, and wondered where on earth he could have picked up such common language.

"Why would you say such an ugly thing?" Mrs. Silva asked.

There really was no reply that Mohan could articulate except what he believed, *he deserved it,* which, Mohan knew, could not be said in front of the boy's parents nor his mother, who had not expected him to be familiar with the kind of language he had used. He wished fervently that his father were there for surely Mr. Silva would have taken his side, would have understood *the provocation,* as he often put it, but his father had gone to visit his sister. Mohan shrugged.

"I am sure he did not mean it," Mrs. Canagaratnam said. "Boys, you know . . ." And she was quiet for a few moments. Then she cleared her throat and said, very quickly, "It is just that, in these times, I think this sort of thing must be dealt with right away. That's why we came." And she looked at her husband, who nodded.

"Of course," Mrs. Silva said, "I am sure he did not mean it. We are very decent people. He has not been raised to use language like this."

"Yes, the language," Mrs. Canagaratnam said, and drank her tea.

After the Canagaratnams left, his mother cuffed Mohan on the side of his head and asked him where he had learned to talk like that. "From the Bollings?" she asked, and when he shook his head, "From where then?" followed by, "I'm so embarrassed. To have Tamil people come in here telling me that I've raised a son who talks filth!" She all but sobbed as she explained the shame of this many times over to Mohan.

Mohan stood there feeling a little sorry for his mother and trying, but failing, to regret what he had done and what he had said. All he could think was that it stood to reason that a mealymouthed *ponnaya* like Jehan would run crying to his mother. So when he was dispatched to find his brother, Mohan was grateful to leave, and each step away from the sight of his mother, and how much he had upset her, made him feel as though he was escaping both his transgression and the fallout.

When he walked in to the Bollings' house, Suren was playing "Ob-La-Di Ob-La-Da" and all of them were singing. The Bolling twins were twirling around with Devi, clapping their hands, and even Jith and Rashmi were swaying in time to the beat. Suren looked up and took his right hand off the guitar for an instant to wave him over, saying, *Come in, machang!* And Mohan felt that it was completely natural for him to walk over and join them, to leave his troubles and concerns behind for a while. He didn't sing, but when Jith glanced over at him, Mohan smiled and tapped his brother lightly on his shoulder.

It would not last, this armistice, and both Mohan and Sonna would find themselves on the outside looking in again, one by choice, one unwittingly, and the Herath children, too, would drift away from the Bolling girls, but, for a while, Suren's guitar brought all the children of Sal Mal Lane together, and we can be grateful for that.

A Visit to the Accident Service

After Mrs. Herath was reassured that she had got Suren's disobedience under control, and after the children were just as reassured that they could outwit their mother, things settled down in the Herath household and everybody returned to their routines.

Suren, comforted by his small brigade of admirers and fellow miscreants, concentrated on improving his skill at the piano and the guitar. Furthermore, when his talent with the guitar and vocals was revealed at a birthday party of a friend, Faizal Adamaly, Suren found yet another way in which he could flout his mother's rules, this time in the form of a pop band he named "White Lies."

Rashmi, who had taken up needlework in earnest, used her spare time to make dresses for Devi's doll and embroider designs into her mother's serviettes, an activity that made Mrs. Silva draw herself up to her full height and say to Rashmi, and whoever else was near, *It all started with me on that very first day, isn't that so, darling?*

Devi, who did not like being still for long, spent much of her time climbing the Asoka tree, which was now such an important part of her play that its life was guaranteed. In its lower branches she would sit to read and suck on sweets or eat olives and mangoes with chillies and salt, her face puckering from the sourness. From its highest branches she would look up and down the street and in through windows and doors, alternately pretending that she was a princess surveying her kingdom, or a spy. Every now and again, she pretended to be a ghost, not answering when her name was called, staying absolutely still. If some unknown person walked by on the road below, she would rustle the leaves, though she could not keep from laughing out loud when her victim stepped back and away from the noise, searching the branches.

Nihil continued to visit with Mr. Niles with a small change. Whereas he used to sit and read in silence, now, on those days when Mr. Niles's pile of handkerchiefs was high enough to indicate a favorable disposition, he sat and read *To Kill a Mockingbird* aloud to him while Mr. Niles listened, a smile playing upon his lips, now and then a murmur of appreciation escaping. Still, it wasn't until Devi tripped as she was coming into the house with her music books and cut her lip, that Nihil remembered to tell Mr. Niles about what else he could see besides his backward words.

Devi tripped over the garden hose that had been left out by Mrs. Niles earlier that afternoon because it had begun to rain just as she started to water her flowers. Nihil's immediate concern for his sister was drowned out by Mr. Niles yelling something very loudly in Tamil, which brought Mrs. Niles running to the front door, her arms outstretched, before Nihil could even pick up Devi's books from among the row of red ixora bushes where they had landed when they flew out of her hands. By the time he gathered the books and rescued the pencil he had sharpened for her just before they left their house from where it was lying in a shallow ditch at the edge of the Nileses' garden, Devi was limping away without a backward glance, the upper half of her body wrapped up in Mrs. Niles's yellow sari *pota*.

"Put the books near the piano and come and sit, son," Mr. Niles said, his voice back to its usual low, soothing depth. "Aunty will take care of her."

Nihil knew the truth of this immediately. Yes, Mrs. Niles would mend his sister, put some balm on her mouth, give her one of her mint lollies, and Devi would finish her lesson in high spirits, the drama of her story clenched tight and ready to be unfurled at the dining table that night. Her swollen lip would be the end of her childhood habit, the raggedy salt-sour taste of it the antidote to her lip-sucking, succeeding where all the lectures and prescriptions tried thus far had failed.

Nihil wiped his palms on the front of his denim shorts. "I sometimes know, I think I know, what is coming in the future for my sister, for Devi," he said, trying to be as precise as he could. "I can tell what is going to happen before it does."

"Did you see that she was going to fall?" Mr. Niles asked, his fingers reaching for one of the handkerchiefs stacked next to his bed. Today, the pile was low and his speech was effortful.

Nihil frowned. "No," he said, defensive. "I don't know what is going to happen, exactly, just what happens right afterward. If it is very bad, like falling, I don't know it."

"And do you see anybody else when you see these things, or do you only see your sister?"

"My sister. The other people come as names. Only Devi comes as her whole self."

Mr. Niles was quiet for a while and Devi's music took up the space between them once more, interspersed with the sound of Kala Niles's palm against the side of the piano; she reserved the use of the metronome for Suren and Rashmi. When the music stopped while some instruction was being imparted, Mr. Niles gestured to the handkerchiefs with his eyes.

"These are washed every night by Aunty. She hangs them up to dry and wakes up at five to iron them. Every morning when the two of them, Aunty and Kala Akki, help me to this chair, I find these handkerchiefs here. It doesn't make me more comfortable, or prevent the tears, or cure me." He held Nihil's gaze for a long while, then asked a question. "Why then do they do it?"

Nihil regarded Mr. Niles; he had no answer. Furthermore, having asked to be told what he knew, he could not imagine why the old man was ignoring what he had said. He decided to try again.

"I know the things that I can help her with," Nihil said. "I know what to do to help her with her tests, with music, with the children in the neighborhood or my parents or her friends. I know what she will do after something has happened, like today. I know that she will stop sucking her lower lip and that she will talk in a certain way about it tonight."

Mr. Niles sighed and it was a painful, broken sigh. "These things you know, they come from being afraid, do they not?" He nodded his head slowly, up down, up down. Then he reached up and drew the fingers of both hands through his hair, sinking them an inch or two into the soft waves, then drawing them back toward the back of his neck and repeating the move until he had massaged his entire head.

Nihil considered the question. Was it fear that made him know what was in store for Devi? If it was, then he would be instrumental, he felt, in causing things to be.

"No, Uncle, it's not because I'm frightened. I just know things," he said, finally, deciding to come down on the side of what he sensed was the truth. As he sat quietly, thinking about what Mr. Niles had said, Mrs. Niles brought out two cups of tea on a tray and set them down on the high table next to her husband. But when she had left and Nihil tried to give Mr. Niles his cup of tea, he waved him away. Nihil sat back down. He said, "I know what Devi is going to do and what people might do to her."

Mr. Niles, who had shut his eyes, was quiet for so long that Nihil decided he had grown tired and fallen asleep. He passed over the Harper Lee book and picked up the *Archie* comic book he had borrowed from Mohan, who had shelves of them, and began to read. Then Mr. Niles spoke, pausing once to beckon Nihil to get his cup of tea for him.

"I need these handkerchiefs, but I don't need them to be ironed and placed here, so neatly, with such order that it seems that they are unnecessary or are not intended for such a thing as wiping these tears. I don't need as many as I see here each day. Two would probably suffice, maybe three. If two or three were given to me each day, that would be a sufficient quantity of caring. All of the rest, the washing, the drying, the ironing, the neatness within which I begin each quiet day, that, son, is love. Love is for the person who loves, not for the one who is loved."

Nihil listened intently. Somehow, what was said about the handkerchiefs was really being said of him, but he did not understand, so he stayed quiet. *Devol si ohw eno eht rof ton*, he pictured, not for the one who is loved. *Devol si ohw eno eht rof ton, devol si ohw eno eht rof ton*, he said in time to their steps as he walked Devi home and then returned for his own lesson.

After that conversation, he decided to keep a notebook in which he could record everything he knew, and when the knowledge came to him, as a way of quantifying the extent and depth of his prescience. At first he drew four columns, one for each of his siblings and one for himself, but by the end of a month the one column that had anything in it was Devi's, so he turned to a fresh page and drew three columns: *What I know, When I Knew It, What Happened*. Some things he wrote down:

Devi was going to get caught passing a note in class and be sent to the principal's office, where she would have to stand facing the wall through an entire period and miss PT, which she loved because she was such a good runner and didn't ever mind sweating.

Raju and Sonna were fighting, and he was not certain what this might have to do with Devi but because they appeared, he wrote their names down.

Devi was going to get hit on the back of her head and have to get two stitches.

Devi was going to have an accident.

Devi was going to have an accident.

Devi was going to have an accident.

"I think Devi is going to have an accident," he told Suren at last, not knowing what else to do with this repetitive bit of knowing that had no accompanying details.

"Yes, she will," Suren said, mildly. "She is always having accidents."

"This is a real one," Nihil said, "a very bad one, I think."

"Do you think or do you know?" Suren asked, looking up from the paper airplane he was folding; he was sitting on his bed, his chin resting on one knee, the other tucked under his hip.

Nihil squinted his eyes against the sun, which was coming through the thick yellow curtains in their room and covering his brother and his airplane and bed in golden light. It seemed to be a time for positive thoughts, not negative ones. "I think I know," Nihil said, trying to incorporate the best of both possibilities.

"Let us see if you only know."

"Then what?"

"Then I suppose we can be extra careful of her."

Nihil lay down on his own bed, arms under his head, and considered this option. It seemed wise, after all, to wait until things were more certain. She had been doing fairly well these past few months, and except for the possible stitches, there was nothing to worry about. The principal, well, that was ordinary stuff, the kind of thing all of them had suffered, with the exception of Rashmi; she never transgressed.

The stitches, however, qualified as The Accident when it happened.

"Fifty-two, fifty-three, fifty-four, fifty-five!" Rose yelled as she passed the plank of wood from one hand to another, behind, then in front of her body. Suren threw the ball underarm and she hit it down the road, the most desirable location for a hit since the natural incline made the ball gather speed as it went, taking the corner at a regular pace then ricocheting off Old Mrs. Joseph's gate and careening away as though possessed. Nihil chased after the ball. Up ahead of him, Sonna was standing in his usual place, leaning against the side of his front door, his arms crossed in front, balancing his weight on one leg, the other braced behind him on the door frame, watching their game.

"Got to pump the arms. Make you run faster!" he called to Nihil. "Go! Go!"

Nihil tucked his lip in, pumped his arms, and speeded up, wondering if the others would let Sonna join their games. He picked up the ball and turned to throw it. "Maybe you can join us when we play cricket," he shouted over his shoulder to Sonna.

Sonna pushed himself off the door and began to walk toward Nihil. "I use' to play . . ." he began, but Nihil did not hear the rest for there was a commotion up the road where Rose had been calling out her runs and where now everybody was gathering in a clump around Devi, including a very agitated Raju.

Mohan called down the road to Nihil and beckoned him over with his arm. "Devi has cracked her nut!"

Cracked her nut. Those were the words that he used. As if Devi were to blame for it. Nihil ran back, knowing, knowing, that she would need those stitches, that forever and ever there would be a raised ridge on the back of her head, that his younger sister would become a timid player at these kinds of outdoor team games, more and more so until she gave them up altogether and took to something else, something that would involve only her own body, only the things she could control. Like dancing, or riding a bicycle, or running.

If Sonna followed, and he did, part of the way, Nihil did not notice. By the time Nihil reached her, Devi was crying, but not as much as she would have if she could see the quantity of blood that was seeping down along her thick but boy-short hair and turning the white dots on the back of her dress completely red. Their parents were not home, and so Nihil ran to Mr. Niles and begged for help.

"I can't drive anymore, son," Mr. Niles said, speaking quickly. "Go and ask Jimmy Bolling to come and take my car. The keys are on top of the fridge. Go!"

It was still a time of neighborliness and small hurts, the kind of reparable injuries that everybody understood and wanted to heal and so they all went together to the Accident Service with Devi. Sonna did not go; he kicked the dirt and said nothing as he watched the car roar down the street, his father at the wheel, steering with his right hand, the top of his left arm propped in the open window. Suren and Mohan sat in the front seat, while the rest of them, Jith, Rose, Dolly, and Nihil, sat in the back, Devi balanced on Nihil's lap while he pressed an old pillowcase to the back of her head, and Jimmy Bolling swore and cursed his way through traffic and, once he got to the hospital, swore some more until he had half a dozen attendants running this way and that wondering how on earth they could appease such a large and disgusted and quite possibly foreign man and make him stop. Nihil waited outside with the others until Devi emerged again, walking hand in hand with Jimmy Bolling, who was swaying a little, both of them beaming.

"Icy chocs for everybody, what do you say?" Jimmy Bolling said, chucking Devi under her chin.

"For everybody," Devi said and laughed. "I got two stitches but I didn't even feel anything," she said proudly, showing off the back of her head, where, in a small square section where her hair had been shaved off, there was now a plump dressing held in place by a bandage that ran across her forehead.

So this must have been the accident he had foreseen, Nihil thought. He felt someone watching him and when he looked up, saw that Suren too was smiling. His grin widened as he realized that his brother was thinking the same thing, sharing in the relief that The Accident was one that was entirely manageable.

When they returned to Sal Mal Lane, Raju, called back into service to his great delight, was sent off to fetch the icy chocs, for which he had to go beyond the bridge, since the one store that carried things that needed to be frozen was Sunil's shop, and where he added the eight chocs to the ever-growing list of items that had already been sold on credit to Jimmy Bolling.

While they waited, the children discussed the visit to the Accident Service, a place they had never seen, the violence and sudden tragedies that were required to enter it being so far out of the normal course of their lives. They talked about all that they had observed while they were there, crouched into one corner in fear as people were rushed in on stretchers, screaming in pain, with broken bones and one alarmingly silent man with a knife wound who only grimaced, baring all his teeth as he clenched his fists. The sight of so much that was worse than what had brought *them* there made them less anxious about Devi, who joined in by relating the stories from inside the surgical ward. Around them, the road, still fresh from a downpour that they had missed while they were at the hospital, released steam as if in good humor, the smell of asphalt and damp earth mingling. There was a lush humidity in the air, everything washed clean but in a childlike fashion, a quick bath to take away the most obvious dirt that still left the scent of play and the outdoors untouched. Above them, the skies clouded and broke in uncertain streaks and tinged the evening with a purple glow. The lateness of the hour and the excitement of the evening made the Herath children call out for more games and though Devi could only watch, they played for a while longer, running barefoot up and down the road, playing impromptu made-up games. They laughed at having escaped with such a small injury, without knowing that this is why they all felt so giddy, wrapped up in the euphoria of the unscathed.

Raju, when he returned, took great pleasure in handing out the icy chocs to the children, making a show of serving the Herath children first, and of them all, Devi, with an overwhelming display of deference. It was not until Raju was almost done that Jimmy Bolling realized that he had forgotten to buy one for his son, which did make him feel bad, so he covered it up by yelling at him.

"Where for me, Daddy?" Sonna Bolling asked as they all crowded around the *siri-siri* bag full of the already softening rectangular green-and-silver packages of ice cream. He asked this from a safe distance, but then, overcoming his fear of his father in the presence of a such a special treat, he came forward and reached into the bag.

Jimmy Bolling used his good arm to shake Sonna's hand until he dropped the ice cream back into the bag. "You don' need icy chocs. These are for the kids."

Nihil, unwrapping his own icy choc, watched Sonna walk away down the road. "Uncle Jimmy, I can give him my one and I can share with Suren," he said, already deciding and beginning to follow Sonna.

"No! No! Don' be silly," Jimmy Bolling said. He grabbed Nihil roughly by the arm and hauled him back to the group of children, who were now deep in their enjoyment of the white insides of their chocolate-coated blocks of ice cream. "He's a bloody thug! Thugs don' eat icy chocs!" And Jimmy Bolling laughed heartily and tipped his cowboy hat, quite as though he spoke from personal experience. Nihil, though he would have chosen to share his treat with Sonna if he had been allowed to do so, was just as easily caught up in the delight of the other children, and so he, too, turned his back on Sonna.

And even though the Silvas were not in the least bit happy, and they said so, that their sons *Had taken off like hooligans with that mad man,* and also, to Mrs. Herath, *Gosh, Savi, should put a stop, no, to all this fraternizing between our Sinhalese boys and those Burghers and Tamils?* even they could not dampen the excitement that their sons felt at having participated in such a momentous occasion and one celebrated by icy chocs.

The next time Nihil went to piano lessons, he felt cheerful as he chatted to Mr. Niles, describing the day's events, the ride to the hospital, the sweet taste of icy chocs afterward, even the care with which Raju had unwrapped Devi's icy choc for her.

"Everything feels better now," he said. "I knew she was going to have an accident and now she has had it and it was okay," he added.

"What else do you know these days?" Mr. Niles asked, smiling. "Do you know who will win the election? Tell me it isn't JR." He shook his head gravely. "I don't like the way he talks about the country, you know. Tamils this and Sinhalese that. Those are not the words of a peacemaker. Those are not the words to use when you want to have a single country, and I think we're headed for real trouble if we end up with that man."

"No, I don't know those things, only my father does," Nihil said, "but he doesn't like JR either so that's good."

"Yes," Mr. Niles chuckled, "that's good. Maybe there are more people like your father and me than there are people like those Silvas and that boy, Sonna, Jimmy Bolling's son."

"Sonna is not a bad person," Nihil said, slowly, remembering.

Mr. Niles raised his eyebrows. "He has been harassing everybody down this road, son. You must watch out for him. I can't go out but, sitting in this veranda, I can hear more than most people think I can. I hear the way he talks to his sisters when they are next door at his uncle's house. And I know how he talks to Raju, too. It's a shame."

"He talks like that but he's not bad," Nihil insisted, his brow furrowing as he tried to decide how much to reveal to Mr. Niles. "He saved me from being hit by a bus," he said, finally, sensing that the full drama of what could have happened might persuade Mr. Niles.

Mr. Niles nodded and lowered his eyebrows. He pulled his shoulders toward his ears in an exaggerated shrug. "Perhaps he's not as bad as he seems. But I still expect you to be careful, son. There's a bad strain in him."

Nihil wished that Mr. Niles did not believe the worst of Sonna. Sonna had quite possibly saved his life; besides, he seemed nicer overall. Sometimes, if nobody else was looking, Sonna would even wave to him as they all waited for the school buses. Still, something in Mr. Niles's watery eyes told him that he was not ready to be convinced, so he said no more about Sonna.

"What do you know about your sister these days?" Mr. Niles asked again soothingly, as though he understood that he had upset Nihil.

"I know one more thing right now, and that is that Devi is going to get in trouble at school."

"Can you help her, then?"

"No need to," Nihil said, feeling sanguine for a change, Sonna, too, forgotten. "We all get into trouble at school, it's nothing special. She will be fine."

Mr. Niles tapped his pile of handkerchiefs and nodded. "It is good that you don't try to save her from everything. Otherwise, how would your sister ever know what to do when she is alone?"

Nihil said nothing. Devi was never alone except for when she was at school, where the most that could happen was a trip to the principal or the whispering of jealous girls, but he did not feel the need to correct Mr. Niles.

Our Lady of Perpetual Sorrows

Nihil was right. Devi was never alone. Or, at least, she had never been alone. However, Devi, like all the children down Sal Mal Lane, including Raju, who was to all intents and purposes not much more than a child himself, only played by the rules so long as she had no reason to disobey them. Thus far, nothing had happened in her life to make it necessary for her to step outside the neat boundaries set for her by her sister and brothers. Not far away, though, a day of half-truths and secret journeys was waiting.

In her heart of hearts, Devi knew that her brothers were made unique by certain imperfections, Suren who preferred to lie rather than to face conflict, Nihil who spent too much time reading about cricket, revisiting scores and calculating batting averages rather than playing the game. Yet the sibling she went to school with was Rashmi and, therefore, her daily reality was not a comforting sense that she, too, could be permitted a few imperfections but rather Rashmi's unblemished record elevated by repetition—as comparison and standard—by the nuns. Being marginally accomplished in the laudable skills, maths and science, and gifted in the one usually consigned to the lowest rung, creativity, Devi was not destined to become the haloed favorite that Rashmi had been from the minute she had first sat down in her preschool class with her neatly filled notebooks, rarely the trace of an eraser mark, and deferential manner. Devi did not have the sixth sense that would tell her when a lay teacher or a nun was walking to class, her arms laden with books, so she could do what was expected: leap out of her chair and offer to help. She spent more time decorating her curvy Sinhala script than she did in making her sentences grammatically correct, constantly mixing up her *mi*'s and *mu*'s until her Weerodara exercise book was a blur of red ink. She shone only in her English class with efforts that went unremarked upon since they exceeded the expectation of rudimentary competence, as well as the understanding of the teacher assigned to instruct them in Basic English. Was it a surprise, then, that she copied her answers during mathematics? She did not think so, but nobody was asking her.

"Minoli Nugegoda!" The teacher's voice summoned the class monitor with obvious disapproval. "Take Devi to Sister Principal's office. Right now. With this note."

Devi and Minoli walked silently out of the classroom and down the corridor outside. As soon as they were out of sight of their classmates, they became conscious, without being able to put a finger on it, of time and authority. Row upon row of classrooms were filled with the industry of schoolwork, each child and each teacher playing their role, each human being somehow entirely cocooned in their own pod of understanding. Everybody else was in their place, doing what they were supposed to do, the whole combining into a sort of impermeable, yet transparent, bubble of good sense. Except for the two of them. They had been sent out to wander down hallways where they had no business being. They held hands and turned a corner before they opened the note: *Caught Copying. Also Disobedient. Needs Punishment—Yours Sincerely, Mrs. Sylvester,* the note read, and, the damning *P.S. Rashmi Herath's Sister!*

"Every first letter does not have to be in capitals," Devi said, sullen and unrepentant, her voice clear in the silent hallway, "just the first letter of the first word of a sentence. Or names."

"Now don't go and say that to Sister Principal. You'll get it," Minoli advised, both in awe of her friend's grasp of the language and fearful for her fate in the dreaded confines of The Office.

They took the long route past the tuck shop and paused to breathe in the smell of the savory buns and pastries being produced by the convent staff. Then they stopped to hold their noses and use the bathrooms before, having run out of ways to delay the inevitable, they reached their destination.

"Copying?" Sister Principal looked up from the note. She adjusted the band across her forehead that held her veil in place over her long, serious face. "Why would you do such a thing? From whom did you copy?"

Devi made no reply. She was a Herath; they did not betray their friends. She flashed a look at the photograph of Jesus Christ that hung above the principal's desk, a blue rosary draped reverently over it. Beneath it, on a shelf set into the wall, was a stack of novenas printed on tissue-thin paper. She did not dare turn her head, but she turned her eyes as far as they could go and looked through the window. There was the stone grotto that held a life-size statue of the Virgin Mary, a flickering blue bulb lit before it all day and all night long. A carved inscription read *Our Lady of Perpetual Sorrows.* She enjoyed sitting with Our Lady of Perpetual Sorrows for a few minutes before school began, liked the notion of endless sorrows, which sounded both desperate and strangely soothing. She also liked to touch the "magic" stone at the foot of the statue, the one rubbed smooth from decades of schoolgirls caressing it, asking for good grades, boyfriends, and breasts. She made a mental note to touch it again tomorrow. She would not ask for anything—she rarely did—she would simply thank Our Lady of Perpetual Sorrows for friendship. Friends from whom to copy mathematics.

The Sister Principal turned to Minoli, when it was clear that Devi would not answer. "From whom did she copy?"

Minoli's lower lip trembled, as though she too were being implicated. "Not me!" she said before bursting into tears.

"See now? You've made her cry," Sister Principal said, beckoning the other girl over, taking her hand and soothing her against her body. "Don't cry, darling, you haven't done anything wrong. Come now, don't cry." She turned to Devi. "If you had to go to confession you wouldn't be sinning like this, lying and cheating and then not even having the humility to be sorry for it. I don't know what this school is coming to," and she petered out into muttering about religions that had no standards for their followers.

Devi regarded the scene with stubborn equanimity. Crying was not an option she would choose, ever. She held out her palms before she was even asked to do so and braced herself for the sharp hurt of the foot ruler that landed five times on each, clenching her teeth and widening her eyes, which remained dry. Then she walked back to her class without even rubbing her palms together once.

Rashmi made Kamala boil water and then applied warm compresses to Devi's hands as soon as they got home, even before lunch. They sat together on the steps outside the back door, still in their white uniforms and their striped school ties.

"You don't need to copy. You just do it because you are lazy," Rashmi said, though not as if she expected any change in Devi's behavior. This Devi took as Rashmi's good-girl way of condoning what she had done.

"I don't like maths or science or Sinhala or Buddhism. I only like English and social studies," Devi said, as though this expression of preference were sufficient to release her from the usual rules for those other, less desirable, subjects.

"You can't choose like that in grade three. You can pick what you like when you finish your O-levels."

Devi looked at her sister and marveled at the way in which she conducted her life, free of tribulations, and never ruffling anybody's feathers; not their parents', not the teachers', not Sister Principal's, not the neighbors', not Mrs. Silva's, or even Sonna's, who, Devi had noticed, though he did not speak to them, looked at Rashmi with a disturbingly longing expression whenever she walked by. She wondered if it took work or if it came easy to Rashmi, this way in which she flowed through the days, competent and serene.

Later that day, Nihil commiserated as they sat on the back porch, dipping Marie biscuits into their evening tea, staring at the brown-orange brew and the way it swirled inside their white porcelain teacups. They had to raise their voices a little to be heard above the sound of Kamala's *ekel* broom as she swept the pink and yellow flowers and leaves that drifted down from the sal mal trees and settled in the gardens of all the homes down the lane, work that had to be done twice each day.

"It's okay. You didn't really get into trouble anyway," Nihil said, and Devi felt happier. This was her kind of response, to be grateful for the worse that had been avoided rather than bemoan the bad that had happened.

"I wanted to tell her that friends help friends, but I don't think Sister Principal has any friends, so I didn't," she said, sure that Nihil would understand this line of reasoning, that had the Sister Principal experienced real friendship, she would have understood the copying.

"Don't try to talk to principals. If you do they'll tell Amma and Tha and then you'll be in real trouble."

They sat and chewed, thinking about Real Trouble: wordy sentences of remorse rewritten one hundred times, always one hundred times, no playing outside, and, when things were really bad, the sensation of their mother's school slippers on bare skin. Yes, there was no need to bring that to pass, Devi thought. Maths was not worth that.

"Can you help me with the stupid subjects?" she asked Nihil, who nodded and continued to drink his tea.

"Helping" became, like everything else, a joint effort. Suren taught her maths, patiently breaking every sum into its composite parts until she no longer saw them as problems but rather as patterns. Rashmi taught her Sinhala and Buddhism, tying them together with Jathaka tales full of princes and vanquished demons until the language became an expression of faith, and scripture a version of known fairy tales intended to soothe pain rather than dictate life. Nihil sat beside her and listened to her repeat the stories that she made up from the facts passed down to her in social studies, the other foot of the compass she used to outline her world, its better half being the language she chose to describe it. Her parents responded to her advancement into the rank and file of their gifted older children, each according to their own preoccupations.

"All A's and B pluses!" her mother exclaimed, holding Devi close on the day the report card came home. "Even a B plus in maths! I'm so proud of you, darling." She kissed the top of Devi's head, breathing in the smell of sweat and play.

"Why no A in Sinhala?" her father asked, ever conscious that mastery of the native tongue was a prerequisite for true nationalism.

Suren, Rashmi, and Nihil, whose own report cards barely elicited a response—they were expected to be superior—stood by and said nothing; they had already decided exactly how they would indulge their sister as a reward for her achievements.

Devi's Report Card

And here it was: Devi's day of rebellion had arrived. The report card, which had finally turned from an embarrassment—a feeling that Devi had religiously expressed, but only because she understood that it was expected that she would be ashamed—into a source of pride, made Devi bolder. She had information she wanted to share with the neighbors that she did not feel required the accompanying voices of her siblings or even their presence. She waited until Rashmi was deeply absorbed in the Nancy Drew mystery she was reading, ducked behind the fridge to hide from Kamala as she passed by on an unknown errand, opened and shut the heavy front door, holding the new brass handle in her hand and turning the latch soundlessly into its groove, tiptoed through the front veranda, opened the gate, and ran down the road.

"I got six A's and three B's!" she announced to the Bolling girls, who were taken aback by her sudden arrival in their midst, bursting through the half-shut door to their compound without even pausing to knock.

"Gosh! How did you manage?" Rose said through a mouthful of rice. They were still in their school uniforms, though they had loosened their ties and unfastened some of the buttons. "In my class mostly Tamil girls get such good marks."

"We barely got two C's each and all the rest D's!" Dolly informed her, following that up with her customary gale of laughter.

"Sit, darling, sit. Where's your brother?" Mrs. Bolling buttoned the top of her bright red shirtdress before stepping out to look up the road. She shut the door and came back in. "Never see you without Nihil. Takes good care of you, doesn't he? Such a nice boy," she said and smacked Sonna lightly on his head, as though it were a deserved reprimand for a crime he was sure to commit sooner rather than later.

"Oww, Mama!" Sonna rubbed his head and frowned. "You're always comparing me to them! But I'm not like them!" he said.

"I know," his mother replied, and smacked him again to confirm her agreement as well as her disapproval of this difference between her son and the Herath boys.

A small argument erupted as Mrs. Bolling and the twins discussed in which ways, exactly, Sonna was different from the Herath boys, and in the ensuing noise, Sonna, who happened to be sitting right next to Devi, looked at her curiously. He had never been this close to one of the Herath girls before. Devi, dressed in a drop-waisted blue-and-white-striped stay-at-home dress and a matching Alice band on her head, looked like a well-loved doll. She had taken her body-wash before going on her adventure, and she smelled fresh, a mix of baby powder and sandalwood soap. Something about that scent stirred Sonna. He felt an overwhelming urge to take her hand and lead her back to her home where she would be safe. Safe from dust and dirt, from cars and buses, from rude boys and crude words, safe from the people in his house. He offered her his glass of water and breathed out.

"Where's Nihil?" he asked at last.

Devi took a sip, then tucked her lips in as if this could excuse her from answering, but he asked the question again. "He's at home," she said. "He's very, very busy today. And Rashmi is busy and Suren is also busy. Even Kamala is busy. That's why I came alone."

"Don' go walkin' aroun' by yourself. It is not safe. Nihil must 'ave told you, no, about the bus an' everythin'?"

"Yes, he told me, but I'm not going near the buses. Don't worry. I just came here to tell everybody about my report card."

Sonna glanced around the table at his family. He smiled, filled with pride, though none of them could have known why he was so pleased.

Devi turned fully to face Sonna and made her announcement again. "I got six A's and three B's."

"Those are very good marks. Nihil mus' be very proud of you," Sonna said, smiling.

"Yes, he taught me, and Suren and Rashmi too. They all taught me."

"Then you wait here, I will go an' get a strawberry milk for you," Sonna offered, surprising himself. He had no money and he would have to steal the bottle, but what was that compared to being able to bring a treat for a girl like her? "I'll go an' come then I will take you back home, okay? Mustn' walk by yourself," he said, and got up from the table, feeling important. He pictured himself, Devi's hand in his as he walked over to the Heraths' house and returned her to her family. They might invite him for tea, offer him biscuits on a tray. He whistled a tune as he went, a melody he had heard Suren play and that had caught his imagination though he did not know its name, "The Skye Boat Song."

Devi, who would ordinarily have cheered up at the thought of the sweet drink, had just had a glass of fresh lime juice at home, a drink she had cajoled out of Kamala on the merits of her report card, and so she simply watched him leave. It would not do to wait for him to take her home; if he did, everybody would know she had crept out of the house by herself. Real Trouble reared its ugly head. Devi tuned in to the voices left behind.

"Wonder what the Silvas got," Dolly said.

"Not Silvas, you are only wonderin' what Jith got!" Rose teased her sister.

Dolly tried and failed to hide her smile. "Must 'ave done well, no?" she said.

"Gosh, I don' know about Jith, but Suren must 'ave got good marks for music again this term," Rose said, her thoughts fleeing from the boy her sister had a crush on to the one who was always on her mind. "When he plays his music it's so nice, no, Mama?"

Devi listened to the discussion, which revolved entirely around Suren's music, his voice, and his long list of desirable traits, a conversation conducted with each person around the long table shouting louder than the next. Nobody here, it seemed, was interested in her grades but for Sonna, and even he had left. She cracked the door just wide enough for her to squeeze out and stood contemplating where she could go next.

She gazed down the lane and thought about visiting the Silva boys, who had become much more friendly with her and her siblings, but then decided against it; they lived too close to her own home. Next door to the Bollings were the Bin Ahmeds, but they were so quiet and kept to themselves and in any case she only met them during Ramazan and the Sinhalese and Tamil New Year when the families exchanged sweets. She continued to stand, weighing her options. The wide, main road beyond the Bin Ahmeds' house was uncharacteristically quiet and empty for a few moments before three vehicles went roaring by. She was almost about to turn back when, in the distance, she saw Lucas shuffling toward his hut. She ran to the edge of the road, her heart picking up its beat at the prospect of crossing the busy road that she had never been permitted to even stand beside without each of her hands being held by a sibling, one on either side. She had to try several times before she managed to dart across between a motorcycle, two buses, and a car. To avoid walking along the road, which had even less space that could be described as a pavement on this side, she stepped carefully through the loose barbed-wire fence that bordered the property, holding the wires apart and still managing to scrape herself slightly. She rubbed the scratch with spit.

"Lucas Seeya!" she called out, catching up with Lucas just before he stepped into the wattle-and-daub veranda of his hut. She couldn't see Alice, but she could hear her voice and the sound of her washing a pot somewhere behind a grove of plantain trees.

"*Appoi!*" Alice said. "Good that the Tamils are being taught a lesson. Should have thrown them out long ago. Think they own this country. Have you noticed, all the good shops are Tamil. Cloth shops. Goods shops. All Tamil."

Devi, confused for a moment, wanted to ask Lucas how a shop could be Tamil, a detail that she felt could be introduced to her social studies teacher since it had not thus far been discussed in class. Perhaps her teacher didn't know this; it would be another opportunity to impress her. But she was prevented from asking the question by the barrage of scolding that spilled out of Lucas's mouth, which frightened her into simply nodding or shaking her head in affirmation and denial.

"Devi Baby! What are you doing here? By yourself?" he asked. He stepped carefully down the uneven steps to his house and walked a little way past her to stare up Sal Mal Lane, which was visible from the Ratwatte compound. "Is something wrong?" he asked when he returned. "Then why are you here without Nihil Baby? You are not supposed to cross that road! You know that, right? And anyway, why are you coming to our house? This is not a place for you to be! Okay, okay, don't look so scared. Here, come, come," he said, and escorted her up the steps, taking her hand in his. "I'll give you ginger beer. You sit, and I will go and come with ginger beer."

Devi was too afraid to say that she did not like ginger beer, its sting and fizz far too strong for her taste, or that her belly was already full with her lime juice. Besides, Alice, dressed in her customary soot- and curry-stained cloth and blouse, had emerged with two pots, one in each hand, consternation further souring her already disapproving features.

"Ah, this is Devi Baby, no. What are you doing here? Where is that man? Lucas Aiyya!" she called out. "Lucas Aiyya!"

"Lucas Seeya went to bring ginger beer."

Alice spat a stream of betel out the side of her mouth. "Ginger beer? Did he offer tea?"

Devi shook her head, though she did not want to cast any blame on the old man. She wished she had not come. She should have turned around and gone home. Or to Kala Niles. But no, she would have to get past Mr. Niles and he would definitely notice if she showed up without Nihil. Uncle Raju, she thought, her face brightening, she should tell him! He was always so impressed with everything that her family did, but he was clearly most especially fond of her. Why hadn't she gone to see him first and saved herself all this trouble?

"Everything is good, Devi Baby?" Lucas asked, holding out the lukewarm bottle of ginger beer that he had already had opened at Koralé's shop. "Bring a glass! Bring a glass!" he said to Alice, as though delay combined with a lack of finesse might make Devi decide against the beverage.

"I got six A's and three B's!" she said, sipping the ginger beer through a straw and deciding that she would at least thank the old couple by sharing her good news.

"Not like that, must get all A's, no, Devi Baby? Like your *aiyyas* and your *akki*. I have heard that they never get even B's!" Lucas said.

Devi swallowed the rest of her drink in several long gulps, holding the glass in both hands and wheezing from the effort between mouthfuls. She wiped her mouth on the sleeve of her dress and giggled after the burp that followed. "I'll go now," she said, standing up.

"*Deiyyo saakki!* You can't go like that. I must come and put you to the other side," Lucas said. "Wait a bit, I will go and get a shirt and come."

Devi sat back down to wait. She listened to Lucas bickering with Alice, a low resonance of voices that were most unthreatening as though this was a form of communication, not disagreement. Nothing like when her parents argued, she thought. Their arguments, always about the government or each other's families, woke her from deep sleep and made her get up and pour water from the boiled and cooling bottles in the fridge or pee with the door to the bathroom open, making as much noise as she could in the hope that they would stop. Sometimes they did, other times they did not. When they did not, she woke up Rashmi and the two of them woke up the boys and sometimes Devi would cry and ask Suren to go and stop the arguing. He never did. He simply sat next to her and stroked her head. She wondered if Lucas and Alice had ever had that kind of fight. She doubted it. There was an air of calm about their hut. She looked up at the thatched roof and counted four *beedi* and one cigarette tucked in between the woven coconut fronds that made up their roof. The bench she sat on was lined with an old sari and several mats so that it was almost like a cushioned sofa. The flies buzzed outside and there was a quick smell of sewage that came and went and then came back to linger a while longer.

"Okay, now I'm ready. Let's go," Lucas said, holding out his hand. He was wearing a smart striped shirt in blue and white that Devi recognized as one that had once belonged to her father, and he had unrolled his sarong so it fell to his feet. He shuffled into his slippers, which had been repaired multiple times and quite crudely, the string all in different colors.

"That stink is back," Alice said, coming out from the dark room from which Lucas had just appeared. "Those slum people are constantly throwing their dirt into the canal and that's why. Devi Baby, maybe your father can fix this problem for us?"

"Don't ask these questions from Devi Baby!" Lucas said. "I will ask Master Sir. These things men must talk between men."

When Devi looked back, Alice was still standing on the top step, her hands planted on her waist. She had resumed muttering.

"I can walk from here," Devi said after they had crossed. As far as she could tell, it had taken Lucas just as long to get across as it had taken her, but she was grateful for his help nonetheless.

"No, no, I will take you all the way home," Lucas said, eyeing Sonna, who had just arrived at the bottom of the lane. He was carrying a bottle of pink milk that, even from afar, looked deliciously cool to Lucas, whose mouth watered at the thought. He swallowed and glared at Sonna, who was staring at them in a way that made Lucas uneasy.

Devi's concerns were elsewhere. "If you take me home then they will know I crossed the road and I will be in trouble," she pleaded in a whisper. "Please, Lucas Seeya, don't tell."

Lucas looked down at her. "Okay. But then you must promise me. Promise Lucas Seeya that you will never cross that road again. You understand? Never again."

"I promise," Devi said, her convincement absolute; the things she needed, her siblings, her friends, her home, they were all on this side of the street after all. And school and birthday parties she was taken to, so there was no chance that she would ever want to cross that street again. "I really promise, Lucas Seeya," she said again.

"I will walk you past Mr. Bolling's house," Lucas said, glancing back again at Sonna, who was still watching them, and Devi relented. When they reached the end of the Bollings' aluminum-bordered compound, she ran up the road and turned and waved, then hid herself in the Silvas' fence, pressing herself into the plants until she was sure Lucas had gone back home before darting back across the lane and opening the gate to Old Mrs. Joseph's house.

The sand and gravel driveway had been swept clean in patterns and she didn't want to disturb it, but she couldn't linger there or else Old Mrs. Joseph would summon her to the main house and she would never be able to tell Raju about her report card. She decided to make a run for it, but did so along the zigzag path made by the broom, so she would make the least possible disruption before arriving at the garage, where, she hoped, Raju could be found. She was elated to hear his grunts and the thud of barbells. Raju's weight lifting generated a sound that the Herath children had, as all the children of Sal Mal Lane had before them, grown to find comforting. Behind his mother's gray painted gate, at the end of the sand and pebbled driveway, inside the garage that had never sheltered a car, Raju grunted and heaved and dropped weights so reliably that it had become the music of their last games of cricket, their last run down the lane with their kites, or their last whispered conversations with their new friends, before they had to go back into their respective houses. For Devi, so full of need at this particular moment, the familiar sounds were like a favorite bit of music.

The front of the former garage was a wall with a door that was set into one corner. She knocked on the door and waited, clapping her hands together several times very softly as she listened for a response.

"Coming! Coming!" Raju yelled from inside before he opened the door.

Devi considered the possibility that this was one of those moments when her mother would have said that she, Devi, had lost her *common sense*. For there stood Raju not merely in the same exercise trunks in which he had first greeted her and Nihil when they moved in, but, additionally, glistening with what appeared to be oil and sweat, rivulets dripping down from his hairline and his belly. The trunks were soaked. She arched her body back slightly at the pungent odor that permeated the space, but before she could think of an excuse to leave, Raju spoke.

"Devi! Come come come! Come inside and sit!" he said, looking past her and then seeming to accept the fact that she was, indeed, alone. He cleared a space for her on a rattan chair that hung from a rafter at one corner of the garage, moving ceaselessly as though fearful that she might leave if he stood in one place. "My goodness. Didn't expect a visitor. Normally don't come, no, normally only I come to visit your place. Mummy's home?"

Raju always referred to her mother as *mummy* whenever he spoke of her to them. Even though Rashmi had told him several times that they did not call their mother mummy but, rather, Amma, *like good Sinhalese children should*.

"Don't know," Devi said, realizing that she had been gone for a while between the visit to the Bolling girls and the one to Lucas, and that it was quite possible that her mother had come home already from her after-school classes. She regarded Raju, who had sat down on the top of two steps leading down into the garage from the backyard of the house. He wiped himself with a towel, mopping his face and chest and underarms that were thick with hair.

"I came to tell you that I got six A's and three B's," she blurted out because, though some bit of good sense and intuition was telling her that her presence here alone was entirely inappropriate, she couldn't help but deliver her news. "That's the first time that I got such good marks. They all taught me, that's how. Otherwise, I usually only get an A for English and an A for social studies because those are the only ones I like."

Raju's eyebrows arched in wonder. "Ah? Really? Now you get such good marks? From a school like that, with all those good teachers, such good marks are a big thing, you know." His mouth turned down even farther than usual to express the degree of awe that he clearly felt. "You must be very proud. Mummy also must be proud. And Daddy must have got you chocolates and everything? Ah? Got chocolates?" Raju smiled.

Raju's smile, despite the grotesque nature of its separate parts, conveyed genuine gladness, and Devi concentrated on that. She could no longer smell the stench that had repulsed her before, and now that Raju's towel was draped across his knees and covered the lower half of his body, he looked as though he was halfway dressed. She relaxed into her chair and answered him.

"I didn't get chocolates, but Nihil said that later after homework, he would give me two of his Marie biscuits when we have tea. And I am sure if he gives me two, then Rashmi and Suren will give me two also. Then I'll have six. Plus I'll have my five and that way I will have eleven Marie biscuits!" She grinned at the prospect.

Raju shook his head from side to side, obviously as delighted as she was about the bounty that awaited her. "Now what can Uncle Raju give you? I must also give you something. I'm also proud of you. Such a small girl and you have done such a big thing!"

Devi's fears evaporated and her grin widened. This was exactly the kind of reception she had hoped for and been unable to secure from Rose or Dolly or Lucas. Here was a person who understood the magnitude of her achievement. She drew her legs up and tucked them under her, then reached out and pushed herself off the solid punching bar that had been mounted on the side of the post next to her. She swung back and forth, content.

Raju Refuses to Be Demoted

If in the wake of Devi's newfound status as a sibling worthy of her older brothers and, especially, older sister, all that happened was that Rashmi no longer had to murmur in commiseration on those occasions when she had to go to the staff room to deliver a message and when Sister Helen Marie drew her aside to share some misdeed traced back to Devi, or when Miss Atukoralé beckoned her over to show her the ugly script that Devi had produced, Rashmi would have been satisfied. But no, Devi's good work at school had resulted in her turning into a peregrinating menace at home. The tale of her crossing the road without permission and all that had followed had been relayed to them by Sonna, who came right up to them as they played French cricket to share the details:

—One of his friends had told him that Devi had almost got hit by a bus when she ran across the main road to see Lucas. The fact that the bus was a 109 had seemed particularly relevant, as if the gods themselves had sent the rarely seen bus as warning.
—Lucas had served her drinks.
—She had spent half an hour visiting Raju, who, they all must know by now, was not to be trusted.

Whether Sonna shared all this out of real concern for Devi's well-being, or whether he shared it because he knew, everybody down the lane knew, how closely the older Herath children, but particularly Nihil, guarded their younger sister, or whether he wished to get Raju and Lucas into trouble, the Heraths could not decide. Nihil believed fervently that it was the second of those reasons. Rashmi believed just as ardently that it was the last of those reasons. Nobody imagined that it was the first reason, that Sonna was genuinely concerned for Devi, that having already saved one Herath child from an accident, he felt responsible for the safety of another as well, particularly this one who had sat and shared her important news with him. Nobody thought that Sonna had, himself, been just as terrified as Nihil might have been to see Devi cross the road with the frail old Lucas, and to realize that she had, indeed, gone across that road by herself. To believe that would require the sort of generosity that Sonna had not had enough opportunities to earn and, in any case, everybody was more concerned with Devi's safety than with the bearer of the news, and so Sonna went back to his house without so much as a thank-you, all the Heraths turning away, intent on demanding an explanation from Devi. Even Devi, Devi on whose behalf he had quarreled with Sunil after having been caught stealing the bottle of strawberry milk for her and on whose behalf he had then earned a beating from his father when the incident was reported to him, even she did not look at him once.

"I told you to stay," he said, making one last effort, this time to place himself alongside the older Heraths, to speak as an older brother might.

And in response, instead of an explanation as to why she had left, her eyes welled up at his having betrayed her to her siblings. This confused Sonna so deeply that he took to his bed for the rest of the day, refusing food until his mother suggested a doctor, at which point he sat up in bed and yelled at her and everything went back to the way it had been before.

Even the Silva boys who had gathered, along with Rose and Dolly, as Sonna spoke, were shocked.

"Even I don't cross the main road without Mohan," Jith said, as he bounced their ball on the ground.

"It's hard even for me. Even I'm scared when I cross that road," Mohan conceded, and when all the children seemed taken aback by this statement, he added, "Even for you, right, Suren? You're scared too, aren't you?" All three of the older Heraths nodded in agreement. Yes, yes, yes.

"Did you really go to all those places?" Dolly asked. She caught the ball when it bounced out of Jith's reach and smiled at him as she returned it.

"Mad Raju's house, that's the worst," Mohan said. He would have said more but he saw Mrs. Herath walking up the road and so he only said, in warning, "Your mother's coming," and the children dispersed and resumed their game, for no more could be said in her hearing.

The kind of end that might have awaited their youngest sibling from the wheels of the buses and cars that traveled at such speed around the blind bend to the right of their lane, or the ingestion of water not sufficiently boiled, for they assumed that it had been tea that had been served to her by Lucas, and Devi would share no details, were as dire as what they feared might have happened to Devi should their mother discover that she had visited any of these places without a chaperone.

"Why would you do such a thing?" Suren asked as they took up the issue again the next day. He looked particularly serious with his hands

tucked into the pockets of the khaki longs he was wearing, having just returned from a dress rehearsal for a school production of *The Sound of Music*
in which he was playing Friedrich.

"You know none of us is supposed to cross the road!" Nihil said, his
voice close to tears. He was so glad that she had returned to them intact and
safe that he stroked her head, but roughly, his anxiety about her obvious
disregard for what might have happened getting the better of him and making him want to pull her hair instead.

"You are not to leave my sight," Rashmi added sharply, wondering simultaneously how this was going to be arranged and whether she should
have said "our," not "my."

Suren joined the older Herath children. They were united in their disapproval as they sat in a row on his bed, which had been freshly made
with sheets that the *dhobi* had brought just that afternoon in a crisp stack
of starched laundry, all of it tied up in newspaper and twine. Devi glared
at them from Nihil's bed, where she, defiant though she was, could not
help caressing the yellow-and-white-striped bedding; it was so smooth
and clean and she needed its tactile comfort. Rashmi, observing, knew
that this lack of repentance was not to be taken lightly. She turned to her
brothers.

"We have to make sure that she is never away from us," she said.
"Never. When she's in school, I will watch her, when we are home, we will
all watch her."

"You can watch all you want. I'm big. I can also walk up and down the
lane. Just like you," Devi said, crossing her arms in front of her chest and
scowling.

Devi was the picture of impenitence as she sat before them, her eyes
set, but Nihil could tell that tears were being held back though she would
never let them fall, not in the face of this kind of berating by her siblings. He
wanted very much to help her out of the corner into which she had painted
herself, to say something kind, maybe take her hand and say *it's okay*, so
she could cry and promise not to disobey their rules, but he held firm.

"No," Nihil said, thinking only of her safety, "you are *not* allowed to
go anywhere without us."

"You can't stop me," Devi said. "I can go right now!" And she stood
up. Nihil stood too, and pushed her back down onto the bed, his palm on
her belly.

"No, you can't," he said. "If you do we will tell Amma and Tha what you did and then you will be in real trouble. Do you want to be in real trouble? Because even I won't help you if that happens after this."

Rashmi looked approvingly at Nihil, whose contributions to these kinds of discussions usually led to his taking Devi's side so she ended up feeling championed rather than punished. "Yes, that's exactly what we'll do," she said. "None of us will help you."

Suren laced his fingers together in his lap as though in meditation. He said, "We are proud of you and your report card, but you are still small. You cannot run all over the place without telling us, okay? Okay?"

"Okay," Devi said, still pouting.

"And you can't go and visit that half-naked Raju," Rashmi added. "Okay?"

Devi did not agree, no matter how many times Rashmi said "Okay?" and this, too, was troubling to her. If Devi hadn't agreed to this specific demand, she clearly did not feel bound to obey, and if that was the case, what was the point in the larger promise of curtailing her activities?

Despite their initial reaction, with Suren increasingly wrapped up in his rehearsals, maths tutoring, and music lessons after school, and Nihil satisfied, it seemed, to gain a confessional relief from sitting with Mr. Niles and unburdening all his worries and tales about Devi's bad behavior to him, Rashmi felt decidedly alone in her crusade against the relationship between Devi and Raju. Over the next months, she had many chances to be reminded of her failure to elicit the right response from Devi—yes, she would not visit Uncle Raju—as Devi was located and hauled back home, the last time by her ear as she yelled *Uncle Raju is my friend!* as she was dragged away from Raju's garage, as soon as he had shut the door, and toward their own front gate. Which is why Rashmi felt that the matter had to be taken to the source of their troubles.

Visiting Raju was not something Rashmi would willingly have undertaken unless every other avenue had been explored. While all of them either knew or suspected that Raju was that curious mix of kind but mentally disabled and, therefore, untrustworthy adult, it was Rashmi who was comfortable with the idea of rejecting Raju wholesale. Something about his unaesthetic physicality and sense of coming undone irked her orderly mind. She was only willing to concede good so long as its human form stayed far away from herself and her siblings. After Raju had come to hang over their decorative white gate, bordered on each side by a high-growing hedge, and talk to their mother while she watered her plants in the evening, Rashmi had to fight the urge to send Kamala out to wipe down the gate. When he was served tea, she made sure that it was poured into a special cup that she had marked on the bottom with a smear of red nail polish she borrowed from Rose. When he stood just inside his gate and watched them play French cricket, she tried as often as she could to hit the ball hard and fast toward his gate until he backed away and went inside his garage to lift weights. To realize then that Devi was so pleased to disobey her older siblings just so she could spend time with Raju was more than Rashmi could bear.

"Uncle Raju gave me sugar sticks from Koralé's shop," Devi boasted. "I sat in the swinging chair and ate them."

"Why did he buy you those things? You aren't a beggar. You don't need things like that from people like him," Rashmi said.

"Rashmi, you are jealous because he likes me best and won't bring sugar sticks for you. Next time I'll save one for you. Uncle Raju is a good person." And Devi skipped away up the road, her rope snap-snapping in time as she relived the sensation of the chalk-shaped sweet in her mouth, the way it dissolved in sections as she sucked on it, the taste of sugar lasting until the very end.

Well, there was not going to be a next time, Rashmi decided, as she sat Devi down between her brothers, whom she had summoned from their respective preoccupations for this occasion, and left to go and speak to Raju herself.

The thuds from inside the garage were now muffled by a thick length of foam that Raju had secured from somewhere to line his floor. The foam was yellow with brown stains and gave off an impression of damp that nauseated Rashmi as she stood at the door, staring at Raju's surprised face.

"My goodness! New visitor today! Come come come. I will have to make a nice place in this corner now for all you children," Raju said, backing away from Rashmi and pointing to the corner where the swinging chair hung motionless and expectant. Rashmi pictured Devi curled up into that seat. Underneath the chair there was a fine dusting of powdered sugar and, already, a row of ants were marching toward it from a crack in the floor by the door to the garage. One wall was dedicated to posters of Bruce Lee and Muhammad Ali, a particularly large one of the latter with the phrase *flies like a butterfly and stings like a bee* written in a white flourish over his black body. They, like Raju, were bare-bodied. Unlike Raju's, their lower garments were decorous.

Rashmi put out her hand, palm up. "Raju . . . Uncle Raju, I have come to discuss something important."

Raju's face recreased to depict both alarm and concern. "Why why? What has happened? Tamil people coming? Mama said they are going to start a big war in the North! She said they'll come here too. But how to come? We're already here, no? But your daddy, he must be knowing something else, no? Government and all? Tell tell, Uncle Raju will put on a shirt and come." He took a few steps and then came back and smiled at her, a little sheepishly. "Now that I am friends with your family, I don't go anywhere without khakis and short-sleeved shirt, you must have noticed, no? Only inside I dress like this. For the bodybuilding." He laughed and disappeared again, calling out over his shoulder, "Wait here, wait here."

Rashmi imagined him wagging his head as he went. She smoothed the back of her skirt before she sank into the hanging chair; it was one of her best skirts, a maroon velvet one, and she had put it on with the hope that it would make her seem even more stern than she planned to be. Carefully avoiding the ants, she left her feet, safe in their black ballet flats, on the ground, so the chair did not make its rocking motion. She also did not lean against its back. She fiddled with the white silk collar of her blouse.

It was true that this was the first time in a long time that she had seen Raju in his barely dressed state. She thought about that for a little while, then wondered what Raju meant by Tamil people coming. Where were they coming to? Perhaps she would ask Mrs. Niles if she knew anybody coming from the North. Then again, maybe it would be better to ask her father, as Raju had suggested. Outside, there was a sudden clap of thunder and she stood up, went to the door, and looked at the darkening sky. There was no rain yet. She hoped it would stay dry until her mother returned home from school. Now that she had taken over additional duties as the teacher in charge of several clubs, she was rarely home before three thirty or sometimes four o'clock. Rashmi sighed, wishing that her mother could just be an ordinary teacher again, the kind who boarded the school buses when their students did at the end of each day and went home to their families. Why did her mother spend so much time in school? Why did she have so many places to go to even on the weekends? If she stayed home, perhaps Devi would too. When she became a mother, Rashmi decided, she would be less careless. She would have both money and children, prestige and domesticity. All it would require were a few good choices.

Raju appeared in the doorless frame of the entry to the garage from the backyard. He was dressed in khaki longs and a yellow short-sleeved shirt. "Now better," he said, "washed up also a little."

Rashmi felt that, indeed, things were looking up. When he put his clothes on, Raju became the good adult, not the half-mad one. Her spirits lifted and she felt slightly kinder toward him. "Uncle Raju, I have come to ask—"

"No, no," he corrected, his eyes grave, his palms out and facing down, "Not to ask, to tell. Because Uncle Raju doesn't know anything. I only know when your mummy or daddy tell me. Or Lucas. Sometimes he tells also. And Mama, but she doesn't know much about important things, about the government and all. About the neighborhood, of course, I can listen to Mama. She knows everything."

Rashmi cut in and spoke as fast as she could. "I have come to ask you to tell Devi not to visit you here anymore," she said. "We don't like it." She crossed her arms in front of her, bracing for the protest she was sure would come.

What Raju might have thought of her request, however, was not immediately shared because just then there was the sound of voices and Devi burst in, Nihil and Suren swift on her heels. Rashmi stood up and went over to them. Devi's eyes were full of tears and the boys were simultaneously berating her, pleading with her, and attempting to console her. Devi ran over to Raju and wrapped her arms around one of his.

"Uncle Raju is my friend!" Devi wailed. "He always has time for me. He never tells me to be quiet or go away!"

To Rashmi's surprise, Raju's own eyes became moist. "Don't cry, darling, don't cry. Uncle Raju is always your friend. Come now, you sit on the chair and I will rock you," he said, his voice reverting to its usual mellifluous cadences. Devi let herself be led to the chair, where she sat and regarded her older siblings, tears still sliding down her cheeks in erratic rivulets.

"We don't want her coming here by herself," Rashmi repeated with as much resolve as she could muster under the circumstances. "It is not appropriate for a little girl like her to come here. It smells bad here. Besides," she added, "when you are in here, you are never properly dressed!"

Raju seemed to take in Rashmi's own formal attire for the first time. He looked up and down each child in turn, then glanced around the garage as if realizing, at last, the incongruousness of the room in which he was entertaining well-dressed people like them. He shook his head from side to side. "Rashmi, you are right. This is not a place for you children. Especially not a little girl like Devi. Next time she comes, I will make sure that she sits in the veranda," he said.

Devi said, "I will come and visit Uncle Raju there!" She wiped her face and smiled.

Rashmi looked at Devi, wondering if she or Raju remembered who else occupied that space. Either they did not or neither cared.

"It is better if you came and visited my sister at our house," Suren said, his voice a mixture of suggestion and welcome. "You can even bring her *seeni kooru* there."

Raju looked at Devi. "Even that I can do. Anything at all you ask, Uncle Raju will do for you children," he said. And that was that.

Was he really that happy? Rashmi wondered as she walked home in her usual place, the left of the row, Nihil to her right, Devi between him and Suren. Raju had made it sound as if he had been elevated rather than demoted. Rashmi, centered as she was in her perfectly arranged world, knew as little about the desires that lived within people like Raju as she did about raising children. Year upon year upon decade of nothing but the same, the same dashed hopes, the same slights and injuries, had emptied all hope from Raju. Until the Heraths moved in, until Nihil talked to him, until tea was served to him by their mother, and until Devi visited him. His cup was brimming over, and nothing that anybody could say or do could diminish that.

Tigers

Raju kept his promise, and Rashmi had to content herself with the fact that they could now at least monitor Devi's activities and ensure that Raju did not encourage her to do anything foolish. He arrived the very next afternoon, dressed in a purple T-shirt and an old pair of long shorts that his cousin Jimmy Bolling had discarded and that were held up by a belt. He was carrying not only a bag of *seeni kooru* for all of them, but also the entire hanging chair complete with its tangle of ropes.

"I brought this to hang on your Asoka tree," he said. "Then Devi can have it."

"It will rot when it rains," Nihil said, stuffing his hands in his pockets, trying not to be tempted by the sweets so he could concentrate on what would be best for Devi.

Raju beamed and tapped his head. "Aha aha, but Uncle Raju has thought of everything. I went to Koralé and he took me to the *burusu kadé* and look, the coir man made it waterproof!"

Rashmi brushed her hand over the rattan but could not confirm that it was any different than when she had sat in it, so she said nothing. Either it would rot or it wouldn't, but what did it matter? She had Devi under control and that was what was important. So she humored Raju while he made a great show of fetching laborers from Koralé's wood-chopping business to shorten the ropes and hang the chair just low enough that Devi could climb into it with the aid of some of the lower branches, but too high for her feet to touch the ground when she sat in it. Rashmi glanced at the sweat glistening off the bodies of the two men who did the work and summoned Kamala to serve everybody cool lime juice instead of tea, which they sipped with their backs to her and her brothers and sister and even Raju, as if embarrassed to be seen drinking something so delicious in front of them. Mrs. Herath, who was inside, sitting at the dining table and grading papers, sent Kamala out again with a plate of pineapple sprinkled with salt and pepper, and this, too, was consumed discreetly by the men.

"First time I'm drinking cool drinks in your house," Raju said, slurping the last of his juice. "Usually your mummy gives me tea."

"We don't call our mother mummy," Rashmi said. "We call her Amma."

"Because we are Sinhalese children," Devi said, from her perch in the chair.

Mohan, who was listening from his veranda, called out his agreement, "Yes, real Sinhalese children know what to call their parents." He came out and stood by the low hedge that now divided their driveway from the Heraths', a hedge that was trimmed and watered in turn by Mrs. Herath and his father. It was due for pruning and the top layer of thin branches grazed his chin. Rashmi and Suren lifted their hands in a wave.

"But," Raju said, frowning, "Tamils also call Amma. Both call Amma. Only Burghers like my nieces and nephew call mummy and daddy."

"Tamils probably copied from the Sinhalese," Mohan said, but his voice was drowned out by Nihil's.

"Some children in my school, even if they are Sinhalese or Tamil, they call their parents mummy and daddy," Nihil announced, as soon as he had finished his drink, sucking the last drops out by balancing the whole glass, upside down, on his face.

Rashmi removed the glass from his face and placed it on the bright striped tray that Kamala had left behind on a stool. "We can't control what other people do," she said.

Raju, growing ever more comfortable as he sat with the children, almost like a close member of the family, he felt, said, "But you children don't say *akki* and *aiyya*, no? I have noticed. Most other Sinhalese children don't call brothers and sisters by their name."

Rashmi drew herself up to her full height. "What we decide to do in our family is a private matter," she said, and there was no doubt, no doubt at all, that Raju did not belong in the warm glow of that *we* and that *our*. In the silence that followed they all heard Mrs. Silva calling for Mohan from inside their house. As he turned to leave, Devi spoke.

"When are the Tamils coming, Uncle Raju?" she asked, pushing herself off from the tree and then crouching down in the chair to avoid banging her head on the trunk when the chair swung back toward it.

Rashmi looked at Raju with keen disapproval. Had he been filling Devi's head with these nonsensical tales too? "They are not coming," she told Devi. "I asked Mrs. Niles. She said no relatives are coming from Jaffna."

Mohan, already halfway to his house, called out, "Yes, I've heard, Tamil Tigers. We have to be ready."

"My god. Not relatives! Tamil Tigers!" Raju said at the same time.

Devi erupted into laughter. "Who are Tamil tigers?" she asked, "Do these tigers speak *Demala?* I'll have to go and tell the Nadesans," she said, and hopped out of her chair. She ran to the gate. Rashmi stopped her.

"You are not to go out of this gate without one of us, remember the promise?" she said. "If you want to visit the Nadesans, you can take Nihil and go. But don't go and tell them silly things like tigers who are Tamil. They will laugh at you."

"Then your daddy hasn't told you about them?" Raju asked, looking even more worried than usual. "How come? All over the news these days. Even in the papers they are writing about them. Daddy must know more than the papers, no?" He wiped the sweat off his face with the edge of his T-shirt, revealing the round hairless belly beneath. "Very strange that he hasn't told you all about what is happening. He has even given Lucas all kinds of information, I heard. About the Americans. CIA is everywhere now. Even in the old British places!"

"Who are these tigers?" Rashmi asked, though she was loath to admit that she was lacking in any sort of knowledge that had filtered its way into a skull as thick as Raju's, loath also to admit that their father hardly ever shared information with them if only because none of them had the patience to sit through his convoluted lectures.

Raju stood up to go. "Better ask your daddy. He must have a reason for not telling you, so I don't want to tell you and get into trouble. Maybe they are not coming. You ask Daddy and then you can tell Uncle Raju also. Because I don't know everything."

Rashmi opened and shut the gate behind Raju, then opened and shut it again behind Nihil and Devi. Devi had decided that she wanted to visit the Nadesans anyway and ask if they would let her play with the powdered dyes they kept for Deepavali. For his part, Nihil hoped that there would be enough time to stop by and ask Mr. Niles about these tigers before he forgot.

"Don't talk about tigers," Rashmi called after them and felt gratified that Nihil turned and waved. She smiled. She liked the way he was coming along. "He doesn't worry as much as he used to, does he?" she asked Suren, pulling her dress over her knees and to her ankles as she sat down next to him on their front steps. For a few minutes she managed to look like a little girl free of cares.

"He worries," Suren said, "but since he started writing things down in that notebook he seems to feel more in control. Maybe that is why he doesn't talk about those things that much now."

"Mr. Niles helps him too, I think," Rashmi said. She wondered if she ought to find out what exactly Nihil talked about with Kala Niles's father, but then decided against it. What was there to trouble her about Mr. Niles, after all, a man who could not even get out of his chair without help? Worrying about Devi was difficult enough for all of them; there was no need to add a new worry about yet another sibling. She gazed absentmindedly at Suren and noted that there was a thin rip in the seam in the shoulder of his shirt. She drew her fingers over it and suggested that he give it to her to be darned when he took it off at the end of the day, her sewing was improving, her embroidery too, she would like the practice.

They were still sitting there when Sonna came into view over the top of their gate. "Mummy sent me to ask if Devi is okay," Sonna said, though he did not meet their eyes and did not look as if he cared if their sister was well.

"She's fine," Suren said. "Tell your mother that Raju is visiting her here now. That will make her happy."

Sonna nodded but did not go away. His glance met Rashmi's and she wondered if there was something else he wanted to say. She contemplated asking him to come in, but in the wake of their recent rescue of Devi from Raju's malodorous den, and the invitation extended to Raju to visit their house on such a regular basis, it didn't seem prudent to invite Sonna in, too, so she said nothing. Another time, she thought, her eyes taking in what she could see over the top of the gate, his hair combed, his face at ease. When things settle down. Maybe he's not so bad. She sat silently while Sonna's eyes washed over them, their garden, the walls of their house, their roof, and then turned up toward the sky as if watching for rain. After a while he looked away from them and walked down the road. In the quiet he left behind, she could hear the irregular footsteps of the hand-me-down boots he had taken to wearing, one heel worn shorter than the other.

Sonna Remembers Everything and Nothing

Let us follow Sonna down the road and observe not the exaggerated swagger of his walk but rather the set of his shoulders. If we peel away the tatters with which he dresses himself, if we wash his body clean of his disguises, if we touch his scars with love and regret as a mother might as she prepares a son's body for burial, if we listen not to the words he speaks but to the yearning in his silence, we will see that Sonna is just a boy, one poised to step away from or toward us.

Nobody had told Sonna to go and check on Devi. He had thought of it all on his own. He had wanted to reassure her that he was a responsible guardian. He had wanted to make sure that she knew that he had hurried back as fast as he could with the bottle, that he had every intention of taking her back home, unharmed, but that by the time he had wrested the bottle from Sunil after a prolonged fight, Devi had fled, gone first to Lucas, then to Raju. Why she had sought out Raju, he could not imagine; the thought of a child like her, uncomplicated, sweet, sitting around while someone like Raju, hideous and stupid, threw weights about the place made Sonna shudder. Sonna had wanted to communicate to Devi's siblings that he had tried to prevent all of it.

As he set out for the Heraths' house, he slowed his steps to avoid coming face-to-face with Nihil and Devi, who had just set out to walk up the street. He did not feel able, yet, to speak directly to them. The older Herath children, closer to him in age, were more likely to understand him after all. Just before he reached the Heraths' gate and still hidden by the foliage on the Silvas' fence, he paused again. From here, he could see Suren and Rashmi sitting on their front steps. The mandevilla that Mrs. Herath had planted on either side of the opening to their veranda when they had first moved there, and then trained along V-shaped trellises, now cascaded from the cement overhang that shielded the veranda from the rain. It provided a red-and-white bower within which the two older Herath children sat, talking. Sonna could not hear what they were saying, he could just barely hear the low tones of their voices, Rashmi's, pitched a little higher than Suren's, wrapping around her brother's words, setting them in order. As he watched, Rashmi leaned toward Suren and caressed his shoulder. She said something to him that made Suren smile and shake his head. This was a different Rashmi. It was not how she looked when she walked down the street or came to Sonna's house; then she seemed untouchable. Emboldened by this, Sonna stepped forward to inquire after Devi's health, though as soon as he began to speak he lost all confidence and did not say what he wanted to but, rather, what he thought they would prefer to hear.

Lying in bed after he returned from the Herath household, ashamed of the tears he had brought to Devi's eyes, and then the lack of welcome from the older Herath children, he tried to understand what had happened, how, exactly, his good intentions had backfired. His mother came in with a cup of tea.

"Sonna, get up and drink the tea and I will change the sheets on the bed," she said, setting the cup on the floor beside him. "Drink soon or the ants will come."

"I don' wan' new sheets now," he said, feeling tired.

"Why? Daddy jus' brought from the *dhobi*. Get up, get up. I can make it quickly, then you can lie back down."

Francie Bolling leaned over and shook the leg nearest to her lightly, her palm over Sonna's right ankle. Something about that gentleness enraged him. He jerked his leg and flung her hand away.

"Leave me alone!" he said. "If the sheet is filthy, let it be filthy. The whole damn house is filthy anyway. Why bother 'bout sheets?" And he scowled at his mother.

His mother straightened up. She murmured "Then nex' time when you get up I will make the bed" as she left the room. Sonna's outbursts had long lost their effect on her after the first few times he had set upon her, trying to assuage some other hurt that he would not share with her. She did not cry anymore.

Watching his mother leave, Sonna felt his anger dissipate. The coir fillings in the mattress poked through the thin cover and scratched his skin, and for a moment he wanted to call her back and ask her to make the bed. He waited for this feeling to pass and, after a while, his thoughts returned to the one thing that came to him when he was in this kind of mood: he remembered the way the bat had felt in his hands when he used to play cricket at his school, back when he still cared enough to wake up and make it there by seven thirty each morning. And although his parents and sisters had never attended a single game in which he had played, he could still recall what it felt like when the other boys at school cheered for him, when everything else dissolved and in its place there was only himself, a boy, and his game. This was the memory that usually took him away from the present and made him feel as though his life was other than it was, but today he could not lose himself in it. The story slipped out of his grasp and the images were replaced by a scene in which he swung his bat repeatedly at a ball that nobody he could see was bowling at him; the stands remained empty no matter how hard he looked up into them, how hard he tried to refill them with the crowds he remembered.

Outside his door, he could hear the radio, and the singing made him think of Suren, the way he strummed that guitar and sang his songs. He had picked up Suren's guitar once, the one time he, Suren, hearing the sounds of a temple parade passing by on the main road, had left it on the dining table and gone out with the other children to watch. Sonna remembered how the guitar felt, bulky yet light, an utter mystery. He had held it up in his arms to feel the weight of it, held it against his body to feel its lightness, but when his fingers caught in the strings and released an unfamiliar note, it had sounded discordant. And still he had held it, tracing its lines, until he heard Rose's voice outside and he put the instrument down and went to his room.

Rose's voice. Why had there never been music in his life when even she had found a way to celebrate hers with song and dance? Why did his mother treat him like a problem that she had not asked for and did not deserve? Why was it that, for as long as he could remember, his father had been disappointed in him? No matter what he did or did not do, the one emotion Sonna could see in his father's eyes was a cruel sort of anger, an anger that seemed to have everything and nothing to do with him. And there he was again, fending off the first memory he had of his childhood. He was seven years old and chasing Rose in a game of catch. He saw, again, his arm outstretched and almost on her, Rose tripping and falling on her face, a cut above her lip, a tooth being knocked out and his mother shrieking.

"My god! My god! Come, Jimmy, come and see! Rose is bleeding!"

His father, still lean then, came striding out of the house, where he had been drinking since morning with a friend who had stopped by, and yanked Sonna by his hair and shook him in midair like a squirrel, bellowing in his face, "What have you done, you little shit? What have you done to your sister?"

His head ached when he remembered this. It ached from the hair being pulled out of his head, it ached from the pounding inside it as he struggled to explain that she had tripped, that was all.

"That is all?" his mother shrieked. "You have ruined her life! Now forever she will have a scar! How will she enter the pageants like that? She's ruined!" And more tears.

"She's not pretty enough to be in beauty pageants," his father said, his voice soothing, but this merely angered his mother more, rousing her to such a pitch that she slapped her husband across his face.

They had fought for the first time, Jimmy Bolling dropping Sonna to grab Francie and drag her into the house and then to leave in a further rage, driving off with his friend, only to have the vehicle turn over before it reached the bottom of Sal Mal Lane. Sonna remembered that sound, the immense thud with which it overwhelmed all the other sounds around him, including his own cries, and how brief that deafening had been. He heard his father cursing, the words unintelligible, the sounds guttural and fierce, and himself standing still for what seemed like a long time, listening. When he finally ran over, he had seen that his father's upper body was twisted back and he was pinned underneath his friend's jeep, the front passenger side of the vehicle flattening his left arm. Above his elbow the strong muscle that his father had flexed so often to his delight seemed flat and bloodied, the rearview mirror crushed and twisted around it, the weight of the jeep pressing down. A section of flesh from his forearm was caught between the glass on the window and the bottom half of the door, that mysterious sliver of space into which the glass moved when the window was opened. Sonna had felt that pain, the sharpness of it, the way there was nothing he could do to alleviate it. The flesh above and below that vice bulged unnaturally, and blood, neither bright nor dark, just strangely ordinary, dripped and ran over all of it. And he remembered wondering when his father had cut his finger, for he noticed that he had a thin antiseptic sticking plaster around the index finger of his left hand, which now lay twitching in the dust before him.

He lay there, screaming, looking up, his eyes fixed on Sonna's face. "Get this off me, you motherfucker. Get this off me! Get this fuckin' jeep off of me!"

Sonna pushed against the vehicle with all his might, the wheels now still. The driver's side of the vehicle was up in the air and his father's friend, Denton was his name, was trying to climb out of the open window. Each time he tried, the jeep rocked and seemed to press down further on his father.

"Stop, Uncle, stop!" Sonna said, panting with effort, and, even after his mother and the Bin Ahmeds and even Lucas had joined in and not even all the combined strength of the adults could get the jeep off Jimmy Bolling, and they had to wait until Lucas brought help from some men in the Elakandiya, Sonna had understood that somehow it was he alone who had failed his father.

Sonna trembled as he relived that day, a day from which, no matter how many other days had followed, he could not drain the slightest emotion. All of the anger, the screaming, the accusations, the very ugliness of his sister, her face swollen, her mouth open in a ragged square of piercing wail, the bloody, crumpled muscle and sinew of his father's arm, his howls of pain, all of it had taken up residence inside his head. And though Sophia picked him up and wiped his tears, he had not even known that he was crying, and though his mother never mentioned the incident again, after that day, everything changed in the house.

His father stopped trying to teach him how to be a strong man, filling small pots with sand and gravel, testing his tiny biceps, correcting the sway of his walk, the pitch of his voice. His father simply ignored him. It was as though Jimmy had decided that if his daughters were not beautiful enough for pageants, then his son was never going to amount to anything he might respect, and, further, that if he himself would never be able to use one of his arms, then Sonna need not try to impress him by using either of his. There was nothing to do but figure out what a boy could do if he were no longer preparing to turn into his father. Nothing Sonna studied at school gave him an answer. The books were full of stories about other kinds of people, the maths he struggled with, his homework was left undone, the writing, though passable, was only that. Nobody cared. He stopped going.

Sonna drew his palms down over his chest, over his belly, and back again to where his skin, smooth and untouched one moment, turned into four thin paths the next. Whenever he asked his mother about them she only said soothingly, *Scars will fade, Sonna, don' worry* and turned away. He had asked his father once, and only once, and his father had said *Because you deserved them, that's why*. Sophia always said *Don' you remember?* He remembered hunger, a child-voiced request for food and a fork in his father's hand. He remembered bleeding. He was almost certain that it had been his father who had drawn that fork across his stomach in one quick, vicious movement, a movement so instinctive that surely it had not been premeditated. But nobody would confirm that story for him and he had come to see those scars as being his. He was born with them, and that was an easier story.

He curled into a ball, his fingers knotted together and held tight against his stomach. He could hear movements outside, footsteps, someone putting down a comb, the gate open and shut, water poured into a glass. The day felt late. He had curled up this way the first time his father had beaten him, when Sonna was nine. He had made it through by fixing his gaze and concentrating not on the strength of his father's raised right fist but, rather, on the stub of his half arm, something about its helplessness serving to make the beating less hurtful.

"Sonna, you sleepin'?" Rose's voice.

His mother's, cajoling, "Suren an' Rashmi came an' gave us some pineapples an' some chocolates also."

And now, Dolly. "Uncle had got from somewhere an' they had extra. You wan'?" She came into the room, holding a chocolate set in its own pleated gold foil cup, something so elegant it did not belong in his sister's palm.

Back into his mind came the scent of sandalwood and baby powder, light-blue-and-white stripes, a clear voice telling him about grades and eyes filling with tears. And with it came a sudden sweetness to imagining what might have been possible, so he continued to lie there, within that memory, thinking about all that he was powerless to change but wondering if this gift of luxury was a sign of better things to come. He reached out his hand and took it.

And so, despite the unfortunate events that led him to be seen not as he wanted to become, a responsible, caring boy, but rather as he had always been, a ne'er-do-well the neighborhood was forced to tolerate, Sonna continued to try. Each morning he stood outside and watched the children leave for school. He waved to Nihil when he could, and he nodded to Suren, though he never smiled, even when Suren did. In the evenings he was back at his post to watch the children play. Which is how he saw Rashmi run down the lane toward him, leap into the air, and take a catch. Mohan was now out and Sonna, observing, cheered.

"Nice catch!" he called to her.

She smiled with real delight, a rare thing for Rashmi, a smile that transformed her entire demeanor.

"You're a good player," he added. "Rashmi, no?" And he felt lightheaded, being able to call her by her name.

She wasn't ordinarily a good player, this was a fluke, but no fifteen-year-old boy like Sonna had ever had the nerve to talk to Rashmi. She smiled again, tossing the ball from hand to hand, listening, thinking Sonna wasn't half so bad, especially when he was properly dressed as he was right now. Like Raju, she thought, when they are clean and dressed they don't seem so bad. She wondered if she should invite Sonna to join their game. She looked at the ball in her hands and she looked back at Sonna. Just then, they both heard the sound of the water-ice man. Sure enough, there he came, his sa-. rong tucked under, his wooden box balanced on the back of his bicycle.

"You like *ice-palam?*" Sonna asked.

Rashmi nodded, caught up in the moment, this half-captivated, half-imprudent exchange, and because it was the polite thing to do. The man did not sell Elephant House *ice-palam*, he sold water-ices. Water-ices were not to be purchased, let alone consumed. They were made of unboiled tap water. Probably from the nearby river. Rashmi shuddered, stuck in her predicament. She looked up the road. The others were arguing about scores. Sonna stopped the man and bought a twenty-five-cent serving of bright-blue water-ice. The man scooped it onto a wafer using his hand and gave it to Sonna, who carried it reverently over to Rashmi. Her hand slipped a little as the exchange was made and she dropped the ball. Sonna caught it. He took her outstretched hand in his and he placed the ball delicately in the center of her palm as though it were a treasure he had found for her. His hand was different from anything Rashmi had ever felt. It was neither gentle nor hard, not soft like hers nor competent like Suren's, it was warm and ragged and full of some nameless longing. There was a world behind that fleeting touch that disconcerted her. He seemed suddenly too-much-boy to her, with his boy voice, his boy clothes, his boy hair, and his boy smells. She was suddenly too-much-girl.

"Thank you," she said, at a loss now for what else she should say, though she wanted to stay in that moment, too much of everything around her, including herself, which meant she could not bring that water-ice, that unknown water-ice made with unfamiliar water, to her lips. "Don't you want some?"

Sonna shrugged. "No, I don' like," he said, though he did like it and wanted it, he just did not have another twenty-five-cent coin with which to buy some for himself.

"Goin' to melt if you don' eat it soon," he said, smiling, trying to sound as if it was just good advice, not like he cared.

Behind her the teams divided again and she heard Jith call out her name, startling her back into her ordinary life, the life where nothing was too much, everything was in balance. She thanked Sonna once more and began to run up the road, the ball in one hand, the water-ice in the other. Did she trip or did she drop it on purpose? Sonna could not tell. All he could see was that before she had taken even a single mouthful, the water-ice dropped from her hand and she turned, shrugged apologetically, waved, and then picked up her pace to run back to the game. The neon-blue lump stayed long enough to imprint itself in his head then melted swiftly into the hot asphalt.

Sonna was still thinking about that moment when he walked up the lane that night to ask his grandaunt, Old Mrs. Joseph, for some cubes of ice for his father's drink, an errand he had grudgingly agreed to perform because the twins were not at home. He was about to open the gate to Old Mrs. Joseph's garden when he glanced over at the Herath house and saw Rashmi seated in a chair on the veranda, reading a book. She played with a strand of hair as she read, absently twining it around each of the fingers in her right hand, passing it from one to the other in a mesmerizing sequence. She stopped only when she had to turn a page. And though he could hear faint end-of-day noises from other houses, the shooing of a stray cat, the shutting of a creaking window, a hand jerking it shut in sharp squeaks, even the sound of the Silva boys being called by their mother, Rashmi's quiet activity made the evening feel calm and manageable to Sonna, and he did not take his eyes off her. Once, she looked up from her book and stared out into the darkness, narrowing her eyes as though she could sense that she was being watched, but she did not leave. Sonna stood there until someone called her name from inside the house and she got up to go and he stood awhile longer, until the light in the veranda was switched off.

Perhaps it was because Old Mrs. Joseph, too, had been changed somewhat by the new family that she did not tell anybody, not Raju nor Jimmy Bolling nor even Sonna, that she saw him standing there on that night and on many other nights to come, gazing at the Herath household, waiting for someone or something. And if Rashmi sensed that he was there, she, too, said nothing, keeping this first secret from her brothers and sister as if in regret for the fact that she was not the kind of girl who would ever be able to accept the kind of treat a boy like him could give her.

1981

Blue and Gold

With a brother like Nihil as her guiding star, it stood to reason that the biggest excitement in Devi's life thus far would take place during the 102nd Battle of the Blues, the annual cricket match between Royal College (public, Buddhist), and St. Thomas' College (private, Catholic), and that it would begin with a disagreement over cricket.

On the first day of the three-day match, everybody in the Herath household was up by dawn except for Mr. Herath, who only appeared at the match halfway through the second or third day if he appeared at all. He didn't participate in these kinds of bourgeois capers. He participated in things where his presence was distinctive and noticed and where it could, conceivably, alter the course of affairs. Appearing at a cricket match to cheer and get drunk with half of the thirty thousand other people there was not one of those occasions so he rarely indulged himself in it.

"Amma, Kamala has packed all the food but I wanted iced drinks, not iced water!" Devi said, coming into her mother's room. She stopped short at the sight of her mother, who was dressed in a turquoise blue silk with tiny yellow peacocks embroidered over the fall and the *palu*. "You are wearing blue and gold!" she said, clapping her hands.

Mrs. Herath smiled at her daughter. "Yes, darling, today's the day to wear these colors, after all."

Devi clapped her hands again. "Yes! We are going to win! Nihil gave me his old flag so I have my own flag now," she said. She ran away, then came back to show her mother the bright flag with its three broad stripes of blue, gold, blue.

Mrs. Herath smiled at her, then looked back in the mirror. She bent her knees slightly, stepped on the edge of her sari, and straightened up again. She turned around and looked over her shoulder so she could see the back. "Devi, can you kneel and pull down the edge of my sari? It's too short." Devi came closer, breathing in the orange, rose, and sandal scents of her mother's Elizabeth Arden perfume, Blue Grass, which she reserved for special occasions, for events that were more important even than weddings. Pausing, before she knelt down, to take another deep breath of the perfume and let it fill her up, Devi felt immediately that this match was going to be momentous in her life. She knelt beside her mother and tugged at the sari until it was the right length. Then, still holding the memory of that scent in her nose, she wandered out, the soft drinks forgotten.

Nihil came into the room. "Amma, can we go? We'll be late. The Silvas have already left. I saw them go and they waved and said we would be late and that we should hurry!"

Indeed, Mohan had said, "If you don't hurry, you'll miss everything," by which he meant the time when the cricketers came out to throw and play a few balls right beside the stands.

"I'm taking a special pen to get my souvenir signed," Jith had added, and flashed a smart-looking click-on, click-off biro at Nihil. He let Devi play with it for a few moments before he snatched it back and ran away to catch up with Mohan.

As far as Nihil was concerned, being at the match a few hours before it began was not only desirable but necessary. Although he no longer went to cricket practice, he went to watch every game he could, copying the moves and replaying them in his head until he was convinced that were someone to hand him a bat or a leather ball he could save any game. Another young Royalist had once saved the big match by batting for four hours straight when even the spectators had given up and defeat was all but expected. Nihil had always imagined that someday he would become such a player, the one a team could rely on, but that could not happen until Devi was old enough. By then it would probably be too late.

Mrs. Herath, seeing how Nihil's shoulders had suddenly slumped, laughed. "Don't be silly. How can we be late? It is not even eight yet and the match doesn't start until ten. We'll leave in about half an hour," she said.

Nihil sighed, unable to tell her where his thoughts had taken him, for surely that would earn an *I warned you, didn't I?* Instead he stood in front of his mother, staring at his reflection in the mirror. He ran his hand over the fabric of his shiny dark-blue shirt with its motif of golden chariots. Suren came in and stood beside him, his arm around Nihil's shoulder.

"See how nice both of you look in those shirts?" Mrs. Herath said. "This way, I can always tell exactly where you are."

"Don't worry, Amma, I will look after Nihil," Suren said.

Mrs. Herath finished strapping her wristwatch on and spoke brusquely. "Yes, but I'll also be using the binoculars!" She rummaged in the almirah for a few moments and turned around holding aloft a pair of binoculars.

"But those are Tha's! He won't want you to take them to the match," Nihil whispered.

Mrs. Herath glanced over at her husband, who was, miraculously, still sleeping through all the excitement, and pressed her fingers to her lips. "Shh. He won't know we took them," she said.

The borrowed driver eased the borrowed car slowly down the narrow road, conscious of the importance of his cargo both human and inanimate. As they passed the Bollings' house, Sonna crossed in front of their car.

"That boy never seems to be at school," Mrs. Herath said, thoughtfully. "At least Rose and Dolly go to school."

"Maybe he's going to the match too," Rashmi said. "He might be going with friends." She said this though she knew that Sonna would hardly be going to a match that did not involve his own school and that, further, he did not seem to have any friends. Although she had wanted to defend him, the words only made her feel worse about the water-ice.

"Like us," Devi said, considering that she and her sister had no business being out of school either.

Nihil, Devi, and Rashmi twisted in the back seat to observe Sonna, who had crossed back and was standing in the middle of the road, staring at the slow-moving car. Nihil waved, a small and cautious wave, and though Devi followed suit, Sonna did not wave back.

"I feel sorry for him," Rashmi said, feeling as though she had added to Sonna's troubles somehow.

"I think he could be better," Nihil offered cautiously, sitting back down, "even if he's not very nice now. Maybe if he joined us when we play he might learn how to behave—"

"I want you to stay clear of that boy, you hear me?" Mrs. Herath said, cutting short Nihil's good intentions. "No good can come of him. Francie told me just the other day that they even had the police come and visit them because he had stolen a bottle of milk from Sunil's shop. Nothing but trouble, she said."

The children said no more, in unspoken agreement that if Sonna's mother herself had complained to theirs, there was no argument they could come up with on Sonna's behalf.

Mrs. Herath felt compelled to add, "A mother knows," the sort of enigmatic statement that had always been useful in the corralling of children.

The first day of the match came and went in its usual manner, the backs of the stands filling with boys and men waving flags and dancing in time to the music being belted out by hastily hired "bands." Since payment came in both money and alcohol, fairly quickly the music was hardly recognizable as such and the singing more caterwaul than song. Devi joined in, raising her voice with glee as she sang her brothers' school song, stretching out her *e*'s and *a*'s until Rashmi thought she sounded more like a villager just learning English than a convent-educated girl from a good family like theirs. When lunch was called, Suren and Nihil went by in a blur of blue and gold during the boys' parade around the grounds.

"Look! Rashmi, look!" Devi yelled. "They are carrying Suren and Nihil on their shoulders like flags! *I* want to go in the parade," she added, after they had passed, fingering the trim on her dress. "I want to go with Nihil."

"Don't be silly," Rashmi said. "Bad enough we are here with bogus excuse letters. Imagine if the match nun saw us in the parade?" She shivered, picturing the particular nun assigned to monitor the activities of convent girls at the match, her eyes glued to the television to see what she could see. "Just be happy that we get to come."

But confining Devi took more than common sense. On the morning of the second day, while her mother was wrapped up with her friends and Rashmi was busy storing their baskets of food and drink under their seats, Devi slipped under the ropes and out of the short gate separating the grounds from the stands and tried to blend in with all the little boys fielding the leather balls while the cricketers warmed up. She was so thrilled with herself that she was completely unaware that the boys were nudging each other and laughing at her until Nihil came up and called her name just as she braced herself to catch a ball that had rolled toward her. Hearing his voice, she forgot to fold one knee sideways and cup her palms. Instead, she squatted. The ball rolled between her legs and toward another boy.

"Bokku! Bokku!!" a boy yelled next to her, the visor of his blue cap tipped up.

"Girls can't play cricket!" another added.

"What are you doing here?" Nihil asked, taking her hand. Devi broke away from him, flew at the boy who was nearest to her, and kicked him in the shins.

"You are stupid idiots. I can catch balls too." She aimed kicks at any boy who came near her. She was like a resplendent yellow wasp, a flash of color amid a field of green and white.

In the end it took two cricketers to break up the melee, which concluded with one of them carrying a squirming Devi back to her mother.

For the rest of that day Devi was forced to sit between her siblings, the two boys voluntarily giving up their boys-tent life to manage their difficult sister. On Saturday, the final day of the match, thanks to her complete lack of regret about what had happened, Devi was left behind.

Raju's Gift

If only Devi had behaved that day at the match. If only she had been content to respect the boys-only boundaries that had been set up and venerated for a century and two years. If only Lucas, not Raju, had been left in charge of her on the third day of the match. But it all happened this way and not in those other ways. Devi misbehaved, Raju was chosen.

Mrs. Herath summoned Raju to *watch over Devi like a hawk, the little vixen, she'll be off like a bullet if you take your eyes off her,* and he took the task so seriously that he ran home, showered, and, despite the heat, returned dressed in a long-sleeved button-down shirt and his best belted khakis and his late father's polished leather shoes with laces, his sparse hair wet and slicked back.

Nihil told Raju confidentially, before they left for the game, that he had gone over early morning to tell Mr. and Mrs. Niles about this punishment, just in case Raju had any need to get additional help from them.

"Devi just would not listen," Nihil had told the old couple. "Now maybe she will learn. I don't like to leave her, but there is nothing to be done. She is too stubborn."

"You run along and enjoy the match, son," Mr. Niles had said. "Tell Raju to come and talk to Aunty if he needs anything. And Kala will be home after school as well."

"It's not fair," Devi confided to Raju when the flurry of departures was behind them and the reality of her punishment had set in. "They all get to do what they like and only I never get to do what I want." She was wearing Nihil's clothes, a pair of black shorts and a dark-blue shirt, the colors of the rival school. It was a protest that none of her family had commented on, not even Nihil, which had stung her most of all.

"They are just trying to take good care of you, darling, because you are so special, that's all," Raju said, using his gentlest voice. "Isn't it better to stay at home and have fun than to go and sit in the hot sun all day long watching cricket?"

"I love cricket!" Devi said, looking at Raju as though he had lost his mind. "I love to go to the big match. And now I will have to wait a whole year to go again. And they may not even take me."

Raju watched her swinging back and forth in the chair hanging from the Asoka tree, her hands clasped around the paper bag of Delta sweets he had brought for her. Clearly the swing and the toffees were insufficient to make up for the egregious sin of having been left behind. He racked his brains for something else that he could do for her, something wonderful that would make having had to stay home with him to watch her seem just as exciting as being allowed to go to the cricket match with her mother and her siblings.

He could get her hair clips, he considered, then rejected that idea. Devi was not the kind of girl who cared for that kind of thing; she was an Alice band kind of girl. Icy chocs, he mused, gazing at the sad face before him. No, that had already been used up when she got stitches; it had to be something new. He entertained the idea of taking her up the road to the Sansoni house and helping her to climb the wall so she could pick a ripe guava, but then put that thought out of his mind, berating himself for even considering such corruption of innocence. He let his gaze wander around Mrs. Herath's splendidly maintained garden, all along the stiff and neatly pruned hedges, winding in and around her pride of Japan, her ixora, her jasmine and gardenia, the spotted mauve, yellow, and white dancing orchids hanging from lined coconut husk pots from the jambu tree, her collection of citrus bushes, limes and oranges, the fruity scent of those flowers designed to remain a safe distance from the rosebushes she had grown with Kala Niles's help, the mandevilla flowers hanging above him, her feathery green and white and purple ferns, up the Asoka tree, and back to Devi without anything of worth coming to mind. Devi continued to sit, rubbing and clacking the nails of her fingers together. Rub rub, clack clack, rub rub, clack clack.

"I can hear the postman," she said suddenly, looking up, "can you? Maybe I'll get a letter from someone. That will be exciting."

"Do you have a pen pal from abroad? From Australia?" Raju asked, even that being possible for the Herath children. He pulled out a handkerchief and mopped his forehead and neck. He considered rolling up the sleeves of his shirt but decided he would hold that in reserve for when the heat got worse.

"No," she replied. "Only Rashmi and Suren. Not even Nihil gets letters. Not even from our grandmother. She only writes to Rashmi." She added this fact to the list of injustices perpetrated against her by her family.

"How about we write a letter to Nihil then?" Raju said, his face brightening. "That way he'll be happy when he gets a letter and maybe he'll write you one."

Devi considered this and then shook her head. "He already lives here," she said. She popped another Delta toffee into her mouth and tucked it into the back of her cheek, letting the melting caramel syrup drip through her mouth, waiting for it to make her feel better.

Raju could not find anything wrong with this line of reasoning so he planted his chins in the palm of his right hand and stared glumly toward the gate, listening to the postman's bell drawing near and then nearer until it stopped in front of the Heraths' house. He stood up and went to meet him. He opened the gate and greeted the postman noncommittally.

"Ah, Mr. Raju, you also have moved houses now?" the postman asked slyly, looking through the bundle of letters in his hand, very slowly, before extracting several bills and letters and tapping them together on the handlebar of his bike.

Raju was too preoccupied to catch the postman's jibe at the way in which he, registered-mail-signature-required letter in hand, had discovered Raju's father, Silver Joseph, with his mistress in this same house the afternoon before they had committed suicide together.

"No," Raju said. "I'm looking after the youngest while the Herath family is at the big match. She is a bit sad and I'm trying to think of something to cheer her up." Raju contemplated Devi from afar.

The postman peered over the gate at Devi, who spun slowly in her chair. "Ah, Baby! Why you sad, Baby?" he asked in English, then reverted to Sinhala. "Baby, if you sit crying like that all day, your face will become sour like a billing fruit!" he said. "Then what will your Amma say when she comes home and finds a billing and no little girl? Ah? Ah?"

Devi tightened her lips but the smile leaked out nonetheless. "Then she'll have to make billing *achchaaru*," she called out. "And nobody will know where I am and they'll all be looking for me and in the end they'll be so sad that they left me here to become billing."

The postman laughed along with Raju. "You want to come for a ride with postman uncle?" he asked. "I will take you up the lane on the handlebar," he said. He turned to Raju. "Shall I take her?"

Raju's face went through several changes as he considered the wisdom of allowing Devi out of the gate. If he ran behind the bicycle, then he would be keeping her in sight, wouldn't he? Besides, here was Devi running up to them, already kicking off her sandals and slipping out of the gate. And here was the postman, wiry as he was, with his trousers held in place by a thick belt tightened around his narrow waist, strapping his stack of mail to the rack of his bike and hoisting her up onto the handlebars.

"Yes," Raju said, quickly, just before the grinning postman took off up the road with the happy, laughing child. "Yes, I will let you take her once only, up the street," he said, starting to walk quickly behind the bicycle, his arms flapping at his sides, the fingers spread wide, a frown on his forehead, his head, too, tipped over even farther than usual with worry.

"Uncle Raju, look! I can go without even holding!" Devi said, lifting her hands in the air.

"No! No!" Raju yelled. "You madman, tell her to hold on!"

The postman laughed and said something to Devi, who shook her head and held on to the handle behind her back. Not that it provided much support, but it was better, Raju felt, than being completely out of control. The postman took her up the lane to the Sansoni house and then down the road to the gate of her house and back again several times before he stopped.

"Now that's enough, Baby," he said, panting, over her pleas for more. "Postman uncle will faint if I try to pedal one more time."

Devi slipped off the handlebars reluctantly and stood beside Raju to watch the postman wheel his bike away, his shirt plastered to his back, to resume his work. There was no trace of sadness left in her face and Raju felt extremely glad about that. As they stood there, Sonna, wearing a dirty white shirt that flapped in the breeze, strode out from Raju's gate, leaving it unlatched behind him.

"Ai! Sonna!" Raju called out, feeling respectable and responsible and in full control. He gestured toward his house. "Lock that gate behind you!"

"You lock it," Sonna said, coming to a stop.

"Always causing problems," Raju muttered as he left Devi's side and crossed the street to latch the gate. It had been a long while since he'd felt the brunt of Sonna's bullying. He had almost forgotten what it felt like.

"Don' know who is causin' problems," Sonna said, "puttin' a small girl like her on the pos'man's bike. Left to look after her but don' even know how to look after yourself."

Raju had crossed back to stand next to Devi, who took his hand in commiseration, instantly comforted by the familiarity of his palm, the odd softness of its fleshy mounds. "Uncle Raju looks after me properly," she said, addressing Sonna. "He brings me sweets and he dresses nicely and he comes to our house and has tea and sits with me."

"Wait till your brother hears that he put you on the pos'man's bike. That will be the end of your Uncle Raju." Sonna glared at her, wondering if she was sufficiently scared, enough to stay out of trouble until her sister and brothers got home. No, she didn't look it. "Good thing too," he added, "otherwise one of these days he'll get you into real trouble. Don' know how you can stand to have an ugly man like him nex' to you all day long."

At this Devi's face screwed up into a glower. "He's not ugly. *You* are ugly," Devi said, stamping her foot at him as if she was trying to scare away an insect.

Sonna stood rooted to the spot and looked at her in genuine amazement. Then he turned on his heel and stalked off. "Do what you like," he said, though they could not hear the words, all they could hear was muttering: "You go an' ride aroun' with the pos'man. I don' care. Did it once, did it twice, three times already I tried. For what? You stay with that fuckin' fool. See what happens." He broke off a sprig from the araliya branch that was hanging over the road from the tree at the edge of the Silvas' garden and flung it away, his hand covered with the milk-white sap that continued to drip from the broken limb behind him. "*I'm* ugly? *I'm* ugly?"

He reached his house, kicked the front door open, and went inside. He strode up to the long mirror in his mother's room. In his state of agitation, his eyes on fire, he did look frightening. The precise ballpoint pen drawings he had made on his body now seemed uneven, the design blotchy in parts where the ink had smeared. He hit himself several times in his stomach, bracing for each punch. He buttoned up his shirt. He tried to calm his face. He was *not* ugly! He wanted to scream it out loud; instead he began to cry, sharp tears evaporating on his cheeks before they had even registered their arrival.

Raju, who had waited until Sonna was out of sight, looked down and stroked the hair off Devi's face and tucked a stray tendril behind her ear, grateful for her support, thankful that Sonna had left. He opened the Heraths' gate and took Devi inside.

"Can you find another bicycle, Uncle Raju?" she asked when they had taken up their previous positions, Raju on the front steps to the house, seated on a folded newspaper to protect his clothes from the red floor polish, she in the hanging chair.

Raju shook his head. "Only bicycle I know of is in my house but it doesn't work," he said. "Daddy's Raleigh, but," he twisted his open palms in opposite directions, "not working."

"Can't you make it work?"

Raju did not know what, exactly, the matter was with his late father's bicycle. He had never ridden the bike, it being full sized and built for a tall man, but he had imagined that he might use it someday and so he had brought it inside and leaned it up against his mother's chest of dry goods. It got some movement every day when their servant girl struggled to push it aside to take out dried chillies and spices while shooing away cockroaches, and then dutifully returned it to the spot where Raju's father had been accustomed to putting it; what had once belonged to the dead was sacred. He could ask Mr. Bin Ahmed, he thought, a vague memory of his neighbor once riding a bicycle rising up before him. Or perhaps he could take it to Koralé and see if he could tell him what to do about the bicycle to make it work. Or Lucas, he could ask Lucas, who might have a considered opinion, having been there when the Raleigh was first bought, brand-new and gleaming black and silver when Raju was just a teenager himself. He looked at Devi. If riding a bicycle could lighten her mood, surely it was worth trying.

"Devi," he said, deciding right then and there that he had not only the authority but the intelligence to make such decisions, "if you can promise Uncle Raju that you will stay inside the house with Kamala, I will go and see if I can fix the bicycle right now."

Devi smiled. "Of course I will stay with Kamala. It's too hot to go outside now anyway," she said, as further evidence of her intent to comply, such unpromising heat stacking up before her like the bars of a cage. "I'll ask Kamala to give me kurumba and I'll wait inside. Even if you don't come back till after lunch I won't come outside. I'll read Rashmi's Enid Blyton book. She borrowed it last week and she hasn't even let me touch it but I know where she hides it and she's not here, so I can read it. Okay? You go," she finished, and gave him a push. "By the time you come back, I might have even finished the whole book!"

Raju fairly ran down the street to fetch Lucas, whom he found sitting in the shade of an areca nut tree, his pale red sarong rolled up tight between his legs and tucked under his bottom, scratching the few hairs on his bald head and staring with some belligerence at the sky.

"Mr. Raju," he said and nodded, though he did not stand up.

"Lucas Aiyya, I have come to ask if you will look at my father's bicycle."

"Eh? Bicycle? What for a bicycle now? I can't even walk!" Lucas said and chuckled, real amusement flooding his age-gray eyes and spilling over into the lines of his face. "I can't even walk, Mr. Raju, haven't you noticed?"

"Not for you to ride," Raju said. "For me. For me to take Devi Baby up and down the road."

Lucas continued to sit, but he stopped laughing. He shook a finger at Raju. "Devi Baby is not supposed to leave the house," he said.

"I know, I know, I'm the one who is looking after her. Whole family went for the big match, and I was told to look after Devi Baby because you know how she is, quite naughty sometimes," he said, laughing, then turned serious. He corrected himself. "But only sometimes, not always. Most of the time she is a very good girl."

Lucas stared at his feet as he took in this sudden wealth of information: that Raju still had his father's bicycle, that the Heraths had gone away for the day, and, most important of all, that they had left Raju, not him, Lucas, but Raju, in charge of their younger daughter. Youngests were the most beloved, the best protected. So how was it that *this* youngest, such a flower among all the other youngests around, had been left in the care of a spilling-all-over-the-place man like Raju? He retraced the last several weeks in his mind. Had he done something wrong?

Yes, true, Alice had feigned a headache on the one day that Mrs. Herath had sent for her and he had taken Alice's place to help the Heraths' woman in the kitchen for a big party they had given for some teachers. And, true, Alice had pretended not to see Mr. Herath when his driver stopped the car on the way to work right next to them and asked after his, Lucas's, health. What was wrong with that woman? She was constantly ruining everything. And now look, after all his hard work to cultivate his special status, the youngest had been handed over to Raju. Then again, he reasoned, maybe there was more to Raju than he had suspected. After all, look at all the things that Koralé had changed since Mr. Herath came to live. No more foreign cigarettes, donating wood to the temple once a month, paying the laborers more after Mr. Herath got Koralé a contact to bring in coconut oil and kerosene too, all these were good things, weren't they? Even the Bolling girls seemed to be dressing properly. And Old Mrs. Joseph had told him that one of them even had eyes on a Silva boy. All these things, surely, had to do with the way the Heraths organized their world. So why not Raju? The Heraths did everything right. Raju had obviously been chosen because he was the best for the job.

Lucas stood up and dusted off the back of his sarong. He looked approvingly at Raju's buttoned-up shirt and his leather shoes. He saluted Raju. "Let's go, Mr. Raju Sir. I will come and look at your bicycle."

When Lucas arrived and asked Old Mrs. Joseph's servant girl to dust the cobwebs that wrapped around the wheels and between the bars of the bike, two large spiders scurried off and Raju skipped out of the way with a yelp. Even when it had been wiped down, the bike seemed crooked and insufficient to Raju. Lucas took the bicycle, looking as though he, too, did not believe it would be adequate as a vehicle for a youngest.

As Raju watched Lucas go down the road, he experienced a disconcerting moment of imagining that it was his father, not Lucas, who was wheeling the bike as he had done each morning when he left for work, his gait erect, his handsome face ready for the day, even on that last day when he left, as usual, but did not go to work; he had simply walked the bike across the street, leaned it against the short parapet, and gone in to kill himself. Raju had been tasked with the business of removing the bike in the wake of the discovery of the two dead bodies, before the two separate funerals. Neither family had gone to pay their respects to the other bereaved, the betrayal so humiliating for both the widow and the widower left behind. And now here was the bike come out of hiding, and if it were to be repaired and if it were to be functional again, if a girl like Devi could sit astride it and be wheeled up and down the street, why then perhaps Raju could forget its previous last day of use. He continued to stand in the burning heat while he waited for Lucas, now anxious, now hopeful, until Lucas returned an hour or so later.

"We had to wait until one of the men took it to Sunil's shop to get the parts oiled," Lucas said. "See how it looks now? Shining also. Koralé got his son to wipe it down properly with some kind of polish. Now it looks good enough to put Devi Baby and ride. But," he held up a finger and made his face grave, "be careful. Youngest child, and you are in charge, Mr. Raju Sir. Anything happens, you are to blame, not me. Not Lucas Aiyya. Don't come crying."

After the sun had gone down a little, but before the others came home, when the shadows filtering through the great leafy sal mal trees fell more gently on the lane, Raju escorted Devi through the gate and settled her on the seat of the bicycle, proud of the fact that the bike stood firm on its rest while he made sure she was safe. While she waited for him, her mood improved and equilibrium restored after her ride with the postman, Devi had discarded her traitorous clothes and put on a blue divided skirt and a yellow T-shirt, and looked more like herself. Raju rolled up the sleeves of his shirt, put his arms around her, kicked off the rest, and held on to the handlebars as he wheeled the bicycle up and down the road, not minding the sweat pouring down his face and gathering in all the crevices and rolls of his body, not minding that his arms and legs began to quiver with the effort of supporting both her and the weight of the bike, not minding anything at all but the fact that Devi was happy, that he had been the one to drive the lost cricket match out of her mind. Neither of them paid any attention to Sonna, who sat in front of his house in a chair he had dragged out.

An Odd Alliance and a Little Romance

If Devi's friendship with Raju raised any eyebrows, the one so youthful and expectant of good things, the other so devoid of symmetry and hope, we may take comfort in the fact that Old Mrs. Joseph, who knew more than most, said nothing about it. Indeed, if there was anything that eased her heart, one crushed so irreparably by the person it had chosen to love, it was the sight of her son going about his day with purpose. A purpose that was not attached to something impossible like a title he would never earn, but something simple and achievable: indulging a child who needed him in her life. So she watched Raju as she did all the neighbors, alert to any sign of things being amiss, and glad at the end of each day that nothing was. At night, on those evenings when she stayed out late on the veranda, a silver-gray cardigan wrapped around her against the slightest breeze, she watched Sonna.

Sonna's vigils had continued, though it seemed to Old Mrs. Joseph that the calm that had seemed to descend on him on that first night appeared to seep out of his body as the weeks and months wore on. Now, when he stood there, staring, he often seemed agitated rather than soothed by the scenes that unfolded in the lit-up rooms of the Herath household, the ones visible from the street: the veranda, the living room, the boys' room, each its own stage with its collection of immovable props and cast of characters. She watched Sonna and wondered if it distressed him to see their sometimes routine, sometimes disarmingly affectionate interactions with each other. If, as he watched Suren help Devi practice yet another piece of music she was struggling to master, or Nihil and Rashmi laugh over some joke he could not hear, or they played cards together, what he saw was not simply four ordinary children growing up together in a family, but children whose kindness toward each other formed a wholeness that he would never experience with his own siblings. Now if he relaxed against her gate, it was only on those occasions when whichever Herath child that was visible was alone, engaging in some inward-focused activity like reading or writing or, in Rashmi's case sometimes, sewing. He never lingered if Suren played the piano; something about that music seemed to irk Sonna.

Soon enough, though, Old Mrs. Joseph's passive observation of Sonna and Raju gave way to witnessing the development of an unlikely and disturbing alliance, this one forged between Sonna and Mohan Silva.

Sonna's small crimes had resumed, one by one, in the wake of his last exchange with Devi. Why her words and no other had convinced him that it was useless to try to be that other boy Nihil had spoken of, the good one, who could say. Whether he knew it or not, what Sonna set his heart upon now was a dismantling of harmony, which he recognized only to the extent that it did not, and clearly never would, include him. He watched his sisters seek out the safe haven of the Herath household and forgot that their visits had once seemed like a blessing to him, the way they had allowed him to experience something of the workings of that family. Lucas's air of contentment grated on him. When Suren came to his house and played his guitar and sang his songs, all the women in his house and the Herath girls listening as they never listened to him, it was all Sonna could do not to charge into the room, grab the guitar, and smash it to pieces. He was upset most of all by the trust that allowed Raju to push Devi up and down the lane on a bicycle, a trust that no one had ever placed in him. What made Devi so blind to Raju's ugliness? She never seemed to feel a single moment of revulsion as surely she should. What made an exacting girl like Rashmi give Raju free rein to come and go as he pleased? It confirmed what Sonna feared most: that not even the Herath children, who were so kind to everybody, found him worthy.

"Someone left dog droppings in Mr. Bin Ahmed's mailbox," Mr. Niles told Nihil one afternoon. "You know, there is only one dog down this street, and he belongs to the Sansonis. Who could have done such a thing?"

Nihil avoided Mr. Niles's gaze when he said, "I don't know who it could have been."

"And," Mr. Niles said, keeping his eyes on Nihil's face, "just the other day, Kala told me that the Tisseras' paper had been stolen and that they saw it lying open on a chair in the Nadesans' porch. They could see it from their veranda. What do you think of that?"

"Did they get it back?" Nihil asked, avoiding the real question.

"They did not ask, but Mr. Nadesan had taken it back and said they did not know how it got there. Someone is trying to create problems for our neighbors and I think you know who that person might be, don't you?"

Nihil shrugged and said he did not know, but it was clear that he did and that Mr. Niles and all the other people down the lane did too.

In these activities, Sonna had an admirer: Mohan.

Mohan had got into another round of trouble at school, this time during a history lesson, and over a comment he made about the Tamil king Elara, who had been defeated by the Sinhalese prince, Dutugemunu.

"We fought that Tamil until the water around Anuradhapura turned red with blood," he said. "That's how much was sacrificed. In the end, Dutugemunu won. That's what's coming."

He refused to acknowledge to the class, as part of his apology, that King Elara was referred to in the chronicle of the country's early history, the *Mahavamsa*, as a just monarch and one whom his Sinhalese subjects had respected, and that though the battle had been bloody, Dutugemunu himself had honored the dead ruler by building a monument to him. Instead, Mohan had simply taken the week of detention in stony silence, boasting to his father that he saw it as a price he had to pay for telling the truth.

"You are different from these other Sinhalese boys who think the same things but have no guts to say it aloud," his father said. "You're a true leader. I am proud of you." He patted his son on his back and commented on how tall he was becoming. "Beginning to look like a young man, son," he said.

After that incident, Mohan began to look for more ways in which he could distinguish himself further from *the other Sinhalese boys*, the nearest being Suren and Nihil, the Tisseras' son being too young to count. Although he had always found Raju abhorrent, he now sharpened the barbs he flung at him, adding those that referred to his race to his usual comments about his mental disabilities and girth. Old Mrs. Joseph, like Jimmy Bolling's father, had been born to a Tamil mother and a Burgher father, but she had claimed her mother's Tamil race when she married Mr. Silver Joseph, himself a Tamil, and so Mohan felt justified in calling Raju *a full-blooded Tamil*, and crossing him off his list. Additionally, Mohan invoked Jimmy Bolling's grandmother's race and began to refer to the Bolling house as the *half-breed house*. He had never befriended the Niles family, and the Nadesans, by virtue of their privateness, were a threat. It was clear to him that the Tamils were taking over and, moreover, they were taking over his lane. He wished that the Herath boys would feel as he did if for no other reason than that there was not much fun in being a leader without anybody to lead. There was only one other possibility: Sonna.

Now, as Sonna's activities graduated to the sort of misbehavior that appeared small but had the potential to stir up the right type of conflagration, Mohan paid him more heed. He observed both what Sonna did to disrupt their neighborhood and his estrangement from his own family, which allowed him, Mohan, to separate Sonna from whatever aspersions Mohan cast upon the Bollings and their mixed race. He took to nodding at Sonna whenever a new prank was executed, hoping that the nod would suffice to communicate his approval. Sonna, isolated once more in a space not entirely of his choosing and yearning for an equal to call *friend* rather than a collection of hooligans to run amok with, was easily won over.

And yet, though both Sonna and Mohan, each for his own reasons, were determined to stir up trouble, and though the kind of trouble they longed for would be swept away by an avalanche of violence neither could have predicted and neither would, in the end, welcome, their dissatisfactions were balanced out by the equally determined efforts of another pair of children: Jith and Dolly.

Nobody could be certain, at first, but in the end everybody agreed that Jith had taken a real and very public shine to Dolly, a liking confirmed by his having intentionally missed getting her out during a game of French cricket, even though her plank of wood had flown out of her hands and her legs below the knees were unprotected and ripe for it. These details had only come to light because of the ruckus that had erupted between the two teams, Suren, Rashmi, Rose, and Jith on one team, Mohan, Nihil, Devi, and Dolly on the other.

"You din' get her out!" Rose and Rashmi screamed in unison.

"*Machang*, how can we play if you won't get her out?" Suren inquired, as if reason might be able to prevail where the visceral fighting instinct that defined the national character, particularly when it came to cricket, even this watered-down version of cricket, had obviously failed.

Even Raju, about to turn away from watching them and go to his garage for his evening session of weight lifting, was appalled. "My god, Jith, you can't play like that if you want to win!"

Sonna, watching from his usual station, leaning on his father's fence, laughed, and even he only laughed because he assumed that Jith had simply made a mistake.

Dolly felt herself fairly levitate with delight at having caused the scene and as she turned her smile and grateful eyes to the one boy who had ever done anything nice especially for her—the Heraths did not count since their kindness was meted out universally—she appeared in the likeness of a pleasantly featured girl and not *a bovine* as Jith's mother had been describing her to them since before either of her sons could talk, further cementing his affections.

"That's okay, I'll get out," Dolly said, sacrificing her stay at the wicket on the altar of his honor. The game resumed but there was a certain electricity to the air that reached beyond the strip of road on which they were playing and found its way into all the houses down the street. It was a disturbance, the shape-shifting kind that, if not curtailed, would, without a doubt, lead to nothing but chaos.

In the Bolling house that night, Rose made the announcement right after the bread and dhal were dished onto their plates: "Dolly is smiling all the time because Jith likes her."

Both Francie and Jimmy Bolling looked up with great interest. One of their daughters had snagged a Silva? A real, solid Silva boy? Francie Bolling reevaluated the features of Dolly's face, the potential curves of her body, found them favorable, and exchanged looks with her husband.

"Don' go an' act like a tart now," Francie said, finally. "If he likes you then he can come an' talk near the gate. You are not to go to his house, I'm tellin' you. If I find out—"

"Mrs. Silva will be shot with her own shit before she lets Dolly near her house, Mummy, don' worry!" Sonna said and laughed, though with a certain bitterness. First the Heraths had welcomed his sisters into their home as easily as their Muslim neighbors folded roasted cashews into the *watalappan* during Ramazan, and now Jith was interested in Dolly? He decided to visit Raju after dinner, see how far he had got with his stupid weight lifting.

"A very strange thing happened today," Rashmi said in the Heraths' house as the children sat with their mother—their father was held up at yet another ministerial meeting—and waited for Kamala to clear away the plates after dinner. "Jith didn't throw the ball at Dolly to get her out even when he could have."

"She agreed to be out anyway, so what does it matter?" Suren said, amicably, sopping up the last of his soup with a chunk of bread and handing his plate to Kamala. He washed his hands in the bowl of water that she placed before him.

"Jith likes Dolly," Devi said. She shared her mother's enthusiasm for the rehabilitation of the Bolling girls; she was particularly happy that the French Cricket incident had occurred while Dolly was wearing one of her old Alice bands, a red-black-and-white-striped one.

"There'll be hell to pay when Aunty Rani finds out," said Mrs. Herath, not imagining that she would in any way be associated with Jith's choice of a girlfriend.

"What was all that noise I heard?" Mr. Silva asked, after his wife had walked around the table serving everybody. She settled down in front of her plate of noodles and salmon curry and began picking out the green chillies, which she did not like but he loved, and putting them on his plate. He passed the MD chilli sauce to his older son. "Was there some trouble?"

"Nothing," Jith said, and rubbed his palms nervously on the front of his shorts. He knew what would be in store if his mother found out.

"Jith didn't get Dolly out, that's why. Everybody started shouting," Mohan explained.

Mrs. Silva felt the vaguest touch of anxiety. She swallowed her first mouthful of food quickly. "Didn't get her out? Why not?"

Jith did not reply, so his brother did. "Nobody knows. She had no bat or anything, she was just scoring with her hands and her legs were all bare and he could have reached over and touched her leg with the ball but instead he threw it up the lane so Dolly was able to bend almost to the ground and get her bat back." Clearly, at this early juncture, Mohan's concern was more with the sad outcome of the game than the disappointing preferences of his brother, let alone the fate that awaited Jith.

Mrs. Silva, who had stiffened at the mention of bare legs and touch in the same sentence describing the proximity of her son to one of the Bolling urchins, felt a well-nursed rage rise in her chest.

"That damn Savi! She's the one who started all this with her English lessons and giving them clothes and everything. From Bernard's she bought those clothes! Now they must be thinking they are fit for anybody. Even my sons!"

The inhabitants of Sal Mal Lane all spent a restless night, the degree of unrest depending upon closeness to the subject. The next morning, everybody woke up in a bad mood.

"If you hadn't been letting those creatures into your house, getting them all dolled up like one of our children, my boys would never have paid any attention to them!" Mrs. Silva suggested to Mrs. Herath from her veranda the next morning, her voice far louder than necessary.

"If your boys were a little smarter and spent more time with their books and less time on the roads, then they wouldn't have been interested in them in the first place," Mrs. Herath countered from her perch in her veranda, surprised that she had been implicated in the whole affair.

"I *knew* this would happen. I told my husband from the start that your family was trouble," Mrs. Silva continued, tugging the hem of her white blouse until it sat straight and smooth over her chest. "Singing hymns and running around with that mad Raju, sending the children to a Tamil teacher for music when there are so many good Sinhalese teachers around, not to mention entertaining those half-breed urchins in your house. Now see what you have done."

Both Old Mrs. Joseph, who was riveted to these goings-on, and Mr. Niles, who could not help but hear, listened to the raised voices. Mr. Niles, who had no view of the lane, could only imagine what had taken place, and would have to wait for Nihil to come and tell him all about it, but Old Mrs. Joseph, who *had seen this coming* for a long while now, was delighted by the scene. She could tell that though Mrs. Herath and Mrs. Silva continued to throw barbs at each other, neither of them was sure, exactly, if anything had transpired between the children, but they were certain of one thing: the usual lines had been crossed to who knew what end.

There was no help for it and, truth be told, it was probably for the best anyway, but a few hours after that sharp exchange of words when it was clear that both parties were still simmering, there were two survey-ors measuring the shared driveway between the Heraths' and the Silvas' homes and by afternoon there was a *baas* hired by the Silvas to build a five-foot wall, which meant that the hedge that Mrs. Herath had planted there, and that had served them so well as a friendly separation, had to be cut down. To console herself, Mrs. Herath hired some *baases* of her own and added a higher dividing wall between their house and both the adjoining houses behind and to the left so that, in effect, the Heraths would dwell in a U-shaped compound bordered by three walls, one of which—the one that separated them from the neighbors they had never met behind their house—was embedded with broken glass to ward off whatever feet might climb over such certain demarcations. The hedge in front completed their voluntary incarceration.

A week later, upon the advice of Kala Niles, Mrs. Herath brought the *baases* back and had them put up a fourth wall—albeit one that was short enough to mirror the Silvas' wall—on the outside of her front hedges. And though it had the unfortunate outcome of hiding her beautiful gardens from her neighbors, Mrs. Herath consoled herself with the fact that the hedge kept the front wall hidden from her view. She also made it a point to invite the ladies down the lane, with the notable exception of Mrs. Silva, to have tea, and had Kamala serve it to them on the veranda so that they could enjoy the sight of her outdoor spaces, and pressed small bunches of flowers or cuttings from her plants into their hands before they left.

"House looks much better now," Raju said to Suren as he joined the two older children, who were standing on the road gazing at the changed landscape. "Now all you children will be much safer, and anyway all the posh people have walls and gates. Good that your father got it put in."

"My mother is the one who got it put in," Rashmi said, wishing that Raju would go back to his weights and stop staring at their house, their cricket matches, and them. Try as she might, Rashmi had yet to shake her disapproval of Raju.

In the weeks that followed, there was no interaction between the Silva and Herath adults, but the children continued their games, though with one modification: they moved French cricket to the top of the lane, right in front of the grove of sal mal trees whose barbed-wire fence had recently been removed. And while this meant that Raju could no longer see them, which made Rashmi glad, it also meant that, much of the time, the ball ended up in the grove of trees and play had to be stopped while they all searched for it, moving piles of leaves and flowers with their feet as they went. This activity gave Jith and Dolly many opportunities to interact, and, since the exploration of this space was still a novelty, none of the other children paid them much heed, not even Mohan. Indeed, the children began to find reasons to not find their missing ball, but rather to dangle from the ropey twists that made up the branches of the sal mal trees, the upper part of the trunks entirely hidden by the cascading tangles of bark and leaf and flower, which, in an arrangement, would look overblown, but which in their grove seemed merely an appropriate abundance, a benediction of their play.

"Look how the branches pour down, like hair," Devi said, and reached up to tug at the lowest tendrils. She dragged one thin and tender loop from the nearest tree and tied it to another from the tree next to it. Her knot held for a few moments, then snapped as the branches sprang back.

"Like curly an' wavy hair," Rose said, "won' stay straight like that."

Old Mrs. Joseph could not see up the road, and Mr. Niles could only hear faint sounds of their play, and both of them had to imagine what it might look like up there, at the top end of their road. Mr. Niles had some assistance in this from Nihil.

"Rose takes the fallen flowers and picks off the tops and plays he loves me, he loves me not," Nihil told Mr. Niles.

"Who is the 'he'?" Mr. Niles asked. "Is it you?"

"Suren," Nihil said. "I'm not old enough for her. But he doesn't love her."

"How do you know?"

"Suren loves music," Nihil said, simply.

So Mr. Niles closed his eyes and imagined Rose, alone, whispering to herself as she went, not looking where she was stepping, trampling dozens of other possibilities as she focused on the one flower in her palm, taking in its complexity, the yellow-tipped pink stamens at the ends of the cobra head–shaped center guarding the miniature white *dagoba* at its heart. He imagined the powdery feel of the butter-yellow florets around that *dagoba*, the way they were supposed to represent a crowd of worshippers, and although it was a flower sacred to Buddhists, not to a Catholic like himself, Mr. Niles was soothed by this image.

Old Mrs. Joseph, who had once enjoyed walking up and down the road in the evenings, and who had always lingered among the sal mal trees, felt that it was fitting that the children had discovered the shady grove.

"Half the time they don't play," Raju told her. "They walk about under the trees. Sometimes, if it has been dry for a few days, they even take a mat and sit and do homework there. Not Mohan, but the other children."

And Old Mrs. Joseph pictured the children sitting beneath the trees, open books and papers rustling in their laps, their pencils and erasers lost among the flowers. She imagined the children not caring about such things, knowing that that they were replaceable.

Mrs. Herath and Mrs. Silva did not break their silence toward each other until Vesak day in May. On that day, Mrs. Herath supervised not only the hanging of colored paper lanterns with their lit candles on the trees and bushes of her garden, but the lining of the top of the new wall between the two houses with a row of oil lamps. Not to be outdone, Mrs. Silva dispatched Mohan to find some for their house as well.

"Koralé's shop will be closed. Just go to the back door," she said.

While she waited, Mrs. Silva moved the Heraths' lamps farther toward their side to make room for hers. But though Mohan was able to persuade Koralé to sell them enough lamps, there was no time to immerse them in water, which meant that the new clay absorbed all the coconut oil poured into them and Jith and Mohan were kept busy refilling the lamps through the night, an extravagance that drained some of the pleasure she felt from Mrs. Silva.

"It looks quite nice with all these lamps, doesn't it?" Mrs. Herath said from her side of the wall, after the lamps were arranged. She was standing by her gate, watching Mrs. Silva's activity.

Mrs. Silva, caught by surprise, was terse. "Yes, it does," she said.

"Have you all gone to temple yet?" Mrs. Herath asked, noting that Mrs. Silva, too, was already dressed in white.

"We go early," Mrs. Silva replied, as she fussed with a wick. "Fewer crowds and we can see everything."

Mrs. Herath thought that the beauty of Vesak was to be part of the crowds in the streets, and to see the lights, both on the *pandals* illuminated with bulbs and in the temples filled with thousands of lamps, lit and relit by waves of children and adults, but she decided, in the interest of reconciliation, to keep these thoughts to herself. She was about to say something else, comment on the pleated lanterns the Silvas had used, perhaps, or the neatness of the arrangements her sons had made with them, when Dolly and Rose came out of the Herath house, where they had gone to wash their hands after helping with the oil for the Heraths' lamps. Mrs. Silva, too, had been trying to think of something pleasant she could say, but the sight of the twins rendered her speechless. She turned and went back into her house and as a result she missed what she looked forward to most during Vesak: to sit in her veranda and look at her lit-up garden while listening to *pirith* from the temple.

For the third year in a row, the twins, in borrowed white dresses, went to temple with the Heraths. Though they had to be reprimanded once by Mrs. Herath for ogling a boy, the rest of the time they lit incense and lamps, placed their share of flowers on altars already piled high, and brought their palms together in prayer though what they prayed for, and to whom, the Heraths could only guess. The Herath children and the twins talked animatedly as they walked home afterward, begging Mrs. Herath to let them stop at a *dhansala* here for a drink, a *dhansala* there for some food, neither approved, but when they reached the quiet of their own lane, they fell silent, their eyes on the flickering candles and lamplights they could see in the Silvas' garden.

After seeing the twins to their house, the four Herath children lingered by the dividing wall talking, their heads swiveling first to one garden, then to the other, their faces illuminated by the double row of lamps on the wall. Some of the lanterns held candles that sent out sparks as they burned, some defect of the wick or touch of moisture preventing them from settling down; others held candles that burned with a steady flame, and those would last through the night; still others held candles that tipped, slightly, threatening to set their wax-paper cages on fire. Yet, though several lanterns did fall to the ground in a sudden burst of flame, their wire edges hot to the touch, none burned as the children watched and their last image of the evening was one of tranquility as they left the fairy-tale gardens behind and reluctantly went to bed.

In the dead of night, unseen even by Old Mrs. Joseph, who was already asleep, Sonna walked up the street. He had been offered *kassippu* for the first time by one of the men in the slums, and he staggered a little as he walked. He saw Mrs. Silva alone by the wall, filling both her lamps and those of the Heraths with fresh oil, her face reflecting the peace of the night. Though most of the candles had gone out in the hanging lanterns, thanks to her effort the wicks still burned brightly in the lamps on the wall. Sonna slid to the ground along the side of Old Mrs. Joseph's gate and watched them long after the last chants of *pirith* were over and the roads themselves had grown still, right until the last lamp went out.

Old Mrs. Joseph's Triumph

By the time the Heraths had grown accustomed to the walls, and the long-promised ivy had been planted along the length of the one facing the Nadesans' house, Mrs. Herath had tired of Jesus Christ. The advent of Sathya Sai Baba and the accompanying *bhajans* became, therefore, the theme song of conflict to Mrs. Silva. Unlike the Heraths' other activities, their music could not be contained by the freshly painted walls and the brand-new roll-in, roll-out gates that shut off the entire section of their driveway.

Though they had recovered a semblance of cordiality toward each other, Mrs. Silva continued to disapprove of Mrs. Herath's haphazard pursuit of *strange religions* and, more importantly, her continued encouragement of the Bolling twins, which spoke to her not of Mrs. Herath's kindness to them but of her disloyalty to the Silvas. The music that came pouring out therefore found Mrs. Silva nearly constantly in a state of both shock and dismay, at the center of which sat her younger son. Whether Jith had given up his—clearly fleeting, it had to be—interest in Dolly or not, Mrs. Silva could not find out; holding herself above the rest of the residents had the unfortunate side effect of making them inaccessible to her. It was another month before Mrs. Silva, reconciled to the move, announced her intention to visit the one person down the lane who would be able to give her the full story about her son.

"I'm going to visit Old Mrs. Joseph," Mrs. Silva said, one day in July, raising her voice slightly so that her husband, tending as he did incessantly to their garden, could hear her.

Mr. Silva stood up and wiped his hands on a rag hanging from the pocket of his old blue denim long shorts. The ferns that Mrs. Herath had given him, and that his sons and the Herath boys had planted, were thriving, and he had just separated a few of the plants and put them in a bag to be shared with one of his colleagues when he went to work the next day. Looking at the bag now, he wondered if the building of the wall would affect the sharing of plants; he had been following Mrs. Herath's success with a hybrid Elaine with iridescent leaves that turned crimson as it matured, and a pale-green echeveria with pink outlines, and he had been hoping to be the happy beneficiary when the time came for her to whittle them down.

He was grateful that he had got a Brazilian snapdragon from Mrs. Herath before the whole business of the wall.

"Did you hear me?" Mrs. Silva asked.

"Yes, yes," Mr. Silva said. "Old Mrs. Joseph. Is she sick?"

"No, I just thought it would be good to visit her, you know." And she stopped.

Mr. Silva nodded slowly and continued to wipe his hands, looking down and away from his wife. Hearing the concern in his wife's voice, he forgot his plants and instead felt a sudden surge of regret that he had encouraged her to befriend the Heraths that first afternoon, that they had aided and abetted in the whole sorry business of their arrival. Well, there was nothing that could be done about it. He sighed and looked approvingly at his wife, her prejudices and pompousness suddenly appearing as virtues that he deserved to have in a spouse.

"Yes, better go and have a talk with her. Get to the bottom of this."

Mrs. Silva brightened and rose from her chair. She went into her pantry, unlocking it with a key from a bunch she carried tucked into her waistband, and chose a tin of Maliban cheese buttons, a nice cheerful blue tin with a trim of red diamonds that would surely delight Old Mrs. Joseph.

"Good afternoon, good afternoon, coming for some information?" Old Mrs. Joseph said, her mouth tilting with more than a little scorn at her visitor and her offering. She was seated in her chair, dressed in her usual garb of a long pastel skirt and top covered by a blue floral floor-length housecoat that had buttons from collar to hem.

"No, what nonsense! I just wanted to drop in and see how you are doing. Haven't seen you in a while, after all," Mrs. Silva said and glanced toward the nearest mussaenda, which had filled out considerably, as if blaming the tree for the dearth of neighborly conversations between them.

Old Mrs. Joseph wondered if she should offer Mrs. Silva a cup of tea and some of her own cheese buttons from a tin that she had been saving, just to make Mrs. Silva uncomfortable. Just then, Raju, hearing voices, came out onto the veranda and swept them up in an effusive welcome.

"Oh! Aunty! So good of you to visit here. My goodness, brought biscuits also. What for? We are neighbors, no? You shouldn't have to bring gifts to visit neighbors!"

"Hello, Raju," Mrs. Silva said, wincing at the title of *Aunty* being given to her by a man who was only a few years younger than she was but thoroughly satisfied by the look of withering disapproval that crossed Raju's mother's face.

Raju, too, noticed and backtracked. "Of course, not to say that we must not be formal. It is good to be formal. More civilized. After all, we are not like my cousin, Jimmy Bolling, their type of Burgher people, no, Mama?" He felt a little thrill uttering those words, thinking specifically about Sonna. He warmed to the topic. "Yes. We shouldn't even be interacting with those types. But what to do, Aunty, when we are related like this? You understand, no? Not like you all, we can't avoid, no?" He turned his palms upward, fingers spread, and twisted them away from each other to demonstrate the exact degree of helplessness in this matter of being related to undesirables.

"Raju, go and ask the girl to make some tea for us," his mother cut in. "And ask her to bring some cake!" she added to his retreating back.

Raju flinched as he shuffled off. If his mother didn't tell Mrs. Silva, he would, he thought. Yes, as soon as he gave the order for tea he would go right back out and tell her everything. Serves her right, thinking she's above everybody, never even looking at him when he stood by the gate each evening, acting like he wasn't there. So unlike Mrs. Herath, who always stopped to say hello, called him by his name, and even gave him tea. See how things worked out? Did the Herath boys run after his shabby nieces? No, it was a Silva boy who got caught.

"How are things with you, with the house?" Mrs. Silva was saying when Raju reappeared.

"The house?" his mother asked, incredulous. "What could be the matter with the house? It's been standing all these years, hasn't it? And after I'm dead it will still be standing. Why, are you thinking of buying it after I'm gone?"

Mrs. Silva looked fondly over at her own house, regretting her visit, regretting the expensive tin of biscuits.

"Aunty, you must be worried about your son, about Jith and Dolly," Raju began, unable to contain himself. "But don't worry. Soon it will be over I'm sure. I will keep an eye on the situation. I am always here. See how nicely I look after the little Herath girl?"

"What situation? There's no situation that I know of," Mrs. Silva said, shocked by the very thought of it and, worse, by the idea that other people might be assuming there was a situation when she was quite sure there was none. She had only come here to confirm the nonexistence of a situation.

"Well then, if there is no situation, we can talk about something else," Old Mrs. Joseph said, choosing a topic with no clear margins possible: "Did you hear what happened last week? Some Sinhalese hooligans belonging to the police and army burned down the Jaffna Public Library. Nearly one hundred thousand documents, hear that? *One hundred thousand* documents. Palm leaves, manuscripts, gone. Poof!" And Old Mrs. Joseph flung her hands into the air, indicating the papers, the smoke, the disappearance.

"Yes, Aunty, did you hear that?" Raju asked, reminded now and freshly upset over the news of all that mayhem. He pulsed his knees together, apart, together, apart. "Two police officers killed, and for that they burned the library, I heard."

"Not just the library. The Tamil party head office there. The office of the local paper there, *Eelanaadu*, was also destroyed. Even statues in the town, of Thiruvalluvar, Auvaiyar, Arumuga Navalar, all gone, knocked down!" Old Mrs. Joseph continued. She leaned forward toward Mrs. Silva, her tone accusatory. "You heard about all this? Ah? You heard?"

Mrs. Silva said nothing and Old Mrs. Joseph continued bitterly. "Bloody fools looking for trouble. That Velupillai Prabhakaran, calling himself the leader of the Tamil people, pah! Not *our* leader, *we* didn't vote for him. Who asked him to be *our* leader? He's behind the *whole* thing, instigating violence everywhere. I am positive. Otherwise who killed those police officers? See what happened after that? He's looking for a war. Going to get a war, too."

Mrs. Silva was silent for so long that Raju felt obliged to answer even though he could not figure out if his mother was more upset about Velupillai Prabhakaran claiming to lead the entire Tamil race or the burning of a library and the dismantling of the statues of Tamil luminaries. "No, Mama," he said, as soothingly as he could, "I hadn't heard all these details. I only heard they were having little little problems," and he rubbed the tips of his fingers to give her a visual, how tiny were his imaginings of these problems. "What will happen now?"

"Nothing will happen. Nothing ever happens except that we have the same people shouting about this and shouting about that, then we have posters and elections, and then, once more, nothing happens."

"But this time around I think definitely the country is—"

"What is this thing, this situation, between my son and Dolly?" Mrs. Silva said, cutting Raju off with what she hoped was an air of brusque competence, as if the tone would be sufficient to squelch the whole business. The fate of the Jaffna Public Library was not her concern. Nor was the fate of the statues of Tamil philosophers and poets. What mattered was the here and the now, and that consisted of Jith and, god forbid, Dolly.

"Oh, I'm sure there is no situation, none at all," Old Mrs. Joseph said, leaning back with great pleasure. "Only situation for us to worry about is trouble brewing in the North. Soon, I'm told, it will all come spilling here, to Colombo. To our streets too!" As if in confirmation, a sudden gust of wind sent a flurry of sal mal petals and leaves drifting down the lane to settle in difficult corners like gutters and windowsills.

Raju, as usual, betrayed the old lady. "No, no, there is!" he said, glad to return to a topic close at hand and entirely manageable, unlike that of marauding gangs in faraway Jaffna, buildings in flames and falling statues. "Whole lane is talking about it. Even Koralé. I heard they are meeting at the bus stop before school and also after school. One time, Sonna said, because he sees everything, you know how he is, watching the whole lane like a hawk, he said Jith even cut his after-school maths class and they went to see the Tamil film at the Empire Theatre!"

"Tamil film?" Mrs. Silva fumed. "What Tamil film? My sons don't even know Tamil." Her tone of voice implied that mastery of the Tamil language would have been considered a blotch upon their character.

"That's the thing," Raju intoned, wonder in his voice at the depths to which the Silva boy had sunk. "Back-row seats."

Mrs. Silva was both mightily roused and as deeply weakened. Was that pity in Old Mrs. Joseph's eyes, or scorn? And Raju, was he savoring this delivery of information or petrified at having to be the bearer of such tidings? With him, one could never tell. The Josephs' servant, a wiry dark-skinned girl from the estates, brought a pot of tea and a plate of cake out to the veranda and held the tray out to Mrs. Silva. Mrs. Silva helped herself to a piece of cake, but she balanced it on the edge of her saucer; she neither ate nor drank. Old Mrs. Joseph, on the other hand, slurped the tea through her dentures with gusto. Raju, too, made unseemly noises as he ate and drank, smacking his fleshy lips together after each sip.

"I will put a stop to it," Mrs. Silva said, her eyes moving from one to the other. "Ginger, if you don't mind, I will ask Raju to report everything to me, straight to me, as soon as he hears."

If Mrs. Silva had imagined that using the pet name that Old Mrs. Joseph's late husband had used would soothe the old lady, she was mistaken.

"You can ask him anything. He's an adult. You don't need my permission," Old Mrs. Joseph said, her voice hard, looking away from them.

Raju sank farther into his chair, an expression of grim solidity, welcoming the weight of the responsibility that was being offered him. "I will do it every hour if I have to, Aunty," he said, looking soulfully at Mrs. Silva, who cringed. "Already I know almost everything up and down the lane."

"Knowing is one thing, preventing is quite another," Old Mrs. Joseph said. The ominous silence that followed her statement lasted until Mrs. Silva rose, without having drunk her tea, and left their house, bidding them a short and begrudging good-bye.

But what, exactly, were Jith and Dolly up to? At the Tamil theater, while they did sit in the back row, the one reserved for lovers, all they managed was a brush of hands and a resting of heads. At the bus stop—before and after school—their communication was almost entirely silent, there being no privacy possible among the school children who gathered in their various school uniforms, season tickets for the school buses in hand. When they played cricket as they now did only until that hour of the day when Mrs. Silva returned from her job at the People's Bank, Thimbirigasyaya branch, they continued to favor each other until the rest of the children decided, unanimously, to avoid the ensuing trouble by putting them on the same team. Their affection was communicated primarily through notes that they gave each other. Dolly, by leaving hers wedged under a brick at the far end of her father's aluminum fence, Jith, by leaving his in a split of a branch in the anchoring tree of his father's garden, a still-young araliya, a branch that reached out to the lane as though aching to break free of the confines of that household and the ideas of its inhabitants. It was a reflection of their innocence that they had not been more careful.

> *Darling Dolly, Yesterday I had a term test and got half of the questions wrong because I was thinking of you! Tomorrow I have another test. I might fail. I am going to have to study today, otherwise the teacher will tell my mother! So I can't come to play French cricket. I hope you score a lot! I'll watch from the window when you go up the road to play. If you see me, you can wave. But only if my father is not there! If you like, you can send me a reply today. I can pick it up when I go to buy bread in the evening. Love, Jith*

This was the first note that Mr. Silva dug out. He folded it back in its careful quarters and eighths and put it back in the tree. To tell his wife would be the right thing to do, but then again, what was there to even talk about? The kids were just being kids, talking about term tests and games. The two words of concern were, of course, *darling* and *love*, but even those were standard issue. Had there been some kind of originality apparent, something to suggest that their infatuation had given rise to some greater expression than they had previously been capable of, then he would worry, then he would tell her. This, he decided to keep to himself. But as a concession to his wife, Mr. Silva decreed that his boys were no longer to join in the games of cricket.

"You are getting too old for that anyway. You should be practicing to try out for the first eleven," he said, uttering the words even though he knew that neither of his sons possessed the level of discipline or talent to even make the B team.

Without the Silva boys, and with the ever more diffident Devi, who, in the wake of her head injury seemed jumpy around the bat and ball, the game spluttered and eventually petered out, and the children threw themselves with gusto into kite season, turning their faces away from the uneven slope of the road and toward the smooth potential of heat-filled skies as if by choice, not necessity.

Kite Season

The gusty wind that dominated a short respite from the monsoons was beginning to tease the children of Sal Mal Lane. It tugged at their school uniforms, inverted umbrellas held against the sun, and combed and recombed their hair, first this way then the other. It whispered *stay! stay!* to them as they stood waiting for their school buses, shivering in the cool morning hours, a request they tried not to hear. They giggled as their skirts and shirts lifted this way and that, their books fell out of their careless hands, and the ribbons tied into their braids and ponytails, blue and white for the Herath girls, green and white for the Bolling twins, refused to stay in their knots. But each evening the children acquiesced. They put down their books, put on their home clothes, and went outside. They went to fly kites.

On the first of those afternoons, Nihil turned to the back of Devi's *parisaraya* book and, after carefully placing a half ruler against the side to leave a margin big enough so that the soon-to-be-torn paper would not disengage its partner on the opposite end, carefully removed a page from it while Devi watched. Both their tongues poked out from the sides of their mouths as the delicate task was accomplished, even though it was Nihil who was in charge of the execution. He drew three columns, marked them morning, afternoon, and evening, and then wrote out a schedule for Devi that included studying her times tables and reading in Sinhala in the morning before school, practicing her piano pieces, homework, and studying after school, and reciting her *gāthā* and reading in English in the evening. Devi read the instructions over his shoulder, her face more grave by the second.

"There is nothing for me to do but study study study!" she exclaimed at last and threw up her hands and stamped her foot for emphasis.

"No, I have left plenty of time for you to play," Nihil told her, directing her attention to chunks of time that she had missed under the overwhelming press of even larger blocks of time dedicated to homework and refinement. Not only was Nihil proud of his neat timetable, this was just the sort of protest that he had been expecting, so he was prepared. "Today, for example, during your free time, you can help me to build the new kite!" he offered. "It's going to be your kite. I already got tissues in your favorite kite colors and the frame is ready too."

Devi, the future forgotten in the face of the fun to be had *right now*, clapped her hands and set off in the direction of the kitchen, calling out to Kamala to "boil some water and get some flour and salt, we are going to make kites!"

The construction of Devi's kite was something to behold, with its layers of blue and silver tissue papers to one side, the frame—prepared by Suren and Rashmi in advance—on the other, and the still-steaming homemade glue in between. The kite, when it was finished and decorated with tissue-paper tassels cut a little raggedly by Devi, and with neat tissue-paper bows made with her usual flair by Rashmi, was by far the most elegant of the kites that the children brought out to fly that year.

"Nihil, you hold the kite and I will throw the stone," Suren said.

"I want to hold the kite!" Devi complained. She looked at Rashmi, who was leaning against the parapet wall outside the Sansoni house. She was there along with all the neighborhood children, even Sonna, who, though he was standing apart from the rest, had shown up for the launch of this particularly beautiful kite. Rashmi, watching Sonna and lost in her own thoughts, did not come to Devi's assistance.

"Once I get the kite up you can hold the string and fly it," Suren promised, as he positioned the tips of Nihil's fingers on the kite that he was holding aloft. When he was sure that Nihil had the kite just right, Suren walked down the street throwing the reel of kite string over the telephone wires that crisscrossed overhead to and from the houses that were fortunate enough to own telephones. He stopped when he reached the last lines, those that ran between their home and the Nileses', and called out that he was ready. "On three!"

The kite lifted cleanly and without fuss from Nihil's outstretched hands while all the children turned their faces skyward.

"Suren really knows how to fly kites," Rose said and fiddled with the red plastic belt she had put on over the pink dress that Mrs. Herath had donated to her. Dolly, also clad in a hand-me-down, hers in mauve with white edging around the collar and sleeves, wished to add a similar compliment but refrained for fear of hurting Jith's feelings. She glanced quickly at him and looked away; he was scowling.

"When I'm big I'm going to join the army," he blurted, saying it as though he had been wanting to say it for a good long time.

"The army? To fight?" Dolly squeaked.

"What else men, if you join the army you don' sit and look at films, you fight!" Rose said. She shaded her eyes with her interlaced palms and continued to watch the lift of the colors in the air with a certain reverence. The kite drew complicated designs against the sky as Suren tugged it this way and that, snapping the string and making it dance, now whirling with elegant swoops, now moving forward in quick darts like a sword thrust against some unseen enemy.

Rashmi who like all of them had been shading her eyes to watch the kite, dropped her hands when she heard what Jith said and turned to stare at the Silva boys. They were wearing identical orange-and-red-plaid shirts with their jeans; they seemed particularly volatile.

"Why do you want to join the army?" she asked, the kite having faded into insignificance in the face of this troubling adult statement from Jith, who was, after all, just fourteen years old.

"We're both going to join," Mohan said. "First me, because I'm older, then him."

"Why are you joining the army?" Nihil repeated Rashmi's question.

"Yes, who is there to fight?" Devi added, all interest in her elegant kite wiped away by the vision that had replaced it with Jith's words: the Silva boys decked out in army fatigues, carrying guns and marching up and down their street.

"Who? The Tigers! You all don't read the news?" Mohan said, scornfully.

"We haven't heard—" Devi began, but Rashmi stopped her by putting her hand on Devi's shoulder.

Rashmi had gathered further information about the Tigers from friends at school, a much more reliable source than her busy father, no matter what Raju believed. She had learned, for instance, that the public library in Jaffna had been burned, and though some of her friends had argued that almost all the holdings were duplicated in the archives in the capital, still, the burning of a library had struck her, a bookish girl herself, as being particularly villainous.

She had overheard Raju explaining all this to Devi just the other day, as she, Rashmi, sat in the veranda of their house. "Mama says the Jaffna library was burned because Prabhakaran is terrorizing everybody," he had said to Devi, who was climbing the Asoka tree and hadn't seemed in the least bit interested in the topic. Rashmi had been just about to ask Devi to have a sense of *decorum* (a term Rashmi had picked up from the nuns) and keep her dress between her legs as she climbed, but she had been too shocked by his words to manage Devi.

"How?" Rashmi had brought herself to ask Raju instead.

"He killed police officers," Raju had said, but he had no response to her *why*, so she had asked one of the Tamil girls in her class, Kumu Jacobs, what she might know about the topic.

"Appa says that there were riots in 1956," she had told Rashmi, her face serious as they stood together near the netball courts during the interval. She fiddled with Rashmi's tie as she talked, trying to smooth a wrinkle that had appeared right beneath the knot under her collar. "He said it happened after the Official Languages Act. Appa says it meant Sinhala only."

"But we have all the languages in school and everywhere," Rashmi had countered. "It's not Sinhala only. Everything is always in all the languages, even the road sign to Sal Mal Lane!"

"I know," her friend had said, "that's what I think, but when my mother tried to say that Appa shouted and said she was wrong and they didn't talk for a lot of days."

According to her friend's father, all the Tamil leaders had walked out of parliament and decided on a *satyagraha*, and that, the announcement of a fast unto death, had made everybody unhappy and all the bad feelings had come to be concentrated on a settlement in the Eastern Province, in Gal Oya. From her social studies teacher, Rashmi had learned that the settlement was begun by building a dam across a river and creating forty thousand acres of irrigated land.

"After it was created," Mrs. Atukoralé, the social studies teacher, had said, "the government was able to give homes and land to nearly five thousand people. Can you imagine, Rashmi? Sinhalese people, Tamil people, even the Veddas, all living peacefully in fifty small villages." Since Rashmi had heard all the details of the riots from her friend, she was not persuaded by Mrs. Atukoralé's description of this wonderful place. In Rashmi's mind, such a place with so much water ought to have been able to cool whatever tempers were being stirred, but they had not; she imagined this area as being entirely dry, the water evaporated.

"It all began with rumors," she had told her siblings that very night. "Because they were all new there, I suppose, nobody trusted anybody else. Kumu said that her father said that someone said that a Sinhalese girl was raped and made to walk naked in Batticaloa by a Tamil mob and that caused the Sinhalese to attack all the Tamils."

"What is rape?" Devi asked as she sat across from Rashmi, fanning herself with a newspaper that she had folded into neat pleats.

"All her clothes were taken off," Nihil said to Devi. "That's rape."

"I heard from Pradeep that the people were told that a Tamil army was going to take over the Sinhalese part of the settlements in Gal Oya and that was what caused all the burning," Suren said.

"Whatever it was, it was a terrible time," Rashmi said, remembering how she had been so deep in conversation with her friend that they had both missed the bell at the end of the lunch interval and both been punished for being late to class.

And Suren had learned, and faithfully informed his siblings, that the riots of 1956 were soon followed by widespread violence in 1958.

"At least the Gal Oya riots were only in Gal Oya," he said to the others, who had sat in a row on Nihil's bed to listen to this news. "Tha told me that the prime minister had tried to make peace with the Tamil leader but the UNP leaders had protested and he had to break the pact he had made. But Tha didn't tell me that in May of that year, and even after the government declared an emergency in June, there had been problems all over the country," he said. "Tha didn't tell me that part. That Pradeep told me in school."

"That's because Tha likes the Bandaranaikes," Rashmi said, generously. "Anyway, *I* heard the riots were because the government tried to re-settle four hundred Tamils in Polonnaruwa among Sinhalese people, after the British closed their naval base in Trincomalee."

"What kind of problems?" Nihil asked, the details of these goings-on too much for him to absorb, and choosing to concentrate on something easier to digest, something with a simple term like *problems.*

"People running around burning buildings and killing people," Rashmi explained, though she wasn't sure this had happened, it just seemed that if something so terrible was happening all over the country then surely it had to involve fire and murder, her two worst fears.

"In Jaffna and Batticaloa the Tamils killed Sinhalese people. In other places the Sinhalese people killed Tamil people," Suren told Nihil, breaking it down even further as if identifying the perpetrators of these events would make it all seem a little less terrifying to all of them as they sat in their pajamas, washed and ready for the night in their mostly peaceful home.

Nihil resolved to ask Mr. Niles about all of these things, but he was unable to do so for a long time because Mr. Niles got the flu and not only was he unable to sit beside him—Mrs. Niles shooing him away with a *Don't come close, darling, you'll catch it too*—Mr. Niles himself seemed far too weak to even greet him as Nihil stood by the door, let alone talk. Had he been able to, Mr. Niles may have told Nihil the truth. He might have explained that the matter of language, not of street signs but of education and examination, had been manipulated by both Tamils and Sinhalese in turn, the one alongside the British colonizers, the other after the colonial power had been driven out. He might have told Nihil how he had felt during those riots in Gal Oya, and he might have given Nihil something else to think about, found some way of soothing his anxious mind. Without Mr. Niles to talk to, however, Nihil was left with his disquiet.

Devi, listening to her siblings, tried to suck on her lower lip but the activity had long ceased to calm her so she pulled it out again, thinking about blood and burning buildings and women like her mother being forced to walk around naked. That night she crept into Rashmi's bed to sleep.

All of these things and others that Rashmi had heard from her peers and her older brother had given her a picture, albeit one that was distorted in the same way any picture that is missing vast swaths of its original colors is, and she felt able to respond to Mohan with a certain aplomb.

"Yes, we know," she said. "All the Tamil leaders have walked out of parliament. Mr. Amirthalingam and even some of the Sinhalese leaders like Mr. Muttetuwegama. His daughter knows one of the girls in my dance class. She told us. There are some Tamils fighting the government, but I think the government has enough soldiers. I don't think they need you to join," she said and then added, practical to the last, "You might get killed."

Jith shuddered and Dolly looked alarmed. "Don' get killed, Jith, let the soldiers who are already there do the fightin'." She did not know if these allegations were true or, indeed, who was fighting whom; all she knew was that, a few weeks ago, sitting in the last row of the Tamil cinema, she and Jith had planned to elope and get to Australia somehow when they turned eighteen and how would they do that if he went and got killed?

"We aren't cowards," Mohan said, swaggering a little. Although all of the older boys' voices had cracked, his had finally settled into a manly depth that gave his words more weight. He was also taller than all of them, and muscled from a year of steady work on his physique every afternoon after school in the back veranda of his house. The two, voice and body, combined to make him seem particularly authoritative. "You are too young to understand but all of us should be prepared to fight. Even Suren. You should tell him. Better get ready now."

The three Heraths closed ranks and said nothing. To suggest that Suren do anything besides draw forth music from instruments, or by lifting his voice, was a travesty that they fought daily at home what with their mother's constant push to turn him into an engineer. Around them Rose and Dolly, too, talked animatedly about the prospect of war and how Suren should be saved from such a fate.

Mohan took a deep breath. War could not come fast enough for him and if he could do his part to hasten its arrival then he was willing to do it. "We should stop going to the Tamil people's houses," he declared, pointing down the road. "All the Tamils down this lane, they are probably helping the Tigers."

Suren, who had brought the kite down when he realized that none of his siblings were interested in flying it anymore, strolled up just in time to hear this statement. He continued to wind the line in its intricate weave around the short stick in his right hand, twisting it back and forth with an elegance at odds with the topic at hand. The kite lay on the road beside him. Devi came over and picked it up and held it before her like a shield. Suren finished winding the thread and tucked the bundle into the front appliquéd pocket of Devi's dress.

"These are our neighbors, Mohan," Suren said. "Why should we stop visiting them?"

"Yes, and they are our friends, too." Nihil added. "Mr. Niles is my friend." He surprised himself by saying the words out loud. It had never occurred to him before then that the largely stationary Mr. Niles could play that role, only that he felt comfortable in the old man's presence, that he was the repository for all his boyish tales and questions. He considered, with growing alarm, the possibility of his time with Mr. Niles being cut short.

"Who will teach us piano if Kala Akki doesn't?" Rashmi asked, arms crossed and standing straight in the blue jeans she now wore routinely as her stay-at-home uniform.

"And Uncle Raju is my friend and he's Tamil. I'm never going to stop talking to him." Devi said, peering over the top of the kite to cast a defiant look at both Mohan and Rashmi.

"You just watch what you are saying when you are with them, that's all I'm saying," Mohan muttered, taken aback by this show of support for people he had begun to see as enemies. He beckoned to Jith and walked back to his house, mulling over the conversation. Even though he had always had his suspicions about the Herath boys and their namby-pamby approach to life, he had thought all it would take was the right information for all the children to join him, the Herath boys, too, swept along. He had envisaged a leadership role in the war, one conveniently located, and entirely manageable, in his own neighborhood. Now what was he going to do?

On their way home, Nihil waved the others on and stopped at Mr. Niles's house. Inside, all was quiet and Mrs. Niles opened the door to him with a finger over her lips. Mr. Niles was fast asleep.

"Is he getting better?" Nihil whispered.

"Little by little," Mrs. Niles whispered back. "Maybe next week he'll be able to talk." She stroked his head and smiled but did not let him come in. Nihil walked home without being able to discuss any of the things he'd learned from his brother and sister, nor to be comforted by Mr. Niles telling him, as he was sure he would, that Mohan was wrong, there would be no war.

A Night of Rain and Talk

That night at dinner, the conversations in two of the houses unfolded with a certain similarity in their undertones of worry and concern.

"Ma, Jith and Mohan are goin' to become soldiers an' get killed!" Sonna announced. He had been standing just too far away to hear what the disturbance was when the discussion took place, but he had got the whole tale secondhand from Rose by grabbing her by her French braids, a style Rashmi had introduced to her, and threatening to cut off her hair, something he hadn't done in so long that she had been terrified half out of her wits and blurted out every last word to him.

"Poor Dolly. Who will take her to Australia now?" Rose teased.

"Don' know what Jith sees in her," Sonna said. "She's never goin' to Australia anyway. Who will take a mad creature like her?" It started to rain as he was talking and, mercifully, Dolly did not hear the last part of what he said. The shower deafened them all as it fell against those parts of their roof that had been fortified with sheets of *takarang*.

"Rose, go an' put the buckets out," Francie Bolling said, raising her voice. "In Sonna's room there's a leak, an' in the kitchen. Check in the other rooms too. Might have to use a cooking pot if there are any other leaks."

A drop of water fell on the table just then, followed by a quickening series. Sonna ran into the kitchen to get a pot. Before long, the rain settled in to sweep across rather than fall upon the house and the whoosh of its lashings was accented intermittently by the sharp sound and echo of the single drops of rain falling into the deep receptacle.

"Gosh, good thing we are all home," Francie Bolling said. "In this kind of rain, there is no staying dry out there, even under a big umbrella. Comes from all sides."

"Mama!" Dolly said, close to tears and unconcerned with their leaky roof and people caught in the rain. "Mohan says that the Tamils are gettin' ready to attack us!"

"The Tamils?" Jimmy Bolling bellowed. "Why on earth would they attack us? If they wan' to attack anybody they'll be attackin' the government jackasses." Jimmy Bolling routinely described all politicians in any government of every party as jackasses. Whether he thought this particular set of jackasses deserved to be attacked or whether he thought they just happened to be the jackasses available to be attacked was anybody's guess.

"Mohan says that we should stop having anythin' to do with the Tamils down the road. Nileses, Nadesans, all of them. Even Raju!" Dolly wailed.

Rose, who had returned from her errand, flopped back down in her chair. "Those Silvas. Can never rest unless they're angry at somebody," she said, soothingly.

Francie Bolling sighed. She watched Sonna wipe crumbs off the table and onto the floor and she did not stop him or say anything about having to get up and sweep all that out right away on account of the ants. He stood up and replaced the bowl of plastic flowers, red roses and lilies, that she removed from the center of the table during meals, and though in his haste some of the sand from the bowl spilled onto the floor, she did not say anything about that either. She clutched the glass of cheap wine that Jimmy Bolling had procured for their consumption and looked at Dolly.

"Don' worry, Dolly doll, you can still go to Australia, I'm sure, when you are big enough." She was silent for a few moments, considering her wine. "Doin' so well we were. Down this lane. Girls happy, boys happy." Her eyes met Sonna's as she said this, so she modified her statement and added, "Mos' of the time," which did not exclude him but did not include him either. "So well we were doin' even Raju becomin' decent and now this Tamil stuff. Don' know why those Silva boys are like that."

"Heraths made such a nice kite, have to say," Rose said into the depressing silence that followed. "An' din' even get to fly it properly with all this talk about soldiers and armies."

There was an ominous note to the next words from Sonna. "They better be careful, otherwise those Elakandiya guys from the slums might bring it down."

With that, talk shifted to a discussion about the various problems associated with having a slum full of shanties just beyond the main road; at least that was something everybody in the household could agree upon. Even Sonna, who knew several boys his age who lived there and who called him friend, was able to say that he wished that the slums were cleaned up and the inhabitants sent somewhere else to live. Some of his associates there seemed to spend more time in jail than out of it, and he was not inclined to fall into the same pattern, though, while they continued to live so close to his house, he did not know how to extricate himself from the alliances he had made with them.

In the Herath household, after the same announcement about the intention of the Silva boys to join the army, Mrs. Herath shook her head. She served each of the children some chilled fruit salad that Mrs. Niles had sent over, the mangoes, papaws, and bananas all cut in identical squares and drizzled with the slightest touch of vanilla and sugar. It was delicious and she would have preferred not to have to discuss the Silvas just then. Her children, though, were not to be deterred by the sweet treat.

"Mohan said he would join the army first and Jith would follow after," Nihil said.

Mrs. Herath sat down with her own bowl of fruit salad, resigned to the fact that talk about the Silvas was going to disrupt her evening. "They are getting old enough to make such decisions," she said, "and it is not as though they will make it to university, unfortunately. I suppose it is better that than doing nothing at home and getting into trouble."

"But fighting *is* trouble, Amma," Devi said, shouting over the sound of the rain that began just then, going in seconds from a few quiet drops, each with its own individual plink, to a roaring downpour that drowned out her voice. "You always tell us not to fight."

Nihil, Suren, and Rashmi got up and ran around the house shutting the windows and pulling the chairs away from the edges of the veranda, stopping briefly to watch the rain that was coming down in an angry, slate-colored slant, like the kind of drawing a child hurrying to complete a picture might scribble with his pencil. Ordinarily, this would be their cue to get out pieces of old cardboard and pages from exercise books and begin to build the paper boats they could track from their windows along the clean, shallow drains that bordered their house, rescuing the soggy vessels with sticks and rulers pushed through the bars of windows from within the dry safety of their bedrooms. But this was not an ordinary conversation, and Nihil, in particular, wanted to clear up any misperceptions that Devi might have about the nature of Mohan's comment.

"This is a different kind of fighting," Nihil said after they all returned to the table. "With guns."

"I know with guns. I know soldiers means guns," Devi responded, piqued.

"Is it true that there is going to be a war with the Tamil Tigers?" Rashmi asked, taking the matter into her own hands and looking directly at her father, who was sitting by the brass chess table and squinting at a newspaper that he had, surely, already read.

This was the type of question that the Herath children rarely put to their father. It was the kind of opening through which he would stroll, in excruciatingly slow motion, dragging them this way and that through arcane historical fact and anecdote until, seemingly hours later, their mother rescued them with a sharp summons to undertake some other onerous chore that would appear to them to be a delight by comparison. Yet now, her siblings rightly assumed, Rashmi had asked one of those questions because there was no help for it. That in itself was disconcerting.

"Hmmm," Mr. Herath began, but was rendered silent by a long burst of lightning that lit up the outdoors like strobe lights signaling distress. All of them, even the adults, put their palms over their ears in anticipation of the thunder that would follow. After it had passed, Mr. Herath spoke again.

"You know about the TULF, the Tamil United Liberation Front? All the Tamil political parties are now united under that one name. They came to the forefront in 1977. You were too young to remember," he said, looking at Nihil and Devi in turn. His brow furrowed as he looked at Rashmi. "Maybe even you, Rashmi, you may have been too young. But that was the year in which they got eighteen seats in parliament and Amirthalingam became the leader of the opposition—"

"God, yes," Mrs. Herath interrupted. "I remember even my Amma cursing Mrs. Bandaranaike. She said, *See what happens when you vote for those left types? Leader of the opposition is now a* Demalā! She was so upset about the whole thing!"

"We shouldn't call them *Demalās*," Devi said, thinking in particular of Raju. "That's not nice."

Mrs. Herath clucked her tongue, half-apologetic. "*Demalā* just means Tamil person," she said, stroking her daughter's hair. "It's just a word. *We* don't have problems with Tamils after all."

Devi moved away from her mother, sure that she was aware of the disparagement intended by the insertion of the twisted Sinhala term into the English. Even the term *Tamils* was bad enough, Devi thought. Something about the way it took away the precise up and down relationships she had with Raju and Kala Niles, and merged them into a group that she could not recognize, upset her.

"Anyway, it was not their fault, those Tamils," Mrs. Herath said quickly. "It's the fault of the SLFP. If they hadn't messed up this country with all their Communist nonsense from '70 to '77, then the Tamils wouldn't have got in."

Whether this was enough apology for the *Demalā* comment was not clear because Mr. Herath resumed talking after a relatively brief digression in support of the SLFP, its leader, Mrs. Bandaranaike, and the policies of nationalism so harshly denigrated by his wife.

"The Tamil parties gained real power only after they met in Vaddukoddai, the year before the 1977 elections, and adopted a resolution announcing that they support a separate state. That is what led to Amirthalingam's victory," he said, and drew deeply on his cigarette. "Big promises to the Tamil youth if the TULF gained significant power."

"So is there going to be a war?" Nihil asked, seizing the opportunity to speak when his father paused to take a long drag on his cigarette. As usual, he wasn't interested in these details. He just wanted to know for what eventuality he needed to prepare himself and Devi. "When is it going to start? Where will they fight? Will they close the schools?"

Mr. Herath continued, in his fashion, as though nothing had been said to interrupt his flow of thought. "In 1975, Velupillai Prabhakaran killed a former member of parliament, who was also the mayor of Jaffna. That man had done a lot of good for the people in that area. He got them better prices for their agriculture, built the roads, built the stadium." He took several more drags on his cigarette and considered how best to describe the complexities of communal politics and guerrilla warfare to his children, all four of whom were looking at him with such quiet intensity, Nihil and Rashmi in particular. Suren was listening, but his was a reflective kind of listening, not demanding answers but also not willing to accept any given at face value; he would walk away from the discussion coming to his own conclusions. Mr. Herath let his eyes drift over to his younger daughter, who seemed poised to hear something simple from him, something comprehensible that she could relate to her own life, to her small frivolities, and, of course, to Raju. Mr. Herath pictured her relating all their conversations to Raju. He looked up at the ceiling with a little anxiety, then he settled on a one-line, watered-down version of the truth.

"Prabhakaran, whose whole premise was armed struggle, was not happy with all that because the mayor belonged to Mrs. B's party, the SLFP, and he favored the parliamentary process. Alfred Duraiappah. That was his name."

"Poor man," Mrs. Herath interjected. "Wasn't he entering a Hindu kovil for prayers when he was killed? Imagine, how vicious, to kill a man on his way to a temple?" She rested her forehead on the tips of one hand as she said this, imagining.

The children too imagined, each according to age and reading, Suren seeing the mayor of Jaffna beheaded with a glittering sword that caught the sun, his head rolling toward the steps of a bright Hindu kovil adorned with carved gods and goddesses; Nihil picturing him stabbed to death, an *Et tu, Brute* on his lips; Rashmi, thanks to all the talk of soldiers earlier that day, seeing Mr. Duraiappah shot in the heart by a firing squad. Only Devi imagined the mayor intact and unblemished, simply alive one moment, dead the next.

Like his children, Mr. Herath was quiet for a little while, contemplating the villainy of the murderer and his wife's penchant for interrupting. "Anyway," he said at last with a sigh, "the Vaddukoddai resolution fired up the Tamil youth and in 1977 we had those riots."

The power flickered and died just then in the wake of another round of lightning and thunder. There was a general stirring and much bumping into each other, as well as the usual screams of fear and delight from Devi, until Kamala brought a flickering light to the table, the candle stuck on the top of a bottle full of cumin, for which she was berated, which was then replaced by an empty upturned bottle that had once contained, the frayed old label declared, wood-apple jam.

Staring at the soft light, Suren remembered hearing about the riots. He was nine years old and two Tamil boys in his class had started fighting over the question of who had begun it all. One boy, he couldn't remember his name, said it was the fault of the Sinhalese police officers who were demanding to be let into a carnival without tickets, somewhere in the North. The other boy, Pradeep, had said no, it was the Tamil people who beat up the Sinhalese officers first. The thing Suren hadn't been able to figure out was how anybody could be so angry at a carnival whether they had or did not have tickets, so angry that they could bludgeon, loot, and murder, as the boys said they had done.

Mr. Herath addressed Suren. "You remember, Putha, some years later, when we went to play that chess tournament at St. John's in Jaffna, how much tension there was in the air?"

Suren had not noticed anything in the air. He had been paying attention to the ocean, whose waters rippled in shallow waves for miles of a kind of green-flecked blue he had never seen anywhere since. A piece of music had come to him as he watched the movement of sunlight upon the pebbles and smooth sand below the water. A song sung by a mother about a son whose father was unknown. The idea that the gift of shells from one father and the gift of beads from the other could be threaded together to adorn the same child soothed him, particularly within the drift of this particular dinnertime conversation:

> *veralen kiri kavadi soya kenek puthuta gena denava*
> *thavath kenek paata paata pabalu kaden gena enava*
> *e kavadiy e pabalui eka noolaka amunanava*
> *evaayin havadi sadaa puthuge ine palandinava*

"I remember the tension!" Nihil spoke up. "I remember that everybody was looking at us when we got down from the buses and also when we got back into the buses. There were even soldiers at the Jaffna fort."

"I don't remember anything but the boring boring boring chess and the loud loud loud chess clocks, and we only stayed at the ocean for a little while," Devi said sadly.

"We didn't go there to have fun, that's why," Rashmi said. "We went to watch the tournament."

"So boring to watch chess," Devi said, and smiled when her mother laughed beside her. She stole a look at her mother, forgiving her for her earlier comment and, seeing that it was permissible, even while Kamala was still clearing the dishes, slumped toward her into a cuddle.

Rashmi looked over at her father. "Why did the Tamils kill the mayor when the mayor was Tamil too?"

"Not the Tamils, Prabhakaran," Mr. Herath said, after a deep inhale and exhale of cigarette smoke. "Velupillai Prabhakaran, who was leading a terrorist outfit from the jungles of Jaffna. Prabhakaran is Tamil, Prabhakaran's group is Tamil, but not all Tamils support Prabhakaran."

Devi said, "Uncle Raju is not Prabhakaran," and wiggled with cozy satisfaction in her mother's lap.

"The mayor was killed because he represented the old way, trying to make changes through politics, through parliament. Prabhakaran's lot don't think that is working."

"Is it working?" Nihil asked.

"And now we have to have a war?" Rashmi asked at the same time.

"No, there won't be any war," Mr. Herath said, gauging the level of interest as well as the available answers and choosing Rashmi's question.

"The Tamil moderates in Jaffna will get rid of the bastard; the TULF will return. They'll continue negotiating."

"Good, then the Silva boys won't have to join the army. I'll tell them tomorrow," Devi said.

Rashmi was not convinced. She was not convinced because her father continued to smoke and think and think and smoke and didn't pick up one bit of reading from the stacks of material around their house. This was not the behavior of a man who was sure of anything. And Suren was not convinced because, while he had not felt tension in the air in Jaffna, he had felt tension in the air around Mohan, and that was much closer to home and seemed to carry with it the malice of intention. Nihil was neither convinced nor unconvinced. He sat through the rest of dinner wondering about the soldiers at the fort in Jaffna. Several of them had been Tamil. If both Tamils and Sinhalese were guarding the same public fort, how could there be war?

Ah, the conversations between parents and children, the way they unfold, always with good intentions, rarely with complete honesty. Which of these stories that the adults told was true, which false, which details spun to fit a certain way of seeing the world, which to fit another, we cannot say with any degree of surety. To know what effect the murder of that mayor of Jaffna, Mr. Alfred Duraiappah, had, we would have to ask his family, his neighbors. To know what effect the burning of recorded history had on the world, we would have to inquire of generations as yet unborn. For now, there was a man who had taken up arms in Jaffna, a mayor who had been assassinated, a library that was gone, and the only verifiable thing was this: there was trouble, and it was drawing close, for in the Silva house, the conversation went differently.

"Those fools don't believe that there's going to be a war," Mohan scoffed as he served himself a pile of rice and curry by the light of an oil lamp they had placed in the middle of the table.

"Which fools?" Mrs. Silva asked, shivering a little in the algid air brought on by the rain outside. She wrapped the fall of her sari over her shoulders and poured herself a glass of still-warm water from the *guruleththuwa* on the table.

"The Heraths. They think they know everything. About kites and war and everything. But they don't. They don't know anything. Wait until the war comes here, then they'll come running to us for help," Mohan said, though his hand shook a little as he added extra gravy to his plate.

"Maybe they will come around when they have all the information,"

Mrs. Silva said. Lately, despite the evidence of the Heraths' lack of judgment regarding matters of race and class, as evidenced by their continued involvement with the wrong kinds of people down the lane, Mrs. Silva realized that she missed the small chats she had once enjoyed with her neighbor.

"Maybe there won't be a war," Jith volunteered, a little timidly. Frankly, he wasn't a wargoing type, though he had not argued when Mohan had told him they were both expected to join the army. He was happy having a nearby girlfriend and planning his life in Australia with Dolly. Thanks to starstruck descriptions that Dolly had culled from various friends who had heard of people like herself, Burghers, who had made the great migration Down Under, Australia had taken on the form of a great escape, unthreatening and simple, exactly the opposite of the future painted for him by his fight-ready older brother. He listened to the rain outside and wondered if Dolly had made any paper boats. He couldn't wait to get up from the table and make one of his own. He had been saving a sheet of glazed red demi paper just for this purpose.

"There is going to be a war. Definitely. Good thing we'll have the two of you in the army," Mr. Silva said, tampering with, though not entirely ruining, Jith's pleasant thoughts of rain, Dolly, and paper boats.

Mr. Silva's knowledge of this war came from conversations at his place of work, from the resentful mutterings of some of his colleagues, mostly Sinhalese, and the anxiety and bravado among the rest of them, mostly Tamil. To these conversations Mr. Silva added his own daily observations. He noticed when a Tamil man gave up his seat more readily for a Tamil lady on the bus in a gesture that communicated an alliance to which he was not privy, and although he did not patronize their shops, he was sure that the Tamil shopkeepers served their Tamil customers before they tended to the Sinhalese ones. He noted that there were more Sinhalese beggars than Tamil ones. He counted and was satisfied to note that his suspicions were right: the Tamils owned the most lucrative businesses in the country. Clearly, they had it coming.

"Yes, bloody Tamils need to be put in their places," Mrs. Silva added. "The more who join, the bigger the army, the better off we'll all be. Keep them where they belong. Have you seen the shops in Pettah? All the best ones owned by Tamils."

"Why go to Pettah? Even here, down this lane, the Nadesans have the best property," Mr. Silva said. "Thought we were lucky getting the Heraths but come to see, even they are like the Tamils."

Indeed, it was the Silvas and the Bollings who had the largest acreage, and, since the Bollings' compound was a simple area of space unadorned with plants, except for their share of sal mal trees, it was the Silvas' garden that could claim to be the best property, stretching as it did in all its verdant and well-tended splendor, all the way down to the end of the lane, enabling Mr. Silva to have space for a grove of plantains and two mango trees—the fruits of which had only been shared with the Heraths—in addition to a large pond bordered by sugarcane, into which he had introduced goldfish. The reference to the Nadesans' being in possession of a superior property was, therefore, a blatant untruth, though neither Mrs. Silva or the boys contested his statement.

The following day, as if to give them all a visual reminder that the end of innocence was near, Sonna's predictions about the delinquents in the slums came true; they brought down the blue-and-silver kite. He took it upon himself to tell the Herath children about it.

"Those fellows roll the top of the thread, near the kite, 'bout three or four feet in glue, then crushed glass, then send it up. No chance agains' that." He grinned as he said it. "Not jus' yours, all the kites aroun' here they got."

Devi cried and Nihil put his arm around her. Rashmi wondered why anybody would come up with such a vicious pastime, but she didn't ask. Sonna, having said what he had wanted to, the news so hurtful, found that the satisfaction he had felt evaporated as soon as he stopped speaking and merely left him feeling empty and desirous.

"Let's go home," Suren said. "I learned a new song and I will play it for you." And in this way he soothed his brother and sisters.

Ramazan: Before and After

Thanks to all the talk of armed struggles and wars, and the downing of their best kite, a sadness hung like a pall over the children. It was Raju who reminded them all that Ramazan was not far away and this cheered them up, for at least the Muslim holiday promised a return to something both familiar and enjoyable. They began to count the days left until the fragrant and lavish feast that would be shared with them when the month of fasting had ended.

"Ruweena fainted in school today," Devi announced one afternoon as she hopped from one pile of sal mal flowers to the other, releasing their fragrance, but undoing all the work that Kamala had done to sweep the backyard. "Sister Principal forced her to drink lime juice and eat toast with marmalade. Ruweena said marmalade tastes horrible." She looked over at Suren, Rashmi, and Nihil, who were sitting on the back veranda to their house, drinking their tea and doing their homework. "I don't know why they have to fast at all when they have food in the house." Devi tried to make her words sound like a statement of opinion but it was obviously a question and Suren answered her.

"Muslims fast to learn discipline and take care of their spirits," Suren said, after taking a few sips of his tea.

"And Ramazan is celebrated in the month that the first verses of the Qu'ran were revealed to the Prophet Muhammad. That is why during Ramazan the mosques read the entire Qu'ran in the evenings." This was said by Nihil, who had learned these details from Mr. Niles.

Mr. Niles, who was still recovering from the flu, had managed to over-rule his wife in the business of letting Nihil sit beside him during Devi's lessons, and just a few days ago they had spoken briefly about the holiday of Ramazan. He was still unable to talk for any great length of time, however, and after a short conversation and the imparting of this bit of information about what their Muslim neighbors were celebrating, he had given Nihil a new book from his collection and asked Nihil to read it aloud to him. The book, *The Children of the New Forest*, by a man named Captain Marryat, with its tale of deprivation and adventure revolving around four children like themselves, appealed to Nihil, who forgot, for a moment, what they were discussing, as his thoughts fled first to Mr. Niles and then to Cromwell's England and forests the likes of which he'd never seen.

Devi's insistent voice shook him out of his daydream: "I haven't heard them recite the Qu'ran and I always hear the *Allah hu Akbar* from the mosque," Devi said. "You must be wrong."

She began to hop in and out of an elaborate length of hopscotch squares she had drawn in the earth with the edge of her rubber slippers. The afternoon sun filtering through the trees dappled both her and the backyard, and flower petals and leaves continued to fall singly and in bunches as a slight breeze picked up. Kamala came out and smacked her forehead at the mess that Devi had made, but she did not complain; she simply picked up the *ekel* broom and set about sweeping again.

Nihil laughed. "Of course you couldn't hear them, silly, you aren't Muslim and you don't go to mosque. You have to be inside the mosque to hear them." He turned to Suren for confirmation. Suren nodded.

"It is a good holiday, I think," Suren said. "What can be bad about spending time in prayer and doing good work?"

"How do we know they do good work?" Devi asked, tiring of her game and coming over to sit beside them. She opened her books and pulled out her half-done homework. "What kind of good work? Bin Ahmeds, do they do good work?"

"We don't have to know what they are doing," Suren said, "only they do. And their god. He probably knows too."

"Who is their god? What's his name?" Devi asked, as she tipped her head to look at her map of the world, the oceans already colored carefully in varying shades of blue pencil, and the Nile, the Amazon, the Mississippi, the Yangtze, the Euphrates, and the Ganges drawn in a deep green crayon through the land masses.

"Muhammad," Nihil said.

"Allah," Suren said.

"I read that Ramazan is the name in Arabic for the ninth month of the year," Rashmi burst out; she had been listening and trying to think of something important to say and felt pleased with herself for having such a rare tidbit of information and one she had finally remembered.

"I didn't know that," Suren said. And the rest of the afternoon was spent discussing what they did and did not know about Muslims, Muslim traditions, and Muslim food, chief among that last category of unknowing being the way in which their Muslim neighbor made their *watalappan* so perfectly, the custard just firm enough, the syrup thick, and the spices lingering on their tongues, making them shut their eyes with pleasure.

Before they could taste those treats, however, the ruling party did something that had never been seen in the history of any country. Even the adults on Sal Mal Lane, accustomed as they had become to all manner of outrageous behavior from their elected leaders, were taken by surprise: government officials discussed among themselves and passed a vote of no confidence in the leader of the opposition.

"Bloody idiots," Mr. Herath fumed when he came home from work that day and then, noticing that the only person in the veranda was Rashmi, he dispatched her to fetch her mother from the side garden where she was busy finding cracks and crevices in the wall into which she could press the ivy that was growing robustly under her care.

"Bloody idiots," he repeated when she arrived, though with a little less intensity. "Did you hear? They went ahead with the vote today. Maithripala Senanayake even pointed out to them that the leader of the opposition need not have the confidence of the government. That's the whole point!" And he banged the side of the front door, a completely uncharacteristic move for him and one that startled his wife.

"I heard, yes, the Silvas told me about it. What did the UNP imagine would happen after this fiasco?" Mrs. Herath asked rhetorically, giving up on the idea of soothing her irate husband and throwing herself into the fray. "The government can vote all they want, but if the members of the opposition have confidence in their leader there's not a thing the government can do about it."

"The Speaker wouldn't even listen to Maithripala's protests," Mr. Herath said, sitting down heavily on a chair in the veranda, still dressed in his work clothes. "Just one member of the government voted against it. Shelton Ranaraja." And after that they both sat there in silence, thinking about the day's events, about their friends who belonged to the opposition, about themselves, until Kamala brought out their evening cups of tea.

Three days later, a group of Tamil militants attacked a police station in Annaikoddai, killed two police officers, and took most of the firearms. The irony of the fact that the attack targeted a Muslim and a Tamil constable alongside two Sinhalese constables was lost on everybody. It was Lucas who sallied forth to Sal Mal Lane with the news.

"Constable Jayaratne's body has been brought to Ratnapura and now riots everywhere, Sir!" he exclaimed, arriving on the doorstep of the Herath household to deliver the information. In his state of distress he had forgotten to let down his sarong before crossing the road. He stood there with it rolled halfway up his thighs, his emaciated legs poking out underneath, leaning against the door frame and panting for breath.

"What?" Mr. Herath asked. "Riots? Where?" He was getting ready to leave for work after his lunch break, and he stood with a bundle of files in one hand and his hard-cased rectangular briefcase in the other.

"Yes, Sir. After the Annaikoddai attack, Sinhalese gangs are hitting back now! Everywhere! Ratnapura, Balangoda, Kahawatte, even in the coastal areas here and also in Batticaloa and Ampara! Even the estate Tamils." He wheezed for a few moments, shaking his head, commiserating. "How can they attack the estate Tamils, Sir? They are the poorest! I have seen! I, Lucas, I have seen them. Poorer even than me!"

"Suren!" Mr. Herath called out and, receiving no answer, called out to the other three children in turn "Rashmi! Nihil! Devi!" Mrs. Herath had not returned from school or else there is no doubt that he would have hollered for her too.

The four children lined up in front of their father, even Suren, who had joined them reluctantly, his loyalties to his parents having grown ever thinner with each passing day when the promise of a musical career was not discussed or even remembered. They were given instructions to run to their neighbors.

"Go and tell Uncle Sansoni, Uncle Tissera, Uncle Silva, Uncle Jimmy, and Mr. Bin Ahmed," Mr. Herath instructed.

"Why not the Nadesans and Uncle Raju?" Nihil asked.

"Nadesans and Raju are Tamils. They should stay indoors, along with Mr. Niles and that family," Mr. Herath said.

"Silvas said that Jimmy Bolling is also half Tamil—" Nihil began, but his father stopped him

"Just do what I'm asking you to do for once!" Mr. Herath said, raising his voice.

"What am I supposed to tell?" Devi asked, bouncing up and down on the balls of her feet, excited by the charge she could feel in the air around her.

"Tell them that there are riots in the outstations and we must stand at the bottom of the lane to prevent any problems here. That's all. Go!"

"I want to tell Uncle Raju!" she said, fear quickly replacing excitement.

"You can tell him after," Rashmi said as she took Devi's hand and ran out of the gate. As they ran, they saw Mohan and called out to him, telling him what they had just heard and asking him to get Jith and come with them to round up the neighbors.

"We're all going to stand at the bottom of the lane, like a parade!" Devi shouted.

"Tha says there might be trouble here," Rashmi said.

"I know there's trouble," Mohan said, walking away from them. "I'm going to see what's happening." And he ran away from them to catch a bus toward the Galle Road, looking for others like him who wanted more trouble, not less.

Their precautions proved unnecessary; nobody came to destroy their homes, burn, loot, or otherwise plunder the things that belonged to them. But an air of expectation remained, a stirring unrest that hung over their every move. The children continued to play but they argued and picked fights just as frequently, and Devi, in a fit of unreasonable rage, even went so far as to bite the Tisseras' son on his arm when he chased and caught Nihil in a fair game of catch. Dolly and Jith continued with their trysts, so the Herath children took Rose on, an outlier sister of sorts, to liven up their days with her bad English and cackles of laughter. None of the adults commented on the fact that Mr. Silva, though he had been asked by none other than Mr. Herath himself, had refused to join their neighborhood patrol. *Every man for himself,* he had said, *that's how it is these days. Better if we each watch our own homes. Tamils can watch theirs. Enough and more of them down this lane, isn't that so?*

Was it any wonder, then, that even the adults tried their best to distract the children with thoughts of Ramazan, dragging out this respite for as long as they could? Even if it meant that the entire neighborhood would lean on a single family, the Bin Ahmeds, the only Muslims down Sal Mal Lane? Ramazan, celebrated on September 11 of that year, took on the nature of a balm for all of them, and the Bin Ahmeds rose to the occasion. It had always been their lot not only to accept the heaping trays of food brought for their consumption by the three Sinhalese Buddhist and Hindu Tamil houses—Herath, Silva, and Nadesan—during their New Year in April, but to also provide all three of those families as well as the Sinhalese-Catholic, Tamil-Catholic and Burgher families—Tissera, Joseph, Niles, Bolling and Sansoni—with deep bowls of *watalappan* at the end of Ramazan. This year, Mrs. Bin Ahmed took special care over the making of the sweet, bringing out her best bowls in which to steam the puddings.

"How many *watalappans* will we get? I think three," Devi asked and answered her own question as they took their lunch.

"Why three?" Nihil asked.

"Bin Ahmeds and Tha's two friends, Uncle Rizvi Mohamed and Uncle Esufally."

"They don't have to bring us *watalappan*. They don't live here," Nihil said.

But he was wrong. The Heraths did get three bowls of the sweet dessert, the syrup from the steamed treacle and cardamom pooling thick at the bottom of each. Mrs. Herath gave one away to Alice and Lucas, who inhabited a world in which the passing of desserts between Muslim, Sinhalese, and Tamil was neither common nor expected, although those who were lucky enough, as this couple were, to have patrons—such as the people on Sal Mal Lane and Mrs. Vithanage—usually enjoyed the treats that came their way during the differnt holidays, and shared them with those who were less fortunate.

"Ah, thank you, thank you," Lucas said, as he bowed his head a few times and accepted the white bowl from Mrs. Herath. "It is kind of you to share with us. We are old but we also like desserts!" He laughed as he carried the bowl back to Alice, who clucked her tongue in disapproval but ate a heaping plateful with deep and silent enjoyment after first having placed a saucer with a bit of *watalappan* floating in it out for the crows in the way she had become accustomed to doing, to appease the spirits. *That's what my mother taught me and that's what I'm going to do,* she said, with a certain haughtiness, to Lucas, when he lamented the waste.

It would be a fine thing if desserts could serve to sweeten not just tongue and imagination but life. That year, however, not only did their treats prove fleeting, even the return of the bowls took place with a certain forced gaiety whose effervescence, no matter how deserved by the impeccable quality of the dish and the grace of the giver, seemed ill-advised. The discussion, after gratitude was expressed and Mrs. Herath lingered as expected on the Bin Ahmeds' doorstep, was not about how much the children had enjoyed the *watalappan,* though they had, but about the possibility of war.

"Soon the real rain will start. North-West monsoons will be here," Mr. Bin Ahmed said, looking at the skies even though there was nothing there to indicate that a torrential downpour was imminent and even though the monsoons he mentioned were several months away.

"Yes, rains . . ." Mrs. Herath murmured, knowing what was being intimated. She looked at his neat house, the garden so basic and yet so pleasing, with its wall topped with purple bougainvillea, the soil covered with sea sand and tiled to mimic the desert homes of the dry zone. She tried to think of something else that she could say to these neighbors who kept so much to themselves and yet emerged with such generosity each Ramazan. Nothing else came to mind so she repeated herself. "Yes, the rains will be here soon. We won't have to water the flowers so much."

"We can make more paper boats then," Devi, who had accompanied her mother, said, hopping on one foot as she chased a smooth stone across the short paved walkway to the Bin Ahmeds' bright-blue front door.

"Hope there is no trouble for us, down our lane," Mr. Bin Ahmed said, though it was not just a wish, it was also a request, and they both knew it. "Government and Tamil party both wanted the District Development Council elections and the TULF won, even though the government's representative, Thiagarajah, was killed by the militants. But the Tigers don't want any political negotiations and they opposed TULF all the way. Lot of violence on every side. Now the Tamils don't know whom to believe, the Tigers or the TULF. I am afraid that eventually somehow they will bring all these troubles here."

Mrs. Herath took in Mr. Bin Ahmed's small frame, his comb-over, the graying threads of hair glistening with oil to keep them in place. He was a short man, just about an inch taller than she was, a man at ease with his aging, but a frail-looking one. She felt sorry for him.

"Why should there be, Mr. Ahmed? We haven't caused any problems for anybody, after all, isn't that so?" Mrs. Herath said, inhabiting her Buddhist upbringing for a while, and thinking about karma. She reached behind her and tugged the fall of her sari away from Devi, who was trying to fix it to her own head like a veil.

Mrs. Bin Ahmed came out and Mrs. Herath thanked her for the dessert.

"That's a lovely color on you, Mrs. Ahmed," Mrs. Herath said, fingering the pretty orange sari that Mrs. Bin Ahmed was wearing.

Mrs. Bin Ahmed smiled. "It belonged to my mother's mother!" she said. "In the old days they made things to last."

"Yes, you are right. One of *my* best saris is one that belonged to my great-grandmother," Mrs. Herath said.

They continued to talk for a while longer about preferred fabrics, favorite colors, the impossibility that anything they bought during their lifetimes could be good enough to last and be handed down to a third generation.

Mr. Bin Ahmed waited until they finished exchanging pleasantries and then said slowly, "It's not that we have caused problems, it's that other people want to cause us problems. That's the real issue here. Look at all of us, living peacefully down this lane. Look at our family. We don't bother anybody."

Just at that moment Sonna strode out from the Bolling house, kicking the door shut behind him. He looked over at them, and hacked and spat into the dirt. Then he stopped and lit a cigarette in full view of the three adults. They watched him until he had walked to the end of the road and turned the corner.

"Yes," Mrs. Herath said, "we live well here, for the most part, but there are bad eggs everywhere. Whatever our differences, our lane is a safe place. We should try to be careful and keep to ourselves, stay away from all these problems that are going on in other places."

That *we* was a charitable inclusion. Mrs. Herath knew that each family shared a different physical and emotional reality and that, between them, her family name made her less uncertain in the face of the news from the North. Still, despite their many differences, until now they had all found a way to balance their own rituals and devotions and languages with those of other people. Soon it would be time for Deepavali again and, this year too, Mrs. Herath was sure that Nihil and Devi and perhaps even Rashmi would go over to the Nadesans' house to help them decorate their home and light oil lamps around the designs they painted on the ground. Later in the year, her children would surely be asked to help with Kala Niles's preparations for Christmas, Suren would play carols on the piano in the evenings, and all of them would sing. Wasn't there harmony in that?

"We are the first house down the lane," Mrs. Bin Ahmed said, finally. "If people come to attack, ours, here at the bottom of the lane, will be the first one they'll take."

"War is for soldiers. We shouldn't worry. We are simply living our lives," Mrs. Herath said. "Don't worry about these things now."

Devi, who was still playing some game that involved hopping, chimed in with "Only Mohan and Jith are going to join the army down our lane," but the adults paid her no heed, which made her stop moving so she could listen more carefully, to see if she could gather anything worth sharing with her brothers and sister.

Mrs. Bin Ahmed spoke up, taking Mrs. Herath's hand to emphasize her point. "Last time when Lucas gave the alert we were all prepared to defend our lane. But this time I have heard the lane is dividing into separate groups and we are being put into the Tamil group."

"Nonsense. We are united as always, Mrs. Ahmed. Nothing has changed."

But things had. Everybody knew it, even those like Mrs. Herath who wanted so desperately to believe in the continuity of the old order that they repeated such words to whoever would listen. Things had changed. They had changed in these ways:

Rose told Dolly who told Jith who told Mohan that Kala Niles had told Raju not to go and watch TV in the Sinhalese people's houses, which meant, specifically, the Tissera household, since they were the only ones who owned a TV.

The Silvas added two more feet to the L-shaped walls bordering their property and topped the back one with reels of barbed wire that kept even the birds away.

A young Tamil man who had boarded with the Sansonis after their son left for Australia, and had arrived from the North, roared up and down Sal Mal Lane on his motorbike without checking for the presence of children, making those who were playing outside leap into hedges and scratch themselves in the process.

Mohan no longer spoke to Raju, Old Mrs. Joseph, or any of the Nileses.

Lucas told the Niles family that Sunil's shop would not give them credit. He didn't have to say why.

Lucas also told the Heraths that the Tamil owner of Sinappa Stores would no longer issue credit to them. He didn't have to explain to the Heraths either.

Alice would not cook for anybody who had anything to do with Tamils, which meant she cooked for nobody, including, on some days, if she had seen him in active conversation with Raju or the Nileses or the Nadesans, for Lucas, who was forced to walk to the tea shop and ask for steamed bread and sambol.

Mrs. Ratwatte fired all her Tamil girls and sent them back to the estates and replaced them with Sinhalese girls from Kandy who had to be taught the art of batik making from scratch. She considered this a service to her race.

Most telling of all, it became rarer and rarer to hear Tamil being spoken in the streets. It was quite possible that, in all of Colombo, there was only one Sinhalese boy, Suren, attuned as he was to the interplay of sounds, who noticed and mourned the absence.

That year during Christmas time, when the Heraths gathered around the piano to sing the carols that they did not associate with Catholicism, just the season, no matter how many references there were to holy, god, and heaven, the voices that lifted above the top of the hedge and poured into the listeners outside—Mr. Niles, lying on his armchair, Rose, Dolly, Kala Niles, all hidden, and Raju and Mr. Tissera, standing side by side, arms crossed, staring down Sal Mal Lane—filled them not with well-being but with a disquiet at odds with the sweetness of the music.

Sonna's Birthday Party

As if the disturbances between the families down the lane were insufficient, Sonna, about to turn sixteen, demanded a birthday party, which resulted in an exchange of ugly words that all the Herath children overheard because Francie Bolling, who chose her timing by her husband's moods, not by her company, decided to broach the subject on a Sunday when Suren was there playing his guitar.

"What does he need a birthday party for?" Jimmy Bolling thundered, when the issue was brought up by his wife, and his voice cut through the music. Suren stopped playing and they all listened.

"Sixteenth birthday is a big one, after all," Francie Bolling began, her voice cajoling, her eyes on Sonna, who was lurking outside the purple-striped curtain that separated their bedroom from the living room outside. "We had a nice party for Sophia when she turned sixteen even though she had already gone and eloped."

"Shouldn't 'ave bothered with that either," Jimmy Bolling muttered, "runnin' away like a common tart. Wastin' all the schoolwork . . ." He petered out into a grumble, then raised his head. "It's for girls anyway, these sixteenth-birthday parties."

Francie Bolling shifted a little closer to her husband, rumpling the matching purple sheets on their bed as she did so. "But, darlin', our only son, after all," she said, putting her palm on her husband's shoulder as he sat by her on the edge of their bed. The heavy costume earrings in her ears jingled as she moved.

Jimmy Bolling slapped her hand away. "Only son? Only thug! Only fool! Only idiot! You wan' to know what sons are like, look at that Mohan Silva! Look at that Suren! *Those* are sons. This one is not a son, he's a burden. Doin' nothin' all day long an' comin' here askin' for birthday parties."

"Sophia got so I get too!" Sonna shouted, coming into the room. Sonna, wearing his jeans, boots, and suspenders over a thin sleeveless undershirt, looked entirely disreputable and entirely undeserving of attention, let alone a birthday party, even though the shirt had been his way of covering up the worst of the pictures he kept drawing on his body.

Francie Bolling got to her feet quickly and tried to shoo him out, but it was too late. Jimmy Bolling stood up and slapped Sonna across his face, once, twice. "Who do you think you are, comin' in here to *my* bedroom? Who do you think you are demandin' things from your mother?"

Sonna's head spun to the right, to the left, but he planted his feet and faced his father. "I'm your son," he said. "You can' jus' give one person a party an' not give the other one. Sophia got, so I should get too. I have friends I wan' to have." He had to stop himself from saying exactly whom he wanted at the party—Rashmi—though he intended to invite everybody down the lane to cover up that fact.

Suren began to strum his guitar to try to drown out the sound of these words, but Rashmi, shocked, put her palm over the strings of the guitar and shushed him.

"Sophia got so you should get? Friends?" Jimmy Bolling scoffed. He laughed. He put his face near Sonna's and shook it from side to side. "Son, only son, you don' have friends. You have other motherfuckers in those slums jus' like you, other fools jus' like you, doin' nothin' but shit all day. You hear me? Do shit, are shit. That's what you have."

No amount of pleading from Francie Bolling would change his mind. To circumvent her husband, a few weeks later, Francie Bolling invited the Herath children—and Jith and Mohan, though those two did not come—to a dinner she had prepared. *Just to share a meal with you children for a change*, she said to them, not daring to divulge her intention to celebrate her son's sixteenth birthday in this fashion. She added turmeric to the expensive *muthu samba* rice she had begged from Koralé, tempered it with onions, called it yellow rice, and served it up with a chicken curry she got Alice to cook and didn't even mix it all together before she served them her treat on Sonna's birthday.

Since the children had not been told of the significance of this day, they did not wish Sonna a happy birthday or bring him any gifts, they simply washed their hands and sat on either side of Mr. and Mrs. Bolling, that being the last available seating at the table. Rashmi, seated across from Sonna, tried to smile at him but he would no more meet her eyes than smile at her so she gave up and tended to Devi instead, deboning her chicken and reminding her to keep the *indul* from moving above the second manogamy in each of her fingers as she ate, in the same way her mother had taught her.

"Make sure you use just the tips of your fingers to pick up your rice and curry!" she whispered to Devi and, a few moments later, "Tiny bites! Don't eat like some ill-bred villager!"

None of the Herath children, not even Rashmi, paid attention to the grime and disarray of their surroundings; all their weekend visits to play and sing in secret had made cleanliness and order irrelevant. Francie Bolling, however, noticed, because when the Herath children were seated at her table, they threw her dining room furniture and her family into unflattering focus. She rubbed surreptitiously at a stain on the red-and-white-checked plastic tablecloth she had flipped over to the cleaner side just that morning; she kept getting up to rewash first one cloudy glass, then another; finally she scooped up all their glasses and went to the kitchen, where she rinsed them again by pouring the water she had boiled for drinking onto them, and carried them back steaming, scalding herself in the process.

"Mummy, why don' you sit down!" Jimmy Bolling said to his wife. "Been workin' since mornin' an' still runnin' around," he explained to the Herath children. "Nice to have you come for a meal," he added, as he served more rice onto each of their plates. When he ate, his arms concealed in a long-sleeved shirt, both Suren and Nihil noticed that the fact that Jimmy Bolling could only hold his left hand in a fold was not apparent. It rested, like their left forearms did, on the table between his chest and his plate of rice, looking for all the world as though nothing was wrong with it.

"How come we're havin' yellow rice?" Rose asked, unable to contain her curiosity. She was sitting across from Suren and trying to be ladylike, keeping just the tips of her fingers in her rice, just like Devi and Rashmi were doing.

Francie Bolling did not answer, but her eyes flew to Sonna's face and then back again.

"Yes, how come? Times are so troubled these days also," Dolly said, having heard about the troubled times from Jith and assuming that such times must also be associated with a lack of money, since, in her experience, things always became particularly bad in her house when her parents were short of money.

Francie Bolling looked around the table. Sonna was staring at her, but so was her husband, who seemed equally curious about the feast. She said, "No, no reason. Jus' felt like doin' somethin' a little different, keep us all happy." She looked at Sonna when she said that *all*. "Herath children also here," she said, nervously, as Jimmy Bolling continued to look at her.

"No reason, Mummy? Really? We're rich now, so you are cookin' fine things for no reason?" Sonna said, his voice full of bitterness.

"Shut up and eat," Jimmy Bolling said.

"You eat," Sonna said and rose from the table. "Herath children are here so better have enough to feed them. Can' let them go hungry. Might go an' tell everybody we don' have food."

Nihil looked at Sonna and tried to understand when and why Sonna's gentleness toward him, such as it was, had faltered. Sonna had always spared a look or a wave and sometimes a smile for him. Now, he treated Nihil with disinterest. He didn't watch them at play, either, as though he didn't care about their games or how fast Nihil ran or anything at all. It made Nihil sad, and he tried to think of something to say but nothing came except *kced gninrub eht no doots yob eht*, so he said that, hoping to communicate something to Sonna, some sympathy, or to recall that other moment they had shared.

"What is that?" Dolly said, and shrieked with laughter.

"God! Sounds like priests in churches. I never understand when the father starts talkin' in Latin!" Rose said. "You know Latin?"

Nihil shook his head. Rashmi looked concerned. Suren continued to eat. Devi spoke up. "He can say things backward," she said. "He's just saying something backward."

"What did you say, darlin'?" Francie Bolling asked, relieved that Sonna's disruption was being drowned out by this new conversation and trying to ignore the fact that Sonna was still standing by his plate, watching Nihil.

"Nothing," Nihil said, looking up at Sonna. Sonna did not acknowledge Nihil's gesture but he left the table more quietly than his mother expected him to.

As the children left after the dinner, they noticed Sonna standing at the very end of the lane staring at the main road. He was lit in silhouette from the lights of the cars that passed by. Next to him there were two other boys they did not recognize but whose attire, shorts and bare upper bodies, made it safe to assume that they came from the slums beyond the bridge.

"There's Sonna," Nihil said, pointing to him. Sonna was standing so close to the main road that every time a bus went by the hair on his head blew back off his forehead and he seemed to tilt back a little.

"Someone should tell him not to stand near the main road like that," Devi said. "Right, Nihil? Remember that boy you told me about? Down the other lane?"

Nihil looked down at his feet and did not answer her.

"Today is Sonna's birthday," Rose said, gazing at her brother. "I completely forgot."

"Today? Why didn't Aunty tell us?" Rashmi asked, dismayed that they had come to Sonna's birthday celebration without bringing a gift for him.

"What for? You don' need to know," Dolly said, then, "Oh! No, I don' think the nice dinner was for that."

"Yes, definitely not for that. Daddy wouldn' allow, an' if Daddy says no, nothin' happens," Rose said.

Still, as they walked home, the children, Rashmi and Nihil in particular, talked about Sonna's birthday and each wondered aloud if there was something they could give him. The things they thought of were gifts they could not afford to buy: a shirt (Rashmi), a can of Fa spray (Devi), a cricket bat (Nihil).

"We can buy him a chocolate," Suren said at last. "He must like chocolate."

The next evening, Rashmi, the only one who saved her allowance, counted out all the coins and crumpled notes, though she allowed Devi to hold on to one square bronze five-cent coin, which was becoming a rarity, and they sent Kamala to the store to buy the chocolate, which they put into a shiny brown paper bag that Devi had been saving *for something special* and that she gave up a little reluctantly. Suren and Rashmi walked down to the Bollings' house to hand over the gift, but when they got there Rose said Sonna was not home, he had not come back, even to sleep, the previous night.

"Give this to him when he comes," Rashmi said, and handed over the chocolate. "For his birthday. Tell him we said happy birthday. It's a chocolate."

"But will melt, no, if we keep?" Rose said. "We don' have a fridge."

So they took the chocolate back and put it in their own fridge with every intention of giving it to Sonna, but the next day Mr. Herath, rummaging in the refrigerator for something sweet after lunch, saw the chocolate and opened it up and the children were too afraid to say anything about it lest their mother find out that they were fraternizing with *that boy,* and they had no more money to buy another chocolate so they reconciled themselves to feeling ashamed and let it be.

1982

The Cricketer and the Old Man Talk of War

Nihil walked silently beside Devi to the Nileses' house, hoping that Mr. Niles would be well enough to talk to him. He tried to quieten the anxiety that had settled in his chest ever since Suren and Rashmi had talked of troubles, and that rose to the surface every time he stepped beyond the gates of their house without his older brother and sister. Now that someone in their own neighborhood, Mohan, had spoken of war, Nihil felt a sense of danger wrap itself around even their most harmless activities. When he stepped into the Nileses' veranda and saw Mr. Niles looking alert and in good spirits, therefore, Nihil could not help the grin and the relief that flooded his face. As soon as he had shut the door leading from the veranda to the living room, where Devi was having her lesson, Nihil blurted out his question.

"What will happen when the war starts?" he said, before he had even sat down.

The old man narrowed his eyes slightly as he watched Nihil settle down, his books at his feet, his body leaning forward. Mr. Niles's thoughts went often these days to the home he had left behind in Jaffna when he met and married the Colombo-born Rita Schoorman and turned her into Mrs. Niles. He wanted to return to Jaffna to revisit the places that had hosted his childhood, one last time, before it was all over, and the contemplation of war before this could happen was troubling to him. War was an impossibility along such quiet cobbled streets. Men, women, and children who traveled so frequently on bicycles between libraries and schools and markets and places of work, such people did not go to war. What would stir up the passions of people like his mother had been, people who cooked *sambaaru* thick with vegetables, brinjal, pumpkin, and okra, the roasted mustard and curry leaves floating in a broth so delicious that nothing else was necessary? No, war was irreconcilable with what he knew of the North. And yet here was this boy, whose usual preoccupations veered between his young sister and lost games of cricket, here he was, right before him, speaking of war.

"I wanted to ask you about it before but you were too sick to talk then," Nihil said, as he wiped his hands on his jeans; they were clammy from anxiety. "I didn't want to worry you. Aunty told me you needed to rest. But Mohan told us that the war is coming. They are going to join the army and go to war. That is what they said. First Mohan, then Jith." Nihil sat back. Already he felt his fears dissipating. He waited for Mr. Niles to reassure him that there would be no war, but that is not what Mr. Niles said, not exactly.

He said, "People do not go to war, Nihil, they carry war inside them. Either they have the war within them or they don't have it. The thing to think about is do you and I have war inside us?"

"I don't have war," Nihil said immediately, as if he had already pondered this very question, "and my brother and Rashmi and Devi, they don't have it either. Or Rose or Dolly. I don't think they have war. Mohan, though, I am sure he has it. Jith, I'm not sure. And Sonna also I'm not sure . . ."

"Sonna is still a good boy in your opinion, then?" Mr. Niles asked mildly.

Nihil shrugged. "I don't think he's a good boy, but he hasn't done anything bad to me or my sisters and brother so I cannot call him a bad boy."

"That's a fair way of looking at things," Mr. Niles said, and smiled.

"My parents . . ." Nihil began and paused, "I'm not sure if they do or if they don't." Nihil pursed his lips and frowned as he weighed the facts against his parents. They sometimes fought, which put them in the "have war" column, but they also took care of people like Lucas and Rose and Dolly, and that set them in the "don't have war" column.

Mr. Niles continued to smile as he watched Nihil trying to figure out the complex nature of his parents. "Your parents are like you, they don't have war in them," he said, deciding for Nihil.

"Yes, I don't think they do. They're good people," Nihil said and was about to ask about Mr. Niles, to force him to say that no, he did not have war within him either, when Mr. Niles dispatched him on one of his routine errands.

"Son, could you go inside and ask Aunty to make me another cup of tea? Get one for yourself too," Mr. Niles said.

Nihil rose obediently and went to the kitchen to look for Mrs. Niles, who kept him talking while she poured the tea and put two stainless steel mugs on a stainless steel tray for him to carry back out to her husband.

"Uncle *loves* when you come, doesn't he?" she said. She smiled and patted his head. "Here, I just made these. Take two and eat one. Keep one for Devi." She put two fragrant *vadai* on the plate and Nihil's mouth watered at the sight of them, bits of curry leaf and green chilli poking through the crisp ball of fried lentils and flour.

"These are my favorite kind of *vadai*," he said. "Devi's too."

She stroked his face, once on each cheek, and then, drawing her caress to a point, she held his chin in the tips of her fingers. Nihil breathed in the *indul* smell that permeated her hands. She always smelled like that, a scent of curries and water clinging to her, making her seem earthy, somehow, and unlike her husband. Mr. Niles's clothing was kept so fresh and his scent, as far as Nihil could tell, was always a mix of sandalwood soap and Old Spice, both overlaid by the blooms on Kala Niles's rose vines.

"You are a good boy. He has been much happier since you started coming to sit with him. Talks more, laughs more, even eats better." And because saying thank you, like saying sorry, was not part of her culture or his, she left it at that and let Nihil smile his acknowledgment and leave, the tray balanced carefully in his hands.

After he had served Mr. Niles and sat down with his treat, Nihil returned to his topic. "And you?" he asked. "Do you have war inside you?" He wanted to make quite sure that should the Tamil and Sinhalese families down his lane divide into their own groups, Mr. Niles would not be part of it.

This was a difficult question for a man of Mr. Niles's age, who had lived both among those who were exactly like him and also among those who did not share his traditions and beliefs. It had been a good life, a life of public stature absent of humiliations, a life within a community that held him in respect. A life in which a child like Nihil would listen with rapt attention to what he had to say, who would follow direction, seek him out. But it was also a life during which there had been upheavals that had stirred him to anger. Mr. Niles looked at Nihil, taking in his waiting eyes, the legs grown too long for his jeans, his aspect of trust, and he considered the question. To answer it truthfully he would have to ask himself other, more complicated questions.

What was his life like, say, in 1956, the year of the first riots that gripped the Eastern Province? His one child, Kala, was just fourteen years old and his days were full of her doings, his wife's conversations, and the directed-journeys of a husband, father, breadwinner. He stamped seals on official documents, signed his name to bulletins about this and that, and watched the world turn. There was the Official Languages Act with reasonable use allowed for his language, Tamil, there were amendments to the act, there was a *satyagraha*, the nonviolent protest continuing on and on.

And in June? On June 11 of that year? Had he done anything different on that day when the entire country separated like yolks and whites into their own ethnic groups as they responded to the news of the carnage in the faraway town of Gal Oya? Mr. Niles thought hard. He had placed a trunk call to his parents, still living in Jaffna, to inquire about their safety. Neither he nor they had referred to the reason for that call, they had let the long silences in between the *Is everything okay?* and the *Maybe ask Appa to stay home tomorrow,* reveal their worries.

But even from that distance he knew, as the other Tamil inhabitants of Sal Mal Lane, the Nadesans and Old Mrs. Joseph and her husband, knew, what terror had gripped the settlements in the dry zone of Gal Oya, because the compositions of those settlements had resembled the composition of Sal Mal Lane, a mix of Tamils, Sinhalese, and Muslims. How quickly Gal Oya had disintegrated under rumor-fueled chaos, the people arming themselves against butchery with kris knives, their very preparedness guaranteeing the fulfillment of their fears. That year, as though the elements themselves were in agreement that no hope was possible, the South-West monsoons had blown over the Gal Oya reservoir, bringing not a drop of rain but only the scorching named winds that depressed Sinhalese and Tamil peasant alike, making them curse the same winds in separate languages: *yalhulanga* for one, *kachchan* for the other.

What could he know of the hardship of starting from scratch, planting in the earth, manning a boundary, he with his government job, set free to feel only safety and guilt? There had been a brief moment of possibility, he recollected it now, with the Bandaranaike-Chelvanayakam Pact, the possibility of dignity, but it did not last. Nothing seemed to last, to take hold, except fear and people on every side who thrived not on harmony but on disunity.

Two years later, 1958, and twin attacks on trains, one in Vavuniya, one in Batticaloa, one aimed at Tamils, another at the Sinhalese. Somewhere out there the sugarcane fields had burned furiously, and Mr. Niles had wondered about that, that sugarcane burning, whether the air had smelled sweet while all around machetes did their work, all around the train stations ablaze while carved pillars and statues, themselves thousands of years old, looked on.

There was his home, his family, to consider when all the news from the North came not as information but as incitement, and mobs roamed the streets of every town throughout the island, including this capital city where he lived. To barricade the doors and stay inside, or to go out and confront the thugs? To be a householder or to be a Tamil, that had been the choice. And he had chosen his family. Listening to tales of brutality, of burning temples, burning kovils, of men with shirts tucked in who attacked those whose shirts were untucked, of people running, running, he stayed inside.

When the call to his parents brought the sound of fear and desperation to him over a distance that rendered him impotent, what had he done then? He had made calls to his colleagues in parallel posts, those with last names that were like his and those that were not, in Batticaloa, in Jaffna, asking them for their help, learning that help was not possible, everybody was afraid, everybody was being attacked, when there was both a Hindu temple and the Buddhist Naga Vihara burning, when Sinhalese Marxists lay dead beside Tamil civilians, there was no trust left.

But then he remembered the words he had uttered in 1977, just two years before the Heraths had moved in. And, remembering, Mr. Niles squeezed his eyes shut against the boy sitting before him. He squeezed them and still Nihil remained on his mind, Nihil and his question about war. He had said those words in the quiet of his home, *let us move back where we belong*, but he hadn't meant them, not the way they had to be meant for his family to uproot themselves and leave with him. He had not been able to say them with enough force, with finality, because the place that he wanted to return to had been tarnished by the murder of Alfred Duraiappah, the mayor of Jaffna, a man he had admired, and the rise of Prabhakaran, a militant he loathed. Everything was muddied, between his anger at the thugs who belonged both to "his" people who were Tamil and "their" people who were Sinhalese, and all the people he loved who crossed between those two categories, the racial distinctions blurring again and again. And as if all that were not enough, his daughter now grown up and unmarried, his wife moving toward reconciliation to that fact, himself sick. Yes, he had sent up that feeble cry, though he had known even then that there was no home left to go back to, his parents gone, his sisters relocated and living in Batticaloa for two decades.

In the end his own answer had been no. He had built a life here in the city and there was no reason to abandon it. But what had he done with those feelings of disquiet? Where had he put them? It agitated him to ponder these questions, to remember such moments, when to answer *no* to moving had not necessarily translated into an *yes* for staying, only an acknowledgment of reality.

"You don't have war in you either," Nihil interrupted his thoughts, forcing the answer he wanted Mr. Niles to give him. "If you did, I would know," he said. Saying the words aloud, Nihil knew they were true and the last remnants of his fears left his body as he uttered them.

Mr. Niles wiped his face, glad that Nihil could not tell that this time he really was crying. He picked up a fresh handkerchief, blew his nose, and said as clearly as he could, "Yes, you would know, Nihil. You would know if I did, that is true." He remained silent for a while, his eyes closed, slowly turning his back on the upheavals he had just revisited. When he opened his eyes again, Nihil was reading a Hardy Boys book that he had brought with him. Mr. Niles watched him, and as he did so the images in his head receded further in his memory. He was here now, this was his life, the whole and the end of it, in the company of this boy. Nihil, feeling his gaze, looked up.

"Put the book away, Nihil," Mr. Niles said at last, and Nihil obliged right away. When he was in a talkative mood, Mr. Niles was likely to open yet another window into his life by giving Nihil one thing or another from his past: a silver comb that fit into his pocket, a Parker pen with a bottle of purple-blue ink, and books. Always, books.

But this time, Mr. Niles did not share a memory. He said, "I have something important to discuss with you. We know you don't have war inside you, so let us see what you do have in you."

"Nothing," Nihil said, disappointed, twisting his hands, palms up. "I just study and go to school and come home and play the piano and fly kites even though we don't fly kites anymore these days because of what happened with Devi's blue-and-silver one. And I take care of Devi."

"Ah yes, you take care of Devi."

The sentence hung in the air between them. Nihil thought about Devi. He did take care of her, but since her stumble and the resulting placement into Mrs. Niles's arms, he had felt less insecure about her well-being when she came for her piano lessons. Besides, his book of what he knew had remained blank for weeks, except, now and then, something about Uncle Raju. But the something about Uncle Raju was not anything to be taken seriously for, after all, Uncle Raju was everybody's worry. He was Suren's worry for fear that their mother would discover that Devi had traipsed all over the neighborhood and ended up in his stinking garage; he was Rashmi's worry because she didn't like the way he dressed, though even that had ceased to worry her as much since he began wearing his khakis at all times; and he had always been Nihil's worry because, well, Raju was Raju. The one person for whom Raju was not a worry was Devi herself.

"I don't worry about her so much anymore," Nihil said. "Nothing has come to me recently. Nothing bad is going to happen to her." He considered that for a moment then added, "Nothing yet," just in case he was tempting fate by making an all-encompassing statement.

"Then, Nihil, it is time you went back to cricket." Mr. Niles leaned forward as he said this, then leaned back again and waited to see what effect it would have.

Nihil regarded Mr. Niles in the quiet accented by the piece that Devi was now playing: Bagatelle in A Minor, op. 59, a safely watered-down version of "Für Elise." This was something he had wanted to bring up with Mr. Niles himself, this matter of going back to cricket. Two of his best friends were now staying after school to practice with the junior team. One cricketer, Ranjan Madugalle, had made the first eleven at the age of fifteen, and he was not only talented but beautiful. Nihil did not feel he was either, though he did think he had some potential on the talent front, certainly more than either of his friends.

"Ranjan Madugalle went on to play for the national team in our first Test match against England," he said, continuing his thoughts aloud. "Once, when he was playing for Royal, I got his autograph and because he knew my mother, he let me wear his colors cap, just for a few minutes while he was signing autographs for the girls . . ." and he stopped there, adoration for the older cricketer fairly seeping out of his body.

Mr. Niles laced his long fingers together and contemplated Nihil. "Long ago, he was just a boy like you," he said.

"I don't think so," Nihil said. "I think he was always a star batsman."

"Nonsense. Nobody gets to be good without wanting it badly enough. How badly do you want it?"

Nihil flattened his back against the woven cane. How badly did he want it? Had Mr. Niles not heard his footsteps as he bowled while one or the other of the children of Sal Mal Lane waited by a makeshift crease? Had he not heard the children cry out in admiration when he, Nihil, batted? Could he not feel his dreams of not merely driving the ball with such elegance that people would refer to *him* as *a young Madugalle*, but also bowling a fast delivery to a nine-man slip cordon as Australia's Dennis Lillee had done in 1977 against New Zealand and keeping wickets like England's Alan Knott and fielding like India's Sunil Gavaskar, flying through the air to make the game-winning catch? Yes, he had Devi to watch over, but how could Devi compare with *that* moment?

"I was thinking that Devi is probably safe to come here for piano without me," he breathed out at last, knowing that this was what he needed to say, and this was the person in whose presence he could say those words. Then, caught up in the enthusiasm that followed from Mr. Niles, he forgot entirely that he had come to this decision alone.

"Good!" Mr. Niles fairly shouted as he clapped his hands, once, together, his past with its many capitulations forgotten. "Then next time, you stay at school for practice and she can come alone."

"Uncle Raju can bring her," Nihil said, thinking aloud, realizing that neither Rashmi nor Suren was home on Fridays, when he and Devi had their lessons, Rashmi having taken up netball too. "Or Kamala, but I think she would prefer Uncle Raju."

"Yes, Raju is a good person," Mr. Niles said. "You know, he and Kala were children together down this lane just like you are now." His eye began to run again and he paused to rub it with a handkerchief. When he looked up from dropping the cloth into the wicker basket that sat on a stool beside his chair for this purpose, he noticed that Nihil had slumped his shoulders down. "What's the matter?" he asked.

"Kala Akki won't change my lesson, and she can't move Suren or Rashmi because Suren's lesson is too long and Rashmi has other activities after school," he said, his voice, which had taken on a timbre of shy excitement, now flat, "and anyway, Amma will be annoyed if I stop music."

"Oh, don't worry about Kala Akki! I will manage her. She will take you on another day, and you can tell your mother that Uncle Niles arranged the whole thing because he thinks you are a good cricketer! No, tell her I *know* that you are going to be a great cricketer!"

"Tha is buying me a leather ball for my birthday when I'm thirteen," Nihil said. "Next year I'll get it. I can't wait to take it to school and show everybody."

"Well then, young man, there is one more thing you need."

"What is that?"

"Go quietly past Kala Akki, so you don't disturb the lesson, go into my room, open the drawer at the bottom of the chest there with all those medicines, and take out your new gloves!"

Nihil jumped up from his chair, ran, screeched to a halt before he opened the connecting door, then tiptoed through the rooms that contained so much still air, the Nileses preferring to keep their windows shut against dust and insects. He could smell the mild frankincense scent of the *sambrani* that Mrs.

Niles lit each afternoon to keep the mosquitoes away, throwing the crushed resinoid into the coals that glowed in the hand-held metal pan she kept for this purpose. He had some difficulty getting the last drawer opened, the handles having come off. He had to slide his hand underneath the bottom of the chest and ease the drawer out a little bit at a time until he could create enough space on top to grasp it from the front and pull it open.

The gloves were not new, they were white and worn, a little big for his hands, but who cared? He put them on and off a few times, imagining himself putting them on as he walked toward the pitch, his bat tucked under his arm, and taking them off as the crowd cheered when he walked back to the pavilion after. The gloves, with their mix of cloth and cotton and rubber, felt as though they were full of history, full of skill.

When he returned he was grinning, as was Mr. Niles. He felt his heart swell as he looked at the old man; Mr. Niles was more animated than he had ever been during any of their discussions over the past three years. Nihil felt pleased to have brought this much excitement into Mr. Niles's otherwise calm life. It made the old man seem younger. He looked like he could get up and walk.

"Can you walk?" Nihil asked, a question that he had always wanted to ask before but that had never seemed permissible until today.

"Yes, I walk twice a day, with great difficulty and a lot of help from Aunty and Kala Akki, one on either side. I walk here in the morning and I walk back to my bed at night. Some days I think it would be easier for them if I just stayed here and went to bed, but then I would develop other problems and that would be make life more complicated for them," he said. "We don't want that."

"If I play a game of cricket, will you be able to come to see me?" Nihil asked.

Mr. Niles laughed out loud and ran his fingers through his hair, then stabbed the air with his index finger as he declared, "If you make the team, Nihil, I will make them take me to the car, and I will have them drive me to the Oval and I will sit up in the parked car and watch you smash that ball over the boundary line for a sixer!" He swept his arm over his head, indicating the trajectory of that ball.

Nihil's smile widened as he listened, seeing everything, the Oval, Mr. Niles in the parked Morris Minor laughing, himself at the wicket holding the pose as the ball lifted away from his bat, higher, higher, out of reach of hands, of legs, far over the looping rope of the boundary where some boy, a boy such as he had once been but was no longer, would leap from the stands to catch it and take it home and dream of glory. He jumped up from his chair and enfolded Mr. Niles in a fierce embrace. "Not the Oval, not yet," he said, as the old man patted his back and kissed the top of his head, "just the school grounds."

"Ah, someday it will be the Oval. But you must start next week!"

Just like that, it was decided. Devi would come to her lessons with Raju, Nihil would stay after school for cricket, and the worrying would abate and eventually stop. Nihil lifted his face up to the wind as he walked home with Devi after her lesson that day, feeling euphoric, and Devi, seeing his delight, laughed at his side and lifted her chin up in imitation. They breathed the scent of the sal mal flowers as they went, and though Devi did not yet know the full extent of Nihil's bliss, they both felt as though they were walking on air.

Except, of course, that nothing is quite so simple. Fears that he had nourished for so long were not going to stay dormant. A curse invoked at birth about a girl, and one so full of fire and spirit as Devi, was unlikely to relinquish its hold. The care and keeping of their younger sister would occupy them all again, but for now Nihil strode onto the pitch wielding his bat like a walking stick, a grown-man tilt to his young-boy head. He was Zaheer Abbas. He was Roy Dias. He was Gary Sobers.

Out of the Blue, a Variety Show

If Nihil had found some comfort in Mr. Niles's agreement that neither he nor Nihil had war within them, even if the old man had not stated explicitly, as Nihil had hoped, that Mohan's war was nothing but a figment of a bellicose imagination, then he was merely affirming what Suren already felt. For him, the Nileses' home was a place that kept him safe not only from the political storms that were gathering in skies he had no inclination to watch, but those difficulties he was experiencing at home from his engineering-obsessed mother and his otherwise occupied father. Kala Niles's devotion to his piano playing notwithstanding, a devotion he rewarded by his continuing ability to best his previous performances, what Suren really wanted was to introduce her to his new love, the guitar, and, eventually, to move it from the increasingly disharmonious Bolling household to the quiet of Kala Niles's home. He chose to tell her about this in incremental doses.

"Tony Sansoni gave me his guitar to play, Kala Akki," he said as he was gathering up his books to leave one Tuesday afternoon.

"Huh-oh?" Kala Niles made the breath-inhaled-and-held sound she was wont to make when taken by surprise.

"Tony Sansoni told me to keep the guitar now that he's going away to study abroad," he said as he sat down to play a few weeks later.

"Huh-oh? Going abroad? Must be to Australia, no? Burghers, no?" And Kala Niles nodded sagely and smoothed the pleats on the front of her durable blouse.

"I can bring the guitar to show you if you like," he said a few months later, after Tony Sansoni had left in a whirl of farewell parties to which nicely dressed fair-skinned Burgher couples came walking arm in arm like people in English magazines, and one young man came all by himself looking teary-eyed.

"Bring, bring, haven't seen a guitar in so many years now," and Kala Niles chuckled and shook her head, thoroughly amused by Suren's offer.

At last the guitar made a quiet transition from the top of the undusted almirah, where it had been placed by his mother, to the Nileses' house, where it sat in a welcoming corner right next to the piano and waited each day for Suren to come and play it. It was an indication of Mrs. Herath's own growing preoccupation with the news outside Sal Mal Lane that she did not even notice that the guitar was gone.

To understand Kala Niles's response to Suren, we need to understand that there were very few things in her life that gave her much joy. The tennis lessons, though fun and glamorous, made her anxious each time she ran from one end of the court to the other. She imagined, and she was right, that her bottom and her bosom bounced at exactly the same time in exactly the same way and that her tennis teacher's glance flitted from one roundness to the other. The Women's Federation meetings had dissolved in a flurry of drama over a suspected affair between the brother of one of the piano teachers, himself a lay music teacher at the school, and the Sister Principal at the convent down the street. She imagined that a gay life of parties and frolicking awaited her after her conservative mother had passed on and she had found a man worth her while, but, for now, while she bode her time, she loved her garden and she loved Suren. Of these two, she would give up the garden but not Suren.

And why was it that Suren, of all the students she had ever taught, captured her imagination in this way? Sometimes the answer is simple: he made her feel that she was a good teacher whose instructional skills he, gifted though he was, needed and valued. When he sat down on the piano stool, he did so with reverence. When a new piece was placed before him, he listened carefully to what she said about its history, and whenever he finished playing a piece of music, after they had both held their posture for a few moments, his hands hovering over the keys, hers over the metronome, their very bodies hearing the final note until it had receded into silence, he would turn to her and smile. And that smile was worth every incorrigible, talentless child she had ever had to suffer in her fifteen years as a teacher. That smile told her that one good thing was enough to make a life remarkable.

If Suren had asked to bring her a full set of percussion instruments including cymbals, xylophone, *and* a snare drum, she would have said yes. A guitar by comparison was, as far as she was concerned, a sweet instrument, one made for young boys like him to strum while singing love songs to young girls his age. It held no threat to the piano that he had mastered, indeed, she saw it as a relaxing cool-down after an hour of finger exercises followed almost religiously by Chopin, Scarlatti, and Rachmaninoff before any other composers, by Suren's own insistence. So Kala Niles let him play for her, and as he played, she was not the only one who listened. Mrs. Niles listened, the music reminding her of a time before wife, mother, old lady. And Mr. Niles, too, shut his eyes and listened with a full heart, as only someone forced to hear a piano every day for the last twenty-five years could, and, listening, Mr. Niles returned once more to Jaffna, not because the music that was played or the songs that Suren sometimes sang had anything to do with the coastal town of his youth, but because the happiness he felt, sudden, swift-rising, that happiness was one he had only experienced in the North. Sometimes when Nihil came around the corner to alert Suren that their mother was home and he had to stop playing and put away the guitar, Mr. Niles would reach for his handkerchiefs to wipe away tears that had nothing to do with his cataract operation. And in those moments he would feel that he was neither full of war nor full of peace, he was simply lost.

Suren broached the topic he had been toying with for weeks after one of these sessions. "Kala Akki," he began, "would it be okay if some of my friends came and we practiced here?"

Kala Niles, who always sat beside Suren while he practiced, had just taken the guitar from him to place it against the wall. The word *practice* was associated, in her mind, with one instrument: "Practice? They also play piano?" she asked, curious.

"No, no, well, one of them plays keyboards, but actually we are starting a band and we have no place to practice. You know my mother . . ."

Kala Niles knew full well what *you know my mother* . . . meant. Indeed, it had delighted her to know that Suren's guitar playing was a secret being kept from Mrs. Herath, who got on Kala Niles's nerves by being too tidy, too compact, too perfect, and not even miserable-without-a-man to make up for it. It was unfortunate that Kala Niles knew nothing of the brittle disharmonies between Mr. and Mrs. Herath, the kind of disharmonies common to so many long-married couples, for if she had, Kala Kiles may have embraced Mrs. Herath with a warm heart, finding that blissful common ground between single women who wanted something that married women were trying to escape, and both women would have been the happier for it.

"Huh-oh! You want to bring the boys and practice for the band here?" she asked, shaking her head from side to side and squinting while also clasping and unclasping her hands.

"We don't have to come every day—"

"No, can't come every day, no. I have pupils. But you can come on Monday or Thursday," she said.

"Can we come on both Monday and Thursday?" Suren asked.

"Of course!" Mrs. Niles, listening from near the kitchen door, said. "Come and play anytime. After school you'll come?"

"Yes Aunty, after school. If we can play even for one hour that will help us to get better."

"Band, ah?" Kala Niles asked, smiling, "But mustn't stop practicing the piano, okay? If you stop practicing then I will have to put a stop to the band!" She laughed as she said this, at how unthinkable it was that such a thing would come to pass.

The first time Suren came to play with his friends, it was a Thursday and rainy and the practice dissolved into drinking tea—made by Mrs. Niles—and conversation—instigated by Mr. Niles—not to mention too much attention paid to Devi, whom none of the other boys had met before and whom they coddled because they all found Rashmi too intimidating and could think of nothing to say to her. The other Herath children had come to listen to the inaugural practice and, though there was no music played, they were not disappointed; four guitars, keyboards, and a set of drums, these were a sight to behold as they were unpacked by the older brother of one of the boys, Sanaka, and set up in the Nileses' storeroom at the back of the house. The storeroom had been cleared so that the safe and shelves were against one corner of the back wall.

"This way you can practice and even the noise we won't be able to hear too much," Kala Niles said, ushering them into the room, which had no windows but which smelled of incense. "Lit for Saraswati," she explained, pointing to the poster on the wall, as the boys sniffed and looked for the source. "Can't start music without lighting for the Goddess, after all, even band music, any music, we should do it properly." She nodded toward Suren. "Suren knows, isn't that so?"

Suren smiled and nodded. He did know. He would have asked for incense for the Hindu goddess who blessed the arts had there been none lit, sure in the knowledge that a teacher of music, even a Catholic one like Kala Niles, would know all the important rituals and would observe them no matter her own daily religious practices. As he looked around the room, Suren did not feel lighthearted, that was not a way of being that he would ever know, but he felt a lack of tension that made him happy here, in this house, with all his siblings around him, with two old people who welcomed them and cared for them and a music teacher who had space in her heart for all kinds of music.

At the other end of the street, Sonna and Mohan had finally and officially solidified their unusual friendship. Their nods slowly turned into verbal greetings and from there to commiseration and on to discussions of the various people they disliked down the road. To Mohan, that would be any-body who was Tamil, and for Sonna it was his own father, Lucas, Raju, and, for reasons he could not explain, Suren. Mohan justified his prejudices with ease, and though Sonna could illustrate his dislike for Lucas—those insect legs, that balding head—and Raju—such a tangle of ugliness, such cowardice—when it came to his father and to Suren, Sonna felt his words get twisted into knots, so he did not try. Raju, therefore, was the center of the Venn diagram of hate that the two boys put together, but in the empty spaces around, there was plenty of opportunity to torment Suren at the bus halt.

"I saw your girlfriend going for tennis," Mohan might say to Suren, referring to Kala Niles.

Or, from Sonna, "Saw Rashmi talkin' to boys up the hill."

These kinds of slurs were designed, by Sonna at least, not so much to insult Rashmi, about whom he remained conflicted, nor Kala Niles, whom he cared nothing for, as they were to trouble Suren. They failed. The words entered Suren's consciousness then left as though they had never been ut-tered. The only things that stayed were the references to the future that Sonna and Mohan made and that Suren knew carried some truth.

"When the Tigers attack, only person to help your house will be mad Lucas! And bugger will fall over an' die before he can even cross the road!" Sonna said this just as Suren boarded the bus to school and so it followed him all day long and made him extremely anxious for his family.

"Someday we'll get rid of all these bloody Tamils." Mohan said this at the end of a game of marbles that Suren had won, which soured both vic-tory and game.

"When I am in the army nobody will touch my parents. Who is going to look after your parents? Not you. You'll be playing *band-chune* some-where," he added.

"Yes, who will look after your precious sisters? Think they're too good to even talk to us. Wait an' see what will happen to them." Sonna said this with a mixture of anger and hurt that Suren picked up on and therefore was particularly troubled by; it was the kind of combination, he had learned from listening to his parents, that made ordinarily harmless people turn cruel.

Taken together, these utterances clouded Suren's usually calm mind and made him feel alternately angry, sad, and despairing, not one of which was an antidote to their barbs. It was Rose who came to his rescue, albeit unintentionally. As he stood at the bus halt one morning listening to the relentless jibes, Rose began to sing.

"Suren, listen, I am in the chorus at Methodist now. Listen to this, our new song:

> *Flow gently, sweet Afton, amang thy green braes;*
> *Flow gently, I'll sing thee a song in thy praise;*
> *My Mary's asleep by thy murmuring stream,*
> *Flow gently, sweet Afton, disturb not her dream.*

What do you think? Beautiful, no?"

Suren was tongue-tied. She sang with perfect diction. So what if the vowels dragged and the high *c* on that second *Afton* was reached for but not found, Rose was really singing! The strange nasal blockage that made her snort when she spoke disappeared when she sang and also made her voice naturally low and rich. It was the sort of voice that his band members and he had been looking for. Rashmi sang like an angel, but who wanted an angel in a band? And Devi, who could also sing, was far too young and pampered for the work that was needed. But Rose was just that right kind of tattered girl who could make it work.

"What men, don' like?" Rose asked, smiling in her habitual way but crestfallen by his lack of response. "You don' like the singing? Teachers said I'm good!"

"No, no, you are good!" Suren said, as he ran for the school bus. "I'll talk to you after school." From the window of the bus he looked out to see Rose's face bedecked in real smiles, while Sonna said something obviously spiteful to her.

So it was that the band expanded and the Nileses', who before the advent of the Herath family had little to do with the children down the lane and would never have considered opening up their home to its least savory residents, found themselves at the center of all their after-school activities and the wildest of their plans, the most exciting one being the variety show that Rose decided should be organized to celebrate the coming New Year in April. She sat, her heart full as they gathered in the living room around Kala Niles's piano and discussed her plans. She had made sure to take a body-wash and powder her underarms with the Gardenia Talc that she had been given by her mother, and, now that she combed her hair regularly, she looked and smelled positively decent.

"Aunty Kala Akki, you can play the piano," she gushed.

"Just Kala Akki is okay," Kala Niles said, casting her eyes this way and that. "No need of Aunty."

"And Nihil can do a backward song," Devi added, with more than a little pride in a brother with such a specific talent.

"Maybe not a backward song—" one of the other band members began, but he was shouted down by Mr. Niles.

"Backward song is on the program!" he yelled from the veranda.

"Rashmi, can you sing an a cappella solo?" Suren asked, not wanting to leave her out but knowing full well that none of his fellow band members would be able to play a note while she stood among them.

"What solo?" Rashmi asked, troubled, since she was not given to performing in nontraditional spaces such as this was going to be. She rubbed her top lip with her fingers. "I can sing 'The Lass with the Delicate Air,'" she suggested after some thought.

"Don't be mad. You can't sing a song like that for this lane. Sing a pop song!" Nihil said. "How about an old song? An ABBA song? You love ABBA songs."

"I suppose I could sing 'Fernando,'" she said, brightening.

The songs were chosen, a play directed by Nihil was added, subtracted, then added again, Devi and Rashmi decided to perform a Kandyan dance together in costumes they already owned, having performed the same dance at the school concert earlier that year, Suren was going to sing a new song he had learned to play, "Out of the Blue," accompanying himself on his guitar and adding a few variations he had composed, and the whole band, Rose included, was going to sing six songs, which were:

"What's Forever For" by Michael Murphey

"Under the Boardwalk" by the Drifters

"Ebony and Ivory" by Paul McCartney and Stevie Wonder (this was Rose's choice and her solo)

"Yellow Submarine" by the Beatles (a special request from Kala Niles)

"Tennessee Waltz" the Anne Murray version (in the hope that it would *cheer up the old people*)

"Kalu Kella" (for Devi, for whom the song had often been sung as a lullaby by their mother, because she *wanted to hear it sung by a real band*)

"Shouldn't we ask Ranil to join?" Rashmi asked, as she tapped her pencil on the pad of paper in which everything was being written. The pad was left over from Mr. Niles's days as a Government Agent and had his name, title, qualifications, and official address printed in flowing script on the top right corner. "He's so close in age to Devi and maybe he can do something together with her," Rashmi continued. She tapped Devi's head.

Devi, who was sitting on the floor, resting against Rashmi's legs, looked up at her sister. "He can sell tickets," Devi said. She had never quite mended her relationship with the Tissera boy after having bitten him on his arm, and was not inclined to be forced to spend what promised to be such a wonderful evening in his company.

"But he might also want to perform," Rashmi said.

"We can give him a chance at the end. If he wants to, he can sing," Nihil suggested. "Otherwise, if we go and tell him now he'll tell his parents and it won't be a surprise. In any case, he doesn't even play with us anymore." Nobody could dispute that so Devi had her way.

Suren looked around at the assembled group. Every one of them was excited except for Dolly, who remained silent. He knew that she would have liked to ask Jith to join these discussions, to sit in the Nileses' house, which was now the place where all of them gathered after school every day even if they had to come late after chorus rehearsals and cricket practices and a half a dozen other activities, but she could not. Suren had heard Jith tell her at the bus halt that Mohan had prohibited him from speaking to Tamil people and the Nileses were Tamil people, so that was that. *Even you, I don't know, he might say, because of your father's grandmother* . . . and Jith had stopped at that. Love, Suren felt, was spoiled when statements like that were made, but Dolly lacked the language to make such arguments. Suren had watched, saddened on her behalf, as she just looked down at her bright-red painted toenails and sucked on one of the pineapple star toffees Jith had bought for her.

"Dolly, do you have something special you want to do alone?" Suren asked.

Dolly stopped chewing her fingernails and looked up. "Like what, men? I don' have any talent, no."

"There must be something you can do."

"No, can' do anything," she said and giggled. "I'm useless!"

Rose looked over at her sister. Since she had joined the band, she and Dolly had drifted away from each other, she to Suren's world, Dolly to Jith's. "You can dance," she said. "You can dance that dance we learned from the Tisseras' TV, remember? The one from the *Pop in Germany* show, to that song 'I Will Survive?'"

Dolly giggled again. "Yes, you can dance," Suren said. "We don't have enough dances."

Dolly smacked her sister on the arm. "Don' have the song also. Need the song to dance."

"I have the song," one of the other boys said. "I'll bring it on a cassette for you."

And Dolly smiled and agreed to dance for their show.

"My job will be to make milk toffees and I will buy cool drinks," Mrs. Niles said when they shared the final details of their evening with her.

"Make fish cutlets too, Mama," Kala Niles pleaded, with her arms around her diminutive mother who was dwarfed in her embrace. She turned to the children, "Mama's cutlets are the best in the whole country, I can tell you. So tasty!"

Cutlets, milk toffee, cool drinks. Song, dance, instrumentals, plays. An MC (Nihil), a bandleader (Suren), a decorator (Rashmi), and a mascot (Devi). Everything for the variety show was put down on paper, a program drawn up, and Kala Niles went about trying to find someone who could lend them a microphone and speakers (for the singing) and a cassette player (for the dancing) that could be taken outdoors. There was one problem: nobody knew how to tell Mrs. Herath.

"Amma will be furious," Rashmi said to Suren as they put their heads together in their oldest-children way, to figure out how to circumnavigate the issue.

"Let's not tell until the day of the show. No, no, the *evening* of the show!" Devi suggested, ever willing to put off what she called *ugly business*, a phrase she had picked up from her mother.

"Maybe Kala Akki can tell her," Nihil said. "She's the one who has been letting us practice and everything, so maybe she can tell her."

"We can't expose Kala Akki to Amma like that. That's not fair," Suren said.

They went around like this in circles that grew and shrank every time they came up with yet another person to be the bearer of the news until they decided, in the way children always will, to ignore the problem. And it remained that way until the fourteenth of April that year, which was the day on which the Sinhalese and Tamil New Year officially concluded with the end of a day of fasting and the sharing of food and a long list of auspicious times and auspicious directions and auspicious colors, all of which were observed to the last detail in the two Sinhalese-Buddhist households, the Silvas and the Heraths, and the Hindu-Tamil household, the Nadesans, though Old Mrs. Joseph, in memory of her mother, always produced a few treats of her own as well, which allowed Raju to join in the general festivities.

And it was Raju, not out of choice but because he was that type of adult who found himself at the center of conflict, it was Raju who broke the news to Mr. and, more importantly, Mrs. Herath.

"So so, Aunty, are you ready for the variety show tonight?" he asked, as he dropped off his mother's offering of sweet milk-rice made with red rice *and* white rice and cashews, cardamom, and sultanas, a recipe that the Sinhalese families did not use, a good thing, since otherwise the same kind of milk-rice would float between the nine houses and make them all ill from lack of variety. "You can bring some of the milk-rice to have afterward, Mama put extra," he added, and then added further, "Mrs. Niles is making her famous cutlets and even, I hear, patties as well as the milk toffee. Milk toffee of course I'm not a fan," he said, making a face, all that sweetness, "but can't wait for the cutlets and the patties. Mrs. Niles makes the best ones down the whole lane. All the parties when we were small, she's the one who always made them. Even Alice can't make them like that."

Mrs. Herath absorbed all this with a held breath. The words *What variety show?* obviously could not escape her lips without voluntarily demoting herself in Raju's eyes. And if cutlets and patties were being produced by Mrs. Niles, then she would have to get Kamala to produce something of equal measure, Chinese rolls perhaps, and that would be difficult under the time constraints, not to mention the fact that every self-respecting shopkeeper for miles around had closed their business to celebrate the New Year.

"We are bringing cheese and biscuits," she said sweetly, remembering with a rush of gratitude that her husband had purchased two tins of Kraft cheese and several packages of Maliban Cream Crackers, just before the shops closed, as gifts for each of their mothers when they went to visit them for the New Year.

"Oh, cheese and biscuits!" Raju said, delightedly. "Mouth is watering! Then I'll go, Aunty, and get ready. Even Mama is going to come. So nice that Suren organized all this. And my nieces also, Rose and Dolly, also helped, I hear." And he was gone, shuffling down the front steps, struggling with the large gate, escaping into his own world.

Suren knew, when he heard his mother calling him, that the moment had come. She had been told, she had discovered, she had guessed, he didn't know what, but she knew. She called his name in a way that made it sound as though the name itself was responsible for the debacle in which she found herself, as though she felt that if he had been named something else, Senerath, for instance, or Arjuna, he would not have subjected her to this day. But here he was, he was Suren and he loved music and what is more, he loved it enough to lie to his parents. No, not his parents, *to his own mother*. Why was that considered even worse than lying to his father, or to the combined unit? Suren distracted himself with such thoughts as he buckled his belt, tied his shoelaces, ran his fingers through his hair, bowed with a debonair devil-may-care attitude to his three stricken siblings, who, each dressed for the evening, were sitting in a row on his bed, and went out to meet his fate.

No night before then or since can compare. Such music in the voices of children, such laughter in the air, such life. No day in the history of Sal Mal Lane had ever seen a spectacle like that one. The sound of a band playing, a band that was made up of one Muslim boy, two Sinhalese boys, two Tamil boys, and one Burgher girl, Rose, singing her heart out, a girl singing like she knew this was it, this moment, this day, this performance, it was all she was ever going to have to remember when she was old, that kind of music was not of this world. It was the music of days past and days that would never be. The music of still-fast friendships and the absence of tragedy. It was music that Raju might have made had he been differently born, and music that Suren carried in his soul, and music that made Mr. Niles think no longer of Jaffna but of this road, this house, this life, and these children. And though in time to come Kala Niles would feel the whiplash of Mrs. Herath's acerbic comments about having *turned your mother's home into a clubhouse*, on that evening even Mrs. Herath was moved to silence. On that night Mr. Herath listened to all of his children sing, watched all of them perform, and he did not get up even once to smoke a cigarette. Francie and Jimmy Bolling came out dressed in a sari and a suit, respectively, and walked up the road to the Nileses' house arm in arm like the Sansonis did. The Tissera and Nadesan families came, and Mrs. Tissera held her son in her lap, murmuring her commentary into the little boy's ears. The Bin Ahmed and Sansoni families sat together in the dining room chairs that had been collected from all their houses and arrayed in rows by none other than Raju, who sat with his mother in a front-row seat. Even Lucas and Alice were there, sharing the back row with Kamala and Old Mrs. Joseph's Tamil servant girl and the Nadesans' two Tamil servants, who, though they did not understand any of what was being said or sung, cheered doubly hard to make up for it.

Mr. and Mrs. Silva did not attend. They *had another engagement* for which they left early, though their sons couldn't help listening from their veranda, particularly Jith, who longed to watch Dolly dance. And Sonna did not attend, though he, too, listened as he sat in Old Mrs. Joseph's veranda, next door to where the performance was taking place.

From the front of the stage, which was no more than a set of planks laid side by side against the doors of the Nileses' garage at the end of their gravel driveway, the scent of mosquito coils and incense in the air, with his guitar in hand and a microphone near his face, Suren felt that the conduct of his life was finally aligned with his spirit.

Changes

Though Mrs. Herath had shown up with a tray draped with a linen serviette and artfully arranged with cream crackers and Kraft cheese, though she had made lively conversation with the neighbors at whose center she had sat as the seemingly proud parent of the chief organizer, and though she had cheered with gusto as each trilling last note faded away and Masonic declarations hung in the air at the end of each act in Nihil's play, though she had done all that, she was more disappointed in her children than she had ever been in her life. Of course they were all responsible for this, and each one of the four squared his or her shoulders and prepared to hoist the blame upon their backs, but she knew that the root cause was Suren. He, for reasons she could not fathom, had become the viper in their midst, who, with beatific face and dulcet tone, had lured his sisters and brother into the dark place from within which they could not just contemplate but have the brass to execute a *bali-thovila*—that was the only term she could use to describe it, a heathen's salutation to the devil himself, such as they had produced on New Year's Day.

In the interest of fairness it is necessary to note here that before she arrived on Sal Mal Lane, a long time before then, before the Herath children came into being, Mrs. Herath had been a different person. She had spent her girlhood immersed in literature and sports, her days filled with determined successes and, as the beloved firstborn of a large family, many privileges as well as indulgences. With no intimations of disaster allowed near her, these were things that had made her fearless as a young adult. If tastes lay in the direction of depth, therefore, her heart was a bottomless pit inhabited by twists and turns that only the bold would wish to traverse. If color was called for, she could have shamed a flaming tropical sunset out of the skies. But marriage and motherhood, those reliable stabilizers, had changed all that, taking her so completely out of her unfettered world and binding her so firmly and so suddenly within the one that proscribed her movements, that all she had managed to retain of her former self was a firm grasp of her mother's values, the values of an older generation: sobriety, dignity, and overall propriety. Those turns not taken, for travel overseas to study nursing, for pursuing the life of a socialite who loved her game of tennis as much as she loved her ballroom dancing, those turns had been repaved. *The footpath has become Galle Road* she liked to say when old friends stopped by, gesturing in the direction of the artery that ran along the coastal city of Colombo, *no time for dawdling.* She did not let memory bring potential into focus: the promise of balmy lanes leading to tennis courts, the thrill of a cinder track under bare feet flying, the rhythm of her slight body dancing with island grace under the Southern Cross, these things were simply old indulgences, the sort of indulgences that could destabilize the stability she had once resisted. And this show, this production, was the worst of it, a sharp reminder of a certain kind of imprudent joy.

"Whose idea was it to go and practice at that Kala's house?" she demanded to know, though she knew the answer, as well as the answer they were going to give.

"All of us thought of it," Rashmi said, surprising Mrs. Herath; of all her children, Rashmi had been her one last hope.

"Okay, then whose friends were those, those, those creatures who were in the band?"

"Mine," Suren replied, drowning out the chorus of *all of us* from his siblings.

"Yours. So, the practicing was for *your* band with *your* friends so it must have been *your* grand idea, am I right?" she asked. "Am. I. Right?" she asked again of the now silent wall of faces.

"They are my friends too," Rashmi spoke up, her words rushing together. "Two of their sisters are in my class at school, that's how Suren met them. When we all went to the birthday party, you remember? Sonali's birthday party, Amma? I wore that pink dress you made for me?"

Rashmi looked down at her feet as soon as she had finished, scolding herself for her foolishness. This kind of detail was the dead giveaway of a liar. The truth required no embellishments; it was what it was. A dress, a pink dress, no less, and one that she hated as she had hated the color since the age of nine, would have been sooner forgotten than remembered. And since when did Suren and Nihil or even Devi accompany her to birthday parties? She looked forlornly at her older brother. He smiled in that new way he had, as though he was saying *Never mind, cheer up,* and *We'll survive this,* all at the same time.

"They are my friends too," Rashmi repeated.

Mrs. Herath sat up straight, determined to put a stop to the nonsense. "Okay, then what are their last names?"

"Adamaly, Agalawatte, Jeganathan . . ." Suren said quickly.

"I didn't ask you. I asked her," Mrs. Herath snapped.

"Adamaly, Agalawatte, Jeganathan, and the last is Simon," she said, confidently, glad that Devi had taken to calling Dylan Simon "Simple Simon," which had planted the name in her head.

"Simon, Adamaly, Jeganathan" Mrs. Herath spat out each name, her rage erasing her egalitarian worldview. "*Thuppai* Burghers and Tamils and Muslims whose parents we don't even know, are these the kinds of people you should be seen with in public, let alone while prancing, half-naked, on a stage?"

The children stared at her. None of them had appeared on stage half-naked. Rose and Dolly had been *tarted up,* as Rose herself had put it, with clothes borrowed from their older sister, Sophia, but that was the extent of half-nakedness. Besides, if Adamalys and Simons and Jeganathans were not to be associated with when they attended the same schools and owned most of the instruments, then what on earth were Raju and the Bolling girls doing in the Heraths' house all the time? Clearly, their mother was reaching for straws, and if she was reaching for straws then surely they were right to have done what they did. All this passed through their minds as they stood and gazed at her obediently, their mutiny safely behind them.

Mrs. Herath looked hard at them, then cleared her throat, deciding. She stood up. "There's going to be no more band practice anywhere. If I hear that you have been going to Kala's to play guitars and drums and nonsense, you mark my words, I will take the *mirisgala* and smash her piano to bits!"

This was the type of threat Mrs. Herath was used to delivering, but those threats were usually delivered with regard to things they owned. *I'll take the skin off your backside, I'll rip that dress to shreds, I'll burn all your books, I'll cut off your hair,* that sort of thing. But to threaten to smash poor Kala Niles's source of livelihood with the heavy granite stone used by Kamala for grinding chillies? The very thought separated the children from their mother by a measure of deep consternation.

"How will we make sure that Kala Akki doesn't get into trouble?" Rashmi whispered as they all gathered under the sal mal trees up the road and discussed the new rules. The trees filled the air with the smell of buds on the cusp of blooming, nature itself gathering toward the children in solidarity.

"Don't worry about that," Suren said, his voice grim as he leaned against one of the trees. "If it comes down to it, I'll tell Amma that I will stop playing the piano forever if she won't let us practice the band."

Yes, Suren had changed. He was no longer the good boy who did what was expected, he was the boy who knew the power of promise and whom he could hold hostage by the mere threat of refusing to live up to it.

"And also if I can't keep singing," Rashmi added. "What?" she asked, as the other three turned to look at her. "I can sing too, not just Rose and Dolly, right?" She looked at Suren for confirmation.

Rashmi really could sing, at long last. Until then she had only possessed a beautiful voice, but she had lacked the yearning that turned a song into a story until she had performed in the variety show. Suren nodded, and Nihil and Devi looked at Rashmi with fresh regard.

Perhaps it was mere youth that made the Herath children and their friends believe that they were invincible and, also, invisible and inaudible. Or perhaps it was that the younger Heraths, Nihil and Devi, had cajoled Raju, who frankly did not require much prodding, Devi simply had to ask, as well as Lucas and Kamala—both won over by their attendance at the variety show—to assist them in their escapade by standing guard and watching for their mother's return. Whatever it was, their practices continued, though a few times they were almost caught when Mrs. Herath got a lift back home from one student or another, and once Lucas, and another time Raju, failed to see her until the car reached the Heraths' gate and she got out from the backseat. Those times found Raju rushing out of his house in his weight-lifting underpants, something he had given up doing after Rashmi had suggested it, trying to start up a conversation with her until Devi could alert the band members that *Amma's back! Stop! Stop! Amma's back!*

The one person who might have told their mother was Sonna, who, they had begun to notice, always seemed to be at Raju's house when they were practicing; they could see the top of his head above Raju's gate as they walked to the Nileses' house. A few times Nihil had been convinced that it was the sight of him that prevented Sonna from telling their mother and he felt grateful enough to raise his hand in a wave to the older boy, even though each time Sonna only turned away without any sign that he had seen Nihil or his greeting. He did not acknowledge Rashmi, either, even though, full of excitement at having discovered the fissures in her otherwise good-girl reputation, Rashmi made a point of turning to smile and wave at Sonna as they passed.

Down Sal Mal Lane, the change in Rashmi and Suren and even in the previously dependable Lucas and Kamala went unnoticed by the working adults distracted by the constant political upheavals around them. Upheavals that the children knew about from whispered conversations at school or from the newspapers they glanced at and then discarded, their minds on music and cricket. Even Rashmi, who had so recently made it a practice to read the papers, had given it up in the wake of the variety show.

A presidential election was announced for the first time in the history of the country, and posters that carried the elephant, the symbol of the government, far outweighed those of the key, the star, the hand, and the bell, the symbols for the Lanka Sama Samaja Party, the Communist Party, the Sri Lanka Freedom Party, and the Janatha Vimukthi Peremuna, respectively, and those posters with the elephant symbol remained on walls long after they were supposed to have been taken down. All the adults had opinions about this, some, like the Silvas, in favor, some, like the Heraths, against, but nobody felt able to protest.

The absorption of the Prevention of Terrorism Act into permanent legislation added another cylinder of fuel to simmering frictions. And what, exactly, did this Act prevent? It did not prevent acts of terrorism, nor vandalism, nor assassinations. It did not foster communal harmony. It was worded to aid in the detention of individuals *suspected* of terrorism and swiftly became a means to censorship of the press and the restriction of free speech and movement.

Nihil learned of this when he read the newspaper aloud to Mr. Niles one afternoon. "The Prevention of Terrorism Act prohibits the publication of any material, spoken word, or sign whose language could be considered to be designed to incite to violence, or which is likely to cause racial or communal disharmony or feelings of ill-will or hostility between different communities or racial or religious groups," he read, then looked up and asked, "What does that mean?"

An agitated Mr. Niles said, "It means there will be no room for us to discuss right or wrong," and he took the newspaper away from Nihil and flung it across the room, where it fell elegantly, like a lady's handkerchief. Mr. Niles's response startled Nihil and made him stay quiet for a long while until, after he was sure Mr. Niles had drifted off to sleep, he got up, picked up the paper, put it back together, and read the news quietly to himself, saving the sports pages for the end.

Nihil went home to tell his siblings that "Mr. Niles says discussions have been banned by the government," a statement they received without much ado, there being no corresponding deprivation that they could relate the news to; all the same rules remained in effect in their house, and even the neighbors who did not talk to one another did so out of choice.

But Mr. Niles was right. Within such parameters, there was no venue for the airing of grievances or passions, all of which were now tucked away inside homes and hearts that, built as they were for other pursuits, could not contain them for long.

Far beyond their games of hopscotch, cricket, marbles, and catch, things the children of Sal Mal Lane might have paid attention to were happening. Still, they refused, whenever they could, to look up from chalk squares, keyboards, love notes, theme songs, and, in Devi's case, her special bicycle rides up and down the road with Raju in attendance. The children's hide-out, tucked among the grove of sal mal trees, gave them an added sense of being removed even from the words of people like Mohan. They retreated there during the hottest time of the afternoons, to sit in its shade and do their homework or talk, sometimes sharing guavas from Mrs. Sansoni, a bag of sweets from Raju, or raw mangoes that Mr. Herath had brought home from the Sunday market. So long as they showed up to be together, to play together, they could pretend that all the larger concerns, which they certainly knew more about now, nonetheless had no bearing on them.

In the Silva household, what was bad intensified and Mohan brought home leaflets denouncing Tamils. This caused Jith to tremble in his presence and write to Dolly in secret. He dreamed each night of escape while the older Silvas waited for war with a certain smug satisfaction, more sure than they had been of anything in their lives that, when it came, they would be on the side of *the winners*, though every now and again Mrs. Silva glanced wistfully toward the Herath house and wished that she had another lady to talk to down the lane, the kind that she knew Mrs. Herath could be if she really wanted to. Until then, Mrs. Silva had to content herself in continuing to *lay the groundwork*, as she thought of it, making occasional small talk that skirted around the things she really wanted to say in the hope that when it was time, when the full force of evidence was before her, Mrs. Herath would come around to understanding that they, Mrs. Herath and Mrs. Silva, were on the same side. There would be gratitude on Mrs. Herath's part then, Mrs. Silva was sure of it.

Mohan spent more time with Sonna, standing at the bottom of the lane with young men whom Sonna introduced to Mohan as his friends though one or the other of those men was constantly being locked up and bailed out of the Wellawatte prison for misdemeanors ranging from drunken fights to petty thefts. If Mohan found their behavior objectionable, he did not say. He had developed an air of bravado and laughed loudly alongside them at bawdy jokes his mother would have blanched to hear.

"Have you seen the Heraths recently?" he might ask Sonna, egging him on. "They seem to spend all their time at that Niles house."

"Pansy fuckers," Sonna might say, though when he said those words he thought only of Suren. "They don' know anythin' 'bout anythin' but know how to sing pop songs." They smacked each other on the back and thanked their lucky stars that they were not like them, those girly homos, those cowards.

Sonna had also taken to spending nights away from home. He left after dinner and sometimes did not return for days. Neither Francie Bolling, who was afraid of both her son and her husband, nor Jimmy Bolling, who did not care, asked Sonna where he went and what he did when he was gone, though Francie Bolling did accept the wads of money he would bring back and give to her when his father was not around.

And because he rarely saw Sonna anymore and because when he did see him, Sonna was usually in a foul mood, either scolding his mother or yelling at Raju, Nihil stopped waving to him and decided that Mr. Niles was right, Sonna was a bad boy by choice.

"I don't think you should be waving to Sonna," he told Rashmi one evening as they walked to the Nileses' house, she to her lesson, he to visit Mr. Niles to discuss his progress with cricket.

"Why?" she asked, tossing her head and smiling at Nihil, at his concern about whom she chose to wave to.

"He's a bad boy," Nihil said.

"I don't care," Rashmi said. "It's not like he's my friend. I'm just waving to him." And, just to harass Nihil a little, she ran back the way they had come, stood on tiptoe, and smiled and waved with even more enthusiasm at Sonna, then waited to see what he would do. He made no move in response, though he stared at her standing there, her hair brushed out and loose down her back in its waves, the teasing in her eyes, her bangles making music, lost in his own dark imaginings. Eventually, when it was clear that he would not respond, Rashmi turned away, her good humor gone.

"I told you," Nihil said.

Rashmi did not disagree.

Despite their continued difficulties with Sonna, in the Bolling house, with two girls engaged in one way or another with "good" families, Jith having been disassociated from the politics of his parents by a sleight of mind that weighted his timidity more and his origins less, the older Bollings regarded themselves as having done well by their children. They began to dress better and speak more soberly. There were fewer arguments and more appearances in public.

In the Nileses' house, three people were revived by the daily presence of children who slammed doors and creaked gates and muddied the floor and dropped crumbs that brought with them armies of red ants that made Kala Niles get down on her hands and knees at night, rubbing the edges of doorways with kerosene oil in a halfhearted attempt to keep them away. Those children turned the house of the Unmarried and the Dying into a house full of the Future.

In the Herath household, much had changed, mostly for Rashmi, who had discovered what Devi had known all along: life was too short for rules made by nuns and older women for little girls. It took a while for her lay teachers and nuns to realize that Rashmi was no longer the golden girl she had once been, because she had earned that time by doing what every smart student knows how to do: be impeccable in behavior and superior in classwork for the first four weeks of school when teachers were distracted and welcomed any evidence of scholarship, and ride the glory until the end of the year. Not this year.

When the second-term tests came around and the report cards were handed out, the evidence was, well, evident: three B's sat, one under the other, for Sinhala, Buddhism, and Maths.

"I am quite sure that she studied hard for these tests, Sister," Mrs. Herath declared as she sat across the desk from the Sister Principal, Sister Stanislaus, and tried not to look at her husband. Whatever her feelings about Rashmi at home, she refused to allow someone *from the outside* to cast doubt on her daughter's character.

Mr. Herath leaned forward, amicably. "Yes, there is no need for all this fuss. She always gets A's, she'll get A's again." He leaned back, satisfied with his contribution and thinking ahead to the afternoon of meetings he had to attend.

Mrs. Herath herself did not feel up to paying too much attention just then to Sister Stanislaus. Like every other adult in the country, she, too, was caught up in contemplating the outcome of the presidential elections, which were barreling toward them. Right now, her mind was on the possibility of curfews and the necessity to stock up on rice and dhal and tins of Jack Mackerel.

Sister Stanislaus picked up a stack of Rashmi's report cards going all the way back to kindergarten, all of them pale blue, and rapped them on the desk. She then spread them out and examined each one through glasses that perched at the tip of her nose, the long golden beads of the chain on which they were hung swinging gently next to her sharp-featured face. Finding nothing there that could really qualify as a problem, but for this last set of results, she looked up finally and turned her gaze on Mr. Herath.

"Well, you must be very busy, Mr. Herath, with the elections?" she said.

Mrs. Herath stiffened. Her husband had barely made it to this appointment, brushing it off with a *summons to the prime minister's office* comment that even she, despite her years of experience listening to him, could not decipher.

"I am not involved in the elections," he said, chuckling with amusement, "I am an official. My job will be to oversee procedure and verify the count at the polling booths. And vote, of course. I'll be doing that."

"It is unfortunate that the country does not seem to be going the way we want it to," Sister Stanislaus said. Neither of the Heraths said anything, and she continued. "The whole business last year with the riots, you know, it was not easy for our Tamil girls."

"There was no rioting here," Mr. Herath said mildly.

"No, of course not," Sister Stanislaus said, airily, as though riots and convents would never inhabit the same universe. "Not here. Still, unrest anywhere . . ."

"Those were some isolated incidents. The army should have been dispatched right away, but these jokers . . ." Mr. Herath felt a sharp pain in his sandal-clad right foot. He glanced at his wife. ". . . anyway, we'll see. The elections may change everything."

"Oh, *our* girls come from families that support the government, no doubt about it," Sister Stanislaus said, the note of accusation quite obvious. Her hierarchy of alignments was so clear to the Heraths it was almost as if she had listed it off: Catholics of any race, Hindu Tamils, Muslims, and last of all the group to which the two of them belonged, the anti-government Sinhalese-Buddhists.

"Of course," Mrs. Herath said, smoothly, "and my husband works for the government too. As do I, after all, as a teacher I too am a government servant, isn't that so? And our children are all good students," and here she faltered before finishing, "all of them."

"Well, Devi—" Sister Stanislaus said.

"Devi is doing quite well, according to her teachers," Mrs. Herath said, "and we are here to discuss Rashmi."

And though Rashmi was discussed for twenty more minutes, no compromise was struck, for the Heraths would not agree that there was anything amiss with a child with three sudden B's after a lifetime of A's. Fresh on the heels of this meeting, when the new class monitors were being chosen, and Rashmi was not only nominated, the nomination was seconded, and the votes were cast by an overwhelming majority in her favor, the class teacher, a nun named Sister Francesca, decided unilaterally to eliminate the function of class monitor.

"You had to go and open your mouth and talk about governments and jokers, didn't you?" Mrs. Herath berated her husband, when Rashmi told her. "Now they'll be penalizing the girls until they graduate."

"They should go to a different school, then," Mr. Herath said. "We don't need to pay school fees to a pack of anti-Buddhist, anti-Sinhalese . . ."

"It's not about being anti-Buddhist and anti-Sinhalese. It's about keeping your mouth shut. Rashmi was doing so well and I'm sure she would have been made a prefect. Now even that is not certain."

Listening hard outside the door, Rashmi tried to feel a pang of disappointment, but all she felt was sheer delight.

Yes, much had changed in the Herath family, between Nihil's return to cricket, Rashmi's ascent as a performer and her corresponding descent as a scholar, and Suren's steadfast march toward the kind of independence that would never again be controlled by parental expectation, he had shrugged off that yoke conclusively. One person remained the same: Devi.

An Election

Well, one thing had changed for Devi. Thanks to Nihil's return to cricket, Raju was now her constant guardian. Each afternoon, when she returned home from school, and after she had her lunch, and finished her homework according to Nihil's timetable, she went to the gate to holler for him.

"Uncle Raju! Uncle Raju!" she would call, waiting until she could see him to dart outside her gate.

"Coming coming, Uncle Raju is coming," Raju would say, shuffling into his slippers and buttoning up his shirt as though he had been surprised, though he had been sitting on his front veranda since half past noon, a full hour and a half before Devi even got home, reading and rereading the newspaper and waiting for purpose.

Most days, Devi's request was for the bicycle, which had first rested against the wall just inside the door to Raju's weight-lifting room and then, because he was worried that he might trip and break it with one of his barbells, had been moved to the Heraths' unused garage. On those days the procedure was always the same.

"I can ride the bike without you, Uncle Raju," Devi would say, after Raju wheeled the bike out for her. She would stand there, her hands behind her back, dressed in some outfit that Kamala had laid out for her, a freshly ironed T-shirt and pedal pushers usually, brown sandals on her feet, the picture of competence.

"My god, no!" Raju would respond as though this had never been suggested before. "Youngest child, you fall, what will your mummy say? And daddy? Mummy and daddy will kill me! I have to hold the bike."

And hold it he would, pushing the bike up and down the road, sweating and huffing as Devi, now ten and a half and lankier by the day, with her hair pulled into tight braids as she joined her older sister in trying to make her hair grow as long as possible as fast as possible, sat on the bumpy seat with her toes clutching the center bar. The bike, which had developed a thin creak that sounded with each revolution of the wheels, a sound that no amount of oil would fix, provided its own music.

On Fridays he walked Devi over to Kala Niles for her piano lessons and sat and waited in the enclosed veranda with Mr. Niles—who never spoke to him but was, nonetheless, companionable in his silence—until her lesson was over; if Mr. Niles missed Nihil's company, he kept it to himself. He contented himself with listening to the children, their comings and goings, their faraway voices, imagining their out-of-sight play.

On some days it was a walk to Koralé's shop to buy sweets, crossing the main road with Devi carried on his back. On others it was playing 304 with a pack of cards depicting the Indian Pacific rail line, a pack of cards that Raju's father had brought back from a trip to Australia, a trip after which Raju had been convinced that nothing less than a sixty-five-hour train journey over 4,352 kilometers from Sydney to Perth would suffice to distinguish the blessed from the ordinary. Some days there was nothing to do but sit in the swinging chair and talk. On those days Raju would forget himself and bring up the topics that made Devi's siblings reconsider the wisdom of leaving her with Raju every afternoon.

"Elections are coming. Daddy told you who is going to win? He must be knowing by now, no?" Raju asked as he stood up from his usual spot on the front steps and dusted the seat of his pants.

"How would he know? They haven't even voted yet!" Devi said, climbing her bare feet up the rope of her swing. She flexed her toes and wondered if she could get Rashmi to paint her nails pink with the bottle of nail polish that she had got as a birthday present from the Bolling girls.

Raju's eyes widened in alarm. "Big people in the government know everything. Then definitely Mama is right. Bad things are coming." Which sent Devi talking nineteen to the dozen at the dining table about all the trouble that was soon to be upon them.

On another occasion Raju said, "It seems that we are going to have no more elections in our country. People are going to be asked, do you want elections or do you not want elections, yes or no," he said, wagging his index fingers, first the right, then the left. "Then it will be over."

"Only parties have elections, Uncle Raju," Devi said. "There are no question elections." She pushed off the Asoka tree with her feet so her swinging chair spun and spun tighter and then unwound itself at top speed.

"Even Lucas has heard this. You ask him. No, you ask Daddy when he comes and tomorrow you can tell me."

But Mr. Herath was not forthcoming. The question annoyed him and, catching a frown from her mother and warning glances from all three of her older siblings, Devi gave up trying to find out about the new kind of election of which Raju had spoken. Instead, she took to counting the number of times each of the party symbols appeared on the posters plastered on the walls of the Empire Theatre, which she had to pass on her way to school and back, the one that showed Tamil films, the only facing wall big enough to take such abuse even though there was a clearly written statement on each section of that wall, in neat red letters in all three languages, Tamil, English, and Sinhala, that read:

> *Vilambarangal otta koodathu*
> POST NO BILLS
> *Danveem Alaveema Thahanam*

On the day of the presidential elections, the Herath children spent the day at home, coloring maps, listening to coverage of the event on the radio, and watching their father, when he returned after his election duties, for his reaction to the results. They listened as their mother tried to draw him out with various statements.

"Kobbekaduwa didn't have a chance without the Bandaranaikes' support," Mrs. Herath said, and the children felt that this was meant to console their father. "See what happened to the old Left? If Colvin and Wijeweera and Kobbekaduwa had all joined together, they could have beaten JR. Ponnambalam would have taken the Tamil vote and we could have still won the elections." When even this drew no response, she said, "Executive President, that's all we need," and her voice carried more disgust than the children had ever heard in it before, even with regard to the variety show.

And still their father said nothing and they were not sure if he agreed or disagreed or whether there was some other relevant information that they were missing, so they put away their neatly printed election-day map of the country that had come as an insert with the morning paper, and the crayons that Rashmi had been using to color parts of it in like this:

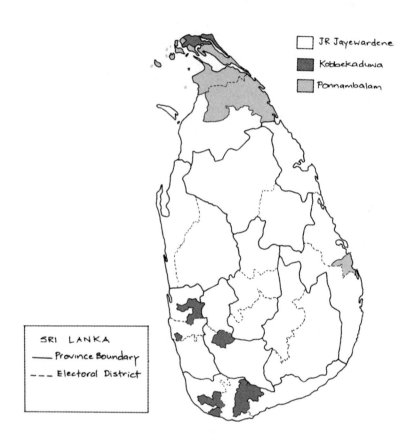

SRI LANKA PRESIDENTIAL ELECTION, 1982
Winners of polling divisions

☐ JR Jayewardene
▓ Kobbekaduwa
▒ Ponnambalam

SRI LANKA
—— Province Boundary
--- Electoral District

as they listened to the news, and went about their business as though it was just an ordinary day that had ended.

Devi, mimicking her siblings and their noncommittal expressions, announced to Raju that, "JR has won, but we will have to wait and see if that is a good thing or a bad thing."

"I don't like JR," Raju told her, shaking his head. He was leaning against the door to his mother's living room while Devi and Old Mrs. Joseph listened. He was wearing a green shirt that day and Devi had assumed that he was a supporter of the new president, since she herself shunned the colors of cricket teams she did not support, so she was a little taken aback. "Mama also doesn't like. Nobody likes except," and he lowered his voice to a whisper, "the Silvas."

"Why do the Silvas like JR?" Devi asked, whispering back.

"Silvas like JR because they don't like us Tamils, that's what," Old Mrs. Joseph said. She looked away from Devi and loosened and then reset her dentures with two sharp clicks.

Devi, who was sitting on the front steps to Old Mrs. Joseph's veranda, turned her face toward the Silvas' house and pointed in that general direction. "They are going to be army boys," Devi said, feeling quite sure that this information was fresh and liking how it all sounded coming out of her mouth, *army boys*.

"Hah. Army boys? That's all that's missing," Old Mrs. Joseph said. "You know what has happened now? JR is going to change the constitution so he and his thugs can stay in power for another six years. Until 1989 we will be under his thumb!" She made the sound of spitting, though no spit emerged from between her lips, and jabbed the thick pad of her right thumb hard onto her left palm. "I'll be dead by then and thank god!"

"I don't think so. I don't think things like that will happen," Raju said, shifting from side to side in a state of agitation while Devi watched first one face, then the other. She liked the thumb gesture and planned to use it on her siblings later that day.

"Happened happened. Already said and done. November fifth. Even our Tamil party, supposed to speak for us, those TULF cowards abstained from even voting, they just let it pass. Only four votes, can you believe it? Four votes against, and those also from the Sinhalese people! Where were the Tamil leaders?" She counted off on her hand, tapping the fingers of her left hand with the index finger of her right hand, "Mrs. B's son Anura, of course, then Lakshman Jayakody, Ananda Dassanayake, and Sarath Muttetuwegama from the Communist Party! Only those four voted against. So who is going to help us now? You tell me." She swiveled around to look at Devi, fixing her with a glare. "Go and ask daddy. *Who* is going to help us now?"

"Tha does not like JR," Devi said quickly, not liking the look on Old Mrs. Joseph's face. "He likes Mrs. B. Since Mrs. B is not there now I don't think he cares."

"Nice not to care, I suppose, for some people." And Old Mrs. Joseph said no more.

Devi's Secret

On a Saturday afternoon in November, after the presidential elections that had disappointed most of the inhabitants of Sal Mal Lane, but before the referendum—yes, there was one, and Raju was right, about the process if not about the question, the question being *Should the present parliament be extended for another six years, yes or no?*, a question that could loosely be translated by most people to mean just about the same thing that Raju had imagined it to be—Mr. Herath borrowed Mr. Niles's Morris Minor to drive Raju to his body-building competition.

Given that members of the armed forces consistently won these events, only Devi imagined that Raju Joseph was going to tear up the competition. Before they left, she gave Raju a medal she had designed and colored in, complete with pin, that read *No. 1 Mr. Sri Lanka* with the word *Champion* below it underlined three times in blue and gold, these being the most glorious colors she could think of.

Mr. Herath simply said, "Just do your best," and patted Raju congenially on his back as he they parted company, Raju to walk toward where the competitors gathered, he to the spectator stands.

The fact that Raju did not place in any category—he belonged neither in the under twenty-one nor in the over forty-five age groups and had to compete with the military men in the seventy-five-kilogram category—and the fact that the other men, by and large, had laughed when Raju strode up dressed in what they called *jungi*, and attempted to pick up his second barbell and failed—these facts were quickly carried aloft by Sonna, who had made it a point to be present at the debacle, riding three buses to get there. They were repeated every time Raju stepped out of his house and walked past Jimmy Bolling's house. Raju took all this in stride, determined to try again, determined to better himself through reading the news and listening to the Heraths, and, most of all, determined to uphold his end of the bargain of looking after Devi. It was that last determination that resulted in Devi nearly losing her guardian altogether.

One day when he was pushing her up and down the road on the old bicycle, Sonna came out of his house and began to tease him.

"Go go go! Build up some leg muscles at leas'. Can' even get a woman so pushin' a girl here an' there, no?" He looked at Devi and hesitated, then said, very quickly, "Better be careful. Might try some funny business with you."

Raju came to a stop, wheeled the bicycle back to the Heraths' gate, and quietly asked Devi to dismount. "Raju Uncle has some work to do darling. I will come and wheel you tomorrow," he said, after he put the bike away.

Something in his tone worried her. She climbed the Asoka tree and balanced on its farthest branch so she could peer down the otherwise hidden part of the road to watch what would happen next.

She saw Raju walk up to Sonna and say something inaudible. Sonna laughed and then Raju punched Sonna in his face. Sonna tried to back off and Raju continued punching and punching and punching Sonna until he was up against the aluminum fence, and with each punch Devi cringed and tears sprang to her eyes because she suddenly felt sorry for Sonna, who looked skinny and weak and just a boy next to Raju, and soon there were Mr. and Mrs. Bolling running out, Mrs. Bolling picking up Sonna but Mr. Bolling, Mr. Bolling only shaking Raju's hand and slapping Sonna across his cheek with his good hand before going back into their house. Sonna shoved his mother away and ran down the street and out of Devi's sight. Mrs. Bolling, who had fallen against the fence, stood up and brushed the front and back of her dress and glanced up and down the road before she went back into their house. Devi watched Raju walk slowly back up the road, and she could see from her perch that when he came up to his gate he started crying. He looked shamefaced and angry and he stood there wiping his tears with the sleeves of his shirt like a child and then opened the gate and went into his garage.

Devi did not know, and why should she, what to do when an adult cried. She and her brothers and sisters had lain awake at night listening to their mother cry sometimes, not often, but even once was too often, wasn't it? And in their company she had felt assured that whatever it was that made her mother cry, she was not to blame for it. But Raju's tears, she was convinced, had something to do with her. What was it that Sonna had said? She couldn't remember. She had always been afraid of him, his way of turning up just when she was doing something wrong, so she avoided him, shut out his words so she wouldn't have to listen. Besides, when she was being looked after by Raju, she only concentrated on her own activities, not his. And now this had happened.

She dried her eyes and stayed a long while up in the tree, grateful for the way it hid her in its firm branches, among foliage and flowers that matched the green-and-white floral print of her skirt and blouse. She picked flower after flower and sucked on them, her thirst unslaked by the minuscule drop of syrup within each bloom, alternately wondering if she should go and see if Raju was okay, though something told her she should not, and peering down the road to see if Sonna had returned from wherever it was he had run to, and wondering whether anybody had tended to his wounds. She watched Nihil go to the gate and look up and down the road, and she listened as he asked Rashmi, who had come outside, if she knew where Devi was. Finally, when she heard Nihil calling for her from somewhere inside the house, she slid down the tree and went inside, not knowing whom to tell or what question to ask.

"Where were you? I was looking all over for you!" Nihil said, when she came inside.

She poured herself a glass of water and took her time drinking it, noisily, with pauses accentuated by the kind of gulps and wheezes that she was far too old to be making. "Nowhere," she said when there was no more water left and she was forced to put the glass down. "I was just in the tree." And she slipped away from him before he could ask her why she had been hiding.

After that incident, though she did not call it that, she called it *That Day*, Raju became despondent. He still arrived, reliably flustered and in his shabby spruced-up state, he still delivered bits of information that Devi carried in turn to the Heraths' dining table, and he still brought her sweets, but there were fewer and fewer occasions on which he would agree to push her up and down the road on the bicycle, her favorite pastime.

"Can't today Devi, didn't you hear? Vijaya Kumaranatunga has been put in jail," and he explained, mournfully, that the handsome and popular actor whom Devi only knew as a film star was also the husband of Mrs. Bandaranaike's daughter, and that the government—JR, to be precise— had put him in jail so he could not campaign for the opposition party.

Devi practiced all day so she could make the announcement at dinner: "Raju says that JR says that Vijaya Kumaranatunga is in a Naxalite conspiracy," she said, making Mr. Herath smoke an entire cigarette and light another one and finish that too before he sat down to dinner and launched into a lecture that referred to multiple political parties by their initialisms, the NSSP, the SLFP, the TULF, the JVP, and the LSSP, not to mention the CP and the ACTC, and which was so rich in anecdote and cross-reference and digression that it wore them down and stripped his children—but not his wife, who did listen to these lectures—of any modicum of knowledge and every last shred of interest they may have possessed to begin with.

"Too complicated," Devi said to Raju the next day. "We have too many parties in our country, that's what I think. Better if we just had SLFP and JVP, because Tha likes the SLFP but I like the JVP because of their parade."

"Ah? You like the JVP?" Raju asked, smiling a little and no longer quite so crestfallen. "I don't like them much. Anyway, now even they have been banned from the elections. Government is banning everybody. Soon we'll have nothing but the UNP," he said.

"Then the Silvas will be happy," Devi said in a whisper, though she did not care either way whether there was one party or ten so long as her world was bordered by flowering trees with branches for her to climb or gather under with her sister, her brothers, and her friends, so long as her swing hung in the same way it did, so long as Nihil kept getting better at cricket, so long as Suren and Rashmi never got caught with their band practices, and so long as Raju kept showing up to take care of her.

This last Raju did, though he did not walk down the street to buy sweets for her if Sonna was outside the Bollings' house, and though he still pushed her on the bicycle, whenever he saw Sonna about the place he found an excuse to put the bike away and play cards.

The referendum, held three days before Christmas, turned out far too many people who remembered the austerity of a previous government, or far too many people willing to intimidate this one or that one or steal ballot boxes or stuff them, or far too many who mistook the symbol the government used, a lamp, for something illuminating and good, because it resulted in a 54 percent win for the government. It gave legitimacy to the executive president, a man who had, upon winning the general election five years before, first amended and then replaced the constitution, to pave the way for an executive presidency—one that would allow him to serve as the head of state, the head of the executive and of the government and the commander in chief of the armed forces—a man who was despised by too many to be effective and too many for the elections to be deemed free and fair, all of which meant that already simmering resentments began to be voiced more loudly.

And perhaps it was a collective despair that lurked about the streets that turned mean and unsafe for ordinary people, people like those on Sal Mal Lane, or perhaps it was only that good attracts the countervailing force of bad, that some people are born to suffer and others not, for, a few days before Christmas, Raju was beaten within an inch of his life.

Revenge

Devi did not know why Raju did not come that day when she called out to him. The Christmas holidays had begun, but nobody else was available to play with her. Nihil had left to play cricket with his teammates at Royal, Suren was deep into practicing a difficult piano piece whose name she could not pronounce but that sounded so agitated that it made her anxious, and Rashmi was writing letters to all her friends, crossing each one off on a list before her.

"Uncle Raju! Uncle Raju!" Devi yelled, and then, when he did not reply, she glanced back at her house to make sure that nobody was watching, and she crossed the street and slipped in through Old Mrs. Joseph's gate and yelled some more, standing outside his garage.

"I don't know where he has gone, child," Old Mrs. Joseph said, her forehead knitted with worry, when Devi finally climbed the steps to the veranda and asked. "He left around two thirty to go and get a bicycle bell from the shop at the junction and I haven't seen him since. Getting a bit worried." She rubbed her furrowed brow and stood up to lean against one of the pillars that supported the roof of the veranda and looked down the road.

"I will go and see," Devi said, though she was not sure how she would do this since she was not allowed to cross the big road with all the traffic or, indeed, go anywhere by herself. She went back to her house and tried to get Kamala to come with her.

"*Aney Baba*, I can't come," Kamala said, pulling her upper lip over her large front teeth. "Madam will be angry if I take you and go down the road!"

Kala Niles, when asked, said, "Don't worry, darling, he'll come home. Must have gone to see the new Tamil film or something like that. You practiced today?" Which made Devi back away and leave because she knew Raju did not go to see Tamil films and no, she had not practiced today or yesterday either.

"If Nihil was here, *he* would come with me to look for Uncle Raju," she said in Rashmi's hearing, but got no response.

At Jimmy Bolling's house she heard a terrible argument before she even reached the door and did not dare go inside.

So there really was no help for it but to go next door and see if Jith would agree to look for Raju. "Jith!" she called, "Jith! Jith!" and when he came out, "I can't find Uncle Raju. Can you find him for me?"

And because his parents had gone Christmas shopping, and, more importantly, because Mohan had gone out with Sonna and this had been troubling him, Jith agreed to go. When he returned, almost an hour later, however, all he would say to her was that Raju was sick and in the hospital, and then he went to Old Mrs. Joseph and told her which hospital.

If Devi were older, wiser, she would have known immediately from the look on his face that Jith was terrified and upset and that the cause of those feelings was something new, some fresh viciousness that he had not previously entertained but with which he was now acquainted and would be for the rest of his life. But she was neither, so she merely tagged along with him to visit Old Mrs. Joseph, and tagged along with Old Mrs. Joseph and Jimmy Bolling when they borrowed Mr. Niles's Morris Minor and set off for the nearest hospital, which happened to be the privately run Sri Lanka Nursing Home on High Street, not far from their lane. Since neither Rashmi nor Kamala had been willing to participate in the search for Raju, Devi decided that there was no reason to tell them where, exactly, she was going, for which she was forgiven after the fact, given the gravity of the situation.

To see Raju on any usual day before or after weight lifting, before or after brushing his teeth and getting ready for the day, anytime, really, was disconcerting to those who were not accustomed to the composition of his face and form and unfamiliar with his benevolence. But to see Raju as he lay on a stark hospital bed, a needle in his arm and every part of his limbs crisscrossed with bandages, to see the brace that separated his neck from his head for, quite possibly, the first time in his life, to see the forearm that was in a cast, and the face that was so bruised no bandages had been applied, only minuscule stitches and clear ointments that glistened and sparkled like unctuous tears, this was a sight for the brave of heart.

Devi stood quite still by the door when she saw him. "What happened to you, Uncle Raju?" she asked in a quiet voice.

"He can' talk," Jimmy Bolling said, his mouth turned down. Old Mrs. Joseph merely sank into a chair and put her head in her hands and began to pray.

Devi stepped forward and touched the cast on Raju's left hand. "Uncle Raju," she whispered, "I went to look for you but you were not there. Then Jith helped me," she said, "Silvas' Jith. He's the one who found you."

Raju's eyes opened and shut once, and no matter what else was said or by whom, they remained closed until it was time for them to leave. He listened to the sound of their footsteps, to Devi's voice, which cut over those of the adults, asking when he might come back home. If he was touched by that voice, those words, he did not express it. He took in the empty room and remained quite still, letting the pain in his body pin him down, lying there as though he were already dead.

Nothing that is good happens because of rumor; rumor is the harbinger and mascot of evil. And rumor had it that evening that Raju had molested a young Tamil girl who lived on Kalyani Avenue, and that *unknown people* in that neighborhood had caught him and beaten him up and left him for dead, which is how Jith had found him, lying face down, whimpering in pain, while a crowd of people from the houses on Kalyani Avenue gathered: Indian Tamils, the kind who dressed with fastidious care and lived conservative and private lives, their voices kept low, their evenings ending early, people who rarely fraternized with anybody outside their quiet neighborhood, which consisted entirely of others like themselves who lived by the same decorous rules. Nobody asked how Jith might have known to look for Raju down Kalyani Avenue, nobody wondered why the thugs on Sal Mal Lane—for Mohan and Sonna *were* thugs, everybody agreed—had no knowledge of the thugs who might be living on Kalyani Avenue, which was, after all, just two streets away from theirs. Nobody asked why Sonna and Mohan grew even more cocky as they talked together, or why several men, not boys, from the slums behind Lucas's house, took to standing at the end of their road, making lascivious remarks at Rashmi and Devi and dark statements about Tamils in the hearing of Kala Niles. Or they did ask, but in a silence decked in horror and fear.

By the time Raju returned to Sal Mal Lane from the hospital, Christmas had come and gone, and though he could now speak, he would say nothing about the assault he had suffered except *I never went to Kalyani Avenue. They took me there*, but who *they* were he did not know and would not guess at though by the way he said all those things it was clear that he had his suspicions and that they were correct.

"Don' know *why* Raju had to go to Kalyani Avenue," Francie Bolling said, the night he came home from the hospital.

"Bugger is crazy, that's why! Crazy and girl-mad!" Sonna, home for one of his increasingly rare visits, and this one had been long, said. "I always knew it."

"But he's not like that," Rose insisted.

"If I ever find out that you were there that day . . ." Jimmy Bolling said, and the trembling of his hand as he served himself a soup with very few vegetables was enough to end all conversation for the rest of that meal and for many meals after that.

"Damn good someone taught him a lesson," Mrs. Silva said, watching Mr. Niles's Morris Minor turn into Old Mrs. Joseph's driveway with Raju in the backseat. "Now maybe the Heraths will stop having him *kusukusufying* with that Devi all day long!"

She and Mr. Silva and Mohan were all standing in the veranda peering through the jasmine plants that now completely wreathed the surrounding trellises, providing scent, shade, and absolute privacy while also enabling them to watch the activities of her immediate neighbors. Jith was nowhere to be found; unbeknownst to anybody, including Rose, he was meeting Dolly on the road leading to the temple, where, incense and oil in hand, they planned to spend an hour or so inside the temple grounds.

"I'm not at all surprised that he got beaten up by the people on Kalyani Avenue. That place is full of Tamils," Mr. Silva said. "All thugs, obviously."

"But he deserved it," Mohan said. "Even Tamils have to fight back."

Neither of his parents questioned Mohan's moment of charity toward the Tamil people against whom he had been conducting such an unrelenting and personal crusade.

In the Herath household, Mrs. Herath prefaced her words with a regretful sigh. "Anyway, Devi, you are getting old enough to look after yourself now, so better stay away from Raju."

"Uncle Raju did not do anything wrong," Devi said, as she bent to fasten her sandals, ready to run out of the door to check in on Raju.

"I know, I know, I am sure he didn't do anything wrong, but in any case it is not appropriate for you to spend so much time with him."

Nihil remembered the references to Raju in his notebook, the notebook that he rarely looked at anymore, his mind so full of cricket, but that he had opened again in the wake of Raju's hospitalization. "Yes, better that you stay here," he concurred.

"Even the Bin Ahmeds say it was Tamil people," Mrs. Herath said, as if Devi's disassociation from Raju had been decided. "They never speak ill of anybody, so they must be right."

"Bloody nonsense," Mr. Herath said, "I don't believe that Raju is capable of doing what they said he did. Lucas told me that it was Sonna and Mohan and some thugs from the Elakandiya."

And Devi knew right then that what Lucas had said was true. *That Day* came back to her in a flash, and that other day when Jith had gone to find Raju, and this day, today, when she was being told she could not see her Uncle Raju. As she listened, some innocence slipped away from her, a sloughing that she was too young to regret, for she knew that she could no more mention *That Day* than she could announce that she had kept a secret from her siblings, no more mention *That Day* than crucify Raju with yet another mark against him. She remained silent and vowed to choose disobedience. Nobody, not Nihil, not her mother, would be able to stop her from talking to Uncle Raju, from sharing information about politics, which she did not understand, and asking for sweets, which she understood with every part of her being, and learning, as she had resolved to do from the very first day, how to ride that bicycle, the one bicycle that existed down the entire lane, the bicycle that interested none of the other children, except in passing, their worlds full of music, cricket, and yearnings that she was still too little to care about.

By the time Raju was free of his bandages, but not of his cast, the Herath children had followed in Devi's footsteps, taking him back into their fold as though his character had never been defamed. Raju, for his part, kept a certain respectable distance that he felt was called for under circumstances he could not control. Which is why Devi was finally able to ride the bicycle without his shuffling step beside her, without his awkward but strong hands on the handlebars, and without his constant instruction.

"The bike is too big for you," he began, holding on to it with his right hand while Devi waited. "Still, with my cast, Uncle Raju cannot take you on the bike. So I am going to show you how to ride it without sitting."

Devi did not need to be shown. She knew how to do the things that all children know how to do without being taught: to climb a tree, to jump into deep water, to break rules, to hide, to take without asking. "I know, Uncle Raju," she said, impatient to get her hands on the bicycle. She bent down and cuffed the bottoms of her new jeans, rolling them midway up her calf.

"I'm ready, let go," she said.

"I got Lucas to take it and get it nicely polished again. Even that noise is now a little less."

"Okay okay." She tossed her ponytail as she said this. These days, when she returned from school, she combed her hair into a ponytail that swung left to right as she walked, the happy result of night after night of braids so tight they hurt her head.

She placed her foot on the pedal, swung her leg over the bar, and took off up the road with Raju yelling "No coming down! Only ride up! Wheel the bike down!"

Which she did, not wanting to upset him, his arm still in a cast, and also because he stood and blocked the way right on the center of the road between his house and hers so that there would have been no way for her to ride the bike down without crashing into him. It was sufficient, this amount of freedom, this forward motion as the wheels turned before her pedals, as the bike carried her up the road, farther and farther, and it seemed that she herself was a kite whose ascent would go on and on.

Mohan and Jith Are Punished

Nothing particularly bad had happened in school that day. Mohan was simply bored. He doodled in his exercise book when he was supposed to be constructing grammatically correct sentences in Tamil, while, next door, the Tamil students did the same in Sinhala during the mandatory period of instruction designated for the study of a *Link Language*. Mohan refused to study Tamil. Instead, he looked around the classroom and considered the backs of the thirty-five boys who sat in front of him. Now that they were in the upper school, all of them wore long white pants and short-sleeved white shirts, and, from where he sat, they looked identical. He decided to classify them. He drew two columns. The first for the Definitely Sinhalese, the second, Definitely Tamil, each subdivided into rich/poor. As he expected, most of the Tamil students were wealthy, and most of the Sinhalese students were poor. Among the poor Sinhalese students he further categorized the Sinhalese-Buddhist students as being the poorest of them all. He included himself in that latter group.

The trouble began when he shared his list with his band of friends during the interval, when the classrooms in the redbrick buildings were abandoned and the children rushed the grounds to play, kicking up the dust and beginning to sweat almost immediately in the heat. Before long, a large area of the school yard was abuzz with the information that new statistics had come to light about the social discrepancies between the Tamils and the Sinhalese in the school. Not much later, half a dozen fistfights had broken out over this information, some Sinhalese-Buddhist children claiming they were just as wealthy as if not more wealthy than their Tamil classmates, some Burgher-Catholics asking why there was no information about them. For the most part, the Tamil students remained silent, neither in affirmation nor in denial, but that did not matter, even the ones who said nothing were drawn into the melee anyway.

Mohan wished that he had been the only one to be hauled before Mr. Gunasekara, the headmaster, when the source of the information was discovered, but no. When he paused to glance through the glass doors before entering the headmaster's office, there stood his tremulous brother, eyes wide with fear, looking like he would piss in his pants. Mohan straightened his collar, smoothed his hair down, and strode into the office. He was thankful that he had recently got it cut even shorter, a buzz like the soldiers he had seen in an American magazine. He looked neither to the left nor to the right, at the shelves packed with books and the filing cabinets full of student records and the walls with framed photographs of groups of prefects whose behavior had been impeccable, who were destined to bring nothing but credit to the school. He stared straight ahead at the brown desk and did not meet the eyes of the headmaster. As he came to a stop next to Jith, he had a powerful wish that the room was larger, that his shoulder was not quite so close to that of his younger brother; he had to resist the urge he felt to shove Jith away.

The headmaster looked up. "Mohan Silva?" And that voice, the clarion voice of Mr. Gunasekara, which had reduced many a stronger boy to tears, instantly halved Mohan's bravado.

"Yessir!"

"Don't run your words together like a damn dolt. Yes, Sir! Try it again."

"Yes. Sir!"

"Better. So you think you are a statistician, do you?"

"Yes, no Sir. I don't, Sir. Not a statistician, Sir," Mohan said, feeling his brother's eyes on him and trying to regain his courage.

"Then are you aspiring to run a security agency of some sort, providing bodyguards to people in fear for their lives?" Mohan, unable to follow the thread of these questions, replied in the negative, no, he was not aspiring to run a security agency.

The headmaster turned to Jith. "Jithendra Silva, is your big brother a statistician, a school principal, or a member of government?"

"No, Sir," Jith replied. Mr. Gunasekara had not acquired his stature within the school by being merciful when punishment had been earned, and although Jith had, truly, done nothing to earn any part of the chastisement that was surely awaiting Mohan, he trembled right then mostly on his own behalf. Despite having known through anecdote and rumor that peeing before seeing Mr. Gunasekara was a wise course of action, Jith felt that his previously empty bladder had miraculously refilled, and for one traitorous moment he wished he was not related to the boy next to him.

"Then how do you think he got these numbers?" the headmaster asked.

"I don't know, Sir. He must have guessed, Sir."

The headmaster turned to Mohan. "Guessed? Is that what you did, you fool? Because you don't have an ounce of intelligence in that thick head you stopped trying to learn anything during Tamil class and decided not only to guess the demographics of the students at my school, you decided to share your bogus information? Is that what you did?"

Mohan knew there was no good response to this question. He kicked himself for not having erased his name on the piece of paper that had been passed around. He had been so proud of his calculations, the nice, even numbers.

"Answer me!" The headmaster's voice made his ears ring.

"NO, SIR!" Mohan yelled, his anger rising to the surface.

The headmaster's voice grew soft and low. "Did you just raise your voice at me, Silva?"

His anger subsided just as fast as it had risen and Mohan felt a warm rush of urine in his underwear. He clenched his fists behind his back and willed it to stop, relieved momentarily when it did. Next to him, his brother's eyes widened in alarm as the headmaster stood up, walked over to them, and slapped Mohan across his face, once, twice, thrice, four times, five times, ceaselessly, Jith stopped counting.

Mohan did not want Jith to wait for him, but Jith did, and so Mohan had to endure his punishment in full view of all the other boys leaving home for the day as well as his younger brother, who stood by the school gates, staring up at the balcony on which Mohan knelt in the full and merciless heat, copying out twenty-three tables detailing the last census taken in the city of Colombo, the previous year. It was a document that the headmaster had secured by calling up a past student, now a minister, and having him deliver it within the hour, so he could teach Mohan something worth learning about his fellow countrymen, besides their race. By the time Mohan was done he had acquired a fresh hatred against the Tamil boys for having caused his punishment, for having been among all the rest who had glanced up as they went home. When he finally stood up to leave, his knees crusted from the crumbling cement of the balcony, scratched in some places, his entire body aching, his face smarting, he realized the headmaster had not even stayed to end his punishment. He had simply told his peon, Nagalingam, a Tamil man who lived in the hostel at the school, to *Take the sheets of paper from that boy, damn fool would have learned his lesson by then,* and left to watch the cricket match, a home game. Mohan refused to look at Nagalingam as he conveyed this message and he pretended not to hear the trace of laughter in the peon's voice. He shoved the papers at him and left.

"I waited for you," Jith said, hopping off the wall on which he had been sitting, as Mohan approached and then walked past him. "I didn't want you to be alone," he said, running to keep up with Mohan.

"I didn't ask you to wait, you idiot," Mohan snarled. "You should have gone. You should have run home to your stupid Dolly and told her all about this."

"I won't tell anybody," Jith said.

Mohan swirled around and Jith bounced off his brother's chest. "I don't care who you tell!"

Jith shook his head, no, he wouldn't tell anybody at all.

Mohan turned away from his brother and wiped a few bitter tears as he walked. "Tamil bastards. Everywhere. Headmaster's pets. Fucking donations. They should get out! Get out of our school. Get out of our country. If I catch a single one of them so much as looking at me tomorrow . . ."

Jith listened to all this and said nothing, not understanding what his brother wanted. It seemed as though if there were no Tamil students for him to be angry at, he would be lost. And yet it seemed he also wanted every one of them to disappear. To where? Sitting on the wall, Jith had composed a fresh letter to Dolly. In this letter he did not talk about love, games, or failed tests.

I am waiting for my brother after school and so I thought I will write to you.
I am afraid that bad things are going to happen very soon and I don't know
if you and I can be together anymore. My brother gets angry when he sees
me talking to you and he does not want me to play with the Herath children
either. He says they are traitors. I wish he wasn't so angry all the time. In
some ways he reminds me of Sonna. It seems to me that they don't want
anybody around them to be happy. It seems to me that if they could make our
lane silent with nobody talking to anybody else they might be happy. But I
don't think they could be happy even then. Maybe they were born to be angry.
I feel sorry for my brother because he doesn't have someone like you to talk to.
Sometimes I think he is angry because I have you and he has nobody. I hope
I see Rose or Devi today so I can send this note to you. —Jith

Mohan said nothing else to Jith on the way home and Jith did not dare to offer him any further solace. He sat beside his brother and tried not to breathe in the faint smell of dried urine on his brother's trousers. As they walked home from the bus halt, Jith was glad to see Rose. He beckoned her over and gave her the note for Dolly. Up ahead of them, Mohan glanced back once then kept on walking.

Sonna came around the corner, and Mohan's spirits lifted. He raised his hand in a wave. "Where are you going?" he asked Sonna.

"Nowhere, just walkin' toward the bakery."

Behind him Mohan heard Jith's voice, calling to him to wait. He turned to Sonna. "I'll come with you," he said.

"Maybe we can go an' see what is happenin' on Kalyani Avenue," Sonna said.

Mohan hesitated. The bakery was one thing, but Kalyani Avenue was quite another. The last time he had been there was when Raju was taken there and much as he had truly relished that moment, he didn't feel like revisiting the place today. He might have changed his mind if Jith had been standing beside him, but he had left Jith behind and when he looked back now, Jith was walking with Rose as if they were a couple, chatting. He was probably telling her what had happened, why they were late, everything. Little shit. Looking up, Jith saw Mohan staring and a moment later Rose picked up her pace and ran ahead of him.

"Come on," Sonna goaded. Sonna's face still carried a faint bruise near his left ear from the beating he had received from Raju, and he touched the spot tenderly, out of habit, as he spoke. "We'll go an' come soon. Won' take long."

"I have to leave my books," Mohan began.

"Brin' the books," Sonna said.

They crossed paths with Jith just then and Jith put his hand out to stop his brother. "Where are you going, Mohan? Nobody is home. You haven't got permission," he said.

Mohan sneered. "I'm not a baby like you. I don't need permission."

"We're goin' to see a girl on Kalyani Avenue, a nice *Letchumi*" Sonna said, and laughed. He reached over and grabbed the backpack off Mohan's shoulder and gave it to Jith. "You take this."

Jith took the bag and walked home slowly, mulling over the day's events. He hoped that the headmaster would not tell his parents. He hoped the other children would not tell their parents. He wanted the incident forgotten. He wanted to be Jith Silva again, not Mohan Silva's brother. And he wanted Mohan to stop going to Kalyani Avenue or anywhere else with Sonna. He looked up as he passed the Bollings' house, but Dolly was nowhere to be seen. He looked back down the road, and since Sonna and Mohan were no longer in sight, he contemplated knocking on the door and asking for her. Nobody was home except for him now, and he wanted to show her the inside of his house, the room he shared with his brother, the music box that had belonged to his grandmother, the goldfish in his father's pond, and the snake skins that he had found wrapped around his father's sugarcane bushes. He wanted to show her the map of Australia that he had stolen out of a *National Geographic* magazine at the library so they could pick out the exact town where they would live. These were things he'd told her about and this would be a chance to show her. Just then he heard Jimmy Bolling curse at Francie Bolling, and the sound of his approaching footsteps.

Jith turned and hurried up the road, went inside, and did not come out again, though he lay on his bed wishing he had the courage to get up, walk back down the road, and ask Dolly if she wanted to come and see his house, which was not a bad place, especially when he was alone in it.

1983

The Last Perfect Day

Nobody could begrudge Nihil his moment. Hadn't he once given up the one thing that delighted him on account of something as unglamorous as looking after his younger sister? Hadn't he been the one, of all the Herath children, to change Mr. Niles's state of mind for the better, a change that, nobody would dispute this fact, had prolonged his life? Tall for his age, with talent that surpassed even Mr. Niles's lofty expectations, Nihil became the youngest player to be selected not for the first eleven but, not far behind, for the second eleven, the A team, as the last in the batting lineup in the upcoming Mini Battle of the Blues.

"Good, good, congratulations!" Mr. Niles said, when Nihil burst into the veranda with the news. Mr. Niles half rose out of his reclining position in excitement, then fell back against his pillows.

"On Friday we are going to play against St. Thomas's A. You'll be there?"

"Yes, of course I will be there," Mr. Niles said, marveling at the fact that he could utter such certainties. Although the initial prognosis regarding his life had been amended in light of the health he had regained during the past years, he knew he had begun to lose the fight. He had kept this knowledge from his wife and daughter by enlisting Lucas to go to the pharmacy at the top of the main road and fill a prescription for a painkiller that he had wrangled out of an old friend, and that he administered himself. This moment, however, called for such utterances.

"We will all have to go then, Papa," Kala Niles said. "Can't send you alone, no?"

"Who will drive?" Mrs. Niles asked, her brow furrowed.

"Kala will drive," Mr. Niles said, surprising his daughter, who wreathed her face in smiles; though she had passed the driving test eight years ago, the occasions on which she had been allowed to take the wheel had been rare.

It was decided. The Niles family would travel together, and the Bolling girls were being allowed to accompany the Heraths, who had hired a van to transport themselves as well as Lucas and Raju, both of whom wanted to witness this magnificent event. Of course all the girls would have to skip school.

The first day of the match dawned long after Nihil had woken up, unable to sleep, gone to the bathroom, drunk water, lain back down, and returned to the bathroom at last to give up on sleep altogether and take his body-wash so he could don the whites that had been laundered and waited for him on the edge of the ironing board. Because he was up that early and dressed that early, he was the first one of all those who lived on Sal Mal Lane to read the news about unrest at the University of Peradeniya, on the main campus tucked into the hills of Kandy. And because he was about to play the most important cricket match of his life, this news was read swiftly and discarded equally swiftly as he turned to the last page of the paper, the sports page, to read what might have been written about him.

"Is there anything about you in the paper?" Devi asked, yawning and stretching as she came out onto the veranda, still dressed in her red pajama shorts and top.

"No," Nihil replied cheerfully, "today they have just mentioned that the match is taking place, but tomorrow there will be for sure."

"You'll have to play really well to get into the paper," Devi said.

"I will," he replied.

"You look like you will," she said, taking in the determined face and neat lines before her. She grinned at him. If ever there was going to be a star batsman, surely this was he. "I'm going to get ready then," she said, fully awake, and went back inside. She returned a few moments later, removing the brush from her mouth long enough to mumble through a mouthful of toothpaste-laced spit, "Bettuh go an' wake Mitter Nilesh!"

"I'm sure they are already up," Nihil said, but went out anyway, practicing one stroke then another with an imaginary bat as he walked, careful not to let any part of either gate, his own or the Nileses', brush his crisp clothing. He listened to the chirping of the early-morning birds and hesitated a moment before he knocked softly on their door. He hoped he hadn't woken them up.

"We're up! We're up!" Kala Niles said, throwing open the door. "Papa has been up since five o'clock!"

Mr. Niles was not in his seat. Kala Niles told Nihil that he was in his room getting dressed in the clothing he wore to weddings and funerals. Nihil could hear Mrs. Niles trying to dissuade him from putting on a tie, too, reminding him of the heat of these March months and other discomforts he might experience were he to be buttoned up quite so tightly.

"All right, Uncle, I'll go and wake up my family," Nihil called out so Mr. Niles might hear him. "Only Devi is up there."

On his way back he met both Raju and Lucas, who were also already dressed for a game that was not going to start for another several hours.

"I'll take Lucas and give him a cup of tea then, that way you can go and wake up the others," Raju offered magnanimously.

Lucas grinned, exposing his mostly toothless gums. He had never been in a private wheeled vehicle before and he could not tell if the excitement he felt had to do with that or the match itself. "Okay Sir Mr. Raju, Lucas will come with you," he said, as he hurried behind Raju, feeling a little uncomfortable in his wedding trousers, though they miraculously still fit him.

Whatever came afterward, Nihil would remember that day exactly as it was, perfect from start to finish.

First, there was that morning of readiness, of what seemed like an entire neighborhood up early and excited for him, and then the drive to the match, the Morris Minor in front, the van behind. There was the arrival at the school gates, and Kadalai himself, the old man who was the undisputed lead fan of the team, his toothless mouth grinning with delight, bowing low as he waved the security guard away and swung the gate wide open for *Ado! This is one of our cricketers!* then shutting it behind them. There was Mr. Niles, who had decided that he could not simply sit in a parked car, no, he had to walk, no matter how long it took him, up to the single set of stands, Mr. Herath holding him up on one side, Suren on the other, he wanted to sit with the group. And when they had walked under the arches, around the basketball courts, past the pool, and onto the open field, there were the perfectly trimmed green oval grounds lined with its white boundary and, best of all, the small crowd that had shown up for the game. Boys from both schools lingered in groups and singles, and here and there Nihil could see the flashes of color that told him that a few girls, too, had come to the game, and that made him feel instantly both nervous and exhilarated.

Later, at the nets, he bowled to a few other cricketers, batted balls bowled to him, and then it was time for the coin toss. Nihil sat for a long time, present but not playing, ready but not called out to play. He watched the game unfold, his spectators, his family, even his heroes forgotten. For now there were just thirteen cricketers on the field, two bats and a single red leather ball flying. The question of whether he would be brought in to play did not cross his mind; there was no other eventuality but that he would find himself at the crease, bat in hand, taking his stance, waiting. He remembered Mr. Niles's faith in him and it made him smile.

As the day wore on Devi came by, bright as a canary in a yellow puff-sleeved dress with a blue sash around her waist that she had borrowed from Rashmi and that therefore hung a little long on her. "Amma sent me with a sandwich for you," she said.

Nihil shooed her away, embarrassed as the other players grinned and imitated her singsong voice. "I don't need a sandwich! The team gets their own lunch."

"Yes, but she said to give it," Devi said, unperturbed. "We have all had lunch. Here, take it."

"*Nangi*, will your Amma send him icy chocs too?" the batsman sitting next to Nihil asked Devi. He was already wearing batting pads and balanced his bat between his legs.

"No," she said, realizing at last that they were making fun of her. She hopped down from the railing where she had been standing and returned to her parents. "Those boys are bullying Nihil," she said.

"Bullying? Why bullying?" Raju asked. He was lifting each arm and fanning himself with a folded paper bag, and he looked like he might be felled by the heat at any moment, but his voice was full of power; he was available and ready to rescue Nihil from his tormenters.

"Not bullying, I'm sure," Mr. Niles said, "probably just teasing because the little one went over. Boys are like that."

Mr. Herath, who had looked up when Devi returned, went back to reading over a stack of reports he had brought with him. "Tell me when he's up to bat," he murmured to Suren, who was sitting next to him.

"I would never go down there," Rashmi declared, though she sounded as though she wished she had been asked to carry the sandwich, which had been returned, to Nihil.

"My god, I would definitely go," Rose said. "Aunty, nex' time send me!" And she playfully squeezed Mrs. Herath's upper arm.

Mrs. Herath laughed and smacked Rose's knee, saying, "Stop it, child, you must behave."

"The game is starting again!" Suren said. "Nihil has still not come off the bench."

"There's time," Mr. Niles said, looking sanguine and cool despite the extra clothing he was wearing; Mrs. Niles had lost the fight over his tie as well as his suit jacket. He tipped the brim of the straw hat he had on, lifted his voice, and artfully coaxed Mr. Herath away from his reports and engaged him in a conversation about work, the work he, Mr. Niles, had once done as a government agent as well as the work that Mr. Herath now did with the Ministry of Education.

While his band of fans waited for him to emerge, Nihil continued to observe the game. On a difficult pitch where the ball had little swing and bounced unevenly, the batsmen were not scoring. That is, his side was not scoring. The afternoon wound on with far too many forward defenses, the bat planted on the pitch, rendering the ball impotent but neither scoring nor getting a player out, and single runs, until another young player took the field. In an innings that included three boundaries and several showy cuts past point, the scoreboard began to sparkle. Looking back, the game was, in many ways, and despite the day yet remaining, already decided by the time Nihil was called up to bat. Yet in equally as many ways, there were chances to lose it, and he rested on his laurels, having avoided doing that.

"Herath! You're up!" the captain called, finally, though there was no need for the reminder, he was the last batsman left, and transformed Nihil from being a boy like every other boy into being *a boy who had played for college*. If he never played another game, if he sat on the bench for the rest of his school career, he would still be that, still remembered by the cricket-mad score-keepers and coaches and prefects and Kadalai and, most of all, most of all, by the mismatched group watching from the stands: Mr. Niles, Mrs. Niles, Kala Niles, Lucas, Raju, his sisters, his brother, his parents, and, sandwiched between them and beside themselves with giggly excitement, Rose and Dolly.

Nihil made his first walk from the pavilion to the sidelines, and from there he strolled casually, as if he had all the time in the world, to the crease, savoring each second. It was exactly as he had imagined it would be. The glance over his shoulder to the right and then the left, taking in the placements, the boys on the field at silly mid on, third slip, and deep mid wicket, the run up of the bowler, who was taking his mark again as he waited, and the sound of the crowd, not a crowd like the one at the big match, but a crowd nonetheless and one that was cheering for him. For him!

The pitch when he reached it was hard. There was a high but even bounce and although he had practiced before on just such a pitch with just such a bounce, he was cautious. He tried to concentrate, seeing not only the bowler but the ball, picturing its polished side angled one way and not the other, picturing the seam side catching the airflow, making it spin this way and not that. Still, the ball came at him much more quickly than he expected, the bat felt heavy in his hands, and suddenly every boy around him seemed to have turned into a giant. No matter, they cheered, out there in the stands, every time he met the ball and hit it, though he was yet to score and though even his hits were few thanks to the consideration of the senior player across from him who ensured that he, not Nihil, remained on strike as often as possible, artfully hitting a single with every last ball of an over so he could cross the pitch and bat, again, until Nihil became comfortable.

Around him the field changed and changed again as the captain of the opposing team tried first a fast bowler then a medium pacer. Each time Nihil and his teammate stood firm. Each time the ball was hit, Nihil did not miss a beat, running when a run was safe, running again if two runs were possible, but staying close, his bat inside the crease as soon as he crossed the pitch. And as the game went on, as the bowlers crossed from side to side and the field rearranged itself and he and his partner met in the middle and exchanged tips and cautions and returned to their wickets, something wonderful happened to Nihil: the game became a game again. He relaxed. His shoulders lost their tightness, his gloved hands their anxiety, and his mind its worry.

Mr. Niles's words rang in his ears: *Long ago, he was just a boy like you.*

He had dreamed of hitting sixers or driving boundaries and he had imagined that such moments would come once he had the power to hit the ball hard enough, but standing there that day, Nihil realized that strength had far less to do with playing the game well than mind did. Did he have the necessary inner quiet that would help him separate the tricky delivery from the easy one, that would give him the ability to time, not force, the shot, to know that at exactly the right time with exactly the right delivery, grace could take a ball farther and faster than brute force?

He did. And he did again and twice more before play was called off for the day. He took his time walking over to his partner and then set off at a slow jog back to the pavilion as the spectators poured out of the stands and he did not mind, not one bit, that the fan running first and fastest was none other than his sister, a streak of golden yellow, the small but significant comet in his life, the one who had stayed safe so he could play cricket.

The People Who Stayed Home

On the second day of the match Mr. Herath, Lucas, Raju, the Niles family, and the Bolling girls, stayed behind, Mr. Niles in some considerable discomfort from all his exertions the day before, though he shook Nihil's hand and sent him on his way to the game with a pat on his back when Nihil went to bid him good-bye. And because they stayed home, their day was experienced differently, for they read the newspapers and heard the gossip and had nothing to distract them from the fear and anger that clouded the skies above them.

In the papers, a plethora of Incidents were discussed. More than fifty individuals, mostly Tamil but also Sinhalese who belonged to the left-leaning parties, had now been detained under the Prevention of Terrorism Act. K. Navaratnarajah, one of those taken in under the act, had died in detention, the papers said. Meanwhile, editorials discussed how followers of Velupillai Prabhakaran, the man who had stood in that jungle seven years before then and declared his disinterest in elections, had bombed five polling booths in Jaffna.

There was an Incident mentioned regarding a government official using the phrase *Para Demellu* during a speech and another official demanding an apology for that insult on behalf of the Tamil members of government. No apology had been forthcoming. An Incident was mentioned about the death of two members of the armed forces in the North, which was an Incident reported along with a cumulative number of those in the armed forces who had been killed since 1981: twenty-two. As though the deaths of people in uniforms merited aggregation, as if any day now, these deaths would round out to a number that would prompt some more severe reprimand, something more visceral than consternation or even sympathy.

A State of Emergency had been called upon, once more, the left-wing papers said, to shroud the nation in further misinformation and fear, and two newspapers, the *Saturday Review* and the *Suthanthiran*, both of which were Tamil-language newspapers critical of the government, were accused of inciting separatist sentiments, and shut down.

The direction in which the country was heading were discussed by ordinary people, the slant of their words depending upon the things that they read in their choice of newspaper, what they heard from each other, and, sometimes, their ethnicity. People looking for less specific reasons, intellectuals writing in multiple languages, brought up other facts to explain what was happening around them: government corruption, the impoverishment, as a direct result of that corruption, of the general populace, the lack of work in rural areas, the impotence felt by workers due to the violent breakup of that nationwide strike not long ago, and the systematic strangulation of the democratic process what with the self-appointment of an executive president and the carrying out of a referendum. These were all brought up and heads were bowed or shaken depending on the political persuasion of the intellectual.

The Incidents mentioned were not all in the same newspaper. The newspapers that carried the news in Tamil had one set of stories, those that were in Sinhala carried another set of stories, and, why not say it, each of those newspapers tended to favor the virtue of those who spoke its own language of print and question the moral fortitude of those who did not. If some balance of perspective were possible, then it would have been possible in English-language newspapers but, alas, those newspapers were filled with the thoughts of people, both Sinhalese and Tamil, whose identities flavored their opinions but who had learned to present their arguments with more spit and polish, which meant that nothing was said overtly, though the implications behind what was said were the same. Ranting about one party or militant group or another was deemed adequate expression of civic duty by all the people writing in all three languages in all the major newspapers, and worse, their predictions of the future were nothing like the one that was coming. Not even close.

For those on Sal Mal Lane, those who were not watching a cricket match, there was the additional difficulty of weighing what was read with what was heard, particularly for those who listened more than they read.

"They say the Tigers are gathering for a big strike," Lucas said, shaking his head. "Maybe it is good that the Silva sons are going to join the army." He had taken to wearing his sarong rolled up at all times in anticipation of some difficulty that would demand swift movement.

"When are they coming?" Rose asked him when she ran into him after a day that seemed depressing and dull after the one spent playing truant and sitting through a cricket match, boys everywhere they looked.

"Soon, they say. Better go and warn Koralé also."

"Tigers are coming in a few months!" Rose said to Dolly.

"What are we going to do when the Tigers come next month?" Dolly asked Jith, after giving him a gift she had made for him, a navy-blue handkerchief on which Rashmi had helped her to embroider his initials, JS, in a flowery monogram script done in hot pink.

"We are ready. We have our Seeya's guns," he said through cheeks bulging with not one but two Delta toffees, a sweet-tooth habit that made his face break out but that he would not give up.

"Guns you have?" Dolly asked, her eyes widening. "Bullets an' all?"

Jith did not know if the guns were loaded, only that they hung on the wall over their dining table. "Yes, of course. All guns are loaded, otherwise what's the use of having them?"

"Silvas have already bought guns," Dolly told Sonna, who said he already knew, though he had not known. He stormed off down the road to see what kind of weaponry he could rustle up, fuming that he had not been told about the guns by Mohan.

"Silvas have gone and bought guns," Sonna told Raju when he almost collided with him coming out of Koralé's shop, Mr. Herath's cigarettes in one hand, his change in the other. "Now you'll see."

"All the Sinhalese houses are getting guns these days," Raju told Kala Niles, worry deepening all of his mismatched features, as they stood together next to the bakery man, buying loaves of fresh warm bread, something they had been doing since they were children, children as young as Nihil and Devi were now.

"Yes, everywhere now people are getting ready," the bakery man said and then, to Mr. Tissera when he came out to buy their bread, "Sir, you got guns ready?"

"Guns? What for?" Mr. Tissera asked in some alarm, and he began to crack the knuckles on his fingers one after the other.

"For anything, better be prepared when the Tigers come," the bakery man said.

"Don't be foolish. Nobody is going to buy guns. From where to buy them anyway?" Mr. Tissera said, but when he went inside he said to his wife in a low voice, "Whole lane is getting ready for Tigers. We also should do something."

"What is there to do?" his wife asked as she sat at the dining table wearing her housecoat and peeled clove after clove of garlic for a garlic curry that she knew Mr. Niles liked to eat and that she made for him now and then, even though it left her fingers raw and aching for days after.

"Better go and ask the Silvas," he said, "they always seem to know everything about troubles." But when he stepped outside he ran into Mr. Nadesan, coming home from visiting his sister, and when Mr. Tissera asked him if he had heard that the Tigers were coming, Mr. Nadesan shook his head sadly and said *We are thinking of going to India, we have family there.* And Mr. Tissera felt too despondent to keep walking down the street to the Silvas and instead came home and lay down in his armchair wondering what kind of uncivilized family might move into the house next door when the Nadesans left because they, the Nadesans, had always been his kind of neighbor, quiet, polite, there when needed, asking for help when necessary, never imposing.

Yes, down Sal Mal Lane there was more talk of weapons and preparations and Tigers than there had ever been. Big words like *atrocities* and *disenfranchisement* were tossed over plates of rice and curry during the midday meal, and nobody at all, not the Bin Ahmeds, not the Nadesans, not the Nileses, not the Tisseras or Mr. Herath and Kamala—for only they were at home that day—not the Bollings, certainly not the outliers, Lucas and Alice and Raju, and not even the Silvas felt safe.

So it was a good thing that the Herath children were able to spend that day watching one of them take the field in a second innings. And even though when the game ended, it did not end with Nihil making the game-winning catch he had hoped to make, his contribution had been steady, he had taken one catch, aided in a run-out, and stopped three fours, nonetheless, when the game ended he was close enough to the wicket to grab the bails and thereby had a precious reminder of the game, this game.

May Day

March, the month of cricket, came and went, and the April New Year after. While the children spoke fondly of the previous year, when they had all grown up and into their future selves in significant ways over the matter of the variety show, no new show was put on. Mrs. Herath was still under the impression that her word was law, the Nileses, though they made their home available for the rehearsals and welcoming to the children, were privately anxious about the news in the papers, and the children themselves had begun to settle into a state of cautious vigilance. It was understandable then that the people of Sal Mal Lane were grateful for the holiday that arrived in May, for the parades and speeches and sense of festivity that came with it were universal and not specific to one family or another.

The banners that unfurled on the first day of May each year were shown on TV, and most of the people on Sal Mal Lane felt that it was adequate participation to watch the day's events from the safety of their drawing rooms. Not Lucas, who always set off to watch the parade organized by the right, the United National Party, with its acres of green, and not Mr. Herath, who went off not merely to observe but, indeed, to march with his fellow Communists of various stripes in the one parade that had space for their kind, the one held by the blue-hued Lanka Sama Samaja Party.

"Long time ago I used to march in the Viplavavadi Communist Sangamaya, VIKOSA, and the Revolutionary Communist League, the RCL. Now they just have a meeting, no marches," he told his children, reminded each year of their dwindling numbers.

"So who goes in your parade?" Nihil asked, but mostly as a courtesy.

"Very few. For old times' sake I would say that the Communist Party May Day parade took an hour to pass by, but it is now probably far less," and Mr. Herath shrugged his shoulders, trying to act like it did not matter.

It was not so much an acknowledgment of defeat as it was a statement about the immense intellectual lack that defined a populace unable to espouse his views. He combed the sparse beard that he grew each April for this occasion and then trimmed to resemble Lenin's on the first of May, though, thanks to his full head of hair and temperate features, Mr. Herath hardly looked the part. The children nodded and avoided their upcountry mother's gaze, for she cared little for their father's politics, and even less for Communists, her few words about either summoned only to soothe some charge in her husband who did care, and deeply, about both.

Despite the fact that every party organized its own parade, the group that eclipsed all the other parties was the red of the JVP, drawing crowds to its parade by the awe-inspiring precision of its armies of identically dressed marching members, holding aloft a sea of red flags emblazoned with the yellow sickle and hammer, their advance slow and inexorable around corner after corner after corner, a seemingly unending stream of virility, color, and command. All the Heraths, except of course Mr. Herath, went each year to watch the JVP parade.

"I see the red! I see it!" Devi yelled, her body leaning half over the balcony of the house where they had gathered, the home of a friend of Mrs. Herath's, which happened to be along the parade route.

"Don't lean so far out," Nihil said, his fingers tight over the bow tied around his sister's waist. He could feel the hard scrape of her backbone through the red blouse she had put on to match the red pedal pushers she had borrowed from Rashmi to confirm her support of the JVP, her skinny body hanging like a pillow over a clothesline. He wished he could go and join his older siblings who were standing by the gate, even though the gate itself was barely cracked wide enough for their bodies to squeeze through.

"Nobody stands in front," Mrs. Herath had said. "If all hell breaks loose I want you to be able to come in and shut the gate." She used that phrase on them, *if all hell breaks loose,* each year that they waited for this parade, and if asked she probably would have said that *all hell* was no more than a few fistfights but, since nobody asked, the possibility of unimaginable chaos loomed large in her children's minds.

In the year of this particular parade, while the children gasped and pointed to the advancing rows, Mrs. Herath considered the fact that they had lived almost as long under a regime determined to fill the shops with things people could ill afford as under the previous one whose reign had been characterized by the rationing of all staples including milk powder, dhal, and rice, and not one imported item to be found except through connections that led to stashes revealed in black-market storerooms. She felt a stab of remorse over those Dankotuwa Porcelain plates her husband had secured for her through just such a deal, regretting her part in causing this blemish on his otherwise untarnished image as an incorruptible civil servant. Thinking about the plates, she also felt bad about her argument with him just that morning.

"At least the children can have cotton-polyester uniforms now," she had said to her husband as they prepared to head in opposite directions, he to his rally of principles and she to her rally of display. "Remember when they had nothing but poplin? What a nightmare for that Kamala to wash and iron every day."

"Better uniforms, yes, at the cost of massive debt," Mr. Herath replied, bending his knees slightly to see his face in the mirror, which was too short for him, and combing his hair. His remarks lacked flair and punch. They were relentless statements of facts. No sarcasm enlivened his speech, no well-turned phrase was summoned to turn the description of some event, some person or circumstance, into anything very memorable. That was his wife's skill.

"Debt or no debt, at least we are living like human beings now, not like beggars, standing in line for everything. Bread lines, ration lines, kerosene lines. Thank god *somebody* drew the line!" she said and powdered her face.

Mr. Herath said no more. He gathered the keys to the official car he kept for use on May Day and election day—the rest of the time it was returned to the ministry in the care of his chauffeur—and went out. He often wished that his wife would decide, one way or another, whether she supported the same people he did, the Left, or not. It would be far easier than having to listen to her commiseration on some occasions, her denouncements on others. As he drove away in a temper, he had to swerve to avoid hitting Sonna, who was wrestling Rose and Dolly on the street in a manner that indicated that the blows and grasps were not in jest.

"Funny how you Communists are still able to travel in cars," she called after him, even though he could not hear her.

Those words, too, lingered in her memory as she looked out over the parade. But her small quarrel with her husband was soon wiped from her mind, for there appeared before her and, more importantly, before her older children, a man dressed in a Tiger suit.

"*Koti enawa! Koti enawa!* " he yelled as he bent low before them.

Rashmi shrank back through the gate and Suren followed. "You can't hide forever. When the Tigers come they will find all of you!" the man yelled, sweeping his arms to describe a wide arc of people, before two men, clearly organizers from the JVP, pulled him off the gate, berated him, and sent him away.

"Why did that man shout like that? Is he JVP?" Devi asked.

"He's not JVP. He's just trying to cause trouble," Nihil told her, though he did not know for sure.

"Maybe he is JVP," Rashmi said. "Maybe they want us to be scared, no Amma?"

Mrs. Herath did not respond, for she did not know either. Were there Tigers coming? For what were they coming? Was there anybody among the thousands of government officials, or even among the thousands upon thousands of youth marching before them, among the dozens of people who lived down their lane, who were happy about the Tigers? She thought about her students at school, who separated now in her mind without much effort into their ethnic groups as they had never done before. She brought each face into focus and wondered which of them might harbor secret hatreds or secret fears, both of which were the same to her. She didn't know. She just did not know. She felt a sudden yearning for her husband, for his clear political opinions; they carried with them the weight of his integrity and conviction and gave her something she could believe was true.

"I don't think he was JVP," she said, wanting to think the best of everybody for as long as was possible. "Why would they want to stir up trouble like that?"

She comforted her children with these words and they returned to watch the rest of the parade, commenting on this drummer, that flag bearer, the impossibly straight lines of so many young people, and they ate lunch, which was followed by a sweet dessert of fruit salad and ice cream, and then they went home to wait for their father, who returned much later, crestfallen over matters he would not share with anybody in the family, his brow furrowed, and who drank half a bottle of *arrack* over several hours all by himself, after even his wife gave up trying to cheer him up and went to bed.

On the rest of Sal Mal Lane, the mood was a variation on Mr. Herath's, if not quite so mournful. Jimmy Bolling held a party with cheap alcohol in honor of May Day, which to him was a holiday, not an expression of commitment to ideologies. Alcohol was imbibed by everybody, including his son and daughters, and this led to the type of brawl for which they had once been famous because Sonna, too inebriated to remember his father's sensibilities, made one of his customary remarks about *bloody Tamils*.

"Who are you callin' bloody Tamils, you fool?" his father said. "You also have Tamil blood."

"We are not Tamil, we are Burghers," Sonna corrected, raising his right index finger high in the air as though he were presenting himself to be counted among the non-Tamils. He laughed.

"We are Burghers," his father repeated, with disgust. "Fuckin' great-grandmother was Tamil and this fucker is talkin' about Burghers."

"Tamils should all bloody move to Jaffna," Sonna said, after nursing this fact for a while. His voice slurred. He pointed in the direction that he believed was north. "Even you, if you think you're Tamil, move to Jaffna. You should take Raju an' that mad woman an' go!"

And though he pushed off his chair and stood to meet his father's on-coming bulk, imagining himself sufficient to withstand the blow, Sonna was soon not merely felled to the ground but dragged to his bed, roped to it, and beaten with one of Jimmy Bolling's belts until he whimpered. That ended the party for the Bollings, who finished their drinks, ate the last of the now cold bits of stringy meat that had been fried up with chillies and capsicums to go with their drinks, and went to sleep without washing any of the dishes.

Rose crept up as soon as she was sure that her father was asleep and untied the ropes around Sonna, for which she received first a fresh bout of cursing from Sonna and then, between more curses, a series of drunken mutterings during which he mentioned all of the Herath children by name, called Mohan *that fucker,* and said Dolly would be far better off if she took up with Suren instead of a rotten Silva. Dolly, listening, only shrugged and asked if Sonna wanted some tea, she could make some for him.

Lucas had been unhappy to hear, given his alliance with the Heraths and his now well absorbed knowledge of the equality of all human beings, particularly those human beings who populated his country, and of the villainy endemic to America and Americans, that his party of long preference, which was also the Silvas' party of preference, the UNP, was talking about banning the JVP, the very party that the Herath children loved to see each May Day, and, worse, were hobnobbing with Americans and luxury goods.

"*Pchah,*" he said to Alice, as he sank his bony body down onto the edge of their bed and unwrapped the spare sarong he had tied around his head to keep it safe from the sun, "country is going to the dogs. Ever since . . ." and here he paused, for he could not quite put his finger on when, exactly, this going to the dogs had begun. "We should never have had a president," he said after some thought. "That was the beginning of all the trouble."

"Not the president, the people are the trouble," Alice said from her corner of the room, hunching as she combed the brittle edges of her hair in preparation for bed. She was in a chatty mood, having spent the whole day in happy solitude. "If not for the people there would be no trouble."

"How can you say that? People are led by the leaders. Leaders have to lead properly. When the president is getting things from America . . ." And he shook his head, at a loss for words to describe what misery might await them with the influx of such goods as had been spoken of by various people he had met at the rally that afternoon. Goods such as fabric that did not need ironing, and boxes of cereal that did not require cooking, and milk powder that would help women preserve their breasts for better things, and on and on until he had felt that his whole life had been lived in a state of lack, a lack he had never felt before this day.

"Go to sleep. We can't worry about leaders and presidents," Alice said, kindly. "I can bring you another cup of plain tea if you like."

"I don't think I can go to sleep," Lucas said, putting his head in his hands. "Too much trouble everywhere. Raju Sir told me whole lane is getting ready for Tigers, and Silva sons told me that Tigers are definitely coming to fight with us. Where will we go?" And saying this he lay back in his bed in hopelessness where, despite his best efforts to focus on all the worrisome things he could not control, nor even understand, Lucas fell asleep.

Mr. Niles did not sleep. He had spent the day listening to the news on the radio and was disturbed by an Incident that had been reported, in which two Sinhalese seniors at the University of Peradeniya, from Arunachalam Hall, named in honor of Sir Ponnambalam Arunachalam, a Tamil statesman who had been one of the first to lead the demand for a University of Ceylon—albeit one that his brother, Ramanathan, had wanted located in Jaffna, where access to it would be largely limited to Tamil students— led a group of other students in an assault against Tamil students at the university. As if that were insufficient information to trouble their listeners, both newscasters, in English and in Tamil, reminded everybody of an earlier incident, some years back, when all the Sinhalese students had fled the national university in Jaffna after the students there had beaten up its Sinhalese registrar, Wimal Sundara. The two events, set next to each other in that way, painted a picture that was unremitting in its bleakness, and Mr. Niles found himself unable to sleep.

He hobbled around the house, sliding his feet forward in small steps, lurching as he clutched one piece of furniture or the other, seeking stability where he was used to being stabilized, on either side, by his wife and daughter. At the piano he stopped for a moment, lost in thought. Sinking onto the bench, he opened the cover. There was only the faint light of the moon through the windows and the shadows cast by the red bulb in his bedroom that Kala Niles lit each night beneath her pictures of Jesus Christ, the Virgin Mary, and the goddess Saraswati, though a picture of Sai Baba, given to her by Mrs. Herath, was also tucked between them. In that luminous dark, Mr. Niles laid his fingers gently on the keys of the piano. He closed his eyes and felt their soft-hard pressure against the underside of his fingers. He moved his hand up toward the ebony keys and felt them on either side of each of his fingers, like a glove. He had never learned to play the piano, had never touched these keys, and yet the music of this piano had been the music of his life. How little he had loved it, how sparing he had been with his praise for his daughter. And yet it had been her skill that had brought Nihil to him, a son whom he loved wholly and with uncomplicated gratitude. He opened his eyes and brushed his fingers along the length of the piano, reaching first to the right, all the way to the end, and then to the left. He leaned forward and rested his forehead on the upper panel above the music rest, feeling the smooth polish of the wood releasing resonance and secrets against his skin.

And that was the last time that Mr. Niles would walk, with or without help, for as he lifted his head and turned his gaze, his eyes caught the edge of the guitar that stood in its case against the wall, and the sight of that guitar reminded him of the variety show that had taken place in his house. It reminded him of all his neighbors, their individual faces as they waited and listened and applauded, as they milled about and shared the food that had no ordained form or taste, for even though it had been New Year they had each brought what they had or what they cooked best. And as those faces settled around him, into their chairs, he heard again the particular solo that Suren had sung, his voice sweet and pure and such words on his lips, words that had fallen lightly on his ears then, Suren's voice and the guitar overwhelming the words. But he remembered now that Suren had sung of regret, about time stolen from children, and blood that is spilled like wine. Was it the words, or was it the sound of those words in a voice as young and sure as Suren's, or the fact that such words should exist? Whatever it was, it made Mr. Niles stand up with an urge to do something, anything, anything at all to keep all of them safe, to keep them singing and making music and talking about cricket.

When Kala Niles and Mrs. Niles came running, they found Mr. Niles crumpled in a heap by the piano, his long legs bent crookedly underneath him.

"Go and get Mr. Herath!" Mrs. Niles said, and Kala Niles ran, not caring that she was in her nylon nightdress which was entirely transparent, to bang on the gate and wake up the Heraths.

"Daddy has fallen down, Uncle, need to take him to the Sri Lanka Nursing Home! Come soon! Come soon!" and she turned away with a sob.

Mr. Herath, returned quickly to sobriety, paused to pull on trousers and a shirt and wake up his wife, as well as Suren and Nihil, which meant that there was enough noise made that soon the whole family was up and Suren was sent to wake up Raju as well. Raju carried Mr. Niles almost single-handedly to the car in his arms, the old man's head resting against his face, the body curled over his belly, and Nihil and Suren holding Mr. Niles's legs.

"I have to come!" Nihil said.

Mr. Niles gritted his teeth and managed to reach over and hold Nihil's hand, giving him permission to squeeze himself into the space between the two front seats from where he held on to the back of the driver's seat with one hand and Mr. Niles's hand with the other.

At the Sri Lanka Nursing Home, Mr. Niles's legs were bandaged with splints to hold them straight, and he stayed there overnight. With the aid of half a Valium that Mr. Herath slipped to him, taking it out of his own purse and snapping it in half with the edge of a fingernail, he fell asleep with Nihil lying next to him and his wife sitting beside him, and Mr. Herath drove Kala Niles home to prepare the house for her father's new level of immobility.

And so, May Day, and the night that brought it to a close, was full not of celebration but of the lit ends of concerns that nudged and burned everyone in equal measure, even the children.

July

Second Lieutenant A. P. N. C. De S. Vaas Gunawardene, Sergeant S. I. Thilekaratne, Corporals G. R. Perera and R. A. U. Perera, Lance Corporals Sumathipala and G. D. Perera, and Privates A. J. R. Fernando, M. B. Sunil, D. N. A. D. Manapitiya, G. Robert, A. J. Wijesiri, N. A. S. Manutange, S. S. Amarasinghe, S. P. G. Rajatilleke, and K. P. Karunaratne

On the evening of the twenty-third of July, thirteen Sinhalese soldiers, a number so well placed in the human psyche that it arranges itself, as though in symmetry, in the mind, were ambushed and killed in Thirunelveli, outside Jaffna, by a group led by Velupillai Prabhakaran. Four mines were planted in a ditch intended for the installation of telecommunications equipment and detonated, from the balcony of a nearby house, under a jeep that was leading a convoy. When the soldiers who were in a half-truck behind got down to help, they, too, were attacked with automatic weapons and grenades. The bodies of those thirteen soldiers, as well as two more who succumbed later, were brought to an undertaker who had embalmed the bodies of statesman and pauper alike, the establishment of A. F. Raymond. They were brought there instead of being sent to their individual villages and towns, to be buried together at the cemetery in the capital city. This group burial was a way of avoiding the possibility of riots breaking out in the fifteen individual villages of the fifteen individual soldiers, but it could have been said that fifteen funeral pyres in one place would raise the heat of the country far more assuredly than any number of simple village ceremonies, no matter how great the provocation.

Everyone would agree afterward that it was a series of events that caused what later came to be known as Black July, but it was the murder of those soldiers that was brought up repeatedly as the reason for what happened next.

If room were made for grieving individual deaths, for remembering the conduct of the lives lost as well as the lives left behind, for sister, for neighbor, for father, perhaps there would have been no crowds pouring out from buildings, from homes, from businesses and train stations and buses. No crowds searching for fact, for direction, for an answer to the *What is to be done?* which, throughout the country's history, had only been uttered as a graceful nod to the fact that nothing, nothing can ever be done for our human circumstances. But there was no time allowed, no time taken. There were only the bodies of fifteen young soldiers, and somebody who had directed their killing.

On that Monday morning, the morning of the twenth-fourth, the children of Sal Mal Lane woke up, got dressed, and went to their respective schools or other activities.

Suren, on study leave for his Ordinary-Level examination, was at the Young Men's Buddhist Association playing in a chess tournament that was called off when one of the parents, arriving breathlessly to take his son home, said, *Thirteen soldiers have been killed and their bodies have been brought to Colombo, there are people everywhere.* He walked out of the building and into the buzz and scream and threat of panic.

Suren walked through it to A. F. Raymond, where the buses were stopped and where the doors were blocked by a large crowd. People pushed against each other, swaying as if they were a single organism, first this way, then another, on their toes, their arms outstretched or wrapped around the shoulders of strangers. He squeezed out from between them and went, as calmly as he could, toward a place from which he might find a bus to take him home. He was jostled by crowds advancing on one side, crowds flee-ing in the other, and so many children in their school uniforms, crying, their heads turning from left to right, looking up into the faces of the adults around them, then wailing afresh when they discovered that they were not their father, their mother, their known caregiver. He joined a group of people to stare up at two firefighters trying to rescue two Tamil men and one woman trapped at the top of a building that was referred to by one and all as the BCC building. One of the men was screaming along with the woman, but the other man, the other man was silent and hung back as though he would rather burn down with the building than be saved. Next to the BCC building an upturned vehicle burned furiously as though the fire itself had business elsewhere and was racing to finish. The two shops behind the vehicle were gutted and destroyed. He came upon a single man being assaulted by a group of at least a dozen men, but he did not know to whom he could go for help, for the only people who were not running were the men who were perpetrating the violence and though he screamed *Stop! Stop!* his words came out in a whisper.

Suren did not find a bus to take him home. He experienced many other such sights intimately, the shrillness of screams as well as the softer cries for help abrading his innately peaceful mind, the sounds like small knives piercing his skin. He answered some of the calls, to pick someone up, to hold aloft a lost child, to carry the bags of a mother moving in the same direction as he was going, but more often than not the task was beyond what he could manage as he walked and walked and walked all the way home, his eyes taking in everything that was in flux before him, the people, the buildings, the vehicles, even the singed trees. The marker that remained unchanged was the street itself, its potholes and pavements, its discarded posters and litter and grime a reminder that, just an hour ago, nothing extraordinary was happening. Suren filled his head with music as he went, trying to block out the things he could not control, trying not to see the things he could not bear to see, but this did not help; it only set all the terrible events to music, and Suren felt that he had grown corrupt, that he had participated in all the cruelties along the way.

As he drew close to home he saw Sonna, who was standing by the side of the road, looking bewildered. Suren wondered if he, too, was trying to get home. He wondered if they could walk together, to gain some strength from each other's company as they made their way back to Sal Mal Lane.

"Sonna!" he shouted, as people, angry with his immobility, shoved him, pushing to get past. "Sonna! Over here!"

But Sonna did not hear. He stepped forward into the crowds and a few moments later Suren saw him in the midst of a mob of men who did not look like they would provide a safe escort. He turned away and kept walking alone; the music returned, and the guilt with it.

Nihil was still at school when the prefects were sent up and down the hallways to tell the teachers that school was being closed, they had to leave and go home because *the bodies of fifteen soldiers have been brought to Colombo and there is trouble everywhere.* Though his first thought was to run out with his classmates and find a way to get to the convent to take Devi and Rashmi home, he decided to go to the staff-room and tell his mother first, and when she saw him she held on to him and would not let him leave.

"We will go home with Mr. Pieris," she said. "He has a car and he has promised to take us home. I called the convent. The girls are safe."

The car moved slowly, pushing past pedestrians who were filling up the streets. As they turned the first corner, Nihil saw that the statue in the center of the roundabout was smashed. The shop where he and his teammates liked to drink plain tea and eat hot hoppers was on fire. People were running down the road toward some sort of refuge, though where that refuge was or who was promising it, he could not see from where he sat. As their vehicle passed the University of Colombo he saw youth amassing in groups, separating and gathering again on the grounds of the campus. He saw a few students clustered around a Tamil girl. They hastily unbraided her hair and tied it into a knot at the nape of her neck. Another girl took her bag of books from her and gave her a different one. She said something to the Tamil girl and he watched her wipe her face. The two girls walked toward the center of the field hand in hand while the other students drifted away. Nihil craned his neck to watch them long after the car had moved on, picking out the purple skirt that the Tamil girl had been wearing, seeing it now in the midst of one group, now in another, until he lost her altogether.

"Don't look too long at anybody," Mrs. Herath said from the front seat.

"I hope they don't stop me and ask for petrol," Mr. Pieris said. "The headmaster said that they were stopping cars everywhere." He was sweating profusely; he had insisted that they leave the shutters up and the car was unbearably hot.

Everywhere Nihil looked now, people were crying out for help, which he could hear but could do nothing about as the car moved inexorably toward home, and Nihil wondered ceaselessly if the other members of his family had made it home safely.

They were stopped twice by mobs who pressed against the car on all sides. The first time it was because Mr. Pieris, accelerating into what he thought was a patch of clear road, almost hit a man who ran across in front of the car. He braked so hard that Nihil's head whipped back against the seat. The man came over to the driver's side, followed by a group of people. Mr. Pieris rolled down the window and Nihil saw that he was trembling.

"*Samavenna,*" Mr. Pieris said, apologizing, but the men told him to shut up.

The car rocked from side to side in the arms of the mob, and Nihil did not feel the welcome rush of fresh air, he felt the heat of their bodies seep into the car in the sweat dripping from their hairlines and in the nervous, angry energy of their movements. Lips drawn away from teeth stained with betel, with nicotine, a few pure white, mouths throbbing with angry words that were so loud that Nihil could not decipher what they were saying. Some of the men seemed unsure of what they were doing, a few looked embarrassed and stood back a little, but they did not leave, no, they continued to stand with the other men. Where had they come from? Who were these men? Nihil did not recognize a single one. But Nihil *had* met some of these men. He had sat at adjoining tables at that same store where he and his teammates had drunk that plain tea. He had boarded buses with them. He had walked beside them. But the people we understand are those with whom we live, not the ones whom we brush past, unaware of their circumstances. Yes, to Nihil there was an *us* and a *them*, as these men put it, but his *us* did not divide along the lines of race, the line that was now being drawn, his *us* lived down his lane, his *them* were screaming at his mother.

"*Sinhalada demalada?*" a man in a blue checked shirt yelled, his voice sharp and hoarse.

"We are Sinhalese," Mrs. Herath said. "This is my son. We are Heraths."

It made Nihil's heart ache to listen to his mother's voice, so full of pleading, so desperate to prove their worth by virtue of their race, their name. He wanted to tell her not to be afraid, he was there beside her, but he dared not speak.

"*Poth pennanna!*" a second man yelled.

Nihil did as the man asked and brought out his exercise books from his bag to demonstrate that they were Sinhalese, not Tamil, and though he also had an exercise book that had Tamil in it, he did not take that one out of his bag.

The second time, he and his mother and Mr. Pieris had to recite Buddhist verses to prove that they were not only Sinhalese but Buddhists as well.

"*Namo thassa—*" his mother began, speaking the opening lines of prayer, the ones every child was taught as soon as they could speak, but she was stopped with the smashing of the window on her side of the car.

The face of the leader of the mob was instantly distorted by the hairline cracks that ran away from where his hammer had hit the pane of glass. He yelled, "Not that! That's too easy! The Karaniya Metta Sutraya!"

And so they began to recite the sutra that spoke the Buddha's words on the matter of loving-kindness, a sutra that they had only ever recited within the meditative quiet of temples, each to him- or herself, or in the company of monks, their musical up and down intonations guiding them from distraction to inner stillness.

> *Karaniya matthakusalena*
> *Yam tam santam padam abhisamecca*
> *Sakko uju ca suju ca*
> *Suvaco c'assa mudu anatimani*

As his mother recited the opening stanza, her voice shaking, Nihil joined in along with Mr. Pieris, until the verse began to take hold, their voices steadied, and the mob let them pass, quietened, it seemed, by their chanting; they did not stop reciting the sutra until they reached the end. And all this while he could not shake off the thought that Devi was not safe.

But Devi was safe. She was walking, even as Nihil reached home, in the company of her father and sister.

Devi had seen nothing so long as she and Rashmi sat within the high gray walls of the convent, behind the massive steel gate that had a smaller door cut into it and that was opened to allow parents in, but one by one, so their identity could be verified, before each child, one by one, could be handed into their care. While they waited, Devi played beside the grotto of Our Lady of Perpetual Sorrows, making wishes and trying to cajole Rashmi to do the same though Rashmi, more attuned to the disturbing energy she felt beyond those gates, refused, she just sat and stared at the gate, willing her father to come for them, her heart sinking a little each time the gate opened and some other girl's father or mother appeared.

"Colombo is burning. We have to be careful getting home," Mr. Herath said to Devi and Rashmi, when he was finally allowed in, the last to get there. He took a hand in each of his and walked away from the gates. The girls looked at their father and were frightened by the anxiety on his face, his brow wrinkled as he glanced this way and that.

When they reached the end of the lane that ran alongside the gray walls of their convent and looked down the road that lead toward Galle Face Green, Devi saw high flames, the buildings beneath now handing off now accepting batons of fire. A bus and a car were both lying on their sides, their innards twisted. Right ahead of them she saw a man being pulled off a bicycle and beaten. She knitted her brow, went inward and silent as she marched by her father's side, running every now and again to keep up with his pace and asking no questions but thinking *These are the troubles that Uncle Raju spoke of. How had he known?* She held tight to her father's hand and thought only of reaching their peaceful lane where everything was going to be where it should be, nobody was injured, nothing was burning.

"Will we be able to get home?" Rashmi asked, her backpack bouncing on her shoulders, her steps quick, her voice urgent. "Where is Amma? Where are Nihil and Suren? Who is burning everything? Why is this happening?"

"Thirteen soldiers have been killed," her father replied, but wearily, as though he too knew that surely the death of thirteen soldiers could not explain this degree of anarchy.

"Where? In Colombo?" she asked, but he did not answer. "Where, Tha? Where?" she asked again, shaking the hand that was holding hers, but he did not respond and she stopped asking.

Mr. Herath was dispirited by the little he felt he had been able to achieve to counter the waves of violence that were sweeping through the city. He had directed his secretary, a Tamil lady, to pick up her daughters from their schools and go home, he had asked his driver to take the chief clerk, another Tamil, back to his home, and he had waited with his friend Mahadeva for the car to return so he could take him, Mahadeva, too, to safety. He had not called the convent until all these things were done, and had extinguished the twinge of guilt he felt when he was told by the Sister Principal, in a voice that betrayed how little she thought of him, that his daughters were the last remaining students waiting to be picked up. Still, he thought, he could have done more and now he felt only two things as he walked. He felt the weight of his daughters' hands in his, the immensity of that responsibility, and he felt the weight of history. First, he had promised his children that there would be no war, that the Tamils themselves would rid the country of Prabhakaran. Next, throughout his life, stuck in what he saw now as a bookish understanding of political movements and their ideologies, he had truly believed that the parliamentary system would prevail, the sharing of wealth and rights would become reality, the people would own and rule the country. Yet around him now, people, those very people he had counted on to stand up for social justice, to march out peacefully someday, en masse, to demand equality for all of them, they were running wild, shattering buildings, overturning vehicles. Around him people were on fire.

An old woman ran past them, her sari coming undone in a stream of red, her hand going from her mouth to the parting in her hair, rubbing, rubbing, trying to wipe away the telltale smudge. He dropped the children's hands and hurried forward to catch up to the woman, to calm her, help her in some way though in what way he did not know, but, hearing the sound of his footsteps, she screamed and ran faster. Mr. Herath fell back. Beside him, Rashmi resumed her questions and to them she added another one.

"Tha, why is she running away from us when we are good people?" she said, and he could find nothing to say.

How strange that they walked, those girls, one silent, one talking, as though such sights were insufficient to root them to the earth and make movement impossible. How strange and yet how natural that their father would keep them moving forward, one step at a time, toward home. Home where safety was guaranteed.

There were very few private vehicles on the road now, and even the buses, when they came by, were packed. When they finally managed to cram themselves into one, the conductor, who took no money, reached half out of the bus to pick Devi up and push her in so she stood on the steps, her face up against the sweaty legs and torsos of strangers. Mr. Herath began speaking in Sinhala to the children.

"Issarahata yanna," he said to Rashmi and Devi, pushing them in.

"Tha! There's no room here!" Devi replied in English, squirming toward him. Her father looked distraught.

"Do not speak to me in English," he hissed at her, in English, as they got down from the bus and started walking again. Up ahead of them a group of men dressed in sarongs and wielding clubs made their way toward them.

"Do you have a lighter?" one of them asked Mr. Herath, in English.

The girls listened as Mr. Herath referred to the man as brother, and offered him a box of matches. *"Naa sahodaraya, gini kooru vitharay thiyenne,"* he replied in Sinhala. The man leaned forward with his cigarette in his mouth and the girls watched their father light it, his hands steady, his palm keeping the flame safe.

Neither Devi nor Rashmi said another word until they reached home, their hands sweating, and the memory of the tightness of their father's grip making everything else recede.

Home

Sal Mal Lane seemed ominously quiet as they turned into it off the main road, which, too, was empty of vehicles. There was a gray pallor to the air and the smell of burning from somewhere close by. There was nobody outside and, except for the shouts of mobs far away, the only sound was their footsteps. The girls dropped their father's hands and ran the rest of the way home.

"Four people went into Kala Akki's place and robbed things," Suren told his father in a state of distress that overwhelmed him again after the initial relief he had felt when he saw his sisters come in. "I told them not to go there, I told them there's an old man there, but they went anyway!"

"Who were they?" Mr. Herath asked.

"Thugs from the slums, I think," Mrs. Herath said, standing on tip-toe on the top step leading to their front door and looking anxiously up and down what she could see of the road. She had tucked the edge of her sari into the waist of her underskirt, something she did when she was agitated. "Same fellows who used to hang around at the bottom of the lane with that Sonna." She called out to Kamala and asked her to shut all but one of the windows in each room.

"I heard them talking to the Silvas before going to the Nileses'," Nihil said. "I heard them say they knew that Mohan and Jith were going to join the army soon. And when they passed our house I told them not to go and they called me bad names and asked if I wanted to die too." Nihil's eyes filled up with tears as he said this.

"Raju is the one who got rid of them," Mrs. Herath said. "He ran inside and I heard him shouting at them and eventually they went away. But I'm afraid they are going to come back in the night."

"Can I go and see Mr. Niles now to make sure he's okay?" Nihil begged.

But he was not permitted to go out until Mr. Herath had sat by the telephone and called people in the police and people in the army and people in government both in Colombo and elsewhere and discovered that, yes, it was true, there was rioting all over the capital and in Kandy and in Bandarawela and everywhere else and there was nothing at all that any-body could do. Nobody, not the inspector general of the national police, who was Tamil, nor the commander of the army, who was Sinhalese, nor anybody else could do anything to stop it. The thugs roaming the streets were people nobody seemed to know and therefore nobody could control. The wealthiest Tamils were safe, barricaded behind sharp, pointed steel gates, walls, and security guards, but no Tamil was safe from fear, not even them. The only places where anything had been done or was being done to save anybody were places where the Sinhalese people themselves, the *we* that certain of his friends mentioned, had gathered in force to prevent the rioting. *We* put up a blockade, *we* evacuated the neighborhood and helped our Tamil friends to find places of safety, they said, and Mr. Herath hung up the phone hoping that the *we* in his neighborhood would have the courage to do likewise.

Throughout that day, the Silvas remained indoors.

At four o'clock the mob returned.

Mr. Herath dropped the phone and went out carrying Nihil's cricket bat, and Mrs. Herath shut the door and sat inside with Kamala, their arms around the children, listening to the voices outside. The children, corralled in this manner, waited, their eyes moving from each other's faces to half focus on pieces of furniture or other items in the room before returning again to a brother or a sister, searching for relief. Devi, still in her school uniform, took off her tie and began to wind and unwind it around her forearm, providing all of them with some respite as they watched her trying to align the stripes just so. She stopped when the noise grew louder and they could hear the sound of a tussle and cries of pain.

Kamala began to recite *pirith*, her voice close to tears, her palms stroking the two heads beside her, but Mrs. Herath pulled Suren and Rashmi closer to her and said, "Don't be afraid, children, he is not alone. Raju is out there."

When Mr. Herath opened his gate, he saw that Raju, brandishing his lightest barbell, had felled one of the men but now was surrounded by the other men, who were screaming at him though they were keeping a safe distance from the swinging barbell.

"I didn't mean to hit him, Uncle," he shouted to Mr. Herath, "I just wanted him to go away. Go away from our lane!" He turned to the men and yelled, his voice hoarse from all the screaming he had already done, first at the Nileses' house and now here, *"Palayang!"*

"Bastard deserved it," Mr. Herath said quickly, then turned to the group of men. "Don't you live in the Elakandiya behind Lucas's house?" he asked in Sinhala.

"What is it to you where we live? Think you own this road?" one of the men said, stepping menacingly toward Mr. Herath, who stood his ground.

"Don't touch him!" Raju yelled. "You touch him and I'll land this on your head too!"

Just at that moment Jimmy Bolling came jogging up the road with two belts in his good hand. "You fuckers, you stay away from my cousin!" he screamed.

Raju, though he had not won the title of Mr. Sri Lanka, won Jimmy Bolling's respect that afternoon for the way he used his barbell, knocking first one then another of the men to the ground while Jimmy himself whipped them with his belt until at last the men, singly and then in groups, ran away.

"They'll come back, I'm sure of it," Mr. Herath said, wiping his face, his voice shaky. They dropped their weapons, the bat, the barbells, the belts, and all three of them examined their own bodies for cuts and bruises. Jimmy Bolling had a thin long gash on his bad upper arm from a knife, Mr. Herath had several sharp incisions and his shirt was torn, the buttons ripped, one sleeve hanging by threads. Raju alone had suffered no injuries.

"We have to get you out of here, Raju," Jimmy Bolling said. "Get your mother an' come, we'll go to my house."

Raju, his shirt stuck to his body with sweat, his face a mix of pride and fear, tried to resist. "I have to stay and guard the house," he said. "Otherwise they'll take everything."

"There'll be no use for the things in the house if you're dead, you idiot, go!" And Jimmy Bolling shoved Raju toward the gate to his house. "They'll be comin' back to look for you after what you did to them. Go now. Fill a bag with a few things an' come."

And though Raju resisted as much as he could, citing first his previous success at saving the Nileses' house and then the rebuttal of this second attack, in the end, Jimmy Bolling took Old Mrs. Joseph and Raju as well as their servant girl to his house, barricaded them and his whole family, except for Sonna, who was nowhere to be found, behind his doors, and sat outside his aluminum fence with Sonna's old bat, which was child sized, a knife, and two of his belts. He held those weapons and he thought that if his oldest son showed up from wherever he had gone to, he would be the first to beat him, for Jimmy Bolling knew without a doubt that Sonna was in the thick of looting. From outside, he listened to his aunt talk bitterly about terrorists and the prevention of terrorism and *Where*, she asked, *Where were the people to arrest the terrorists who were terrorizing people in the full light of day?* He listened to his wife stirring sugar into glasses of plain tea, and he listened to Rose and Dolly relating, yet again, the difficulties they had experienced trying to get home from school.

When Mr. Bin Ahmed came, carrying a suitcase containing irreplaceable documents, photographs, jewelry, and the two trophies his daughter had won for debating, as a child, a suitcase he had packed months ago, during a time when nobody on Sal Mal Lane had expected any disturbances, and when he said, "Mr. Bolling, can we also come and stay in your house? My wife and daughter are very scared. We are right by the road and thugs are going up and down, please Mr. Bolling," Jimmy Bolling yelled at his wife to open the door and shoved them inside. Francie Bolling gave them Sonna's room, and although the Bin Ahmeds had always lived in an impeccably kept house, for as long as they sat there they saw nothing of the grime and mess, their minds entirely on safety.

Lucas and Alice went to Mrs. Ratwatte's house and sat on a bench in her back veranda, alternately mourning the events of the day and talking about the families on Sal Mal Lane, about who among them might be safe, who protected and who betrayed. Of one thing they were sure: Raju and Jimmy Bolling would be able to look after their own houses. It was the Niles family that they worried about the most, even Alice, who, in the face of all that was happening, abandoned the harmless antipathies with which she had entertained herself for most of her adult life.

As the day wore on and the sounds of rioting grew louder, the Nadesans called out to Mrs. Herath from the other side of their half-green wall. Their two servants had climbed to the top of the wall using a ladder and were crouching there, looking terrified.

"Amma! Nadesans are coming," Devi cried, running to her mother when she saw them.

"Open the gate, quick!" her mother replied.

"Not at the gate, over the wall behind," Nihil said, and ran to open the back door. "My mother is coming, don't worry," he said to the Nadesans.

Mr. and Mrs. Herath came out, along with Kamala and the rest of the children, and the Nadesans, dressed as usual in their formal clothes, he in his pressed shirt and khaki trousers, she in a deeply colored sari, a red *pottu* in the part of her hair, were helped down the Heraths' side of the wall by Suren and Mr. and Mrs. Herath, who stood on chairs, all of them turning their faces away to spare Mrs. Nadesan, who was attempting to hold her sari wrapped close around her legs as she struggled in their various arms. The Nadesans filed wordlessly into the Heraths' house and were shown to Rashmi and Devi's room, where they sat, silent and still, their eyes on the floor. They had brought nothing but their national identification cards, their checkbooks, and their passports.

At last Nihil was allowed to leave, and he ran to Mr. Niles's house, Suren close on his heels. "We have to take Uncle to our house," he said, bursting in through the doors that Kala Niles only opened after she heard Suren's voice.

"All of you must come," Suren said.

Kala Niles rubbed her shoulders repeatedly as though she were cold, paced back and forth, and began to cry. "I can't go anywhere. I can't leave my piano. Take Mama and Papa. I will stay here and save my piano."

Nihil went over to Mr. Niles and took his hand, seeing that he was far too agitated to speak. He tried to comfort him, saying, "Raju and my father and Uncle Jimmy are all going to look after the lane," but Mr. Niles shook his head, no, so Nihil fell silent. Instead, he reached up and stroked Mr. Niles's head. He was struck by how clean that hair felt, silken and soothing to his touch, something soft in the midst of all that was going on. He continued to run his fingers through Mr. Niles's hair, half mesmerized, half hoping that his presence would be enough to calm the old man.

Behind him, Nihil heard Suren reassuring Kala Niles. He said, "Don't worry, Kala Akki, we will find a house that has no piano and move your piano there," and he turned and ran and went from house to house asking which family might make room for the piano. And Suren, being Suren, included the Silvas in his rounds.

The door to the Silvas' house was shut and it took a long while for them to come to the door though he could hear them whispering on the other side. Finally Suren yelled, "Mohan! Jith! Open the door!"

Mr. Silva opened the door when he heard Suren's voice. "Can we bring Kala Akki's piano here? The mobs might come back and if they do they might destroy it," Suren explained.

Mrs. Silva, listening from inside, walked to the door and stood beside her husband. She looked scared. "My god! We can't take the piano, Suren. If they see that piano here they will know we are helping Tamil people. Might come and loot our house too! We are just going to shut our door and stay inside. You had better do the same. I don't know what your parents are doing, letting you run around like this!" And Mrs. Silva began to shut the door.

Jith stepped forward. "Are the Bollings okay?" he asked Suren in as low a voice as he could manage while still being audible.

"I don't know. I think so. Yes," Suren said.

"Get inside!" Mrs. Silva said, the fear gone from her voice. She grabbed Jith by his arm and yanked him inside. Before the door shut, Suren caught sight of Mohan, and in his eyes Suren saw all the threatening remarks that Mohan had ever made to him, about wars and his inability to help anybody, including his sisters, all condensed into this one moment. He turned around and ran with renewed resolve. Mohan was wrong. He *could* do something.

The Sansonis and Heraths already had pianos. He found that the Bollings' house was far too full, and besides it was too close to the main road and visible to any of the thugs still roaming the streets. That left only the Tissera family, who, after some initial consternation—*Would the mobs come while they were in the middle of the move? Would they come to their house too?*—began to make room for the piano.

"Uncle Raju," Suren said, after he'd knocked on Jimmy Bolling's door and been let in by Rose, "we're going to need your help. We need to get Kala Akki's piano to the Tisseras' place."

Raju, who had spent his time pacing this way and that in the Bollings' dining area, shuffled into his slippers and marched out with purpose. "I need to go and help the Heraths," he said to his cousin as he passed him. "They need my help," he added, in case this had not been made clear enough. Jimmy Bolling nodded and kept on walking; he was already on his way to join in the effort.

It was a sight to behold, that piano being moved with such care from Kala Niles's house to the Tissera house. For several minutes, while the people on all sides caught their breath, Suren and Mr. Tissera and Raju on one end and Mr. Herath and Jimmy Bolling and Rashmi and Nihil on the other, that piano sat, for all the world as though there was no better place on earth to be but right in the middle of a curving road under skies graying with the smell of loss, and it seemed as though if Suren had sat on the piano bench and begun to play the saddest piece of music he had ever heard, Chopin's Nocturne no. 21 in C Minor, nobody would have asked him to stop, they would have all simply sunk to their knees and let the whole world burn.

Kala Niles did not know that the piano would take a long time to return to her home, but then, nobody was thinking beyond that evening.

"We have to carry Papa," Kala Niles said, once the piano was safely situated against the living room wall of the Tissera household as though music was a part of their daily lives, not something of which they partook by standing outside their neighbors' houses, and after her record player had been taken to the Heraths' house. "He stays on that bed now, so we will have to carry the whole bed."

Once more the neighbors gathered, and Jimmy Bolling delayed returning to his post to help carry the old man, who was disappearing into the thin mattress that topped the plank of wood on which he now spent every moment of every day, being turned and moved by others, never of his own volition. They carried him down the street but held low, unlike a coffin, down and in through the gates to the Heraths' house and all the way through it to the dining room next to the kitchen, which was the only place where such a long bed would fit.

As he was moved down that road, Mr. Niles looked up at the sky. He looked up and he said, "The last time I saw that sky was when I watched Nihil play his cricket match." He said that and he began to cry and he said nothing for a long time after, not even when Nihil spoke to him.

Fire

The third mob arrived just after sunset. Kamala and Rashmi were busy trying to make their guests comfortable when they stopped, cups of plain tea and towels in hand, words fading on their lips at the sound of the men moving inexorably up their road. Perhaps they stopped at Jimmy Bolling's house, for there was a change in the sound made by their feet and voices, a pause of some sort before they resumed their march up the road.

Devi, still small enough to creep through a bathroom window, was just returning from rescuing Mrs. Nadesan's gold wedding necklace from her almirah. After climbing back onto the top of the wall, on Suren's instructions, she pushed the ladder away from the wall so nobody would know that the Nadesans were hiding with her family. She climbed down along the ivy, her body light enough to be held by the still-young roots. She heard the first voices as she began her descent and it made her scramble and slip and scrape herself until she fell into Suren's arms. She gave the necklace to Rashmi, then ran to find Nihil and put her arms around him.

"I'm scared!" she said.

"Don't be scared, they're not coming here."

"How do you know?" she asked. She pressed her face against his chest. She could hear the beat of his heart and it was too loud and too fast for her to be reassured by his words.

"I know," he said, and he was filled with a feeling of remorse, for he did know, now, why they would not stop at his house and that Mohan had been right all along, the war had come. He removed Devi's arms from around his body, but he took her hand and went to join Rashmi and Suren, who were standing at the front window watching their parents, who were now outside their gate.

"What are you doing?" Mr. Herath shouted, pushing at some of the men advancing up the road. "Stop this! These are innocent people, they are our neighbors!"

The children saw a member of the mob break away and come toward their father. The man wore a peacock-blue sari around his neck. The man grabbed their father by the front of his shirt and shook him. They saw their mother plead with the man, her palms together, and they heard her woman's voice high over the others as she turned away from them and called out to the Silvas. They heard their father again, his words, uttered in a familiar voice, clear. "I will not let you do this!" He raised his voice louder and called for help, "Raju! Jimmy!" even though neither of them could have heard him over the sound of the mob.

Nihil, his fists clenched, said, "I can run and get them!" He started for the door, but Suren pulled him back, saying no, he would not be allowed past the gate anyway.

The man shouted something else at their parents and they could not hear what was being said in all the commotion, but they could see the expression on his face; a look of such deep scorn that Nihil felt ashamed for his family. Whatever the man said seemed to take the fight out of their father and they watched as the man pushed him and he did not stand his ground, so he fell against their mother, who pulled him away from the road and shut the gate with a padlock. They listened as each member of the mob outside rattled their gate as they passed, some so fiercely they were sure it would come off its hinges, the air rent with the sound it made, like a giant cymbal beating time. They watched their mother run her hand over and over down their father's back as he leaned against the wall, his face turned to it.

Suren closed his eyes for a few moments as if he were reaching deep within himself for something, understanding, wisdom, anything that would tell him how to help his parents and siblings. When he opened his eyes, he turned to Rashmi and said, "Rashmi, go and make sure the Nadesans and the Nileses are okay." Then he turned to Nihil and asked him to check on Mr. Niles. Devi, he dispatchd to the kitchen, to ask Kamala to make some ginger tea.

Rashmi went and found Mrs. Nadesan rocking back and forth, talking softly in Tamil, her face wet.

"Don't worry, Aunty," she said, "you'll be safe here. Devi brought your *thali*, see?" and she drew the heavy gold necklace out of her pocket and fastened it around Mrs. Nadesan's neck, all the time trying not to hear the sounds outside, of shattering glass and voices lifted in triumph. Mrs. Nadesan only rocked faster.

"Thank you, thank you," Mr. Nadesan said, and Rashmi knew that they would prefer to be left alone, so she went to check on Mrs. Niles instead.

Nothing in the boys' room was rumpled or disturbed. The beds, made by Kamala just that morning, were still neat and creased, the floors swept, the curtains drawn against the heat. It was a serenity that startled Rashmi, who was, herself, in a state of deep agitation though she tried to hide it with a calm expression, the one she felt was required of her at this moment. Mrs. Niles was reciting a rosary, her eyes shut, her mouth moving, her fingers caressing each clear bead, the silver cross resting in her other hand. She looked odd sitting there, bolt upright on Suren's bed as if she were merely visiting, even as she mouthed her prayers.

"Rashmi, tell me, what is happening?" Kala Niles asked, her eyes full of concern.

"Don't worry, Kala Akki," Rashmi said, "you're safe."

Kala Niles nodded and was quiet for a few moments. Rashmi sat down next to her on Nihil's bed. They both listened to the mob outside. There was something particularly wrong, Rashmi thought, with a room that could be this quiet, prayerful thoughts releasing into it, while a few yards away bedlam reigned.

As they listened there was a long series of crashes and Rashmi winced and drew closer to Kala Niles, who said, "Everything will be lost."

Rashmi composed herself. "The piano will be safe," she said, softly. "The record player will be safe. And you are safe."

Kala Niles took Rashmi's hand in hers and stroked it. She tried to imagine if this was true, if the piano, the record player, her parents, herself, if these were the only things that could be lost. She tried to make the guarantee of their safety loosen the tightness in her chest. It did not. For she knew that across the street, what was being erased was the conduct of their lives, and who could ever bring that back?

Rashmi listened to the sound of Nihil's voice as he talked to Mr. Niles, explaining, as though he hadn't done this already, that he would be safe there, that his parents would look after him.

"We will say you are our grandfather," she heard Nihil say, and she wondered if Nihil only cared about Mr. Niles, whether he had forgotten all the other people they were sheltering. She hoped that none of those others were listening to Nihil and was glad when she heard his quick footsteps pass by the door on his way to some other part of the house.

The Heraths, the Tisseras, the Sansonis, Jimmy Bolling, and the Silvas, each family in their own house, listened to the sound of looting. Nihil joined Suren to stand together by the window closest to the Nadesans' house, as though their nearness could provide comfort to the house itself. They stood, their bodies tense, their ears alert, trying to separate the sounds they could hear, one from the other. Voices carried over walls. Voices rejoicing in some particularly precious item, an especially heavy sari rich with embroidery, a set of glass bangles, voices warning each other to watch out, there was broken glass there, step back, be careful. There was no fear in those voices.

Nihil, grown wiser, said, "Sonna could stop these people. He could control them. He's the one who knows them."

"Maybe," Suren said, thinking about the last time he had seen Sonna, earlier that day, at the center of a mob just like this one, "but he's not here."

They continued to listen to the sounds around them, the tinny crash of ornaments hitting the floor, the thud of furniture pushed over, the sound of breaking crockery. These were the types of sounds that ordinarily would have startled them, made the adults around them take a sharp breath before scolding them for being careless. Now Nihil and Suren stood, unable in the excess of sounds to pick out one whose making they could regret in greater measure.

A man called out that he had found two sets of silver knives, did the other men want some? Nihil leaned forward and gripped the bars of the window, the skin on his knuckles tight. "Do you think if we had the Silvas' guns, we could stop them?" Nihil asked.

"We aren't the type of people who own guns," Suren said.

"But if we had them? If someone gave them to us? If we could get the Silvas' guns, do you think Tha could stop these men?" Nihil persisted.

"Maybe," Suren said after some thought. "But it is those types of people, people with guns, who prepare for war. I prefer to be like us."

Nihil did not know what *people like us* meant anymore. He had thought that he belonged to the group he referred to as *good people*. But of what use were good people if they could not prevent the bad people from robbing their neighbors? He wished he had a gun. He would have shot the man who attacked his father, he would shoot everybody. His body began to heave. He wondered if this was what Mr. Niles had meant when he talked about people having war within them. He wondered if he was like Mohan now, a vessel of war.

Suren put his arms around Nihil and stroked his head until he stopped shaking. "It is better that we don't have guns," Suren said. "It is better to save our neighbors than to attack other people's neighbors."

Nihil tried to hold on to his anger but felt it abate as he rested in his brother's arms. He put his own arms around Suren and embraced him. Rashmi came into the room where they were standing, still wondering how a house so full of people, as theirs was now, could be so silent.

"Are they gone?" she asked. "It seems quieter."

They all listened. The sound was growing less, a stray crash here and there, the sound of feet running, this time, away. Then they heard their mother's footsteps. She came into the house, her eyes wet, and said, "They've started to burn the houses down," and she didn't stop any of them as they ran outside, all of her children, she simply kept walking until she reached Mrs. Niles and put her arms around her.

Devi climbed the Asoka tree, Nihil behind her.

"What can you see?" Rashmi asked from below.

"They're setting fire to Uncle Raju's house!" Devi shouted down to them.

"And now the Nileses' house!" Nihil said.

Devi, watching from her perch in the tree, was glad, in the way that only children can be glad, that Raju was not there, that he was safe and being guarded by someone as formidable as Jimmy Bolling. Nihil, sitting on a lower branch, watched with her, and was glad that Mr. Niles was not there, nor the piano, that they were both safe. But even though they tried to hold on to that gladness, they were stirred from within by the sense of their own impotence and that feeling, that helplessness, eventually took over as they watched, unable to do anything but watch, as the two houses filled with smoke from fires lit in different rooms.

Nihil inched higher on his branch. "Kala Akki's rose vines are on fire!" he said, his memory tricking him into smelling not fire but the fragrance of the roses.

Devi and Nihil watched the flaming bushes, transfixed by the way the fire, with its crepitant song, climbed from root, along each twisting limb to flower and on up to the roof of the veranda. It looked like someone was writing in an elegant script, a strange beauty marking the destruction as it went. But when it reached the gutters, which must have held some residual rain, it stopped, and the sound of crashing beam and falling tiles, from Raju's house this time, broke the spell for them both.

Nihil looked up at Devi, who seemed, herself, to be half floating away on the heavy threads of smoke that were now making their way into the neighboring gardens. Parts of her body were obscured and Nihil felt an acute sense of pain as the smell from the burning and the smoke conjured up a vision of a funeral pyre. He tried to console himself once again with the thought that no, Mr. Niles and all their Tamil neighbors were safe, there was no pyre, nothing that was burning mattered. He called up to his sister and asked her to climb down.

"You are too high," he said, "climb down next to me."

"I want them to go!" Devi cried, tears escaping from her smoke-filled eyes, as she climbed part of the way down the tree and balanced herself on the same branch on which he was standing.

"We can't make them go," Nihil said, turning his face away from her so she would not see that he, too, was crying. He wondered if Jith was worrying about Dolly, if the other Silvas were safer from all that he felt knotted and painful inside him because they had never cared about any of the other people down the lane. He wondered again about those guns, for what use they were being reserved.

"Have they gone?" Suren called from below.

Nihil shook his head. "No. There are some left. Others are still running away with things. I can't see what they are taking, there's too much smoke."

Nihil and Devi climbed down and stood with Rashmi and Suren inside their veranda, waiting. After a long time, the mob left and they heard Mr. Sansoni calling them.

"Come soon! We can still put out this fire!" he said, as he ran down the street with a bucket of water. He kept the index and middle fingers of his right hand on his nose as he went, holding his glasses in place. Everybody rushed out at the sound of his voice, even though Mr. Sansoni was so rarely a part of any activity that took place down Sal Mal Lane.

Mr. Tissera came swift on his heels, carrying his own buckets of water, which he filled and refilled at the tap in Kala Niles's house. The buckets dragged Mr. Tissera's arms down on either side and he, a thin man, looked like he might, himself, split in half. It was not until Mrs. Herath asked Suren to get the hose from their garden that it occurred to Mr. Tissera to look for the one that Kala Niles used to water her flowers and use that instead.

"Bring the hose!" Mrs. Herath said to Suren, who was already dragging it out of its muddy inertia, and she stood with the pipe aimed now at one house, now the other, her spray of water crossing every now and again with Mr. Tissera's, while all around her the children, Mr. Herath, Kamala, and the other neighbors threw buckets and pots and bowls of water against the walls until the fires were put out, leaving behind the soggy charred smell of their good intentions married with the ill will that had caused the fires. None of them knew that two of the buckets they were using belonged to the Silvas, nor that it was Mrs. Silva who had brought them out and left them on the street for them to find.

That night, Mr. and Mrs. Herath sat in the front veranda as they always did during the late evenings, pretending to chat. Inside, in the boys' room, where Mrs. Niles and Kala Niles sat, and the girls' room, where the Nadesans and their servants sat, all was quiet. When Kamala and Rashmi served rice and dhal and dried fish and sambol, which, though nobody wanted to eat, was the right thing to serve because it was the food of the soul, the food that everybody no matter where they were from, no matter the circumstances of their hunger or lack thereof, could eat, the Nadesans refused. They were Indian Brahmins and would not eat food cooked in the Heraths' pots. So a packet of Marie biscuits was offered, along with fruit juice made by diluting a mango concentrate that had been in the fridge, and this they accepted.

Nihil sat next to Mr. Niles, feeding him soup whose vegetables had been mashed with a fork in the grooved *nebiliya* that Kamala used to wash and destone the rice. Devi sat beside him and they both tried to get Mr. Niles to talk, but he would not. He simply opened his mouth for his food, wiped his eyes with the one handkerchief he had with him, even though it was completely damp, and remained silent, and Nihil told Devi to go find their father's handkerchiefs and bring them for Mr. Niles, which she did, glad for a task she could manage.

Nothing was communicated during the serving of this first meal except with murmurs and silent offerings of one thing or another, a head shaken here, a nod there, and when the spoons and plates were collected after, the ordinary sounds of clearing dishes seemed unnaturally loud.

Which is why Mrs. Herath asked Suren to play the piano that night. "Play Beethoven," she said, "perhaps that will help them to sleep."

As that night in July came to a close, the strains of Piano Sonata no. 14 in C-sharp Minor, op. 27, no. 2, a piece so familiar it fairly breathed, lifted off the keys and floated tenderly through the house and down the silent street where nobody was listening.

Where Sonna Went

Jimmy Bolling did not, ordinarily, care where Sonna went. Ordinarily he would have been glad if Sonna never returned. But this had not been an ordinary day.

First, Rose and Dolly had barely made it to safety. On their way home, the girls had been confronted by a group of men.

"Nice skin but hair is brown," one of them said, stroking her cheek as Dolly cringed.

"What school?" another said, yanking Dolly's tie.

"Methodist," she replied, beginning to cry.

"Not Buddhist school?" the man yelled.

"We're Burgher," Rose said, taking Dolly's hand in hers.

"*Lansi?* Then why not fairer skin?" another yelled. Despite the time of day she could smell alcohol on his breath.

"Our father's great-grandmother," Dolly began, her voice quivering, but Rose dug her fingers into her sister's palm and stepped toward the men.

"We are Sinhala mix. *Ammata hukana keri vesige putho, thavath kunuharapa ahagannethuwa apita ape paaduwe yanna deepang hukanne nethuwa. Pakaya!*" In a moment of inspiration that sprang not from fear but from fury, Rose unleashed a string of filth that made the men first fall back at the sound and sight of it, this light-skinned girl hurling such raw words at them, then burst into laughter.

"Go, go, go home quickly!" one man said in English.

"If someone else catches you, you won't be so lucky," another one said, pushing them roughly down the road. They had stood there laughing as the girls ran away from them.

Their story when they got home added to Jimmy Bolling's fear. For the first time in his life, he wished his son would come home. He needed Sonna the way any man who has to protect a household of women, children, and an old man, needed the kind of strapping son that Sonna had become. Seeing Jimmy Bolling's distress as he listened to Rose's story, Raju had tried to help. He had brought the Bin Ahmeds' hose into their house and spent more than an hour watering the boundary walls of the Bolling compound, saying helpfully, *If they come with kerosene, we must be prepared,* while aiming the hose methodically in stripes along the fences and onto the walls. He then climbed up on a chair he dragged to the corner of the compound, where the Bolling girls had sat so often while Suren played the guitar for them, and aimed the hose over the fence and onto the side of his mother's house, which sat adjacent.

But, having stomped through the mud and yelled *Enough!* at Raju, and having forced everybody indoors again, and locked the front door, Jimmy Bolling felt the weight of his solitude return. Although he had uttered a few strong words as the looters passed him, he had not tried to prevent them from swarming into the houses up the road, and he had not been able to help his neighbors put out even the smallest fires he could see from where he sat, for fear that Raju or his mother would come out and see what was happening. He had been forced to watch as groups of men ran past him, more than a few of them calling him a *lansi ponnaya* as they went, knowing that for one reason or another, no matter how many knives and belts he had beside him, he would not leave his post to attack them. When first Raju and then Old Mrs. Joseph had asked about the smoke, calling to him from inside, he had yelled *Some trouble down the next lane* and summoned his wife to move Raju and his mother to the farthest room, theirs, and make sure they stayed there, the only protection he could offer them from what was happening outside.

Now, after all that, here he was again, sitting outside his flimsy aluminum fencing, having to guard all these people, and where was Sonna? A curl of fear rose inside him, and with it came an image of his son as a child. Sonna was seven, standing silently by the fence while Rose sat on the ground wailing. Jimmy Bolling remembered that face, Sonna's, the way it had looked, as though the world itself had shifted, somehow. He had watched that face in the side-view mirror as his friend reversed the car and he had watched Sonna kneel down in the dirt and pull Rose close to him. He had held her face and stroked her hair. By the pursing of his mouth he had been able to tell that Sonna was hushing her, whispering *shh . . . shhh*. Jimmy Bolling remembered asking his friend to stop the car, he wanted to go and comfort his son, to tell him it wasn't his fault, and when his friend would not listen, too drunk to care, Jimmy Bolling had lunged at the steering wheel. After that there was nothing but the memory of pain and rage.

Dolly's voice rose up from inside and startled Jimmy Bolling. He jumped as though he had been caught in the midst of some cowardice. He looked up and down the silent lane, then moved his head, stretching out the muscles of his neck. He glanced at the sky. Evening was falling. What would the night bring? Sonna would have the connections to intervene on behalf of his family, he thought bitterly. Bastard knows everybody. Where the fuck was he?

Yes, where was Sonna?

On the morning of the riots, while all the other children got ready and went to school, Sonna woke up in the house of a new friend he had fallen in with a few weeks earlier. They had come together to steal plants from the nursery beyond the bridge and then sell them to households in neighborhoods in Dehiwala. Together, they also stole pawned jewelry from a broker on High Street and sold it to young women on their way to work, accosting them at the bus halt near Russell Stores. Sonna had three hundred rupees so far, from his commission on the sales. When he had enough he was going to start a security business. He had heard from Mohan that this was an up-and-coming industry. *People are scared these days,* Mohan had said, *security businesses will be starting everywhere.* While Sonna did not know exactly how such a business might be set up, he felt he had the necessary credentials to provide security to people. He was street smart, he was strong, he could frighten people.

He was still in that half-awake, half-dreaming state that morning when his friend shook him. "Sonna, wake up, dead soldiers have been brought to Colombo. They're saying riots!" the boy said.

"Riots? Where?"

"Here!"

Sonna sat up quickly and dressed. If there were riots, he knew the Elakandiya mobs would go to Sal Mal Lane. He had to get home quickly. He buckled his belt, threw on his shirt, stuffed his feet into his boots, no socks, and strode down the road. If Sonna had left earlier he would have made it back to Sal Mal Lane, but by the time he got out of his friend's house the streets were filled with people, half of them terrified, the other half terrifying. He saw Suren in that former group. He wanted to call out to him, to ask if he knew if everybody was all right on Sal Mal Lane, but between him and Suren there was a crowd of men among whom Sonna saw people from the slums near his house, their known faces coming into sharp focus against masses of features he could not recognize.

"Ah! Sonna Sir! Come and join us!" they shouted. Two of the men broke off from the gang and came over to Sonna, put their arms around him and half dragged him into their midst.

"*Machang,* I have to go home—" Sonna began, but he was shouted down.

"Home? Now is not the time to go home, Sir! This is the time we have to save our people!"

"We're going to Wellawatte and then coming back this way. You can go home then. Come, come, hurry up!" And Sonna found himself jostled and pulled along by the crowd. He kept glancing back, hoping to see Suren again, but when he finally did see him, Suren was much farther along the road, too far away to hear him even if he called out. He reconciled himself to being swept along by the mob. On the way Sonna learned of the bomb that had killed the soldiers, the transportation of their bodies, and the rioting that followed.

"*Demala huththo,*" they said angrily, "think those bloody Tamil Tigers can kill our soldiers? We'll see about that. There won't be one left when we finish." And they smashed the fronts of stores that belonged to Tamil merchants, and if they could not, if there were steel doors that sealed the store, they poured kerosene under the doors and set the oil alight, never pausing to see if the fire would take hold, or if anyone was inside, moving so ceaselessly from one establishment to the next that it seemed to Sonna that they would not stop until there was nothing left to burn.

During all his declamations against the Tamils, a dislike he had acquired through his association with Mohan and one he had made his own solely to add to the ways in which he could infuriate and distinguish himself from his father, during all that time, Sonna had never conceived of a day like this. He had spoken, as Mohan did, of *troubles* and *someday* and *bloody Tamils,* but his animosities lay closer to home, the bloody Tamils of his words just a stand-in for his father, the person he could not curse quite so readily or quite so freely.

Now, caught in the madness around him, there was nothing for him to do but join in, though he couldn't let go of his fear for Sal Mal Lane and all its inhabitants, though all he wanted to do was run home. He screamed at people he saw along the way, sending them scattering this way and that, he pushed two young boys off their bicycles, he slapped a middle-aged man until he fell to the ground, and he tore through shops sweeping inventory to the floor. Each time he did these things he imagined the Herath children watching and the image of those faces saddened him, and so he bared his teeth and his voice came out louder. He did everything harder, more wild than all the rest, setting fire to rooms before any of the men had a chance to loot. Deep within himself, Sonna was occupying a different frame; he was charging through streets to rescue, not harm, and he came at people like an avenging god until he could no longer tell the difference. He paused once; in the one open shop that the men got to before he did, the owner long since fled, he saw a shrink-wrapped cassette tape of top-twenty songs from 1982 in a pile of cassettes that the men were about to burn and it reminded him of Rose, so he picked it up and put it in the back pocket of his jeans, the one thing he stole that day.

"Kalyani Avenue!" the men yelled as they turned back. "Lane is full of Tamils. Not one Sinhalese house!"

"Let's go there then. Leave the rest to others."

On they stormed, on back down High Street, and on down the hill toward Kalyani Avenue. Sonna, instantly sobered, grabbed the shirt of the man nearest to him, a man whose skin was such an unusual shade of dark that he was named for it. "Kalu Aiyya," he panted as they ran, "I must go home now."

"Why are you going home, Sonna Sir?" the man asked, keeping pace, "there's work to be done."

"I have done enough. I have to go and see if my family is okay."

The man stopped. "Why would your family not be okay? Aren't they Burgher?"

"Yes, Burgher, but my father's aunt, others down the road—"

"Then you come with us when we go there to get rid of them," the man said, resuming his jog, his rolled-up sarong bouncing against his thighs as he ran.

Sonna left Kalu Aiyya behind and ran faster until he came to the front of the group. "Stop!" he said, holding up his arms. "Stop!"

The men bumped into each other as they came to a slow stop. Around them other smaller groups of men and some women were tearing through the streets. There were no Tamils to be seen on the streets now; they had all gone into hiding or run away or were trapped in their homes. An egg-shaped van came speeding up the road and one of the men pulled another away from its path, his arm around his shoulder. Both men shouted at the driver to watch where he was going, couldn't he see he could kill somebody driving like that?

"What, Sonna Sir? What? Tell quickly!" one of the men shouted. One of his forearms sparkled with several gold bangles and he had a peacock-blue silk sari wrapped around his neck. His pockets bulged.

Sonna looked around. The rest of them, too, were carrying their loot upon their bodies, in their clothes. One man kept patting his shirt pocket, which was filled with hair clips and ribbons for some beloved female in his life. Another had a child's yellow-and-green drink bottle slung around his neck. A third had dressed himself in shirts and women's blouses to the point that the upper half of his body seemed bloated in contrast to his thin legs. In one corner there was a man who was using the edge of a sleeve to wipe the blood off a young boy who had suffered some injury along the way. He spat into the shirt and wiped again, then pressed the shirt into the wound. The boy grimaced in pain and the man uttered some soothing words. None of them carried weapons. Weapons, Sonna supposed, were always easy to find. They lay in every house so long as the inhabitants were too scared to pick them up themselves. Any chair, any knife, any bat, any bar in any window. That and the power of numbers. He shuddered.

"What?" the same man yelled. "If there's nothing to say, let us keep going. We're wasting time."

"My lane, Sal Mal Lane, must not be touched," Sonna said, making his voice as powerful as he could, some of the depth of his father's voice suddenly coming out of his mouth.

The men started shouting, arguing. "What is so great about your Tamils? You have Tamils, they must also go," one said. He had sat down on a suitcase stuffed with stolen goods, saris, cutlery, picture frames, even a bell that he had yanked off a tricycle.

"My family is there," Sonna said. "I don't want my family harmed. And there are Sinhalese families there. Tisseras, Silvas, Heraths." He paused and drew a deep breath, "Heraths specially, they will be helping Tamils. They must be safe."

"Who is this Herath fucker?" one man asked, spitting. "Who is this *huththa* who is helping Tamils?"

"He deserves to burn," said another, a man who looked eminently decent except for the dirt and sweat on his khaki trousers and white shirt, someone who obviously held a desk job. Sonna wondered how he had got involved with this particular group.

"We should burn the whole lane," a teenaged boy said. His voice cracked in the middle of the sentence and he finished on a high whine. He glanced at Sonna and added, "Except Sonna Sir's house. He's with us."

"Are you with us?" the man with the sari around his neck asked Sonna. "Because if you aren't with us then you must be like this Herath fool. Helping Tamils. Sounds like that is what is happening here." He used the edge of the sari to wipe the sweat, ash, and dirt off his face, and the blue sari came away creased and grimed.

Another man spoke up. "Sonna Sir has always been with us. If he's asking, we should listen."

The men broke into argument again, some wanting to forget Kalyani Avenue and go straight to Sal Mal Lane to torch all the houses, others saying no, there was more to be done on Kalyani Avenue, those Indian Tamils who thought they were too good for everybody, and what kind of barbarians would burn the houses of Sinhalese people? Their own race? No, this was a time to protect *our* people, wives, children, homes, this was a time to make it clear that not one more Sinhalese soldier would ever be touched by those Tamil devils in Jaffna. If any of the men remembered an attenuating fact, some kindness done or received, some sweet shared, some marriage made within their families with the Tamils, not in faraway Jaffna, which none of them had ever visited, but those who lived among them, they did not mention it. This was a time of just deserts and lessons taught and believing without a shadow of doubt that whatever was done was deserved.

Sonna listened, his whole body alert. If the men decided to turn toward Sal Mal Lane, he would have to outrun them. He did not know what he would do when he got there. Mohan's guns came to mind. If he could reach Mohan, the two of them could get those guns and stand at the bottom of the road. None of the marauding crowds had that kind of weapon. He could keep the lane safe. His father might join them. His heart lifted then resettled at this prospect. He thought of Devi, Rashmi, Nihil, how grateful they would be that he had saved not just one house but the whole lane. He could taste it, that moment, it was so close. He braced himself to start running.

Then the leader of the group, a man who had suffered burns over most of his body as a child, and whose limbs were covered in large patches of pink flesh, and who was, on account, called Sudhu Aiyya, spoke. "You come with us to Kalyani Avenue," he said. "After that we will have to go to Sal Mal Lane. We can't leave out certain Tamils like you are saying. No, listen! Listen!" he said, as Sonna protested. "We will go to Sal Mal Lane but we will not touch the Tamils." A dissatisfied murmur rose up. "All of you listen to me," he yelled. "We will not touch them, but we will have to destroy their houses, there's no help for that. That son of a whore Prabhakaran asked for this, killing our soldiers. Now, they will get it."

"I'm asking for a favor, Sudhu Aiyya," Sonna said, his voice lower now, the threat gone out of it. "Please, you can take everything from Kalyani Avenue—"

"*Oy!* Sudhu Aiyya has decided, didn't you hear?" The man nearest to him pushed Sonna in the chest.

"I will do anything," Sonna begged, "I will burn every house on Kalyani Avenue, anything, but please save Sal Mal Lane."

"Enough!" Sudhu Aiyya said. "You want to burn houses? You tell us which houses to burn. Pick two."

"On Kalyani Avenue?" Sonna asked. "Burn everything! Give me the kerosene and I will burn them!"

"No, on Sal Mal Lane. Pick two."

Sonna felt the world tip and blur before his eyes. Pick two? Which two houses could he pick? What right had he to pick any? If the men were unwilling to leave his lane alone, what hope was there that once they got there they wouldn't attack his mother and sisters, the Heraths, everybody?

Sonna calculated quickly. Raju, how he hated him, how he hated the way he fraternized with the Herath children, the way he held himself straight and seemed to have a purpose in his life. How he hated that he had competed in that weight-lifting tournament even if he had lost. And the Niles family. What was the appeal of a family like that to all of the children, including Rose and Dolly? Had they invited him to come to the variety show? Had they asked if he might like to sing? No, they hadn't. They had left him out as if he was just a mangy stray, unwanted and despised by everyone. But even they had room for Raju. And the Nadesans, who had never spoken a single word to him in their life, who did they think they were? Indian Tamils, they called themselves, high caste, better even than Raju's mother. What right did they have to treat him that way? Did they talk to his sisters? To the Heraths? He did not know. As far as he knew, they spoke to nobody. And yet. Their house sat next door to the Heraths'. If it burned, so would the Herath home. He pictured it, the flames leaping over that wall, setting everything alight. He pictured the children screaming, running out onto the street. He pictured Rashmi. He pictured Nihil. He made up his mind.

"Then burn Raju's house and the Niles house, the two houses past my father's house," he said. "Burn those. Leave the others alone. Leave the people alone. They will all be in the Herath house. Do not touch them." He said this last with a dark passion that seemed to convince the men that he knew what he was asking and what he was willing to sacrifice to make sure they listened.

They turned away more quietly and walked in silence for a while, but when they got to Kalyani Avenue they found their voices again. Sonna did not have to join them in burning the houses down that road. When they got there, the entire street was already on fire. Sonna stood before it and the fear he had for Sal Mal Lane drained out of him. There was nothing he could do to stop any of it. *Eht yob*, he whispered. *Eht yob, eht yob.*

The Day That Followed

There was no need to read newspapers. What was happening was happening to them.

In the late hours of that first night, Mr. Herath, Mr. Sansoni, and Mr. Tissera walked silently down the street. Their footsteps were recorded as they went, traced into the thin layer of ash and dirt that covered the lane in places. Nothing stirred though all around them they could feel alertness, everybody listening, watching, waiting behind closed doors and latched gates. A curfew had been imposed and so they moved quickly and did not speak to each other as they walked under cover of darkness, past Jimmy Bolling, who had fallen asleep still seated in his chair, the belts fallen to the ground beside him. They crossed the road, slipped behind the barbed wire around his property, and knocked on Koralé's back door.

"We need to buy rice," Mr. Tissera said. The Tisseras' house, too, now held its own refugee, the Tamil wife of the editor of a Communist newspaper, who had arrived hiding her face under a helmet and seated on the back of a motorbike driven by a friend. Ever a fearful man, Mr. Tissera had insisted that he would stay up all night playing carrom with his son to keep watch, but had abandoned this post to his wife at Mr. Herath's request.

Koralé poured the rice into three bags and then added tins of canned fish though nobody had asked him for that. No money was taken, though Mr. Sansoni offered and Mr. Herath insisted and Mr. Tissera nodded.

"No, no," he said, pushing the money away. "Not for this."

They thanked him and went back the way they had come, though their first attempt was aborted when an army truck came patrolling slowly down the streets, the soldiers inside looking more scared than any they had ever seen. They stopped beside Jimmy Bolling, hushing him quickly when he cursed at them, startled out of his sleep. They gave him a bag of rice and fish, which he stood up to take. As they walked on they heard him rap on the door to his compound, the sound carrying clear down the silent road, and all three men looked back the way they had come. The other bags of rice and fish were taken to Mr. Herath's house and given to Mrs. Herath, who had made plain ginger tea for them all. After she left, carrying two

cups of tea for Mrs. Niles and Kala Niles, who were still up, the men huddled in the kitchen. Mr. Sansoni was given a chair on account of his age and
girth, but Mr. Herath leaned on the table on which their gas cooker sat,
and Mr. Tissera crouched on a low stool. Kamala, not knowing what to do
if she was not needed in the kitchen while food and drink were being prepared, took a broom and began to sweep the veranda, even though it was
now close to midnight, pausing every few steps to stamp lightly on the floor
to dust off her bare feet.

It was Mr. Sansoni who said it: "We will have to set up a neighborhood
watch." And that was what was discussed in whispers in the kitchen whose
light would not reach the road outside, but whose light and the whispers did
reach the ears of Mr. Niles, who lay far from repose in the area just outside.
If he was inclined to talk, Mr. Niles may have asked what they were planning to protect, but Mr. Tissera did that for him.

"Everything is looted, and the houses are damaged. What is there to
protect now?" He turned up his palms. "Maybe only our own houses. They
may come back for us."

"We have to protect whatever is left," Mr. Sansoni said, running his
fingers through the gray curls on his head. He hadn't washed since morning and he could smell the sweat on himself.

"In other places, people have been killed. Our neighbors are still here
with us. We have to protect them," Mr. Herath said. "Not only from the
thugs who come from outside," he added.

Nobody said anything further as they all sipped their tea and considered this. And if, in ostracizing that family, these neighbors could set
themselves apart from the things that the Silvas had encouraged, then let
us allow them this relief, for it would not last; deep down, they knew that
the Silvas were no more wholly guilty than they themselves were wholly
innocent, for guilt and innocence lived within them all, even their guests.

The next morning the children came out of hiding, and because their lane
was so small, a dead end after all, and their lives so tight, they were allowed to walk outside as a group, and walk they did, marveling at what
had taken place, awe as much a part of their impression as horror. They
passed beneath the sal mal trees, whose lower branches were laden with
singed leaves and flowers as though a fall season the tropical island had
never known had chanced upon them. Their lane was littered with items

that had been dropped or abandoned, skeins of embroidery threads, aluminum molds for making string-hoppers, even an upholstered chair that they did not recognize.

"Must 'ave been the Nadesans'," Rose said.

Suren picked it up and tried to forced the top of the backrest together, but try as he might he could not make it look whole again and he had to leave it lying on its side exactly as they had found it. He said, "We can try to clean Kala Akki's house," and everybody fell in line with him, sweeping charred bits of this and that to the side of the road with their rubber slippers as they walked.

They opened the gate and went in, their nostrils flaring at the scent of singed brick and furniture. The rosebushes closest to the house, not just the vine that Devi and Nihil had seen from their tree, were curled and burnt, but the plants farther away stood lush and green, reminding them all of what had once been. The curved door hung open, half wrenched out of its posts. There was no sound inside except that made by their feet and breath, though outside the birds chirped. Mr. Niles's veranda was littered with ash and wood. A path of torn music books and saris and photograph albums led from the front door to the kitchen. The kitchen was strewn about with rice and dhal and dried spices spilled as though in a curse, a curse for no more cooking, no more meals, no more entertaining, no more existence, no more of anything, not even a backward glance. Except that, in their hurry, the mob had missed the storeroom. Though this space, too, smelled of smoke, the children felt as though they were peering into a cordoned-off room in a museum, the band instruments still set up, the chairs and cushions untouched. Suren shut the door and slipped the bit of wood back through the latch as Kala Niles had always done to hold the doors together.

"What about Uncle Raju's house?" Devi asked him, her brows furrowed. She had tried to open Raju's gate on her way to Kala Niles's house, and the gate, rumpled and curled at one end, had been warm to the touch.

"We will go there, don't worry," Rashmi said. She picked up a painting that had not broken and looped the mount back on the nail from which it had hung, though the wall behind it was now grimy. She went over to the soot-stained window of Kala Niles's bedroom and looked over at the Nadesans' house. "Thank goodness they didn't burn the Nadesans' house," she said, practical. "We can get some of their pots so they can eat proper food again."

"Maybe we won't have to clean there," Devi said, as she looked about the Nileses' house, at all the things that could perhaps be salvaged and all that would have to be swept up. She dusted off the skirt of her dress, unsuccessfully trying to get rid of some black ash that covered a part of it.

But they did have to clean the Nadesans' house, for nothing was where it should have been, everything standing was now not standing, everything full was spilled out, even the flowering begonias were lying face down beside shattered clay pots.

"Nihil and Rose and I can clean Kala Akki's house," Suren said.

"Then I'll take Devi and Dolly and go to Old Mrs. Joseph's house," Rashmi said.

As they left the Nileses' house, they saw Jith standing outside their gate and Rashmi asked him if he wanted to help. He looked relieved and came running up to them, shaking his head in agreement, but he was only able to help them for a short while, for as soon as Mohan realized where he had gone, he came out and ordered him to stop being a fool and to get back in the house before their mother found out, she would be furious.

While the adults engaged in their adult concerns, glad that the children were not underfoot, that is how the children spent that day, wiping and sweeping and scrubbing and trying, as best as they could, to erase what had happened from their surroundings, though what could they do about black tiles and charred walls and what could they do about the tears that poured down Mr. Niles's face and what could they do about the way in which Mrs. Nadesan held Mr. Nadesan's hand with such fear that even they could taste it?

In each house they saw things they had never seen before. In Kala Niles's house they found a carved figurine of the Buddha tucked behind the photograph of Sai Baba, and a locket that contained a twist of fine hair and a baby tooth. There was an old cricket bat made of white willow, signed by someone whose name, Mahadevan Sathasivam, they did not recognize, that had escaped notice because it was tucked far underneath Mr. Niles's bed. The bat was tagged with a note that said in stern yet shaky script, the top arm of the *F* drawn far to the right, and the whole message underlined twice: *For Nihil, on his fourteenth birthday.* They also found two bottles of pills labeled *morphine 30 mg,* one half-empty, one full.

In Old Mrs. Joseph's house they found a wedding photograph in which she looked surprised and delighted. They found silver spoons engraved with the letter J and a rubber-corked bottle in which was preserved the appendix that had been removed from Raju when he was nine, a fact only clear from the labeling. Inexplicably, both by virtue of its having survived the looting and its very presence, they found a gift-wrapped box of watercolor paints. Every now and then, Devi picked up a playing card with a picture of the Indian Pacific train on the back of it and she began collecting these as though they were treasures, her eyes searching for them alone and skipping over everything else.

In the Nadesans' house, to which they all went later in the day, they found nothing that made them pause because, while they had shared celebrations, they had never spent much time inside this home. They moved quickly through it, replacing what was fallen, sweeping what was broken and irreparable, organizing on the table those things that were clearly personal, folding saris and shirts. Suren stacked all the family pictures from the living room on the dining table, then systematically shook out the cracked glass from each frame into a wide-mouthed pot. When he had finished, he called Rose and Devi over to show them how much glass there was in the pot and the girls took turns shaking it to listen to the sound it made. And if during all of this work not one of the children, not even Devi, suffered from a wound, a finger cut on a bit of broken glass, a foot pierced by a nail, it was perhaps because they moved through the houses slowly, as through in a trance, the frivolity and foolish haste of the days past suddenly and utterly beyond their reach.

Later that day, while the others continued in these activities, moving back and forth between houses, Nihil was selected by Mr. Herath to accompany him on visits that he made by walking and taking the bus, to check on their friends in other places. The roads they took were mostly empty, the usual collection of dropped bus tickets and receipts, fly-away paper bags and discarded newspapers augmented manifold by the debris of hurried departures, open suitcases and boxes, not all of them empty, even the occasional abandoned bicycle, the handlebars or tires twisted as though by force to prevent escape. One thing had returned to normal: the smell of the city's air, the ocean breezes, undisturbed in their routines by the events of the previous days, having blown away the evidence of fire.

Mr. Herath took Nihil first to the Hindu kovil in Colombo 4, which had been set up as a refugee center, to see the Selvadurai family, who huddled in a square of space in the far corner of a room filled end to end with people sitting, bewildered, among their possessions. When the Heraths reached them, Mrs. Selvadurai clutched Mr. Herath's hand and asked him if he would take a note to his wife.

"Our children were visiting Sinhalese friends in Nuwara Eliya," she said. "I need to let them know we are safe." She searched in a bag for a piece of paper and wrote a note that Nihil read as he walked beside his father to their next stop.

> *Dearest Savi, Please call our children and tell them we are safe. The number to the place they are staying (Seneviratne) is 0945793. Here, in case you need them, are the national ID numbers for Murugan and for me. 367521974 V (Murugan), 383311907 V (me). I give them to you because I do not know what will happen now and you are my closest friend. —Sylvia*

"Why would we need their identity card numbers?" Nihil asked.

"For identifying them, to say they are citizens," Mr. Herath said.

"But if they have their cards can't they just show them?"

"She is worried that the cards will be stolen," Mr. Herath said, and he did not tell Nihil that Mrs. Selvadurai feared more bloodshed, that their property would be seized, that their children would be orphaned and hosts of other things that he couldn't even comprehend, and that she was simply sharing the one thing that she had to share, the numbers that proved that she existed, that she belonged.

They went to Joseph Lane, where Mr. Vaseeharan, Suren's advanced maths teacher, lived. He was standing near his gate with his head bandaged.

"I told those bloody thugs—they were about to hit me with a broomstick—I told them to find a more noble implement for their brutality," he said, touching his head with pride though his voice shook. Mr. Herath nodded and patted him on the back and they talked at some length about the events of that day. As they walked away, Mr. Herath explained to Nihil that Vaseeharan was the son of the Tamil leader who had first called for separatism, S. J. V. Chelvanayakam.

"The good son," he said, "the brother, Chelva's other son, Chandrahasan, is not a good person." Mr. Herath, as was his practice, looked down as he walked.

"Are we going to see the brother?" Nihil asked, his eyes meeting the eyes of strangers as he went, a trait he shared with his mother. "If they beat up this son, then the other son, the bad one, must be really suffering."

"No, I only wanted to make sure that Vaseeharan is being looked after. Chandrahasan will be fine. He has friends." And Mr. Herath said no more about why he cared about one son, not the other, and why the one who was bad had suffered less than the one who was good, and Nihil himself did not know what questions to pose, in a situation where two brothers could evoke such different sympathies in his father. He walked beside him with many a backward glance at the man he would come to refer to as the Good Son, who waved each time Nihil turned around.

That night, the Herath girls participated in cooking dinner for the first time, using the Nadesans' pots. In the kitchen they peeled and chopped onions and garlic, they learned how to use the tin cutter to open the tins of fish, they were shown how to scrape coconut and how to make two kinds of milk with it, one thin, one thick, and in what order, exactly, to add the spices to the curries that were being prepared by Kamala.

For a second night in a row they served their quiet neighbors, whose diminishment was so apparent, whose anger there was no space for, and whose sadness they could not ameliorate. For a second night, Mr. Herath, Mr. Sansoni, and Mr. Tissera walked up and down the street in turn, torch in hand, waiting for daybreak.

And, for a second night in a row, Nihil sat beside Mr. Niles, with Devi for company, and the two of them talked about the things that Nihil had seen that day, but he would not let Devi say anything about the houses down their lane or what everything looked like outside the walls of their own home, its quiet and its regrets.

Ash

On the third day, Lucas came up the street to say that he had heard that Tigers had infiltrated the city of Colombo and though none of the families down Sal Mal Lane wanted to believe such tales, they discussed strategies and posted Mr. Jimmy Bolling, Mr. Tissera, and Mr. Sansoni at the bottom of the lane while Mr. Herath went to find out the truth.

There was no truth to be had. There were only rumors that nobody could verify or deny: riots in prisons where Sinhalese prisoners were murdering Tamil prisoners; riots in northern towns where Sinhalese women were being murdered by Tamil villagers; disturbances in the southern towns of Matara and Galle and the hill country towns of Gampola and Badulla and even in the holy city of Anuradhapura. Some told him there were nearly three hundred people dead, while others said there were nearly a thousand people dead. Everybody talked about the numbers and the importance of the correct numbers as though that, the correct number, would explain everything. Nobody spoke of the numbers of Sinhalese who had helped, not harmed, their Tamil neighbors, not even they themselves. It was as though the work of a few had polluted them all, as if taking the blame for the acts of others might help dilute their shame. *All it takes is a drop of cow dung to ruin a pot of pure curd*, they murmured to themselves, wondering if it would ever be possible to purify that which had been so badly fouled.

And because the adults who cared for them were preoccupied with the violence of this new day, the children were left alone.

"Has Sonna come home?" Nihil asked, as they sat at the top of the lane in the shade of the sal mal trees.

Unlike the trees down the road, those within the grove were unharmed, and if they sat facing away from the lane on which they lived, they could pretend that nothing had changed. The ropy new branches wrapped and twisted around the trunks as they always had, and though most of the blooms were gone, the scent of those that were still decaying underfoot let them pretend that the grove was flowering. But none of them could turn their back on the road except for Devi, and she only did so because she had never been able to sit still and, even now, flitted from one tree to the other ducking under low-hanging branches and skipping around the trees as she listened to them talk.

"Lucas told Tha that he thought he had seen Sonna hanging around with some men from the Elakandiya," Suren said.

Rose, who was leaning on the trunk of the tree directly across from Suren, said, "Don' know what has happened on Kalyani Avenue. All Tamil houses. Who is there to save?"

"Some Tamils mus' be bad men," Dolly said, but she said this sullenly, "otherwise how come riots?" She got to her feet and dusted off the back of her skirt, leaning forward and twisting around to make sure it was clean.

"You'll get it from Daddy if you talk like that," Rose said, and at this Dolly fell silent; she had witnessed the beatings Sonna had received, for the raised voice, the misplaced word, the lack of speed in bringing something her father called for, and she knew what it meant to *get it* from their father.

"Where do you think he's gone?" Suren asked.

"Still don' know. Daddy says lootin' somewhere. Daddy says he won' let him come back to the house. Ever again, he said." Rose was glad as she said this that Sonna was not home but was, rather, safe somewhere far away from their father, for Jimmy Bolling's mood had been so dark for so long that she knew Sonna would not fare well at his hands.

And since this kind of rupture between father and son was foreign even to Suren, who certainly had accumulated his share of grievances, as all sons did, against his own father, he suggested that they go to Kalyani Avenue, where, if they were fortunate, Sonna could be found, as Raju had once been found.

Imagine a place isolated by design, nobody there to cry out to for help. Imagine fires unhurriedly set at two ends and a neighborhood uncomplicated by difference left to burn. Imagine a ghost town constructed entirely of ash. Imagine houses, still standing, but not one among them that displays signs of human struggle or salvage. Houses whose walls are entirely gray, full of form yet without substance, for if the children touched one thing, a fence post, a door, it disappeared with soft relief like dreams that fade into the dawn, barely a sound that rose like a sob and enveloped the children in gray powder. Imagine the road itself, covered with blown ash, and their footsteps falling in clear outlines as they walk down the road that no one has visited except, for a last time, with fire. Nothing here has been taken. Everything remains as was, the tables upright, the chairs too, the windows opened, lunch boxes packed, handbags on bureaus, suitcases under beds, all of it either burnt through, as far as the fire could go until there was nothing left to feed it, or covered in ash. Imagine all this, then listen to the voices of these children.

"Where did the people go?" Devi asked for them all.

"The people must have gone before they came," Nihil said, and they all knew who that *they* were.

"Were the people saved?" Devi pressed on.

"How would we know?" Suren asked.

"The people were saved," Rashmi said, deciding for them all on a version of a tale that they could live with. "They left and they took nothing, so they must be safe."

None of them could know for sure if this was true, whether the inhabitants of Kalyani Avenue, just up the road from theirs, with nobody to speak for them, had survived, whether all of them were hiding in one of the houses into which they had not gone, or crouching in heaps on the floors of the refugee camps they had been told were set up in government buildings and schools and all the places of worship, the temples, mosques, churches, and kovils. They clumped together in a circle, their backs to each other as though they were under siege from all sides. While they stood there, each of them trying to convince themselves of an everything-is-all-right in the face of nothing-is-as-it-should-be, they were startled by the sound of a dog, its bark unnaturally alive in the midst of the destruction around them.

"Sounds like a small dog," Rose said, as they listened.

"Yes, but from where is it coming? Can't be a house. There isn't even one that is not burnt," Rashmi said, and they all looked down the part of the street they had just walked, and up the next section of it, which went, equally straight, in an L shape.

The dog was found in the very last house, and it was a Pomeranian, formerly white, now singed and covered with ash. A dog that was both scared and happy to see them. A stainless steel bowl was found and washed and filled with water for it, but when they tried to coax the dog to come with them, it refused to go, scampering out of one set of arms after another, yelping. So, to the routine of cleaning houses and cooking, it seemed, the same food over and over again, was added a visit to Kalyani Avenue in between curfews, a visit they undertook as a group that on two occasions even included Jith, to feed the Pomeranian, which waited for them and welcomed them and partook of their offerings but would not leave the house, not even to relieve itself, until one day, when they arrived, they found it lying on its side, dead.

"How could he have died?" Rashmi asked. "Of what?"

Suren wanted to tell them that the dog died of a kind of heartache, but even he could not find a way to say those words without placing some of the blame on themselves, so he let the question remained unanswered.

At the back of the house, Nihil and Dolly, the most determined two of the group, squatted and began digging a hole with nothing more than spoons, pausing to wipe the sweat off their faces and necks. Though the others joined them eventually, it took them over an hour to make a hole wide enough and deep enough for the dead Pomeranian, which they wrapped in one of Mrs. Herath's old saris that they took without bothering to ask.

"Good dog," Suren said, as they stood over the grave, which they had marked by pressing the stainless steel bowl into the soft, loamy earth under a charred guava tree. None of the other children said anything, for what was there to say? Nothing had been saved, not even the last creature left alive down that road, not even when they had done their best to try to make it stay. They walked home silently and did not visit Kalyani Avenue again until, eventually, the ash blew over and covered their footprints too.

Because there was no more to do, nothing more to be cleaned or kept, nothing more that could be said or done, and because all that remained was an overwhelming sense of inadequacy, and because, of all of them, it was Devi who understood the least, she finally went to see Raju. She did not ask for permission to go, for she knew, having asked before, that she would be denied for reasons nobody would share with her.

Raju had not been seen for several days because Jimmy Bolling would not permit him to leave the house. Jimmy Bolling believed that if he did let Raju leave, Raju would walk down to his own house and see what had been done to it and he would tell his mother, Old Mrs. Joseph, and Jimmy Bolling could not have that, not until he could fix up the place a little. That was what he thought. He had not bargained for Devi.

"I need to talk to Uncle Raju," she said, her hair still dripping wet after a bath, the back of her dress damp from it. "I want to see how he is doing."

"He is fine," Jimmy Bolling said, "we are looking after him well."

"I want to see him," she persisted.

"Daddy, she can come an' see," Rose said.

"Nothin' wrong with comin' and talkin'," Dolly added. "All these days they wouldn' let her come."

Devi felt a surge of affection for Dolly who had suffered the loss of Jith, who was no longer permitted to speak to her after Mrs. Silva had discovered that he had joined them to visit Kalyani Avenue. Nobody spoke of or to the other Silvas, who remained indoors except for when Mohan, never Jith, was sent to buy bread or rice, and when he went, he avoided eye contact.

"I can give a message to Jith," Devi offered, when Jimmy Bolling finally let her in.

Dolly only smiled and said, "No, it's okay. Better like this. Daddy doesn' like."

And Devi might have spent some time talking to Dolly about Jith and her father and all the things that had changed but there was her friend running out from Jimmy Bolling's bedroom, a wide grin on his face.

"Devi! I thought nobody would come to see Uncle Raju! To see how Uncle Raju is doing! Every day even Rose and Dolly kept going out with you Herath children. I thought everybody had forgotten us!" He would have enfolded her in an embrace but for the fact that he was not given to doing that sort of thing, his sense of propriety too well hewn now, so Raju contented himself with flapping his monkey-long arms and pacing and being now cheerful, now sad as he asked for news from the outside.

"What is happening outside, Devi? My cousin Jimmy won't let me go out. He won't tell me, girls won't tell me, nobody will talk. Bin Ahmeds also want to know. We have been sitting here for so many days now, listening, smelled smoke even, but nobody will talk!"

And Devi, because she was a child, told him.

And because Raju was, himself, a child, he ran sobbing to his mother and told her, cursing his cousin for having lied to him, for having answered, repeatedly, *Only the Nileses' house was burnt*, when he had asked if their house had been safe from the fires he knew had been set down that lane, he knew it.

"I have to go home!" Old Mrs. Joseph screamed, tugging at her housecoat. "Let me out! I have to go to my home!"

"Stay here and I will take Raju," Jimmy Bolling said, pleading with his aunt and trying to force her to sit back down on the chair in which she had spent most of the past days, hardly eating, sipping cup after cup of plain tea without milk and without even sugar as though in penitence for some crime she had committed, some atonement she was making to unnamed gods.

"You can't keep me here," she said, pushing back against him with remarkable strength. "I have to go home. Raju, son, come! Take me home!"

And Raju, who always obeyed his mother, did. Against his cousin's wishes, against his cousin's strength.

When Old Mrs. Joseph stepped out from behind the aluminum doors of her nephew's house, what did she expect to see? Only what she had always seen. Children playing, hedges growing, the floral litter created by the sal mal trees, Lucas shuffling up or down the street, Kala Niles or Mrs. Herath hurrying to one teaching engagement or the other, Mr. Herath being driven to work, Mohan and Sonna lurking, each in his own corner of the lane. But what she saw that day was not any of those things. What she saw with each weakening step was a lane where the children did not play but, rather, stood in a group and talked about things that clearly upset them, a lane that carried, despite its best efforts, a streak of malice, a lane where, behind singed mussaendas that had lost their foliage, stood a house that was unrecognizable, the one untouched part of it being the garage in which Raju lifted weights, and the side of the house that faced Jimmy Bolling's property; that had been saved by Raju having spent so much uneasy time watering it with the Bin Ahmeds' hose.

Nobody blamed Devi, directly, for the stroke that Old Mrs. Joseph suffered, nobody told her that she should not have gone to see Raju, that she should have stayed away until Jimmy Bolling had been able to do something to restore the house, but she knew that she had been culpable. So she avoided Raju and did not accompany her parents and her siblings when they went to visit Old Mrs. Joseph, who could only move one side of her face and whose speech was slurred and whom Raju tended night and day, wiping the drool off her chin and the curries off her lips.

It was only his way of forgiving her, his way of offering her a little bit of happiness in the midst of so much unhappiness, that made Raju, seeing Devi standing alone by her gate, come to the Herath household while his mother dozed and say to her, "Devi, come, I will let you ride the bicycle all the way to the bottom of the road."

Who knows how things might have turned out had this been a different time, a time when peace was not something to hope for or talk about, but was something that was simply taken for granted. Who knows how things might have turned out had Sonna not come home, not fought with his father, if Devi had not come down the road, her hands tight on the handlebars, her hair flying, her face full of smiles for the one-last-time toward Raju before she went inside to help cook dinner? For Sonna was there and Devi was there and Raju was there, where they should not have been, in a time when no mercy was left.

Flight

There are no houses built of ash on Kalyani Avenue, there are no hot-wet houses down Sal Mal Lane, there are no neighbors grieving, there are no thugs, nothing has been taken that was not willingly given, no flower unearthed that was still in fair bloom, there are no walks down the street in the dead of night, her mother does not cry over a letter she reads over and over again, Nihil does not spend every spare moment beside Mr. Niles's bed, Suren has not given up playing everything but the same piece of music each night on the piano, and Rashmi has not grown older with adult concerns. Everything is as it once was.

The tennis ball bounces against the walls, Nihil yells *How₹at?* Dolly and Jith exchange letters and smiles. There are band practices at Kala Niles's house and nobody knows too much about the Nadesans but what they do know is sufficient and pleasing. Mr. Niles still sits outside on his veranda; his legs are not broken, nor his spirit, and his voice gladdens as he speaks to Nihil. Lucas comes and goes, Alice complains, and Rose and Rashmi dream of singing and dancing to raucous applause.

This is how the world is as Devi rides the old Raleigh bike that used to belong to Raju's father but that has now been gifted, once and for all, to her. This is how it appears as her legs stretch and reach to push the pedals, now on one side, now the other, and she perches over the center bar. There is freedom from fear, and a sense of flying as she turns the bike at the top of the road and comes down, her feet holding steady as the slope of the road carries her forward, gathering speed, to where Raju waits at the bottom to catch her when she brakes.

Raju, waiting at the bottom of the road, sees Devi no longer as she once was but as she has become, a young girl. Her hair has grown long and is pulled back from her brow with a white Alice band. The wind lifts the loose strands off the back of her shoulders. Her arms, always thin, are filling out. Her calves have a curve to them. In her eyes is a little girl and a girl almost grown, for the days of sadness have matured her, too. Soon she will be tall enough to sit when she rides the bike, to come off the seat only to help her get up the steeper part of the road on the old-fashioned bicycle. And as he absorbs these impressions of Devi, Raju tries not to be distracted by the sound of the brawl that is taking place in his cousin's house.

"Get out of my house, you fucker, you piece of shit!" Jimmy Bolling yells, and there is the sound of crockery smashing, the sound of Francie Bolling screaming *Stop! Stop!* and the sound of Rose and Dolly crying.

Devi reaches the end of the road and the bike comes to a stop in front of Raju, his hands reaching out to grip either side of the handlebars to hold it steady for her in case the brakes fail. As she tips toward him, Raju inhales the scent of oranges and roses, the perfume she has stolen from her mother for this occasion.

"Devi, now better stop for today," Raju says, as the fury unfolding nearby continues and makes him sweat. He undoes the top button of his untucked shirt.

"But I have only gone a few times!" Devi says. Does she not hear? Does she not care?

"No, no, you have gone seven times already, I counted!" Raju tells her, still holding on to the bike.

"One last time then?" she asks, her voice so sweet, so sweetly reminiscent of a time gone by. "Please, Uncle Raju. Now it's my bike. One last time?"

And he shakes his head, regretfully, unable to say anything else but yes to such words, to a request for such a small thing. He helps her wheel the bike around to turn it facing up the road, and then he gives her a little push and she is off.

"This is going to be the best one, Uncle Raju!" she calls out over her shoulder and he can hear the thrill in her voice.

"All this time only reason they din' come here and set fire to this dump is because of me! *I* saved this! *I* saved the Nadesans' house too! An' *I* saved the Heraths! I saved all of you!" Sonna yells as Raju watches the bike turn the corner past the Heraths' house. From there he has to imagine her progress, for the rest of the road is not visible from where he stands at the bottom of Sal Mal Lane.

"You saved us? You weren' even here to help! You were too busy lootin'. I'll pull a knife and slice you! I'll slice you to pieces!" Jimmy Bolling shouts and now Raju can hear the sound of flesh meeting flesh, of struggle and slap and grunt and the dry heaving of rage, a struggle that Jimmy Bolling is having trouble winning this time.

"Kill me? You fat fuck? You can' kill me, I'll kill you! I'll kill them all!
I'll kill them with my hands. I don' need a knife! Come here, you *Thambiya*.
I'll kill you too!"

There's a commotion right outside the door and Raju sees the Bin
Ahmed family come running out of Jimmy Bolling's house and flee toward
their own. And behind them he sees Sonna, and behind Sonna, Jimmy
Bolling, reaching out and grabbing Sonna by his hair while he thrashes and
screams words that Raju is not used to hearing, not even from his cousin
in his most drunken state. Words so raw and vile that all he can think of is
that Devi will be turning around, coming back, and that she should not be
defiled by hearing such things.

Nihil, for no reason that he knows, gets up from where he is sitting
next to Mr. Niles and goes outside. He goes outside in time to see Devi,
perfect, whole, and filled with happiness as she sails past him on the old
bike. *I'm flying!* she calls out to him, and it makes him smile to hear that.
I'm flying! For an instant he wants to run, to catch her at the bottom and
ask if he can ride the bike too, so he, too, can be as lifted as she is, as for-
getful of their collective undoing as she is. To fly. And he does run, as fast
as he can, because that thought has been replaced by another, a vision of
loss so terrifying that he knows it is true and he is crying before he has
run ten steps, crying for what he knows is coming and what he knows he
cannot stop.

At the bottom of the road, Jimmy Bolling and Sonna continue to fight.
Raju braces to catch Devi, who pedals down the road though she has been
told she shouldn't, she shouldn't ever pedal down a hill, she should hold
the pedals still, though she has been warned by him, and Raju thinks, *I am
going to take the bike away from her until she is old enough*. And he thinks this
and watches her, something precious, something meant to be cherished and
kept forever, and so he does not see Sonna raise his head from beneath his
father's arms, the arms that are keeping him locked in place, he does not see
Sonna look at Devi and her lovely face, at Nihil, who is already crying,
at Raju, who is so protective, so ready to stop the bike with his own body if
he must. He only hears what Sonna screams, a string of sounds more than
words, sounds tearing out of his throat like those made by a wild animal
trapped too far out of sight and hearing to be released, an animal fighting
to last through the night.

"Raju! Run! They're behind you!"

And he, poor man, always so nervous, so routinely harassed, so recently broken, turns away from Devi to look behind him and therefore he does not catch her, he does not place his body before the bicycle. She goes past him in a flash of bright yellow, the cotton of her dress so airy and light as it brushes his face, herself so weightless when the bicycle meets the bus with a sound that is too loud and she is carried like a feather, back toward Raju, past him, and falls, shattered and bloody, at the feet of the brother who will never reach her in time.

What does it feel like to hold a body so young? What does it feel like to hear the cries that go up from Raju, from Jimmy Bolling, but most of all from Nihil, who has not kept his sister safe? It is to know the suffering of all human life, whose conduct it is to protect but whose natural order is to end. It is to know what it is to love a human being who has ceased to know what shape that love might take.

Nihil holds his sister in his arms and cajoles her to return. "Come back! Devi! Come back! Come back! Come back! Come back!" And he touches her face as he utters these words, and strokes her hair and straightens her dress over her scraped knees, which do not require dressing, and wipes the blood that spills from the back of her head and seeps out through her ears, and he says them as though there are no other words to say but those words, "Come back! Come back!" even though he knows she will not. "Come back!" he cries as he presses his face to her body, his tears falling through her dress and slipping over the ribs below.

It falls upon Jimmy Bolling to find Mr. Herath and tell him about his daughter. And it falls upon Mr. Herath to tell his wife, and he can find no right words but the truth, *Devi is dead.*

In days to come, some would whisper that it was a good thing that Nihil was there when they came out of the house running, though of what use was speed anymore, for what they found was not only a child who was gone but a child who was half-gone, and that half-goneness that Nihil embodied gave them something to focus on. A child half-alive was still recoverable; it was still possible to imagine him being sent forth into the world to live his life, to be, whereas the child lost took up residence within their hearts that would forever be full of memory and devotion to finite time, eleven and half years and not one day more.

Mrs. Herath puts her arms around the body of her younger daughter and Mr. Herath puts his around his younger son. Suren and Rashmi sink to their knees, weeping, kissing Devi's feet, redoing all that Nihil has already done, making her neat, wiping her neck, her head, and saying her name,

Devi! Devi! Little Devi! And there is longing in their voices, as though they wish they had spoken that way to her before then, this day, yesterday, every day that she had not been lying before them so utterly still.

Other people gather. Kamala and Alice, who cling to each other and scream out their pain as women of their status are wont to do.

Lucas comes and weeps and says "Aiyyo! Aiyyo! Devi Baby! Aiyyo!" over and over again until he is led away by Mr. Tissera.

And all the neighbors who were still in the Herath household, all except Mr. Niles, come out of those rooms in which they had sat for days, for no house that was burnt, no jewelry that had been stolen, no albums destroyed, no, not even fear for their own lives can keep them from feeling this pain, this despair that overwhelms them all, so tangible is its presence, so eternal its promise.

Inside the Herath household, the one person left behind, Mr. Niles, tilts his head to listen to the distant voices down the street. And in those voices he hears the unmistakable note of lamentation reserved for mourning the death of a child, and he turns onto his side, the first movement he has made on his own in months. He calls out *Son! Son! Nihil!* He calls and calls though Nihil is not in the house. Though Nihil, even if he were in the house, would not come.

And where is Raju? He is not among those who stand or kneel around Devi's family. He is not on the road, or in any of the houses. Raju is not going to look upon the dead face of this girl he loves, the one who had loved him back, who had considered him her friend, her guardian, her family. He will not look upon her face. Up the main road he runs, a piece of the broken handlebar in his hand, up he runs, no fatigue to stop him, no word of caution, nothing at all until he catches up with Sonna, who has been cowering alone at a tea shop at the top of the hill though he longs, oh how he longs, for his family, for a single friend, and oh how he grieves for Nihil. Nobody stops Raju, no one calls for help, no voice begs for mercy, not even Sonna's. If a doctor happened by afterward, they would have been hard pressed to find where joint met joint, where cheekbone drew away from jaw. When Raju drops the piece of metal in his hand at last, its surfaces slick with blood and hair, not far from where Devi still lies, so loved, so missed, another dead body lies, as deeply unloved, as deeply unsung.

If Only

Devi rests as if in a deep sleep in a casket that her parents have chosen. White satin, pleated and ruffled, and floral wreaths of jasmine, orchid, and rose, frame her entire body. It seems as though she rests not in something made of kaluwara, the swift-burning wood of the South, but rather in a bower of cloud and flower. Her head faces west, there is an oil lamp lit at her feet, and beside the coffin, on a tall curved stand, is a photograph of her in which she looks at the world with a slight smile, though her eyes are full of laughter.

Mrs. Niles sits beside Mrs. Herath, accompanying her through the wake. Every now and again Mrs. Herath begins to talk to Devi, saying a variation of the same words. "Uncle Niles got you this casket, darling. Because of the riots. There was nothing good enough in Colombo, but Uncle Niles—" She does not finish even though this is the one piece of information that she seems to want to share with Devi and even though Mrs Niles takes her hand every time and says *It's all right, she knows.*

Suren and Rashmi sit on either side of Nihil in the chairs arranged along the wall nearest to the front door. Nihil stares at his hands as they rest in his lap, his fingers laced together. *What if,* he thinks, of course he thinks it. And, also, *if only.* These are the only thoughts possible.

What if I had not been sitting beside Mr. Niles?

If only I had not stopped paying attention.

What if I had not played cricket?

If only I had heard her go out.

What if when she passed me, knowledge had preceded the happiness that came over me?

What if, instead of letting her voice lift my spirits, I had let the sight of her make me afraid?

What if.

And, always, *if only* Raju had not. *If only* Raju had not owned a bike. *If only* Raju had not given it to her. *If only* Raju had not looked away. *If only* Raju had not existed.

At first he does not notice Raju come into the room where his sister lies. And he may not have noticed Raju at all had Raju not, upon reaching the casket, fallen to his knees in a fit of sobs, half inhaled, half exhaled, and said, in his musical voice, "Forgive me! Forgive me! Devi, who will forgive your Uncle Raju now?"

In that instance, the words that nobody in his family would ever have uttered, that nobody in their family would have tolerated being uttered by anybody else, escape Nihil's lips, for there are no other words he can think of with which to abuse this man who has taken his sister away.

"Para Demalā!" he screams. He leaps out of his chair and grabs Raju by the collar of his shirt, and Raju struggles to his feet. "You have no right to be here! Get out of our house!"

He shoves Raju, shoves him and hits him with his fist, and kicks at his legs with his bare feet while Raju staggers and does not even try once, not with one lifted arm, to protect himself, he only says, "I am sorry Nihil, I am sorry, I am sorry."

And Nihil would have said more and done more if not for the fact that Suren has pulled him away from Raju, and if not for the fact that Rashmi has said, "Shh, shh, Nihil, don't say such things. Don't say such things."

"Raju was her friend," Suren says, his arm around his brother as they take him into their parents' bedroom and try to make him stop trembling. They cover him with whatever they can find, their father's sarong, the sheet off the bed, as though Nihil has a fever, as though if they could only wrap him up tight enough, hold him close enough, they could contain his grief, they could prevent him from breaking apart.

If Mrs. Niles is insulted by what Nihil has said, if Kala Niles is upset that Raju has been referred to as a Tamil outcast, if the Nadesans are hurt, or Jimmy Bolling, or even Old Mrs. Joseph, who has been carried over from Jimmy Bolling's house, in her own chair, by Mr. Tissera and Mr. Sansoni, to pay her respects to the dead, none of them show it. They simply bow their heads further and sigh.

"Come, Mr. Raju," Lucas says, taking Raju's hand, "not good for you to be here. Difficult for the family. You come another day, another day," though what other day might permit such a visit Lucas does not know.

Mr. Herath sits in the veranda and receives the visitors who come in a never-ending stream, their arrivals and departures sufficient to refresh his memory each time he looks up and sees, written in their faces, the whole story of how his daughter died, how unnecessary has been her passing. They embrace him and he tries to give them what they have come for, a fraction of his heartache, that they may carry it away, but he cannot.

Instead, he asks after their families and they, understanding, say, *I came with Sisil,* or, *Saku's family is safe, they are staying with friends,* or, *My wife is sorry she couldn't come, my mother-in-law is ill,* until there is no more to be said and they turn away to sit beside other friends, and he is left alone.

Mr. Niles continues to lie in the back of the house and Mrs. Niles tends to him, though Kala Niles has moved to stay with the Tissera family. The Nadesans, too, have returned to their own house.

"There is no way to move him and no place to take him to," Mr. Herath had said, when asked by his tearful wife how they were supposed to conduct a funeral and *pirith* and an almsgiving in seven days with Mr. Niles lying there. "He will have to stay here."

From where he lies, Mr. Niles can hear the mourners. He knows when the body is first brought in by the undertakers at A. F. Raymond's, because the house erupts in fresh tears, and Kamala, who is watching from near the back of the dining room, cries out, *"Aney Devi Baba! Devi Baba genavane!"* And he hears Mrs. Herath cry and cry and cry as people come and she rises up to accept their expressions of sympathy and then stands next to them as they hold her hand and wipe their own tears and she sees again and again and again her daughter as though she is freshly dead, freshly brought into her home in a casket. And he feels the weight on Mr. Herath's shoulders, the burden of trying to get his family through these rituals, these days, days that no parent knows how to live through and yet does. Sometimes Suren or Rashmi comes and holds his hand or touches his brow as they pass from the living room to the kitchen and back again. But not Nihil. Nihil never comes, and so Mr. Niles lies and grieves for the loss of the girl in the casket and the loss of the boy who lives.

The Composer

Suren knew that it was important, at this moment, for him to hold his brother up, for who had loved Devi more than Nihil did, but he also knew that his concern for Nihil lay over a store of pain that he was trying to hold in check. It was a firstborn, oldest-son time and Suren stepped into the role. He made sure that plain tea with ginger was being made for the mourners who came, and for those who might prefer coffee he made sure there was always a tray of Nescafé—made from the tins that Mrs. Sansoni had brought, a gift from her son, Tony—being offered. At the appropriate time each afternoon of the three days that the body lay in their home, he went to his mother, helped her to her feet, took her to the kitchen, and coaxed her to eat at least half of a sandwich from the stack that the Tissera family sent. He did not offer her the soft vegetable buns that the Silvas had arranged to be sent to their home, buns that arrived by the box from the bakery owned by Jith's uncle, twice removed. Those buns were served to guests, never to the family, never to the other neighbors, none of whom would partake of anything that could be traced back to the Silvas, though they spoke to them politely as the Silvas, too, took their turn to sit among the mourners through the day. He served his father tea and coffee himself, but he left it to Rashmi to escort Mr. Herath back to the kitchen for food.

It was Suren who consulted with his aunts, and the one surviving grandmother, to arrange for the rituals of cremation. In this work he was assisted by the members of his band and the Bolling girls, who, though they knew nothing of Buddhist rituals, put on their uniforms, the only white dresses they owned, and stayed beside the Herath children, helping where they could. It was Rose and Dolly who joined Jith—but not Mohan—to help hoist the white flags in a zigzag pattern down Sal Mal Lane, one end tied to the largest of the trees in the grove at the top of their road, the other end wrapped around the post of the streetlamp near the Bin Ahmeds' house. It was Rose who, together with Suren, stood at the bottom, her eyes squinting against the sun, looking up at the banner that fluttered above their heads, the one that announced the death, with Devi's name and the words *Vayadamma Sankaara* beneath it.

"What does it mean?" Rose asked him.

"Nothing lasts," he said, simply.

As they went about this work, Suren sometimes stopped to explain to people who asked, people passing by along the main road, that, no, Devi, whose name was shared so elegantly by two races, was not a Tamil child killed during the riots, she was a Sinhalese girl, she was his sister. And when he said this the adults who had asked, whether they were Sinhalese or Tamil, always sighed with relief, which made Suren want to change his answers, to say yes, she did die during the riots, and she did die because of them, for that was the truth of it, but he allowed them their relief and their sympathy and went back to his duties.

Far from all that Suren minded, in the places to which those passersby went, things were discussed in the usual way. The government was blamed by the supporters of the opposition. *The looters had electoral lists with them,* they said, accusing highly placed officials of instigating the riots and, worse, not offering even one word of sympathy after to the Tamil citizenry. The government supporters blamed, alternately, the Left, for stirring discord, and the Tamil leadership that had failed to stop the rise of Prabhakaran. In its own defense, the government listed these things:

That a curfew was imposed immediately to stop the riots.

That it was government property that was attacked first, with trains, buses, and buildings targeted.

That shelter was provided for more than twenty thousand homeless Tamils.

That when that shelter proved inadequate, ships were commissioned to transport to the North those refugees who had families there.

None of the Tamils who were tended to in this manner would credit the government with any good, for how could they when the evil that had happened had occurred on its watch? Some Tamils would eventually leave for Australia, America, and Canada, from whose safety they would prepare to wage a war by proxy, a war that had as much to do with their decision to leave as it had to do with what they had left behind. The poorest Tamils would one day be trapped by Prabhakaran in the North, their lives given over to supporting an unwinnable war. But the largest number remained where they had always been, their lives enmeshed both with the lives of those who had wished them harm and those who had protected them from it.

If it were possible to look down from a great distance and see a pattern rather than individual losses, we could say that more people lived than died, more homes were saved than were burnt, more friendships endured.

But at street level they were all irrevocably damaged, and down Sal Mal Lane that sense of devastation was wrapped up around Devi, a death that could be described by one and all as being senseless, a bereavement that served as a touchstone for other losses.

"Tomorrow is the last day," Rashmi said to Suren the night before the funeral. They were sitting in the front veranda while their parents, alone for the first time, sat with the body. Mr. Tissera and Suren's bandmates were in the kitchen playing a game of cards to stay awake, the Bolling twins had fallen asleep in Rashmi's room, and Lucas was keeping vigil on the front steps, talking in low tones with Banda, the driver who had taken Devi and Rashmi to school when they were younger and who had come as soon as he heard about the funeral and not left since.

Suren nodded. It would also be the first day of all the days when there was no dead body before them, no mourners and lamps and no chanting of monks to give purpose to their days.

"Let Nihil sleep tonight," he said, looking over at their brother who had fallen asleep, seated on a chair, his hands still crossed over his chest.

"What shall we do about Mr. Niles?" Rashmi asked.

Suren watched his sister fiddle with the hem of her white skirt. The threads had come undone and she was tugging at them, unraveling. "Mr. Niles will be carried home after the almsgiving, once the Sansonis and Tisseras have cleaned up the kitchen and the front room," Suren said, though he knew that was not what his sister was referring to.

"I mean about him and Nihil."

Suren shrugged. "There is nothing we can do about it. We can talk to Mr. Niles and we can hope that it will be enough to hear from us. We can't force Nihil to go and talk to him."

"It was not his fault," Rashmi said, after a long silence.

"It was not his fault," Suren repeated, and he was thinking about both Mr. Niles and Nihil. Next to him, Rashmi began to cry. He put his arm around her and rested her head on his shoulder and tried not to think about whose fault it might have been, about whether anybody could be blamed or whether blame was useless, for so long as there was human life, human life would end.

On the day of the funeral, Mrs. Niles and Mrs. Tissera took Mrs. Herath to the back of the house and helped her wash and draped a new white sari on her, though they needed her assistance in draping it in the upcountry

Kandyan style. Then they brought her out of the bedroom to sit one last time beside her daughter.

"When are they coming?" she asked, faintly, of no one in particular.

"The priests will be here at three," Suren told her, and he touched her shoulder so she leaned forward and laid her head against the side of his body and whispered *Aney putha, mage putha,* and he knew she was seeking some strength from him to get through the next few hours, though he had none to offer; everything he had was given to his brother and sister.

"Someone will have to look after Nihil," Mr. Niles said to Rashmi as she passed by him, dressed, for the first time and with Kamala's help, in a white sari of her own.

"We will," Rashmi said, and since she did not have it in her to comfort Mr. Niles just then, she just said that, "We will," and kept on walking.

Mr. Tissera, who had never spent this much time with the Herath family, and certainly had never spent so much time in their bedrooms and bathrooms, helped Mr. Herath to get ready. He sat him down in the chair next to Mrs. Herath and then walked to the back of the room to wait, Mr. Sansoni and Mr. Silva beside him, their wives with the other women who drifted in and out of the rooms in the house as though no space was sacred anymore.

Mohan and Jith stood with their father. Jith focused on Dolly, looking at her whenever he could, trying to detect if she had changed and in what ways. But Mohan, he had come for Devi. He stared at the rigid stillness of her body as though all the excess of movement that she had been known for had been in anticipation of this day. He kept his eyes on her face, on the fingers arranged with a prayerful serenity she had never displayed in life, on her feet, which were dressed in white socks, but no shoes. He stepped away from his father and the line of men around them, and moved toward the casket. He bent his head and tried to think of some words that would make sense for him to say, even in silence. None came, but when he felt his father's hand on his arm, tugging him away, he resisted and he continued to stand there, beside the coffin, until the priests arrived.

At three, Mr. Herath said, "It is time," though he may have been reminding himself, and he helped his wife to her feet and they went forward, the sides of their arms touching, to meet the priests who had arrived with no more than a rustle. Mr. Herath's brother stepped forward to wash their feet.

Suren waited until the priests had taken their place, and his parents and siblings too, before he sat down behind them, letting his mind settle. In his

sermon the chief priest referred to Devi, her youth, her playfulness, and to
her death, and reminded her parents and siblings that the body that lay before them was empty, simply a reminder of impermanence, artificially held
together, something that must, also, be allowed to leave.

"Why mus' they talk about all that? So sad!" Rose, sitting right behind
Suren, whispered to Dolly, who shrugged, having no response.

"Shh! Listen!" her father said, and maybe he thought at that moment
of his own dead son, or considered his wife, who sat beside him now, with
whom he had fought and to whom he had denied the burial no matter how
much she wept and pleaded, and who had in the end pawned her one pair
of gold earrings and given the money to Mr. Bin Ahmed, saying *Please
cremate my son's body and bring the ashes back;* maybe he thought all that
though his eyes were dry.

"It is Buddhism, because they are Buddhist," Mrs. Nadesan said, and
because she wasn't used to whispering, all the Heraths heard her.

Suren thought then that no matter the hymns and the *bhajans,* the religion that informs mourning was probably the religion of the heart.

"Why must we return to life?" the priest asked. "We return to the
people who made promises to us, to whom we made promises, and we try,
again, to fulfill them, to have those made to us be fulfilled by others."

> *Unname udakam vattam yatha ninnam pavattati*
> *evameva ito dinnam petanam upakappati.*
> *Yatha varivaha pura paripurenti sagaram*
> *evameva ito dinnam petanam upakappati.*

They were words that the priest had recited at the beginning, words
Suren understood as having meaning in his life now, not simply as a recitation in Buddhism class: as water flows from high to low ground, whatever merit is done, through good work, through prayer, through offering,
reaches the dead.

Music, Suren thought. For Devi he would compose music, a promise
that he had never made but that, surely, he should have, a good work that
he could perform on her behalf. He thought then of pieces that would in-
form the musical arrangements he could make for her. Melodies alternating
between longing and foreboding for her friendship with Raju, churning
undertones for Nihil's fears beneath top notes that insist on continuity for
the things he could not change, staccato rhythms to depict Devi's skipping rope and her clapping hands, lighter music for the ride she had longed

for on that bicycle, the way she had owned it, the speed, the wind, every-thing, her spirit journeying alone, somewhere higher than the road, the sensation of observing from below and above, leaving the earth, lin-gering there unseen. He listened to the priests, but the voices he heard were those of composers: Debussy, "Jimbo's Lullaby" from *Children's Corner* Suite, Chopin's "Ocean Waves" Etude, Brahms's 8 Pieces, op. 76, Capriccio in B Minor, Camille Saint-Saëns's *Carnival of the Animals,* and more Debussy, Nocturnes I, "Clouds." Suren lifted his bent head and turned his face upward, and as he did so he felt that all that was heavy and sad was here, with him, low to the ground, and all that was light was suspended above, in a space that held Devi, a place he could not reach except through his music.

"When are we going to practice band again, Suren?" Rose would ask in days to come, hoping, wishing that the band had survived. "I found a new cassette tape in Sonna's room with all the top hits from last year. Even "Jack and Diane" and "Physical" it has. Someone must 'ave given him, but he never liked music so it wasn' even open. I took it before Daddy saw. He would have thrown it. We can play it for the band."

"No more of the band, Rose. I am working on something else now," Suren said, as they sat together in the sal mal grove, he with his ruled manu-script paper, composing, she, watching. And though he said this quite kindly, he knew that it was unkind to a girl like Rose, a girl whose voice could only grow in the company of a boy like him. Still, he did not try to do more than he could.

"Never the band then?" she asked.

"I am not interested in the band anymore," Suren said, "but maybe they can play with you once they get new instruments. Do you want me to ask them?"

Rose said, "No, don' worry. Better with you in it," and hid her dis-appointment with muted laughter and a shove against Suren's arm, the one time she had ever touched him. Rose understood it was the end of things, for without Devi the Heraths were not simply three-left, they were one-missing, a circumstance that none of them would ever overcome. So she walked home silently and sat beside Dolly on Sonna's bed, feeling that in some similar way, she and Dolly too had been lessened by Sonna's death. Thinking this, she finally gave in to the tears that their father had refused to permit, and Francie Bolling joined her, not minding the slam of the door as Jimmy Bolling left the house.

Kala Niles did not ask Suren why he no longer wanted to play Rachmaninoff, Tchaikovsky, Bach, why he only practiced scales, arpeggios, chord progressions, finger exercises, why he listened, again and again, to the few records that had survived, Mozart's Concerto no. 23, Chopin's D-flat Major Prelude, and, on the other side, the E-minor Prelude, a single Debussy, Arabesque no. 2, and Brahms's 6 Pieces, op. 118, Ballade in G Minor. She did not express regret over her dozens of other records that had been destroyed; she only said, "Whenever you want, come. Come for free."

Her invitation to Suren came after the moving of her piano, a second time, down the road and in through her gates and back to its old space, which now smelled of fresh paint. The corner next to it remained empty; the guitar was gone. She did not ask about his changed preferences, so Suren told her: "I am composing a piece for my sister."

Kala Niles twitched her lips and blinked her eyes and she said, "I will listen."

In the midst of Devi's funeral and the seventh-day almsgiving, which sapped almost all the strength he had left in him, Suren had learned to navigate between caring for his family and tending to his own heart. Yet though he tried to ignore what was going on around him, Suren could not keep himself from reading the news, which he now knew could never be ignored.

In the halls of government a constitutional amendment was passed requiring the declaration of allegiance to a unitary country: *No person shall directly or indirectly, in or outside Sri Lanka, support, espouse, promote, finance, encourage, or advocate the establishment of a separate State within the territory of Sri Lanka.* Which meant that the Tamil party, whose manifesto expressly declared such a desire to divide, resigned in protest. The government also banned all the left-wing parties.

The Tamils, who continued to live among the Sinhalese all over the island, turned a little more inward, their suspicions confirmed, their prejudices now necessary, and, all around them, the Sinhalese, too, grew harder in their resolve. *Prabhakaran will never win. The country will never be divided,* they reassured each other. *No matter what they do, in the end we'll win.* And though in the decades to come, much was, indeed, done, with towers and hotels crashing to the ground, airports and seaports bombed, buses set on fire, and even the country's most sacred temple attacked by suicide bombers, and thousands upon thousands of innocents both Sinhalese and Tamil murdered, they were right about two things: Prabhakaran lost and the country was not divided.

Whether the war was won, however, was another matter altogether. And peace, the kind that ordinary people had once known, that was not so easy to come by. For even in the aftermath of all that they had witnessed together, Suren still heard Mohan say *good riddance* when speaking about yet another Tamil student whose family had decided to leave the country, and even though Mohan did not sound as sure of himself as he had been in years past, Suren realized that he did not understand the source of Mohan's prejudices nor ever would. He contented himself with the results of the national exams instead, for though he was proud of his four distinctions and four credits, he was even happier to announce to Kala Niles, as though in gift, that the thirty-three students who had achieved either five, six, seven, or eight complete distinctions were all Tamil.

As Mrs. Niles and Kala Niles tended to the slow repair of their house, Suren helped his father to supervise the return of Mr. Niles, who was carried with a further heaviness of heart as though they were not one-less but one-more, Devi with them within each of the people who bore him thus, Mr. Herath, Suren, Jimmy Bolling, and Mr. Tissera. Nihil did not accompany them, and when Suren returned from the Nileses' house and looked for his brother, he found him in the Silvas' garden, systematically ripping up every fern and flowering shrub their mother had given to Mr. Silva.

"Why, Nihil?" Suren asked, his voice weary.

"These are our plants," Nihil said, standing up to face Suren, his face calm.

Suren said, "Leave what is still good alone," and he took Nihil home and left him with Rashmi. He went back and knocked on the Silvas' door and said he would come back and help to put the plants back in the ground and though he brought both Rose and Dolly with him to do this work, none of the Silvas said anything; they simply stayed out of sight until Suren and the girls were gone.

In his own house, Suren found that the mood was ever quiet, even when they spoke, because each member of the family was always in two worlds: the present, which unfolded relentlessly and required routine and schedule and work, and the one that remained within, the one in which Devi was not where she had once been. In that half world Suren posed questions.

To his mother: "They say the school results will be out soon. Do you know when?"

To his father: "I hear that the JVP has gone underground. Do you know anything about the Communist Party members, where they might be?"

To Rashmi: "Are you going to be singing at the ballad festival? There's going to be tough competition, and the boys' and girls' sessions are on separate days."

To Nihil: "I'm going with a friend to watch the match on Saturday. Do you want to come with us?"

They replied, each in turn. His mother said she did not know when the results were going to be out but she was sure he had done well. His father talked about the government, the mess they had made of the country, the violence of it all, but his replies were brief now, they never spoke of anything too far into the future. Rashmi said yes, she had a solo in the Joan Baez ballad and afterward the teachers were going to escort them to listen to the boys when they were performing. Nihil only shook his head.

But in Kala Niles's house, he did not have to work so hard on reminding his family of life and each other. He did not have to wish that someone, Rashmi, his father, anyone, might help him out and take their turn in posing these unimportant questions. All he had to do when he was at Kala Niles's house was to sit at the piano and play while she listened. When he played, and while she listened, Devi was not gone, she was beside them both, impatient for him to finish, impatient to find out what beautiful composition he might make of her life.

An Embroidered Shirt

Rashmi had always had intimations of what her life might be as an adult: secure, successful, and beset by responsibilities to which she would be equal. Nothing would overwhelm her. But that was before she had discovered the pleasure of singing in a band and being a little less good in school, before watching her neighbors' houses burn, before burying the last dog left, and before she had to learn to cook and serve food. Before Devi had left her without a backward glance. Well, that was not entirely true; there had been a backward glance, even if she hadn't looked up to notice it.

"Kamala got cashews. Want to make milk toffee?" Devi had asked Rashmi that day, while Rashmi lay on her belly in her bed in their shared room and wrote about a boy she was getting to know, the brother of a friend. She had shaken her head, no.

"Want to play battleships?" Devi had asked a few minutes later. She had wrapped herself up in the curtain of their room, twisting and twisting until her body hung like a large lime with legs. Rashmi had given her the same reply. *No!* With emphasis.

"You never want to do anything fun," Devi had said. "All you do is sit and read books and write in that stupid diary." And she had unwound herself and stood up. "Nobody here wants to play with me. Everybody's sad all the time, even Raju. All Suren does is bang bang bang on the stupid piano, all Nihil does is talk to Mr. Niles, who won't even talk back to him, and all you do is this. What's the use of brothers and sisters if they don't even play?"

Had she looked back, to see the impression her words had on her sister, Rashmi tried to remember, or had she imagined that look as she watched Devi storm away, dragging the curtain behind her as far as it would go, then sending it flying back in an utterly unsatisfying flutter of green? Had she called out to her and said she *would play, just let me finish,* or had she only thought that she would and had not said it, thinking why did she have to say it because intention had always been accompanied by time. She would play, *after.* After she had finished describing her last conversation with that boy in her book, after she had got it all down. All she could bring back now were Devi's words, those words uttered in that voice, *What's the use of brothers and sisters if they don't even play?* And all she could find in her memory of that day were Devi's feet in red rubber slippers, poking out from underneath her balled-up body wrapped in the green curtain, her footsteps leaving, and then, and then, there was nothing but herself kissing those feet, which no longer had slippers on them.

Rashmi thought about this every morning when she woke up, squashed next to Nihil because she could not bear to sleep in her own room. There was nothing to do about the memory, it was both wound and balm, so she would put her arm around Nihil and wait for him to wake up, listening to his breath come and go, watching his back lift and fall.

"I think of her every morning, as soon as I wake up," she told Suren one morning when it had become unbearable to keep this to herself.

Suren said, "She would like that."

As if Devi were in another room, as if they could share these thoughts with her. "She doesn't know," Rashmi said, softly, so as not to wake up Nihil, who was still asleep.

"She does," Suren said.

"How do you know?" Rashmi asked.

There was silence and then Suren said, "I can feel her here, with us."

"I can't," Rashmi said, feeling more sad than ever. Surely if Devi were in their presence she ought to feel her spirit, she was the sister. How could Suren feel her and how could she not? "Why do you think I can't feel her here?"

"Do something for her," Suren said.

"Like what?"

"You could make something for her. Sing for her. Or you could cook for her."

Rashmi did all these things. She made milk toffee with cashews that she roasted with Kamala watching on, stirred the condensed milk and cream and poured it out into plates lined with wax paper, and cut the toffee into neat squares. Then she gave them away to the Bolling family because nobody in hers wanted to eat milk toffee, which had been Devi's favorite of all the sweets she ate. She sang for Devi, the songs that Devi had always begged her to sing and that she often had refused to sing, not because she wished to be unkind but because a song had to be felt to be sung and on some nights she hadn't felt like singing. She sang when she took her body-wash, her voice echoing in the room as the water splashed over her, and she sang in Kala Niles's house, accompanying herself on the piano with chords that made Kala Niles shudder. As she sang she began to feel Devi with her, listening to her voice, her mouth closing over the impossible sweetness of her toffees, blissful in the knowledge that she was completely loved, but it was her *making of something* that permitted her to forgive herself.

She was sitting on the front steps to their house when the postman came one day, bringing her two letters, one from the boy whom she barely spoke to anymore, and another from her grandmother, with some money inside.

"Every day I think I see her standing here," the postman said, sympathetically. "I remember like yesterday letting her ride this bicycle," and he patted the seat of his bike. "*Chah.* If only I had not offered. I blame myself."

And Rashmi, who was wise now in the way adults are, not with surety but with helplessness, knew that this was his way, as it was the way of all the other people who blamed themselves as he was doing, of carrying away at least a little bit of the guilt that she and her brothers felt. So she didn't tell him he was not to blame, she merely said, "She loved riding that bicycle. It was her biggest treat."

As they stood there for a few moments, heads bowed, Raju came to his gate. The postman looked up. "I feel sorry . . ." he said, looking at Raju then back at her, but he didn't finish the sentence, for how could he tell her that he felt sorry for the man who had not kept her sister from flying down that street and out of their lives? So he pushed his bike up the street, to finish delivering letters to all the houses on the left before returning to deliver the letters to those on the right. And he tried, as all the neighbors on Sal Mal Lane did, to pretend that the Niles and Joseph houses were not still singed and broken, they were exactly as they had once been.

Rashmi stared at Raju. It was the first time she had seen him since the funeral, though Kamala had told her that he had attended the ceremony, listened to the chanting from afar, walked in the funeral procession, far away from those who were close and unsullied, behind those who had known Devi only in passing and even behind those who had not known her at all. Rose had told Rashmi about Sonna, and how Raju had bludgeoned him to death, and how her father, Jimmy Bolling, had said he did not care, *Let the son of a bitch rot. I will not bury him, I will not press charges, I should have done it myself,* and how Francie Bolling had cried and cursed Raju. She also knew that Raju no longer lifted weights, that the weights had been returned to Jimmy Bolling—they sat in the kitchen and were now used as benches by Rose and Dolly when they went in there to help Francie Bolling cook—that Raju rarely left the house, or read the papers, he just stayed beside his mother, who never spoke.

Looking at Raju now, Rashmi tried to feel some anger toward him, but she could not. He was as he had always been, a sad, deformed man whose life had been charmed by the friendship of children such as they were, such as Devi had been, a man who had spent a few years, out of all the years he had lived and all those yet remaining, when life had seemed to offer him something more than mere existence in the company of his hopeless, hopeless dreams.

"Can you take me to a shirt place in Wellawatte?" she asked Suren the next morning as they left for school.

"We will have to go before Amma gets home," Suren said, not asking why she wanted to go, or for what, "and we will have to ask Kamala to keep an eye on Nihil."

"Kamala and maybe Lucas can also come and wait with him," Rashmi said.

That afternoon, Lucas came and sat on the steps to the front veranda ostensibly to read the *Silumina*, but really to make sure that Nihil remained at home, for that is what their parents had asked of them, to *Keep your brother in sight always*. Rashmi and Suren walked all the way to the top of the hill, past the shop where Sonna had died, which was now boarded up, and took the 141 bus to Wellawatte. Most of those shops were still shut, and many of them were gaping holes lined by blackened walls, open to the elements.

"I hope they open these shops again soon," Rashmi said. She saw a nun hurrying down the opposite side of the street and was grateful for the T-shirt she had thrown on to disguise her uniform; they had been in such a hurry to leave the house there had been no time to change.

"The refugees will have to come back from the North first and their houses will have to be rebuilt," Suren replied.

"Do you think they will come back? Will they return to the same houses?" Rashmi asked, stepping around a pile of half-burnt, half-torn notebooks and shelving that must have come from a bookshop.

"I hope so," Suren said. "Otherwise what will happen to the teachers in the Tamil classes? There would be nobody to teach."

"It is sad here without the shops open. Even the market is gone. And look at the kovil. There is nobody outside stringing flowers."

They paused for a while to press their faces to the gate. The kovil was littered with the debris left behind by the refugees, with bundles of rags and shreds of saris and *siri-siri* bags blowing in the breeze coming in from the sea. The kiosk at which they had last seen the flower men, as they referred to them, was now a pile of wood. There were rolls of red thread ground into the sewer drains and tangled on the sharp edges of the broken booth.

"What are you trying to get here?" Suren asked, tearing Rashmi away from the kovil.

"I want to get a shirt for Raju," Rashmi said.

"Then we'll have to go to the fabric part of Sellamuttu Stores, but I don't know if it is open."

"But you didn't ask me why," Rashmi said.

"You must have a good reason," Suren said. "If it is for Raju, it must be for Devi too." He put his hand on her back and guided her across the road between cars and buses that all moved slowly, the drivers curious to see what could be seen.

Sellamuttu Stores was, miraculously, open. Inside, though, there was a Sinhalese man.

"Where's the owner?" Suren asked him.

"They have gone to Jaffna," he said. "I am only a friend. I said I will open the shop and run it till they come back. But I don't know if they will come back. Who would want to?"

"Do you send them money?" Suren asked.

"Not many people come here, so there hasn't been much money. But if it picks up then I'll be able to send money." They both nodded.

"Did they go by ship?" Suren asked, having heard of the transport of Tamils from the refugee camps to the villages in the North.

"Yes," the man replied. "They were at a church in Kotahena and I went to see them there. After a few days they went to Jaffna on the *Lanka Kalyani*. A cargo ship. I heard it took a long time to get there. I hope there was food on the ship."

Suren and Rashmi shared in the silence that followed the man's statement. All three of them wondered about such a trip, what the owners of Sellamuttu Stores might have taken with them, if anything, whether they were relieved to escape or fearful of a journey over the ocean. They considered what they might do under such circumstances and, in the deepening quiet, they settled instead on the feelings each of them carried within, for lost neighbors, for a dead sister.

Rashmi spoke first. "What size is Raju?" she asked Suren.

Suren spoke slowly as though coming out of a deep reverie. "His neck is probably eighteen and a half and sleeves are probably about thirty-four," he said.

"My god. Very strange size," the man said, standing up straight and looking alarmed. "I am not sure I'll even be able to find a shirt like that!" Still, after much searching, which included climbing on stools and ladders, he found a light-blue shirt with just such measurements and Rashmi paid him all the money she had received from her grandmother, which wasn't quite enough but which the man accepted, brushing away her concern with a sideways shake of his head and a *kamak neha*.

Lucas had left before they got home because Nihil had fallen asleep. Nihil spent much of his time at home sleeping; his silences would grow longer and longer until he shut his eyes and lay down and fell into sleep that was so deep that it was often hard to wake him up, a job that Suren undertook. The one time Rashmi had tried to do it he had woken up looking crazed, clutched her arms, and said *Devi! Devi!*

Over the next weeks, Rashmi spent her time after school, and every late-night hour she could manage to spend before she had to go to sleep, embroidering the shirt with blue and yellow threads. In doing so she was reminded of the person who had first taught her to embroider, Mrs. Silva. She felt grateful for that first day, the day when she and Devi had sat with Mrs. Silva and learned how to embroider on small squares of old cloth, the fabric soft in their fingers, the scent of the still young creeping jasmine strong in the early-morning hours and surrounding them all in a cocoon of fragrance.

"You have to hold the needle firmly but the thread lightly, that's the trick to embroidery," Mrs. Silva had said, her own beautiful embroidery set aside while she unpicked the knots from Devi's work and hers.

Devi, irritated by the difficulty of the work, complained. "Why do I have to learn this?"

"Someday when you are a fine lady you'll want to embroider your own linens and baby clothes, won't you?" Mrs. Silva asked.

"No. I don't want to be a fine lady. Rashmi is going to be a fine lady. That's enough."

If Rashmi had known then that she would be embroidering something to remember Devi by, using her skill long before she became A Fine Lady, in fact after she, too, like Devi, had decided that being fine about anything was not that important after all, what would she have done? She looked at the cloth and thread in her hands and felt overwhelmed by the past and by the present. Suren came in and found her, the shirt and skeins laid out neatly on Devi's bed, her hands quite still as she observed the arrangement before her.

"What's the matter?" Suren asked, picking up a few skeins to make room for himself and sitting down on the bed.

"Don't sit on her bed," Rashmi said.

Suren got up and moved to Rashmi's bed. "What are you thinking about?"

"Mrs. Silva," Rashmi said. "She taught me to embroider, and now I'm using it to make a shirt for Raju, but Mrs. Silva is not a good person."

"But she taught you something good," Suren said, playing with the skeins of thread that were still in his hand. "Maybe that will help erase some of the bad things she has done."

"I don't think it happens that way. I think all the bad we do remains next to all the good we do. I don't think you can change one by doing the other."

"Then all you need to think about is doing more good than bad," Suren said. "This shirt that you are making, that is a good thing. Just think about that. Forget about Mrs. Silva."

So she tried. Rashmi embroidered flowers that she copied off one of Devi's dresses, taking one from the box into which they had been packed to be given away, one of her favorites, in green and white; she embroidered chariots she traced off of Suren's and Nihil's blue-and-gold shirts; she embroidered balls balanced on cricket bats; she embroidered kites and hopscotch squares and skipping ropes and, along the hem, with some difficulty, she embroidered the outlines of bicycles.

"When do you plan to give this to Raju?" Suren asked.

"I thought I could give it to him after the three-month almsgiving," Rashmi said.

Suren smiled. "That would be a good time to do it. It would make her happy."

Rashmi did not tell Nihil about the gift she was making, the whys and wherefores. Nihil was untouchable. He was with them and yet absent; he spoke and yet said nothing that anybody could pin a thought to. He went to school, he studied, he took tests, and he slept and slept and slept. His appetite neither waxed nor waned, it was sufficient. Sometimes his friends would visit him and he would talk to them, even laugh with them, but the visits were always short, as if neither he nor his friends could keep up the pretense. So Rashmi was surprised when Nihil offered to help with cooking for the three-month almsgiving.

"Tell me what to do," he said, coming into the kitchen where she was standing peeling onions and garlic and potatoes.

"You don't need to cook," Mrs. Herath said. "It's okay."

"I want to cook. Tell me what to do."

"Here, you can peel these," Rashmi offered, wanting to seize the opportunity to bring him out of the silences he preferred.

"After that?" he asked.

"After that you can help me cook the potatoes and make the *mallun* and prepare the cutlets for frying," she said.

In the kitchen that afternoon and evening, with Nihil beside her, Rashmi listened to her mother and Mrs. Niles and Kala Niles and Mrs. Nadesan talk. Kamala, dismissed from the kitchen, stood nearby just in case she was needed to fetch and carry things.

"We have decided to go to India," Mrs. Nadesan said.

"Really? For good?" Mrs. Niles asked, as she stopped stirring the curry she was making and turned around.

"For good," Mrs. Nadesan said. "Might as well, if we have to leave, to leave for good. That's what my brothers all say. They always said it was better to live with our own people. I wish we had listened."

"You don't have to leave. We are not leaving," Kala Niles said, "even though our house was burnt, not like yours. At least yours was still the same."

"We have no place to go even if we want to leave," Mrs. Niles said.

"I don't want to leave," Kala Niles said firmly, glancing at Mrs. Herath, who had remained silent.

"I don't want to leave either," Mrs. Nadesan said. "This is where we have lived all our married lives, and our girls before they grew up and left, but with all this trouble, better to go now than later." None of the neighbors responded and after a while Mrs. Nadesan clucked her tongue and said, "I almost forgot." She undid a knot at the edge of the fall of her sari and unwrapped a pair of earrings. "These I want Rashmi to have. She saved my *thali*. Come, take them, darling."

Rashmi stretched out her hand and took the earrings, and she did not know if Mrs. Nadesan had forgotten that it had been Devi who had crawled back into her house to rescue her gold wedding necklace, so beautiful and heavy she had to pass it to Suren before she could climb out of that window.

Suren had told her that Devi had asked to hold the necklace again, after, wanting to feel that weight in her hands, pausing even in the middle of all that chaos to admire its beauty. Or maybe Mrs. Nadesan did remember but did not want to mention Devi's name.

"They are beautiful, Aunty," she said, and gave them to her mother, who took them from her and tied them into the edge of the fall of her own sari. And then, not knowing how else to thank Mrs. Nadesan, Rashmi felt compelled to say, "There won't be any more trouble."

"There will always be trouble when we have people like the next-door neighbors around," Mrs. Herath said at last. "But for what it is worth, I want to say that we, our whole family, will be very sad to see you go."

Mrs. Nadesan went over to Mrs. Herath and put an arm around her. Mrs. Herath was smaller, so her mother was completely hidden from Rashmi's view. "Don't be sad, Savi. All of us have cried enough now. We must stop thinking about the past and face what we have to face," she said, but Rashmi could tell that Mrs. Nadesan, too, was crying.

If Nihil was moved by these expressions of regret, he did not make it known. He simply bent further into his task, as he sat on a low stool and made small round balls with mashed potatoes and carrots and finely chopped leeks that had been fried with onions and green chillies and garlic. Rashmi watched his relentlessly methodical work and the exactly spaced time between scooping a bit of the mixture, shaping it into a ball, and placing it in the dish of beaten egg whites, and, after a while, she felt the sadness lift, and she mimicked his pace until all the cutlets were coated with bread crumbs and fried and set out to cool on sheets of newspaper.

Late that night, as she swept the front veranda one last time in preparation for the next day, Mohan came to the doorstep.

"Amma sent these for the almsgiving tomorrow," he said, holding a covered dish out to her. "She made macaroni with cheese."

Rashmi leaned the broom on the wall and walked over to him. She had to tilt her head back to look at him, even when he stood one step lower. His voice, too, seemed much deeper than she remembered. She realized she had not spoken to him in a while. She took the bowl from him and set it on a side table.

"Are you and Jith still going to join the army?" she asked. "Now there's a real war, it would mean fighting."

Mohan looked down at his feet. "Jith is not going to join. I told him he shouldn't do it. He is going to study computers instead. But I have to join.

I don't have . . . I am not good . . . my teachers . . . I am not a good enough student to stay at school," he finished in a rush.

Alice came out of the house, on her way home after helping with the cleaning of the house, and Rashmi and Mohan moved aside to let her pass. They both watched her.

"But there are other things to do without joining the army," Rashmi said, after Alice had shut the gate behind her.

"Like what?" Mohan asked, but not like he thought she might know, more like he was incredulous that she would suggest that there were options he hadn't considered.

Rashmi shrugged. "I don't know. You could learn accounting or shorthand and typing," she said, since these were the things she had heard of, as options, for those who didn't go to university.

"Those are for girls, not for boys."

"Oh," Rashmi said.

There was nothing more to talk about, then, for the two of them. The scent of her mother's roses, grown from cuttings she had got from Kala Niles in gratitude for Mrs. Herath's advice regarding the proper placement of ferns, wafted across the garden. Rashmi inhaled deeply, filling her body with the smell. Mohan shifted his weight from foot to foot, his eyes moving around the room, to the floor, the chairs, the ceiling, and the mandevilla vine that framed the doorway. Rashmi considered asking after Jith but didn't know how to do so without sounding as though she had run out of things to talk about with Mohan, and so, when the silence had stretched out longer than was tolerable, she picked up the dish he had brought, ending the conversation.

"I hope they are all right," he said quickly, "the Niles family and the Nadesans."

"No," Rashmi said, simply, "but they are alive."

Mohan put his hands in his pockets and looked at her. He said, "I miss hearing Devi. She always yelled for Raju at the same time. I would listen for her voice. I didn't know that I had been doing that until—" And he stopped there.

Was Mohan asking her to forgive him? If so, for what? Everybody was responsible for what had happened to their street, so everybody was responsible for Devi. Herself most of all, she thought. Devi was *her* sister.

"If you study harder you can stay in school," she said. She turned and went inside and didn't come back out for a long time to finish sweeping because she knew without having to see him that Mohan was still standing there, standing on the steps to their house, waiting for something none of them could give.

On the morning of the almsgiving, Rashmi stood and listened for the drums that heralded the priests' coming, and watched as Suren washed the feet of each of the eleven priests and Nihil dried them before they stepped into the house. The chanting of the *Mahapiritha* soothed them all then, again in the evening, and once more on the morning of the next day, and when the priest tied the threads around each of their wrists, she felt as though indeed some of their pain had been soothed.

After the priests had been served from the bowls that covered the tables before them, and after her parents and their sisters and brother and relatives and Mr. Tissera too, even though he was Catholic, had offered three sets of the eight requirements for monks, including cloth for their garments, she, Rose, Suren, Nihil, and Dolly stepped forward to donate smaller gifts to the younger monks: pencils and erasers and crisp exercise books. As Rashmi placed the last of these offerings before a young monk, younger than Devi had been, and as she knelt and bowed her head and brought her hands together in worship, she remembered the other offering she had prepared.

Nothing about Old Mrs. Joseph's house looked the same, and in many ways it was worse off than the Nileses' house, which, complete as it was, with a set of parents and a competent child, had slowly had its exterior and some of the interior restored. She and Suren, along with Lucas and Kamala, had gone over and helped Kala Niles to scrub the walls outside, as high as they could reach. The Bolling twins had borrowed Mrs. Herath's garden shears and Mr. Silva's too, though in that case Jith had simply sneaked them out to Dolly, and spent a weekend clipping all the singed and dried rosebushes and vines, and dragging the branches over to the back of their own house to set them on fire, far away from where Kala Niles could see them. Nobody had gone to Raju's house. In that house, much was still unhinged, the doors, the windows, the mussaenda, Old Mrs. Joseph herself, her movements even more restricted than they had been before with only Raju to tend to her, their help from the estates having run away as soon as the last curfew was lifted. Jimmy Bolling brought food for his aunt and for Raju, but Francie Bolling, though it was the food she cooked that was taken in this manner, refused to go near Raju.

The gate to Raju's house was cool under her palm and Rashmi remembered that the last time she had stepped through this gate had been when Devi herself had called out to her to *Come and touch the gate, it is still hot!* She paused for a moment at that gate, neither going in nor leaving. The smells from the warm basket of food in her hand wafted up, each separate curry releasing its own mix of spices. She thought about the special curries each of the neighbors had brought, the eggplant curry from Mrs. Nadesan, the garlic curry from Mrs. Tissera, the dhal from Mrs. Niles, the *watalappan* from Mrs. Bin Ahmed, and she felt hungry for the first time. When she looked up she saw that Raju was sitting by himself in the front veranda. As she pushed the gate open and went in, he stood up, anxiety creasing his face.

"Rashmi, you have come! Is everything okay?"

She said, "I brought you and Aunty some food."

Raju took the basket from her, shaking his head from side to side, and placed it carefully on the ledge that surrounded Old Mrs. Joseph's veranda. He said, "It is kind of you."

"And this," Rashmi started, and stopped. She handed the shirt, in its brown paper bag, to Raju. She knew what she wanted to say, but she did not trust herself to say it.

"What is this?" he asked, and then when she did not say anything further, he opened the bag and drew out the shirt, which unfolded awkwardly in his hands until he smoothed the edges and held it up.

Was it a shirt that he would ever wear? Or was it a shirt meant for looking at? A shirt not for displaying in public but for reading and memory? Would Raju understand its significance? Did he deserve such a gift? Rashmi did not know the answers to these questions. She only knew that whatever Raju did or did not deserve, Devi, lost to them all, would know that Raju was not abandoned to his loneliness.

"This is for you to remember Devi," Rashmi managed to say.

And though she never asked Raju what he thought of her giving, though he did not thank her, as she walked away from him, Rashmi felt that she walked in the company of her sister.

A Small Boy, an Old Man

Nobody knows what is to come, not even those so tied together in spirit that they are able to persuade themselves that they do know. Yet Nihil felt that he had known, all along, and that it had been his dismissal of what he had known that had made Devi ride so fearlessly down their lane. Because he blamed himself, he blamed others, all the others except for Sonna. He could not blame Sonna no matter how many times he tried.

Nihil blamed Raju, for having taken on the business of caring for Devi when he knew how lacking he was. He blamed Rashmi, for not playing with Devi that day or on any other day so that she would not have wanted, not have needed to seek out a companion so flawed and foolish as Raju. He blamed Suren, for not having saved him from this moment, for not having reminded him of his book of worries, for wasn't that his job, to nudge him to wonder why he had written *Raju, Raju, Raju* so often in that book? He blamed his parents for everything; he did not know what specific blame to lay at their feet, so *everything* fulfilled that requirement. Most of all, Nihil blamed Mr. Niles. For who else but Mr. Niles, with his yellowing white hair and his sharp gaze and seemingly sensible observations about war and peace, his batting gloves and talk of the Oval, had made him let down his guard? He must have known what would come to pass, for hadn't it been Mr. Niles who had said to him, all those months and years ago, the words that he had set aside and only now remembered and called forth to damn the old man: *You can't keep your little sister to yourself. She won't stay.* And if he had known, why had Mr. Niles not warned him of the day when Devi would step away from him, not just as a sister might, shrugging off his concerns, but forever, like a spirit who had never intended to stay?

The people around him tried many things to ease his mind.

His grieving mother, who wore nothing but white saris day after day, all the other ones moved to a place where she could no longer even see them, planned a Seth Pirith, which was supposed to placate whatever demons had possessed him and set him free to live again. Nihil listened dutifully while the priests chanted, and uttered the stanzas he was required to utter, but when it was all over nothing had changed.

His father took him to the Soviet-run People's Publishing House, which had not been shut down even though the Communist Party was now banned, and he tried to interest Nihil in books about dragons and people named Baba Yaga and Vasilissa the Beautiful, and he was successful, he thought, when Nihil picked out a book and brought it home. Except that the book was about a brother and a sister called Tutti and Suok who had been separated by force and their story plunged Nihil into a further spell of withdrawal.

Rashmi tried, but only indirectly, by asking Nihil to help her in the kitchen whenever she cooked, and she cooked frequently since that was her solace, and Nihil was happy enough to participate. Still, although he chatted with her as they cooked, and that was reward enough, when the cooking was done he folded into himself and went away to read the same books over again, and did not pick up on any of their conversations during any other time. Not even as they ate the food they had cooked together.

The twins tried, asking for his help with one thing or the other, a maths problem, an essay, even moving their furniture, when they decided that they would occupy Sonna's room, the one farthest from their parents' bedroom. Nihil helped them with whatever they asked—he even advised them how they might arrange their beds—but when Rose gave him a tattered bit of paper she had found in one of Sonna's shirts, and when he opened it up and read it, he grew quiet and went away.

Suren did not try. He sat with Nihil while he wrote in his exercise books, ceaselessly copying lines of poetry, or read, and whenever Nihil appeared present in their room and not visiting some other world of fiction or fact, imagined or real, he played him sections of the piece of music he was composing for Devi.

Of the various attempts that were being made to draw Nihil out, it stood to reason that Suren and Rashmi were more successful than anybody else, for their reaching out came from the heart, from the place that also loved and missed and longed for Devi. Their reaching did not come from trying to make Nihil forget, or from trying to heal him from without as though what he had was a curable illness, not a hurt buried deep in his psyche, the same hurt that his parents were trying to keep silent as they put one foot in front of the other each day, living for the sake of those still alive.

"Taste this," Rashmi said, taking Nihil's hand and tapping it with the edge of a wooden ladle that was coated with gravy. "What does it taste like?"

"It tastes like something Devi would like," he said, after a pause.

"Yes, she would like it. It has cardamom and star anise," Rashmi said, smiling at him. "Those were her favorite spices."

"She also liked to eat cinnamon," he said, smiling back at her. "Do you remember how she used to steal cinnamon from Kamala and chew it when we played French cricket?"

"Yes! And once she spat it out when she was up in her tree and it landed on Raju by accident. He was untwisting her swing." And for a few seconds, not even the mention of Raju was enough to stop the laughter that they shared.

"Nihil, close your eyes and listen to this," Suren said one day. "Tell me what you think when you hear the different sections."

Nihil, sitting in an excessively upholstered but very precious chair that had once been out of bounds to the children but now wasn't, nothing was, all the rules in their house had been abandoned, leaned back and closed his eyes. He listened. As he did, he saw Devi running up and down their street, as happy to linger as she was to walk, skip, or run; he experienced again Devi's exuberance when he played cricket, the way she cheered, half the time not knowing whether he had done well or badly, her enthusiasm tied to his enjoyment of the game itself; he saw the blue-and-silver kite making its own journey through the trees and out into the open skies, out of their hands; he heard her struggles with the piano, the wrong notes she played almost as often as she played the correct ones. He saw her alive.

"That's all, so far," Suren said, as he took his hands off the keys of the piano. "Did you see anything while you were listening?"

Nihil opened his eyes. "I saw Devi," Nihil said. "The way she was."

Suren smiled. "Good. I'm writing this for her."

Nihil stood up and came over to the piano. Suren moved to the side of the bench and Nihil sat down beside him. "Are you just making it up as you go along?" Nihil asked. He played a few notes, then the C-sharp major scale in chords, his fingers hesitating as he struggled to remember the correct placements.

"No, I sit before the keys and I let thoughts of her fill my mind," Suren said, simply, "and then at the right time when I place my fingers on the keys, I know how to arrange them and even though the notes don't make sense in small sections, when I put them all together they do." They sat like that in silence for a while, and it was not a sad silence. Then Suren said, "Find some way to remember her, Nihil." And that was all he said.

But could Nihil do that? If there was a way to remember her in such ways as Rashmi and Suren had found, he did not know what that was. If there was a way to turn back these last months, he did not feel he was blessed with the knowledge of how to do that.

Then, in the dead of one night, Nihil found himself sitting at his desk, the lamp on it casting a rectangle of light. He opened his drawer and there, as though someone had taken it out and placed it on top of all the other books so he might notice it, was his book of worries. He flipped through the written pages, so few! He read and reread the entries, the words about Devi's accident when she had to have stitches and her fall when Mrs. Niles took care of her and of her getting into trouble at school. Why, he wondered, had he never imagined that all these separate things might be simply one thing? One way of living in the world, one set of circumstances that would come together to form what was her life and her death? He turned the last page on which he had written, and smoothed it down. He picked up a pen and wrote *Everything I Remember About Devi*. He underlined it. He left the next line blank and then, in neat and even writing and with a steady hand, he began to write.

Did he remember everything about Devi? Does it matter? What he did remember was enough, for he wrote through the quiet hours, he wrote until he filled the pages of that ruled notebook, the notebook he had started out to fill for all four of them, then just for her, the notebook so thick and solid because he had imagined not only that his fears for his sister would require such a thick book, would require that many pages, but also that such diligent entry would keep her from harm. But it had not. All there was left for him to fill it with was her, as she had been, as he had known her, precocious and smart in some things, not in others, defiant, kind, untroubled by the things that concerned the rest of them—the future, political events, dreams of performance—happy with life, sweet simple life, a devotee of play, and, most of all, beloved, more than all of them, beloved. He wrote of her as he imagined she might have become had she stayed, tall and slender, still as feisty, still as full of girlhood and laughter, still waiting to be told what was what, still disregarding what was told to her. In this life, this life she did not have, she remained as perfect, as incomparable, and as unbroken as she was in the life he knew she had lived. In his version there was no fault line between these two lives. There was only Devi as she had been, Devi as she would be.

There were still many pages left to that book when he finished. And he accepted those empty pages as being not an indication of the lapses of his memory but, rather, the fact that there was no more to be said. When he rose from his chair, the dawn was just breaking.

Outside he could hear the earliest birds singing. In the pink glow of the coming day, Nihil stood underneath the Asoka tree and dug a hole with his hands. He placed the book inside and set it on fire. He sat back on his heels and watched it burn, and the smoke of this small fire, so unlike the fires that had burned the houses down that lane, this smoke did not sting his eyes, it simply lifted and rose between the leaves of the tree she had loved to climb, up and through its branches, up and into the skies. He covered the ashes with earth and he lit a stick of incense over it. Then he stood up and went inside.

"Where is Nihil?" Mr. Niles would say to Suren as he came and went, or to Rashmi when she stopped to say hello to him.

"He's at home," Suren might say, or, more specifically, "He's reading."

"What is he reading?"

"Poems by R. L. Stevenson," Suren would say, or *Red Sky at Morning*, or *The Hitchhiker's Guide to the Galaxy*, or *The Catcher in the Rye*, but never the books of easy, down-to-earth mystery and adventure that he had once loved.

"Is he playing cricket?" Mr. Niles asked this of Rashmi, not Suren, not because he hoped it was true, but because he had to ask, had to know if there was even the faintest possibility that Nihil would go back to what he had loved.

"No," Rashmi said, "nobody plays cricket down our lane anymore. Everybody is growing up." She used that word because that is what she had heard said of them, *All our children are growing up*, by the adults on Sal Mal Lane whenever they spoke about the quietness of the road.

And that growing up, what was it, for the children were still children, full of wishes, wish-fulfillment still imaginable. The growing up was this: each of them had moved away from a simpler past, one where nothing that happened beyond Sal Mal Lane had ever seemed to apply to them. Some had shifted a small distance, like Mohan and Jith; some much further, like Rose and Dolly, who mourned for the brother they had always feared but who had, nonetheless, been a part of them; and still others, like Suren and Rashmi and Nihil, with the wide-open space left behind by Devi, had traveled an even greater distance away from childhood.

"Not even for practice?" Mr. Niles asked, for he knew without having to be told that there would be no more games of cricket played down that road, not for a long time, and that when those games resumed, with other children, he would be gone.

"No, he hasn't gone for practice since—" and Rashmi stopped there.

"Ask him to come and see me." Mr. Niles asked this of Suren.

And because asking was possible though forcing him to come was not, Suren said, "I will ask him to come."

Mr. Niles waited: that day, the next, the following week, the week after that. Nihil did not come.

"It would be a good thing if you went to see Mr. Niles," Suren said.

Nihil looked up from the book he was reading. "I don't want to see Mr. Niles. I don't play the piano anymore and there is no reason for me to go there."

"He is an old man, and he won't be here much longer," Suren said.

Nihil had turned back to his book and this time he did not look up, but he heard. And when he heard those words that alluded to death, he thought of Devi. He thought about the words he might have said to her, *Don't go so fast!* or even *Stop!* He thought of what he might have done as he watched her come, so light and happy, of how he might have thrown himself in front of the bike and how she might have flown off the bike, and she might have hit Old Mrs. Joseph's gate, or might have simply crashed to the ground and bruised her knees and shins and her elbows and palms and might have even hit her head, but she would not have died. He was sure of it, she would not have died.

And if she had lived, what would he have said to her? He would have said what he needed to say to her, the words of chastisement that would keep her safe.

"You were going too fast! I had to stop you!"

"No more of this bike! I'm going to ask Raju to take it back!"

"What is the matter with you? Do you think this is a time to be riding bikes up and down the road? Have you forgotten that our neighbors' gardens are still filled with ash? Have you forgotten that Raju's mother is half paralyzed?"

Ah, yes, those are the words he would have said. He would not have said other words, the words he wanted to say after, after she could no longer hear him.

"Come inside, I will play battleships with you."

"I'll double you on the bike until you can ride it alone."

"You can bring me my lunch at the next match I play."

"I will buy you an icy choc and an ice-palam and a cold bottle of Coca-Cola too."

"You can hold the kite."

How could he have known that they were the words, the only ones, that were worth saying? How could he know, being just a child, being just human with human sight?

And what would Devi have said had she been able to speak? Nihil wondered. If she had been able to say anything at all, what is it she would have said to him?

"I am sorry."

"I was happy."

"It was not your fault."

Nihil closed his book as those words came to him, hearing them in Devi's voice, understanding at last that the love he felt for Devi had always been equaled by the love she had for him. Understanding that she would have kept herself safe had her safety guaranteed his happiness. Understanding also that no such guarantees can ever be made.

The last voice that Mr. Niles heard as he slipped out of consciousness and into the death that had been promised him, the one that had not arrived within the six months given, that had waited long enough for him to meet a boy, such a boy as this, to love him and lose him and have him returned to him again, the last voice he heard was Nihil's. For a day and into the best part of that night, pausing only for the soup and tea that Mrs. Niles brought for him, Nihil read aloud to Mr. Niles.

"Go and fetch the two gray covered books on top of my chest of drawers, son." That was the first thing he said when Nihil pushed open the door and came into the house. He had said that even as he lay there, his eyes shut, knowing who had come though Nihil had not said a word.

Nihil went into Mr. Niles's bedroom, the one in which he hadn't slept for almost a year. He breathed in the smell of clean things, freshly washed, the bed so crisp as though Mrs. Niles expected that on any given evening, her husband might stand up and retire to sleep in his own bed and not remain in quiet rest on the mattress in the veranda. There was no dust there, not on the bureau, or under the bed. Nor on the bat that was laid at the bottom of the bed, the bat that he saw was still tagged with his own name, but that he did not pick up.

"My mother and father gave these books to me when I took my university entrance examinations. We were still living in Jaffna, in my childhood home. These books, they were new then," Mr. Niles said when Nihil gave him the books.

"You were young then," Nihil said, and those were his first words. When he said them, Nihil found that they did not sound loud and strange as he had imagined they would, they sounded as though he had never left this place, this place beside Mr. Niles, who had listened to him and heard him and who had always, even on the first day they met, told him the truth.

Mr. Niles handed the books back to Nihil. "They were written by the Knight of Newbold Revel, Sir Thomas Malory. They are for you."

He did not ask Nihil to read to him, but Nihil did. The tale that he read was one he understood. It was a tale of striving for high ideals amid human frailty, turmoil, and change. It was a tale of betrayal and love. And though he wanted, very much, to start with the last word and read it backward, to say *ruhtra fo htaed eht fo dne eht si ereh dna,* he began with the first words, *It befell in the days,* and he read them forward, whole, as they had been written.

Epilogue

The events that unfolded on Sal Mal Lane involved everybody: the Niles family, the Nadesans, the Sansonis, the Bollings, the Josephs, the Bin Ahmeds, the Tisseras, the Silvas, and the Heraths. They also involved Lucas and Alice.

A man had stood in a jungle clearing on the fifth day of May, in 1976, and he had asked for war. In the years after, men and women stirred by hatreds echoed his call. And though the people who stood with that man and the people who stood with those other men and women had agreed that war was necessary, there were many people who did not.

In the years that followed the events that took place on Sal Mal Lane, there were other children. There were New Year sweets and Christmas cakes and watalappan exchanged among the neighbors. There were Vesak lanterns on trees and entryways painted in pinks and greens and the sound of carols being sung.

There never was again a young girl in a yellow dress imagining flight, and there never was again a piano moved with such love down a dead-end street.

Glossary

achchaaru	pickle
ado	dude (slang)
Aiyya	older brother
aiyyo/aney	Oh dear, or oh no, or, simply, oh
Akki	older sister
akshara	plural form of *aksharaya;* the sound of a letter; usually refers to the sound or letter suggested by an astrologer upon the birth of a child, to guide the parents in naming the baby
Allah hu Akbar	God is great
almirah	a large wardrobe or cupboard used for storing clothes
aluhung	a generally harmless skin fungus that causes patches of discoloration
Ammata hukana keri vesige putho, thavath kunuharapa ahagannethuwa apita ape paaduwe yanna deepang hukanne nethuwa. Pakaya!	You motherfucking sons of whores, unless you want to hear more filth from me, let us go where we are going without fucking with us. Fucker!
Aney Devi Baba! Devi Baba genavane!	Oh, Devi Baby! They have brought Devi Baby!
Aney putha, mage putha.	Oh son, my son.
Appa	Father (Tamil)
Appoi!	Goodness!
arrack	coconut-based local alcohol

baas	laborer, usually carpenter or builder
baba	baby
bali-thovila	technically an exorcism or the invocation of demons using dance, but often used to refer to any unruly activity, particularly if it involves music
band-chune	minimizing the activity of playing in a band; literally, like "band-shmand"
banian	a thin sleeveless undershirt
beedi	a curl of dried tobacco filled with equally dried, coarse flakes of tobacco
bhajan	song of praise to Hindu deities
Bokku!	literally, "ditch"; used as an insult to a fielder when a ball rolls between his legs instead of being caught
brinjal	eggplant
Burgher	mixed-race Sri Lankans; descendants of European colonists from the sixteenth to twentieth centuries from Portugal, Holland, and England
burusu kadé	shop that sells products made with coir
chah	damn (slang)
chee	yuck
dagoba	a dome-shaped structure built over the relics of the Buddha
Deepavali	Hindu festival of lights
Deiyyo Saakki!	May the gods be witness!
Demala	Tamil (language)
Demalā	derogatory term for a person of Tamil origin
Demala huththo	Tamil fuckers
Dhaham Pāsal	Sunday school (Buddhist)
dhal	lentil curry

dhansala	a stall that provides alms to people on their way to temple, usually food, drink, and flowers
dhara mudalali	manager of a small store that specializes in wood
dhobi	laundryman
Elankandiya	"Ela kanda" refers to the banks of a stream; "Elakandiya," a takeoff on that term, refers to a slum near Sal Mal Lane.
ekel broom	broom made for sweeping the outdoors constructed by stripping each frond on the branch of a coconut tree and binding the stiff bark left together
gāthā	Buddhist stanzas in the Pali language
genavane	has been brought
gingelly oil	sesame oil
goma pohora	fertilizer made with cow dung
guruleththuwa	long-necked clay jug into which boiled water is poured for cooling and for taste
hoonu bittara	literally, "gecko eggs"; here, very small candy-covered anise
huththa	fucker
ice-palam	Popsicle
indul	scent left behind by spices or curries when one eats with one's fingers
Issarahata yanna.	Move forward.
Jathaka tales	folktales
Jooli hathay mala keliyay.	Those born on the seventh will suffer terrible tragedy.
jungi	women's panties
kabal lansis	trashy Burghers (mixed-race); equivalent to "white trash"
kachchan	hot, dry winds usually associated with drought (Tamil)
kalu	black or dark

kalu kella	dark-skinned girl
kamak neha	it does not matter

Karaniya matthakusalena	This is what should be done
Yam tam santam padam abhisamecca	By one who is skilled in goodness,
Sakko uju ca suju ca	And who knows the path of peace:
Suvaco c'assa mudu anatimani	Let them be able and upright, the epitome of humility

kassippu	crude, home-brewed form of alcohol
kitul	a palm tree that yields a sap, which produces a thick sugar or treacle
kohu	coir
kolla	boy
kottamalli	coriander, roasted and prepared with water to soothe a cold or cough
Koti enawa!	The Tigers are coming!
kovil	a Hindu temple
kurumba	the water from a young coconut
kusu-kusufying	hobnobbing, fraternizing (slang)
lansi	derogatory term for Burghers (mixed-race)
lansi ponnaya	Burgher homosexual; slang, referring to ineffectuality
Letchumi	Lakshmi, the Hindu goddess of wealth; often used to refer to a Tamil girl (slang)
lungi	a piece of fabric, usually cotton, that is used as a full-length, wraparound skirt; in Sri Lanka, it is worn by older women
machang	friend or dude (slang)
Mahapiritha	literally, "the great prayer"; refers to the Buddha's Discourses, including the three main sutras, the Mangala Sutra (the auspicious factors), Ratana Sutra (the gems), and the Karaniya Metta Sutra (universal love)

Mahavamsa	chronicle of Sri Lankan history from the coming of Vijaya in 543 BCE to the reign of King Mahasena, 223–361
mallun	salad made of finely chopped green leaves
mehendi	henna
mirisgala	a heavy oval stone used for grinding chillies
muthu	pearl (a variety of *samba* rice that resembles pearls)
Naa sahodaraya, gini kooru vitharay thiyenne.	No, brother, I only have matches.
Nangi	little sister
nebiliya	a shallow steel bowl with grooves used for destoning rice
nona	lady
paan	bread
pakkali	servility; literally, "currying favor" (e.g., running and opening the door of the boss's car, carrying his bag, etc.)
Palayang!	Get out!
palu	the section in the front end of a sari, usually heavily embroidered
pandal	a large colorful display decorated with lights; usually erected in public spaces during Vesak, they depict scenes from the life of the Buddha
Para Demalā/ Demellu	Tamil pariah/s
parisaraya	environment (social and natural)
pchah	clicking sound made by the tongue against the teeth
pirith	the Sinhala translation of the Pali word *paritta*, which means "protection"; it is supposed to protect the listener, and is a recitation or changing of the word of the Buddha
pola	farmers' market, usually on Sundays

ponnaya	slur for gay boy
pota	a short term for the fall of a sari
Poth pennanna.	Show us your books.
pottu	mark made on forehead by Tamil women using various forms of dyes or pastes to signify marital status
Poya	full moon day, which is always a Buddhist public holiday
PT	short for "physical training"; also known as the "games period" in schools
Putha	Son
Samavenna	Forgive me
sambaaru	a vegetable curry cooked with a mix of vegetables and lentils; a Tamil specialty
sambol	a side dish made from grinding fresh coconut together with onions, dried chillies, and lime juice
sambrani	natural resinoid benzoin that give off a scent of frankincense when burnt
sari pota	the fall of the sari
satyagraha	fast unto death for a political cause
seeni kooru	a type of candy; literally, "sugar sticks"
Seeya	Grandfather
Seth Pirith	chanting of Buddhist prayers to soothe the troubled
Sinhalada demalada?	Are you Sinhalese or Tamil?
siri-siri bag	plastic bag named for the tissuey sound it makes
sudhu	white
takarang	aluminum sheets
Tha	short version of *Thaaththa*, which means "father"
thali	gold necklace worn by Tamil women to signify marriage
Thambiya	Muslim (derogatory term, slang)
thuppai	half-baked

Unname udakam vattam yatha ninnam pavattati *evameva ito dinnam petanam upakappati.* *Yatha varivaha pura paripurenti sagaram* *evameva ito dinnam petanam upakappati.*	Even as water flows from the high ground to a lower ground, what merit is given here reaches the departed. Even as the waters of a full river reaches and fills the ocean, what merit is offered here reaches the dead.

vadai	savory finger food made of lentils and spices fried into cakes
Vayadamma Sankaara.	All things are impermanent.
Vedda	indigenous person
Vel	festival celebrating the Kataragrama deities
-vem	a common ending to Tamil names

veralen kiri kavadi soya kenek puthuta gena denava *thavath kenek paata paata pabalu kaden gena enava* *e kavadiy e pabalui eka noolaka amunanava* *evaayin havadi sadaa puthuge ine palandinava*	One man brings seashells for him from the beach Another one brings colorful beads from a shop I string these together on the same string and drape them around my baby's waist.

verti	Indian sarong
Vesak	celebration of the birth, death, and attainment of nirvana of the Lord Buddha
vesi	whore
watalappan	sweet dessert made with kitul juggery and coconut milk (Muslim)
yalhulanga	hot, dry winds usually associated with drought (Sinhala)

Acknowledgments

For the gift of time, I thank the Corporation of Yaddo, where this book was written, and the Virginia Center for the Creative Arts, and Pendle Hill, where it was edited.

As ever, I owe Michael Collier a debt of gratitude for welcoming me to the Bread Loaf Writers' Conference; his grace remains my strongest affirmation.

I have the highest regard for my agent, Julie Barer, who never loses sight of the human being— and life—behind the writer; I have taken more time and worked harder because of her. I thank my editor, Fiona McCrae, who is practiced at the art of asking for more by seeming to ask for less; the darlings died happy thanks to her. I am grateful to the gray wolves who have given this book their hearts, particularly Katie Dublinski, Erin Kottke, Michael Taeckens, and Steve Woodward.

Chiro Nanayakkara and Shirani Seneviratne helped with the research for this book. I owe a special thank you to Ranjan Madugalle for sharing his stories of cricket with me. I am especially grateful to architect and friend Susanna Billson, for her clear renditions of Sal Mal Lane and Sri Lanka.

I thank my fellowship of mushroom-loving souls: Leslie Brack, Daniel Brewbaker, Elisabeth Condon, Paul Festa, Edward M. Gomez, Lisa Hamilton, Curtis Harnack, Jane Hirshfield, Jill Lear, Alan McMonagle, David Rakowski, Jonathan Santlofer, James Scott, and Joan Wickersham. I completed this novel, observed the first anniversary of the death of my mother, and danced back to life in their company at Yaddo. The music here is a gift from David, Sonna grew into his story thanks to Alan, and the poetry and compassion are Jane's. This book belongs to them, too.

I am indebted to a host of writers. I mention a few I have counted on both to steady the boat and to sail away from the safe harbor: Mary Akers, Xhenet Aliu, Richard Bausch, Charlie Baxter, Noreen Cargill, Hache Carillo, Ted Conover, Eugene Cross, Lynn Freed, Ursula Hegi, Jenn de Leon, Matthew Nienow, Chang-rae Lee, Charles Rice-Gonzalez, Natalie Serber, Cheryl Strayed, Sara Taddeo, Cindy and Luis Urrea, Brandy Wilson, Elliott Woods, and Clarence Young.

I am infinitely grateful to Christy Beck, Susie Billson, Claire Conway, Pam Laughman, and Eve Weiss for filling in for me in the most important job of all. Likewise, my mother- and father-in-law, Barbara and Jerry Freeman, and aunts, Laurel and Sara Hartman, made it possible for me to leave home, knowing that my four blessings were in loving hands.

Without my brother Arjuna, the thoughtful, musical one, there would be no Suren, and this book would be missing both its rhythms and its quiet. My brother Malinda is my first reader, my fact-checker, my one-line critic, my hero, and, for this book, my muse. My nieces Mithsandi and Dayadi Seneviratne, and Indivara Miltaso, along with my daughters, will recognize some of their words and deeds in those of the children of Sal Mal Lane. There are some aspects of my parents, Indrani and Gamini Seneviratne, in these pages; it would take many books to do justice to the depths of their complexity and the generosity of their hearts, though I can assure them that, despite the many who adore them, the love of their children is greater still.

I am thankful each day for my beloved, Mark. If there is truth to Donne's conceit of the compass, then it is true of you and me: your firmness makes my circle just, and makes me end where I began. I am full of gratitude for the ones I must learn to let go, each to a world of her own making: my daughters, Duránya, Hasadrī, and Kisārā. My words are my history, written for you. Your skies are your canvases—use all your colors!

I am grateful to the people who live down the many small roads of my beloved country; any one of those tributaries might have contained this story. May peace be yours.

A Graywolf Press Reading Group Guide

On Sal Mal Lane

A Novel

Ru Freeman

Discussion Questions

1. Throughout *On Sal Mal Lane*, Ru Freeman uses subtle foreshadowing to let you know the book's outcome will be unfortunate without giving anything definite away. Did you notice this tactic? If so, did you find it successful? What instances in the book can you pinpoint?

2. In conversation with Mrs. Silva, Old Mrs. Joseph says, "knowing is one thing, preventing is quite another" (page 183), which in a way speaks for the book's tragic course of events. Do you think that Devi's fate was inevitable or merely an accident? Or is it inevitable that accidents happen?

3. Harmony is a theme throughout the book, expressed through the neighborhood's union, the children's friendship, and Suren's gift for music. Where else can you detect harmony in the book? How does this speak to the book's larger message?

4. During one of his talks with Nihil, Mr. Niles says, "People do not go to war . . . they carry war inside them" (page 222). Elaborate on what you think this means. Do you agree or disagree?

5. *On Sal Mal Lane* has a third-person omniscient narration that is from the point of view of the street itself. Was this narration effective? Did you find it distant or intimate? How did it allow us to see the inner lives of characters?

6. History and culture are a large part of *On Sal Mal Lane*. How did Freeman interweave these details in her narrative? Did you come away from the book with a deeper understanding of Sri Lanka's multicultural identity?

7. Early in the book Nihil has an encounter with Sonna that changes him. Freeman writes: "What grace there is to give if only the givers knew that they had the privilege of bestowing it. What grace is often given without intention" (page 99). Do you think if Sonna and the Heraths hadn't had so many missed opportunities things would have been different? Could their friendship have saved him?

8. The Heraths and the Silvas have very different worldviews, opinions, and political beliefs. How is this reflected in their children? Is prejudice the inevitable result of such differences?

Cheryl Strayed, author of *Wild* and *Tiny Beautiful Things*, interviews Ru Freeman about *On Sal Mal Lane*

Could you explain the name of the street, which is also the name of the book?

The street is named for the Sal Mal grove that cuts off the lane at its dead end, and for the trees that are found in all the gardens of the homes down that road. There is another significance to the Sal Mal tree—it is the tree under which the Gautama Buddha's mother gave birth to him, and the four Sal Mal trees surrounding his bed turned white when he passed away. It is also a flower said to be favored by the Hindu god Vishnu, and so it is rarely cut down. Further, the Sal Mal flower and its stamen and petals are shaped in a way that depicts people at prayer around the dome of a dagoba. It seemed fitting, somehow, to have this neighborhood nestled in the heart of a grove of such trees, such flowers.

Your novel is teeming with great characters, young, old, Sinhalese, Tamil. Do you have favorites among them?

My favorites are Sonna and Nihil. Sonna was, in fact, a very minor character in the first draft. He came and went very quickly, nothing very important happened to or because of him. Somehow, though, when I read aloud from this draft it became apparent that Sonna had a great deal of potential—within himself and as a character. He resisted being diminished in every revision; he just grew. Nihil was always the driving force behind this story, the inspiration for it, really. Together they embody what I am most drawn to contemplating: this drive we have to keep what we love safe, and the way in which we yearn for things we are rarely capacitated to deserve, earn, or keep.

At the heart of the novel is an unlikely friendship, between the young girl Devi and a neighbor, Raju, a misfit. What was the inspiration for their relationship?

Children. When I was first living in a very upscale suburb in New Jersey, I found that adults always assumed I was my light-skinned daughter's nanny. They never even spoke to me, constantly looking past me to each other. Their children, on the other hand, never made this mistake. They were paying attention to the relationship, to the way I interacted with her. Children anywhere are usually able to see beneath the exterior, to the human being. In Devi's case, she could see that Raju despite his mishapen body and social inarticulateness held only good intention in his heart.

The street, Sal Mal Lane, houses a really wide variety of people. Was your street like that in Sri Lanka? Is that typical of the country?

Yes, my street, also a dead-end though with guavas, not Sal Mal trees, was very much like this one. Most of the country except in the North where the Tigers (the LTTE), held sway, was—and is—thoroughly cross-pollinated. In those areas, through systematic slaughter of entire villages, the Tigers ensured that only Tamils, and only the poorest of Tamils (those unable to leave), continued to live in the North. Elsewhere we lived together, attended the same schools, so on. In some ways that was the true shame of what happened with the riots in July 1983, this way in which all of that had to go on but the insides of people—their hearts, their minds—were transformed. We went on to live together and yet be suspicious of each other. To interact and play and attend each others' religious festivities, births, deaths, marriages, and yet there came into being this reservation, something held back. That earlier time, before what happened, that is the true measure of peace and that is what the country is harkening toward again.

The children in the novel seem to have fairly free range. What advantages does that give you as a writer?

Well, it enabled me to follow them to places where they were not supposed to be! Devi, for instance, crossing the big roads that she is prohibited from crossing, the children rehearsing their band in a neighbor's house, these were really interesting for me, as a writer, to accompany these children that way. As a child I did grow up in that way. We went wherever we wanted except at night. Somehow at night all the rules changed—I suppose it is the same here, too, with curfews and such. But in general there was a real fluidity to the conduct of our days, where we entertained ourselves as siblings and with friends, often doing precisely what we were not supposed to do. I climbed the roof with my brothers, stole fruits from our neighbors (because it was always better tasting when stolen than when freely given), and walked down the terrible big roads to buy hard red sweets with which to color my lips and pretend I was wearing lip gloss.

You write so well about childhood, and about friendships between adults and children. Was that easy material for you to write?

I don't know if it is because I was raised in a culture that thrives because of its inter-generational interdependence, but I have always been drawn to old people. Here in the United States, my life has been illuminated by friendship—both fleeting and deep—with older Americans. I like stories, and older people have them in spades; they can tell me about places and times into which I can imagine myself as a storyteller. On the other hand, I also see everybody as a child. I sometimes catch myself staring at somebody—some man loading groceries in crates for delivery into the back of a truck in Chinatown, NYC, and I see that man as a child whose childhood was suddenly ambushed by adulthood. In everybody there remains that child, utterly bemused by what has happened to them, and yet soldiering on regardless, putting one foot in front of the other, trying to live up to this and that thing that is expected of them (usually by children), trying to forget a righteous path through life. There is something so utterly poignant about all this. It isn't easy material so much as it is life.

The children play cricket and French cricket in the book. What's the difference between the two?

Ha! (that's one). Cricket is played between two teams where the eleven players on one side bowl to and field while two players on the opposite side bat and score runs between the stumps and bails placed on either side of a twenty-two-yard-long pitch. French cricket is played anywhere between any number of people and can be scored individually or as a team, with one person at the crease holding a short plank of wood; the feet are placed together and the batsman cannot move except to hit the ball and then, by passing the plank around their body, scoring runs. In terms of intensity, French cricket is to cricket what a pick-up game in the 'hood is to the NBA.

There's a stellar passage concerning a piano being moved from one house to the other during the troubles—apparently this too happened in your childhood?

There was a family across the street from us whose piano had to be moved because it was their source of livelihood—just the one daughter who taught piano. When it became apparent that there would be gangs roaming the streets and sure to return in the night, and after several Tamil families, including that one, had been spirited away into our homes, there arose this question of how to hide a piano. It couldn't come to our house because we already had one, and it was decided that it would go up the street to the house of a family named Mendis. Everybody gathered to move that piano—it isn't easy to move one even for professional movers, and the damage done to that in the desperate fumblings of laypeople . . . and still, there was this sense of solidarity and hope that was wrapped around getting that one musical instrument shifted from one home, through their garden, out of their gate, up the street, down the driveway and up several stairs into a place of safety. All the men and most of the children pushing and carrying and pausing in between. All but the Tamil families who had to stay indoors, hidden and silent and trusting people whom they had lost every reason to trust.

There's great joy and ebullience in many of the scenes, and examples of great compassion between the characters. And yet throughout, dark clouds are gathering, and tragedy, when it strikes, is very real.

I think of this book not so much as optimistic, but as being a gesture toward what is good. As a nation we were all left bereft in the wake of these riots no matter who perpetrated what, who demonstrated compassion, who was violated. We lost a sense of ourselves, as a collective, being a people whose moral arc bends toward justice, peace, harmony. And though a family like mine may have been able to say that we were good people, we also knew that there weren't enough good people to have made it possible for nothing bad to have happened "on our watch," and it is impossible not to be tainted by that. Acknowledging that these terrible events took place, setting it down as it happened—not as we want to relate these stories for political expediency—is vital to recovering that equilibrium that we once had as a nation. And so—as has happened with some of the Tamil people who have read it—this book has the capacity to lead us both toward accepting what has been while remembering what once was and there is a great deal of hope in that process, for reconciliation and peace.

A lot of people have heard about the Sri Lankan civil war, but don't really know that much about it. What caused it? How did it affect you and your family?

To go into the history of what caused these three decades would be to unpack a history beginning from the mythical stories of Hanuman and Ravana and Sita and Rama and on through the invasion of the Cholas, and centuries of colonization by Europeans, the advent of the British being the absolute worst of it, and racial politics exploited by all sides of the equation. So I will simply say that this war, like all wars (including the wars against Chile and Cuba and Iraq and Iran and Palestine and on), was caused by the powerful and waged against the innocent. It affected my family like it affected everybody. Ramshackle checkpoints became highly militarized ones; we became increasingly suspicious of everybody around us: we avoided crowded places, though, really, there aren't such places in a city like Colombo; and we began to think like suicide bombers—would I get into a packed bus? would I pick rush hour? During some of those years, my school, attended by many of the daughters of the upper strata, was located between the American Center, the Russian consulate, the Japanese embassy, and the office of the Prime Minister. There was this sense that if a suicide bomber wanted to blow themselves up, they couldn't pick a better target. And yet you go to school anyway, you see buses pulled off and some person-by-person search going on, vehicles being searched or surrounded by armed personnel, and you try not to dwell too much on these things, you try to go on.

How have other Sri Lankan writers responded to the war? Has a lot been written about it?

Yes. Jean Arasanayagam in her collection *All is Burning*, Shyam Selvadurai in *Funny Boy*, for instance, have both written about this time. I am partial to these particular books because whether I agree or not with what has been written, they are written by people who were living through these realities on the ground, not peering at it from a great distance. And by that distance I don't necessarily mean physical distance. I mean the distance of heart. I believe that when you write about complex and rending conflicts like the one in Sri Lanka, and certainly when you are sort of spokesperson for a place—as you are in a country like this where few people know what is happening in this country let alone what is happening in a country ten thousand miles away—you have to come to it with a great love for the people of that country or you fail in the task. You cannot come to it with judgment, some pre-conceived notion of the ground realities. So, for instance, Naomi Benaron's *Running the Rift* (about the Rwandan genocide) or Lorraine Adam's *Harbor* (about the plight of Algerian immigrants in an America girded by the misguided strategies of Homeland Security and the PATRIOT Act) are great examples of writers whose hearts are with the people they are writing about, whose hearts ache for them and whose words are not about figuring out right and wrong but laying bare human frailty and human potential for good.

Sri Lanka is many miles away from the United States, but do you see any common threads between the history of your country and the history of ours?

Much of what happened in the wake of 9/11 is similar to what happened in the wake of the massacre of those thirteen soldiers and the riots of 1983, the suspicion and profiling that followed after the towers fell. There was a lot of misinformation and rumors about entire ethnic groups, battles waged over meaningless things—the Ground Zero "mosque" that was really a community center, for instance—rather than really looking at our common ground. Instead of affirming what was good about community and citizenship, there was a massive move toward fear there and here. The larger lesson, as it were, I think is that wars can and do end, no matter how intractable they seem; certainly something that may give Americans hope as they take stock of so many decades of war (albeit mostly waged on foreign soil). It is possible.

You moved to the United States from Sri Lanka in 1990: was that a big adjustment for you? What were some of the most striking cultural differences?

So many things from the way people talked about their parents being some kind of burden, to the lack of a cultural sensibility around the value of education and reading, but mostly money and food. Sri Lankans don't argue over food or money. At college, I was often struck by the fact that only the people who paid for a pizza would be allowed to eat it. It seemed so utterly crass to me to eat while someone in your company was not supposed to eat because they hadn't paid for it. I came to acknowledge (but still not understand nor quite forgive, I must confess), that in a culture where college age kids are spending money they've really had to work for, it might make them more conscious of making that money last somehow, and have a certain lack of regard for those who were freeloaders. But still. That initial shock has plagued me to this day. I prefer to pay for all food at all times because I never want to expose myself to feeling that someone is not going to pay for me, or is going to discuss payment, particularly men . . . I'm cringing even as I say this. I can actually count the number of times I've allowed a man who isn't my husband to pay for my food: twice. Both book people, by the way, a writer, a bookseller.

If you could import one aspect of Sri Lanka to America, what would it be?

Our dependence on the collective in every aspect of life. We really do rely on each other, on our own friends but also friends of friends, to see us through difficulties. Perhaps this is most apparent in times of bereavement; if the parent of a student at a college passes away, the entire class boards buses to go to the funeral even if they have had no interaction with the student. It is a way of demonstrating to the neighbors and extended family the regard they have for the son or daughter of the person who has died. Recently, the father of a high school student who lives down our road passed away and it was very strange for me to see that there weren't hundreds of students coming by to attend a wake (or sit shiva in this case). I think that involvement, however inconvenient, is what makes us feel grounded as human beings, this sense that whatever happens is happening to more than just ourselves, that our lives and our deaths are witnessed and celebrated and mourned by people we don't even know.

And if you could import one aspect of America to Sri Lanka, what would it be?

The peaceful transition of power between one president and another; particularly lovely to behold when the elections have been free and fair, where disenfranchisement and voter suppression and all that kind of stuff has not taken place or has been limited as far as possible. We don't have that spectacle back home, where an outgoing president (for a long time prime minister) exits with grace and a new one comes in. Whatever the political differences, whatever the actual sentiments of each of these people, there is something wonderful about being able to acknowledge the passage of time, the passing of a torch, to spend a moment there before turning full force to the agenda of a new administration.

This interview originally appeared on Amazon.com's books blog, Omnivoracious.

RU FREEMAN is a Sri Lankan-American writer and activist. Her debut novel, *A Disobedient Girl*, was long-listed for the DSC South Asian Literary Prize and translated into seven languages. She has been a fellow of the Bread Loaf Writers' Conference, Yaddo, and the Virginia Center for the Creative Arts. She blogs for *The Huffington Post* on literature and politics and is a contributing editorial board member of the *Asian American Literary Review*. She calls both Sri Lanka and America home and writes about the people and countries underneath her skin.

This book is made possible through a partnership with the College of Saint Benedict, and honors the legacy of S. Mariella Gable, a distinguished teacher at the College.

Previous titles in this series include:

Loverboy by Victoria Redel
The House on Eccles Road by Judith Kitchen
One Vacant Chair by Joe Coomer
The Weatherman by Clint McCown
Collected Poems by Jane Kenyon
Variations on the Theme of an African Dictatorship by Nuruddin Farah:
    Sweet and Sour Milk
    Sardines
    Close Sesame
Duende by Tracy K. Smith
All of It Singing: New and Selected Poems by Linda Gregg
The Art of Syntax: Rhythm of Thought, Rhythm of Song by Ellen Bryant Voigt
How to Escape from a Leper Colony by Tiphanie Yanique
One Day I Will Write About This Place by Binyavanga Wainaina
The Convert: A Tale of Exile and Extremism by Deborah Baker

Support for this series has been provided by the Manitou Fund as part of the Warner Reading Program.

Also Available from Graywolf Press

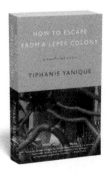

The text of *On Sal Mal Lane* is set in Fournier MT. In 1924, Monotype based this face on types cut by Pierre Simon Fournier circa 1742 and called St. Augustin Ordinaire in Fournier's *Manuel Typographique*. Book design by Ann Sudmeier. Composition by BookMobile Design and Digital Publisher Services, Minneapolis, Minnesota. Manufactured by Versa Press on acid-free 30 percent postconsumer wastepaper.